For S.L.K.
With love, always

Acknowledgements

Thank you to my fantastic agent, Simon Trewin, for selling this book within about three minutes of me thinking up the idea, and to Ariella Feiner and Jessica Craig at United Agents.

Thank you to Cat Cobain for signing me up to a dream publisher at Headline, for astute and passionate editing, and for patience and sympathy when I finished off the book half-blind! Thanks to the Headline team, especially Sara Porter, Georgina Moore and Lucy Le Poidevin.

And thank you to all my family – Mum, Dad, Paul, Stephen, and friends – A.H., David, Walney, Vicki, Lewis, Tom T., Tristan and Lyra.

Prologue

They buried the baby alive.

She was a girl and her mother had sobbed the moment she emerged from the womb. The *devas* had not responded to her prayers for a boy; she must be cursed to have given birth to a girl. A girl born into a poor family was a bankruptcy notice. They would never be able to afford her dowry. They could not even afford to feed her. And therefore she must die.

And so, six days after the baby had gasped her first breath, two silhouettes carried her, concealed under a dirty sari, on to a patch of wasteland in southern Delhi. It was midnight and the unsympathetic moon shone down brightly, highlighting their every move. Her uncle rocked her surreptitiously; her father began to dig. The grave was shallow, barely a foot deep. They placed the baby in the grave. She smiled up at them, dark eyes sparkling, enjoying her novel new cradle. When they tossed the first shovel of dusty red earth over her, she gurgled and giggled. When the dirt flew into her mouth, she began to scream.

A distant noise; some shouts. The two men became fearful. The cover was thin but it would have to do. One last spray of red earth was kicked over her, and they were gone.

She wanted to scream but her mouth was clotted with earth. Tears formed moist brown trickles on her cheeks. She waved her fists and punched ineffectually against her earthy blanket. She craved air like her mother's milk. Her tiny lungs fluttered in panic. And then faltered. She closed her eyes and saw the blue god who had once smiled over her cot. He seemed to be smiling at her now, and suddenly her tomb was filled with light—

Ten Years Later

1

Karina

I'm sitting on a plane to India, enjoying the sort of high that would normally take unimaginable quantities of cocaine to achieve. As we soar into the aching blue sky, I feel like punching the air. It may be a cliché but it's true: today is the first day of the rest of my life.

A journalist from *Elegance* is sitting beside me. She's got ebony hair, her nose is ever so slightly crooked and her lips are hungry for collagen. But she looks elegant in her Dolce & Gabbana suit. And I can't help feeling smug. A year ago my agent plagued *Elegance* with ideas for features. We offered them a story about my plans to start my own clothing line. *No*, they said. A story about my tragic childhood with an overbearing mother. *No*. A story about my secret lesbian crush on Lindsay Lohan (not strictly true but by now I was getting desperate). *No no no.* Don't call us, we'll call you. Today, life is very different. After a bidding war with three other magazines, *Elegance* have paid me *fifty thousand pounds* for this exclusive. It means a whole new wardrobe, a new kitchen and, when I return from this trip – shh – a new nose.

'So, Karina, how do you feel?' Patricia, the journalist, asks.

'I feel nervous. Excited.' Patricia looks rather unconvinced so I add hastily, 'I feel I could cry, I'm so happy!'

She looks pleased and scribbles hard.

'I mean – it's just so amazing,' she says. 'You're about to change the entire life and destiny of a child. A child who could be doomed to poverty, to working in a sweat shop for one pence an hour – and you're going to save them.'

I feel a tiny flicker of alarm when she says this. But I quickly shrug it away. Last night I suffered a terrible panic attack and had to call Clare. She assured me that she had a similar experience the night before she gave birth to her first child. She felt terrified that it would be the beginning of a prison sentence – right up until the moment her baby boy was placed on her breast and she felt a deep wave of unconditional love. And although I'm adopting, I've read countless stories of women who experience just as deep an emotion when they first set eyes on their chosen child.

'I just see the whole thing as an opportunity to *grow*,' I say. I said this in the interview with the woman from the adoption agency and she looked very impressed.

She looked even more impressed when I said I'd donate ten thousand pounds to the adoption agency in Delhi. Adoptions in India can often take a year or more, even with the new regulations to cut red tape. Funnily enough, mine was whizzed through in a matter of weeks.

'So let's just recap on your biog,' Patricia says, eyeing up a press release. 'You're thirty-four—'

'Thirty,' I say automatically.

Then I remember that my agent has advised me to stop lying about my age. He said it would look better if I opted for a 'more mature image'.

'Thirty-four,' I concede.

Patricia laughs and winks at me, and I echo her. But I can't help thinking – will I have to tell men from now on that I really am thirty-four? Will they still fancy me?

'And you started out in showbiz at a very young age – you were only four when you appeared in a Dulex ad.'

'That's me – I was the Dulex girl. My mum pushed me hard.'

7

'Your mother is . . .'

'She's dead.'

'I'm so sorry. So, after Dulex, at the age of eighteen, you were chosen to be a member of the girl band Beppo.'

'Yep.'

'And after seven years of chart success, your group split up. Soon after, you started dating Liam Holt and your relationship hit the headlines. When you split up, you ended up in rehab.' Suddenly there is a glint of steel in her smile. 'And when you applied for adoption, did the social worker who interviewed you know about this?'

'Rehab was eight years ago,' I assert, waving my hand. 'I didn't go there because of drugs – I was just feeling *tired*. Look, when I went to the Priory everyone was in there – Kate Moss, George Michael – it was a networking opportunity as much as anything.'

'And then you went solo and had a one-hit wonder with "Summer Sun" – then, sadly, your follow-up was a total flop and you were dropped by your label.'

'I decided I'd prefer to go into acting – singing has always been a joy of mine, but acting was more of a vocation—'

'But you ended up in a bit part in the British film *Three Weddings And A Wanker*, which went straight to video.'

'Straight to video is not a sin in my eyes. I don't make films just for the money, or for superficial reasons like box-office success. I believe in artistic integrity, in the chance to work with a great director—'

'Including *Bank Job Kung Fu 4*?'

'I did all my own stunts,' I splutter.

'Your fame is in decline, while Liam has settled down with his new girlfriend, the actress Hayley Young. D'you feel that the adoption is a reaction to losing Liam – whom you once described as the love of your life?'

'Absolutely not,' I cry, my anger taking control. Then I swallow, take a deep breath, force a smile. My agent has negotiated sight of a full copy of the article before it goes to press, so I'll damn well make sure it's slashed out if she dares to include it. 'A woman doesn't need a man to make her feel whole – but she does need a baby.'

Patricia looks struck. I'm pretty good at giving lines to journalists. A month ago, when size zero was being debated all over the place, I gave hundreds of anguished quotes about my infamous yo-yo dieting's being entirely the fault of stick insect models. But, in truth, yo-yo dieting is the best PR a celeb can do. Deliberately swinging from anorexia to obesity on a month-by-month basis – and showing off both extremes in low-cut dresses at premieres, or bikinis on the beach – is a guaranteed way to keep your photo in the magazines. Even if the captions are less than flattering.

'And lastly . . .' She hesitates.

She'd better not say it, I think. So far she's avoided the subject, but if she dares to bring it up, I think I'll scream.

'. . . what would you say to those who might claim that your decision to adopt an Indian girl is really just a way of jumping on the Angelina Jolie band-wagon?'

2

Karina

I'd like to rewrite – no, *correct* – history by asserting that I was one of the first people to initiate the celeb-adopting-a-baby trend, second only to Angelina, and way before Madonna. This isn't the first time this has happened to me. Eight years ago I remember I bumped into Kate Moss at a party and she admired the flower-power waistcoast I was wearing. Three days later, Moss left her house wearing something identical and all the magazines were having orgasms over 'the new trend Moss has set again'.

This is my second attempt; the first never really came together.

I'll tell you how the idea of celebrity adoption came to me. I hadn't a thought of Angelina five years ago, on a Saturday night in July, when I was sitting watching TV alone. I remember the night clearly – I had just turned thirty and I was recovering from a week of partying which had culminated in a forty-eight-hour binge-orgy-riot at my house in Primrose Hill. The debris was still littered everywhere: little pyramids of ash all over the floor, cigarette stubs branding my lovely Conran furniture, bottles clanking every way I turned. But I was too depressed to do anything but sit in my nest of trash and filth. The day after my party had finished, my latest crush, a toy boy from *Hollyoaks*, had just dumped me. All the tabloids had exuberantly revealed that he had been two-timing me with his eighteen-year-old co-star all along. Even though I told everyone I really didn't care, it had just been a casual thing, he'd been nothing more than my bit-of-fluff toy boy, deep down I missed his boyish laugh and cute texts. I felt humiliated. I felt *old*.

Thirty is a horrible age to be – not just because of the first flash of crow's feet around your eyes, or the advent of Botox – but because you're forced to look at your life and consider where you are. After my doomed love affair with Liam in my mid-twenties, I had emerged from rehab determined to change. No more drugs, no more messing around. I was going to make it big by the age of thirty. I'd have a house in Hollywood Hills, be married to

Tom Cruise and be earning a salary of twenty million dollars a year. I was hungry and ambitious and determined that nothing would stop me. I was convinced that I had the talent and the drive. I'd been in the business for long enough to know that drive is the more important.

I hadn't thought about the importance of luck. I hadn't imagined that I would keep making the wrong decision at every turn. That the part in the Brit-flick *The Bad Bride* that looked so naff and only paid five hundred pounds would make my rival Melanie Prince a global star. That the song I chose to launch my solo career would fail to inspire the masses to buy the next. All around me, it seemed that Lady Luck was showering golden kisses on girls who went on to become soap stars and pop stars and movie stars and model stars whilst I just hovered in the background, getting a little older and a little more disappointed year by year.

My disappointment began to breed self-doubt. As I sat there on that Saturday night, watching TV, a terrible feeling began to possess me. It had started as a whisper a few years ago, a little voice in my ear at the end of each failed audition. Now it was in danger of becoming a scream.

It's too late, it said to me. *You're past it. You're not getting the breaks. It's not going to happen. You're going to have to sell your house and work in Tescos and accept your dream isn't going to happen.*

It's too late.

I drowned the voice out by grabbing a nearby wine bottle that still had some dregs of red in it and downing it in one. Then I turned up the volume on the TV.

On the screen was a concert. Bono was singing on a big stage in a park. Crowds were screaming praise. A banner behind him said AFRICAN APPEAL. Every so often a red strip would run at the bottom of the screen with a hotline number begging people to donate. Fifty pounds will buy a family a goat and a plough, it said. A hundred and fifty pounds will buy six thousand water purification tablets. A hundred and fifty pounds will also a buy a new Hermès scarf, I thought vaguely. Normally I found these charity appeals quite moving and would always end up ringing and donating. But tonight I was too upset for compassion; I couldn't help feeling sulky and cynical. How lucky those Africans were to have people raising money for them. I'd bought this house in Primrose Hill in my twenties when I was flush with my money from Beppo, but recently I'd been struggling with the mortgage – I could do with a charity concert myself. I pictured Madonna, Bono and Ronan Keating all getting up on stage and appealing to the crowds: 'Let's all stop to spare a thought for Karina and the Louis Vuitton she so desperately needs. Please give generously.' I smiled.

Then Bob Geldof came up on the screen and began talking about the orphans in Africa. I rummaged around for another wine bottle. And then the thought hit me.

I sat up. *What if*, I thought, *what if I were to adopt an African child*?

I mean, all Geldof had organised was a few concerts. And how much effort did a concert really take? All he had to do was phone up a few friends and say, 'D'you want a chance to look good and plug your latest release at the same time?' Who would say no to that? Yet look at how famous he'd become as a result. In fact, he was better than famous. He was seen as a saviour. In our secular Western world, he was our equivalent to Gandhi.

What if, I thought, the way to get famous was not to get drunk, collapse in the gutter without any knickers on and have a breast enlargement, but actually *do good*? Life was all about trends. Moss's thinness was a reaction to the curvy supermodels of the eighties. Everything in our current society screamed Thatcher's legacy; everything was about money and selfishness. What if I bucked the trend and started a new one? What if I made philanthropy as fashionable as skinny jeans?

What if, instead of buying a goat or a farm or a tractor, I actually went one step further? What if I offered to adopt one of those African babies?

Bright butterflies of fantasy began to flutter through my mind. I saw myself being filmed by the BBC on safari in Africa with Geldof, wearing designer khaki. I pictured Geldof saying to the camera, 'Karina – she's just so real. She's been such an inspiration to me . . .'

I was so excited, I called up my agent at home.

'I don't know,' he said, sounding doubtful, 'it sounds like a weird idea to me. I mean, what if you get the kid and you go off it? Can you just give it back?'

'I won't *go off it*! And it won't be an it – it'll be a lovely little boy or girl!'

There was a long pause. 'I don't know, Karina. I can't imagine any of the magazines being interested in this . . .'

'Well, what am I supposed to do?' I cried, my euphoria gushing out of me. Hysteria immediately filled the vacuum. 'I'm thirty and nobody will hire me – *tell me what I'm supposed to do?*'

'I've got you an advert for Persil. Look, it's a Saturday night, Karina—'

'You think an *advert* is going to solve this?' Realising I was on the brink of tears, I slammed down the phone in shame.

I wept, then – but only briefly. I have always been one of life's determined people. His lack of belief in me only inspired me further. When my mum took me to my first audition at the age of four, the casting director told us I didn't have star quality. He said I should give up there and then. But my mum kept taking me from audition to audition, whispering in my ear, 'You *are* a star, you will *never* give up, *never*.' I think that's why I'm so pig-headed now. When I want something, I get it and, as I was taught, I never, *ever* give up.

I spent the whole of Sunday cleaning my house with a burst of fresh, happy energy. This is the start of a new me, I told myself. From now on everything is going to change. You are going to be the most glamorous philanthropist in the country.

I threw myself into researching adoption with huge gusto. Fran and all my friends teased me that I'd never make it past the interview with the social worker. But, of course, I passed it with flying colours. All the frustrated acting abilities that had been stewing inside me for years finally got a chance to be expressed. I gave the social worker a performance of a lifetime, and by the end she said I was one of the best candidates she'd ever come across.

She was, however, a little concerned that I wanted to adopt a severely disabled baby.

'I'm quite sure,' I asserted strongly. To begin with,

I'd decided a disabled baby would earn me double philanthropy points; if I was going to do this, I had to really go for it. But then I'd seen the photos of the kids and felt a genuine flare of compassion in my heart. They were the kids nobody wanted to adopt; the ones who would spend all their childhoods in orphanages with few facilities to help them. They really did need a home.

I kept telling myself it was a wonderful idea, even whilst everyone around me was telling me I was insane. My two closest friends are the girls I sang with in Beppo: Fran and Clare. Recently, however, I've grown apart from Clare, who has settled down, married, had kids and makes her own jewellery for a living. Fran, on the other hand, is the female equivalent of Peter Pan. Peter Pan on cocaine, that is. For the first time in years, however, both of them were in complete agreement. Convinced that I was making a Terrible Mistake. Fran even tried to book me into the Priory behind my back for full-on counselling. Then one day Clare came over and said, 'Show me the papers the agency have sent you.' I showed Clare the photo of the baby.

'Isn't she so *sweet*?' I said.

'No,' Clare said bluntly. 'I don't think that her squinting, cross-eyed gaze and drooling cleft lip are sweet at all. I'm sorry to put it so harshly, but I don't.'

'I don't want a designer kid who looks like

something out of a perfume ad!' I cried. 'I want to help a kid who really needs a home.'

'It's not about looks, Karina – you're not getting me. Look,' she said, pointing to a chart detailing the baby's height, weight and head circumference. 'This looks serious. I'm going to show this to my paediatrician.'

A week later, Clare told me her paediatrician's verdict: the baby's head circumference was so low it was off the radar.

'Look, Karina, I think that you're not as superficial as you pretend to be. I think that underneath your insane "fame philanthropy" motives for this baby thing you actually mean well—'

'Clare!' I gasped in outrage.

'But – *but*,' she interrupted insistently, 'you haven't thought this through. This baby is very, very ill. It's going to need speech therapy, occupational therapy, physical therapy, special education – we're talking practically twenty-four-hour support and care. Imagine the cost – you're already struggling so how the hell are you going to afford it? You'll never be able to go out on the town with Fran. You'll have no time for any boyfriends.'

'I'm done with men,' I snapped, but deep down I knew that Clare was right. Adopting a baby was a big thing as it was. Taking on a disabled one was a huge responsibility I just wasn't ready for.

A week passed and I quietly cancelled the adoption. I told all my friends that the agency had suddenly closed down after a health and safety test and I was heartbroken to have missed out on such an amazing opportunity. My agent seemed relieved; he told me none of the magazines he'd spoken to seemed that interested, and cheered me up when he told me he'd got me a bit part in the new James Bond movie.

All the same, I couldn't help feeling a pinch inside. From time to time I thought about that poor baby and wondered what type of life she was living. Whether she was happy; whether she'd ever found a home.

And then – you know the rest of the story. Angelina adopted her second child and then Madonna got in on the act and soon you couldn't open a magazine without seeing them clutching their adorable little darlings against their cheeks. Every time I saw one, I wanted to yell at passers-by, 'It was *my* idea, *mine mine mine.*'

You can imagine how incensed I was when my agent casually said to me some years on, 'You're thirty-four, you must be feeling broody, Karina – have you ever thought of adopting an orphan from abroad? You'd get heaps of press.'

After I had raved for five minutes, he told me

to shut up and make sure I adopted one from India.

'Angelina's covered Cambodia, Ethiopia and Vietnam, Madonna's done Africa. We need a new angle – a new country. You'd better get in quick: Madonna's got her eye on India right now.'

I went home and thought long and hard about it. By now, I was a little older and wiser. I asked myself, *do I really want to do this? Not just as a publicity stunt – but as a real life choice? Do I want to be a mother?* And then I thought about how lonely I had begun to feel recently, how empty my bed seemed unless it was filled with a man. And how, to my surprise, I had begun to feel tiny maternal pangs from time to time – a baby in the street would provoke a gooey smile and when I picked up Clare's baby I didn't want to hand her back. I realised that yes – I did genuinely feel ready to be a mother.

Clare suggested that, given my obsession with beauty sleep, I might do better with a young girl rather than a baby. It sounded a great idea to me. I decided I was ready. I had just done a very lucrative ad in Japan and I used every penny to make a donation to the agency, speeding it up as fast as we could in order to beat Madonna. Even so, we were surprised by how enthralled the press were. Even my agent was amazed at the revival in my career – 'Fifty K!' he kept crying. 'Fifty K! They wouldn't normally pay this amount for a D-list celeb – I think it's only because you're Liam's ex,' he said, which made me so cross I nearly called the whole thing off.

And here I am, sitting on a plane, next to a journalist from *Elegance*. I am about to adopt Devika. The agency has been sending over pictures of her and she looks like an absolute angel. Over the last few weeks, I've been sleeping with her picture under my pillow and taking it out every morning and giving it an affectionate kiss.

'You know, when Devika was born her parents actually tried to bury her alive,' I tell Patricia. 'Can you believe that? I mean – imagine being so poor that you have to bury your baby, knowing that if she lives you'll starve and she'll end up a beggar or a prostitute.' I stroke her photo, her perfect nose. 'She's ten now and she couldn't get any Indian parents to adopt her because she has darker skin. It's not popular, apparently, because when they adopt they like to pretend the kids are their own.'

'That's such a moving story,' Patricia says. 'I really think you're doing something very special.'

Is it just me, or do I detect a certain doubt in her voice?

I have a funny feeling Patricia doesn't quite believe in me. Maybe it's just the jet lag tiring us out, but she seems to be smiling less and less and that steely glint is making a home for itself in her eyes. Eventually the questions dry up and Patricia's head drops back as she falls asleep but I stay awake, seething with determination and plans. I'm going to show her. By the end of this trip, I'm going to damn well prove to her that I can be the best celebrity mother in the world.

3

Devika

I wake up in the morning feeling as though my tummy is full of snakes – happy snakes and excited snakes and nervous snakes all winding into a big snake knot. I pull out the photo of my new mummy that Mrs Laxsmi gave me. I sleep with it under my head each night. It's got a bit crumpled but she still looks beautiful. I kiss her face and hug the picture to my chest and keep praying over and over, *please, Krishna, please let Karina like me, please let her like me.*

Then the clock says it's five a.m. and Mrs Laxsmi comes round, clapping her hands. She helps us roll up our sleeping mat. Six of us sleep on the mat. I like lying next to Asha because sometimes in the night I wake up and feel her breath like a warm wind on my cheek. But from tonight I will be sleeping in a big bed with a proper white sheet and my own pillow. The thought makes me feel so excited again that I want to jump up and touch the clouds. We go out into the courtyard to have a bath. I hate having baths. When Mrs Laxsmi comes by, I pretend to be pouring the water from the bucket over me, but when she turns away I just scrub my face. Then I put my clothes on. Mrs Laxsmi told me to save my best pink skirt to look my best for Karina. We wash our clothes for tomorrow, scrubbing them in the big iron tub. Soon I will have my own servants to wash my clothes for me. *Oh, Krishna, please let her like me, please let her like me and take me away from here for ever and ever and ever.*

After prayers we have breakfast and do our chores. Mrs Laxsmi says I don't have to go to school today.

'You're so lucky lucky,' Raji grumbles, poking me with his broom. I poke him back and we fight, laughing, and I win!

I will miss Raji when I'm gone. A few years ago, when he was really lucky, he got taken to a cinema, which is a special temple where you can see people dancing and singing on a big screen. From then on, he's never stopped talking about how he wants to become an American when he grows up. He will wear jeans every day and drive a big car and be a famous actor. He's even started saving for the flight, though he's worked out it might take him ten years. He earns extra money by sweeping the yard next door, but so far he's only saved twelve rupees.

Raji and the others go off to school and I'm left alone. Mrs Laxsmi said Mike would help me to practise my English before Karina comes. Mike is called a 'volunteer' which means he visits us in the summer holidays. Last night he taught me how to say 'How do you do' and 'Thank you very much'.

But Mike has gone to the market to buy some batteries, so Mrs Laxsmi tells me to carry on sweeping the yard until he gets back. I hum up at the sky, which is the same colour as Karina's eyes in the photo. *Oh, Krishna, please let her like me.* Lord Krishna will surely help me, for Mrs Laxsmi says Krishna loves me as his daughter. For Krishna once saved my life.

Mrs Laxsmi told me the story of what happened. When I was a little baby, I fell very sick. My parents thought I was dead and they buried me by mistake. I remember waking up in the earth and screaming and a blue god smiling down at me – it's my very first memory. Then I was taken to the orphanage.

I used to pray every night that my parents would realise I was still alive and come and find me. I even started getting up in the night, creeping past the others and standing by the gates, calling out, 'Mum! Dad!' I used to think that they would be passing by in the streets, searching for me, and recognise my voice, then come running up and cry, 'Devika!' Then they'd hold me tight, crying, thanking Krishna they had found me, and take me back home.

Often a shadow would fall over me. I would look up to see Mrs Laxsmi, telling me to come to bed. One night she drew me into her room, sat down on a chair, pulled me on to her lap and said sternly, 'Devika, you are keeping us all awake. Your parents aren't out in the street looking for you. They're not going to find you because they've gone away.'

'How would you know?' I cried, struggling to get off her lap and run back to the gates, terrified I would miss them.

'Some friends of your parents told us that they went away to a country far away. They didn't realise you were alive and now it's too late. You must accept they have gone.'

I didn't understand. I went back to my sleeping mat and curled into a ball and cried all night. I told myself that Mrs Laxsmi was a wicked *rakshasa* who was lying to me and had stolen me from my parents. I even thought about running away. But the next morning Mrs Laxsmi gave me a big hug, her smile so tender I knew she could not have a bad heart. She whispered in my ear, 'Krishna will bring you a new mother. He is looking after you.'

I didn't want a new mother. All I could think

about was my real mother. I drew her face in my head every night before I went to sleep. She had a beautiful face like Saraswati and big black eyes.

Then one day a couple from America came to our orphange to adopt Sheetal. They gave us some *barfi* and sweeties and the man played a piece of wood with strings on, singing songs. We didn't understand a word he sang, but the music sounded good and we clapped and danced. Then they took Sheetal away. I remember we all stood by the gates, waving goodbye. I thought of how they would all sit down together that evening and feed each other rice like a proper family. My heart hurt with envy. I felt guilty, worried my real mother would know I was giving up on her. But I couldn't help it – from then on, I began to picture a new mother. Someone to look after me until my real one found me again.

A year ago, I was nearly adopted. A woman came to visit us. Mrs Laxsmi told me I was in charge of showing her around. 'Maybe she can be my new mum,' I said and Mrs Laxsmi smiled and said, 'Maybe she can.' The woman liked me but she said she wanted a baby. I was too old.

I didn't cry that night. I just lay in bed, watching the fan whirr above me, and thought, Krishna will bring me a mother. He is saving someone better for me.

And now Karina is coming. She has seen my

photo and wants to adopt me! She is beautiful and rich and she lives in England and she is going to take me away and I will live in a big house like a princess. As long as she likes me. I stare up at the skies and pray and pray and pray that Karina will want me.

4

Karina

It was all going so well, until I suffered another panic attack. We landed in Delhi airport at around three a.m. last night to discover that collecting our luggage was almost as random and insane as the early days at Heathrow Terminal 5. Our suitcases didn't even turn up on the conveyor belt – after wandering around for half an hour, we found them dumped in a corner with a cluster of other bags. But we cheered up when the taxi driver collected us. Indians seem very friendly people, for his smile was warm and he gave me a vigorous handshake. But I had to force back laughter when I saw his dashboard – it had little figurines of deities on it, with flashing lights like something out of a Matalan Christmas window display. Really, it looked so garish – you couldn't even pass it off as eighties retro. Patricia saw my twitching lips and said, 'He must be a Hindu.' She gave me a rather stern look. I nodded, putting on a serious face. I didn't realise that they worship millions of funny-looking gods over here.

It was hard to see the scenery in the dark. But as we drove to the hotel, we passed by tents by the side of the road where the homeless were squatting and I felt my heart pinch with pity for them.

The hotel décor, I'm glad to say, was gorgeous: beautiful marble floors and rather more elegant pictures of *devas* on the walls. Patricia and I were both whacked with jet lag, so we said a tired goodnight to each other, then went to our rooms and collapsed into bed. I checked my mobile one last time and was pleased to see I could still get texts – Fran had sent one saying **You got malaria yet? I'm down at P Hill, just snogged Pete Doherty – for shame!**

I texted Fran back and then fell into a deep, deep sleep.

I wake up in the morning feeling hot and headachy. Then I look over at the empty single bed on the other side of the room. Tonight there will be a child sleeping in that bed. Panic rips through me. *Shit what am I doing what am I doing what am I doing*

I'm going to adopt a KID oh God oh God what I am doing?

This is the craziest thing I've ever done. I know I do things on a whim – like *Celebrity Love Island* or stripping off naked for *FHM*'s 'Food & Pussies' photoshoot. But this – this! – this is for life. For the rest of my life. Fifty odd *years*. My panic becomes so intense that I'm close to grabbing my case, running out of the hotel and hailing a rickshaw to take me back to the airport.

Then I remind myself of the *Elegance* journalist next door. If I run now, I'll have to give the money back. And my nose job will be cancelled and that horrible bump will never be fixed. And I won't be in the magazines or get a book deal for my children's picture book about a celebrity princess, which my agent is waiting to sell the moment I adopt. And what about poor little Devika? She'll be left at the orphanage and they'll tell her that I'm not coming and she'll be devastated. I whip her photo out, trying to summon that lovely warm feeling in my heart that she's evoked over the last few weeks. But the warm feeling seems to have vanished – there is nothing but fear.

I sit down on the bed and adopt the lotus. I breathe in and out, in and out, very slowly. I remember Clare's words about the unconditional love that will flow from my heart the moment I see her. The thought makes me smile and touches a maternal chord inside. I remind myself of what all the positive thinking bibles say: taking the biggest leaps are the most frightening, but they bring the best rewards.

I take a shower. As the water cascades down over me, I keep thinking about malaria and typhoid, and even though my arms are puckered from injections I still can't help feeling paranoid. I shower quickly, then jump out and dry myself. I examine my reflection, taking care not to linger on my nose, the sight of which revolts me. My eyes fall to the tattoo on my wrist. I had it done last week, in honour of this trip. It's Sanskrit for '*peace*'. I remember how thrilled I was and I feel reassured again that I am doing the right thing.

Next I get dressed. The *Elegance* photographer is flying in this morning and I need to look hotter than hot. I dress in a peacock-blue sari woven with dazzling gold threads. I spent a good afternoon at my local Sanskrit centre getting the Indian woman there to teach me how to put it on. Then I take an hour doing my make-up, kohling my eyes and scarleting my lips. At the end, I smile at my reflection and think, except for the nose, not bad. Not bad at all.

I could definitely be cast in a Bollywood movie.

Hey, maybe that could be my new career. I could bring Devika back here in the summer holidays to make sure she stays in touch with her culture and shoot a movie at the same time.

The idea is just beginning to excite me when Patricia knocks at the door. She is holding up a ravishing mauve sari and looks embarrassed.

'Wow, you look *amazing*.' She gapes at my outfit. 'Did you get the maid to help you with that?'

'No, I put it on myself.'

'Oh God, really, can you help me? I'm just in a mess – I've got pins everywhere!' she wails, coming in.

Within five minutes, I've sorted her out. She looks quite startled.

'I learnt how to do it,' I said airily, 'so that when Devika's with me, I'll know how to dress her.'

Patricia turns to me with a look of admiration in her eyes.

'You know, you – you've impressed me,' she says, a little sheepishly. 'When I first picked you up, I thought you were just another celebrity looking for a photoshoot, but you really are sincere – and I just want you to know – I think what you're doing is amazing.'

Then, to my surprise, haughty Patricia leans over and gives me a warm hug. As I hug her back, I feel like licking my finger and painting a one in the air. I can always, always win people over, and once again I've succeeded.

* * *

The maid brings up some breakfast for us – two cups of steaming chai and some chapattis with jam. I've had Chai Steamers in Starbucks, but the real Indian thing is something else – my mouth feels rich and creamy with the aftertaste of milk and spices.

'I'll have to get a recipe and make this for Devika every morning,' I declare.

God, I think, I'm glad I chose India. I was worried I might not be able to cope with the spicy food but this is all so fantastic. It's quite a novel thing for me, discovering a new culture. People always think that because I was in a band I've seen the world. In fact, I've only seen the world through the windows of planes, cars and hotel rooms; we were so busy touring there was never any time for exploring. My mum was so intent on turning me into a star, we couldn't afford holidays abroad when I was younger either. So to be out here, meeting locals, tasting a new place, makes me feel like a proper traveller for the first time in my life.

We're just getting ready to go when my mobile beeps. Another text from Fran. I smile and check it. And then the smile vanishes from my face.

Hey just heard Liam is in Delhi too – saw it in Heat. U ok? Fx

'*What!*'

Fran is just winding me up. Surely.

'Patricia,' I say, 'you wouldn't happen to know if Liam Holt is in India right now, would you?'

Patricia looks away and quickly becomes fascinated with fiddling with a pin on her sari.

'I . . . he might well be . . . I mean, he is a jet-setter, isn't he?' she says vaguely.

'This – this is a set-up!' I explode. 'You've deliberately got me and my ex here at the same time to get an extra photo opportunity! I'm trying to focus on adopting my child and you're trying to manipulate things!'

'Don't be so ridiculous,' Patricia objects. 'How on earth would we do that? Liam doesn't give interviews to any magazines, let alone *Elegance*. We're paying you a fortune to focus on you and your baby – this has *nothing* to do with Liam.'

It *sounds* like a reasonable argument. But I've learnt over the last twenty years never to trust the press. Patricia and I sit in a tense silence, waiting for the photographer to get ready, and it seems as though all the good feeling between us has been lost.

Then the photographer knocks on the door. He is a skinny, sweet guy with a dark crewcut who introduces himself as Gerry. We get into an auto rickshaw to go to the orphanage, but I can hardly concentrate on Devika. All I can think of is Liam, Liam, Liam; I stare out at the roads and every time

I see a dark head flashing by (and, as you can imagine, there are plenty of those in India) my heart clenches with fury and excitement. If this isn't a set-up, I simply can't imagine what he's doing here in India – a Bollywood movie? Shooting a video for his band's new single? Or maybe he and his fiancée Hayley are simply seeking spiritual enlightenment – although I remember that when I went through a similar phase and tried to interest Liam in reincarnation, he wasn't impressed: 'I'm not going to go around pretending to be Gandhi and being nice to people and not beating photographers up all because I'm afraid of coming back as a grape.'

Every so often, I'm jolted out of my reverie by the mania of being driven through Delhi. I'd thought India was a Third World country, so I'm surprised by how wealthy the area around our hotel is. Huge, shiny cars honk in the traffic; opulent buildings glitter in the blazing sun. But as we head for the orphanage, the luxury melts into slums and the road deteriorates. Our rickshaw competes with cows and buses; there appears to be no clear traffic lanes, just a speed free-for-all, and every so often we swerve to avoid a hole in the road. I suddenly feel Patricia's hand grabbing mine and squeezing hard.

'Sorry,' she says, giving me a nervous grin, 'it's just – culture shock.'

I smile back.

And then my smile fades. My heart starts to bang loudly against my chest. We've pulled up outside the orphanage. We're finally here.

5

Karina

Outside the orphanage, we find Mr Kaushal waiting for us – the official from the adoption agency in India. He's dressed in a white suit which sets off his dark skin beautifully, and looks quite dashing. He gives me a dazzling smile and shakes my hand so exuberantly I think it might fall off – which perhaps isn't surprising given that I've donated ten thousand pounds to his agency. I thought it might help me shoot to the top of their list of priorities.

'One question, before we go in,' Patricia asks him.

'Of course, of course – anything,' he says, spreading open his hands.

'Your agency is rather on the maverick end of the spectrum – you're not recognised by CARA,' Patricia says, referring to India's Central Adoption Resource Agency. 'Why is that?'

'Lots of agencies aren't recognised by CARA,' he says smoothly, grinning at me as though he thinks Patricia is a bit of a pain. I grin back.

'But the disadvantage,' Patricia points out, 'is that this adoption won't be recognised by the Hague convention. Karina can't put in an adoption order here – just a guardianship order. She has to take Devika back to the UK and put in the adoption order there.'

I see Patricia has been doing some research behind my back. Hmm.

'Yes, yes,' he agrees, 'but this way it's very quick – otherwise it can sometimes take years. We make it all – how do you say in English – chop chop, super fast.' He laughs agreeably and I smile back, relieved: without this wonderful man adopting Devika would probably have taken five years, by which time the whole celeb mum trend will be all over anyway. I had to strike whilst the iron was hot.

'Enough questions,' he says, waving his hand. 'Now Karina must meet her child.'

Oh, God. The butterflies are coming back again.

Inside, we meet Mrs Laxsmi. She's a plump woman with greying hair pulled back in a bun and a sari with a rather tatty hem; she's so lovely that I wish I could drag her away to a designer boutique and cheer her up by treating her to a makeover. She greets us warmly by placing garlands of yellow flowers over our necks. Then she shakes my hand, hugs me and kisses each cheek, which makes me worried she might smear my make-up. The photographer keeps flashing me at every turn and I wish I could instruct him to shoot only from the right so my nose doesn't look so bad.

'We go for guided tour first,' Mrs Laxsmi says. 'Then Devika.'

I don't want a tour. I just want to get this over and done with. My stomach is now on butterfly overload. My palms are sweating. In fact, the combination of Indian sun and fear is so lethal my sari will soon be dripping. But, aware of Patricia's eyes on me, I nod and smile at Mrs Laxsmi until my face begins to hurt.

Oh my God. Is that . . . a *rat* running down the corridor? Make that two. I know this is India, but this is meant to be an orphanage – haven't they heard of health and safety? I've never really thought about what it must be like to be this poor – poverty for me has always been defined as not being able to afford a new pair of boots from Hobbs. I feel sorry for them on the one hand, but another part of me can't help writhing with disgust.

We visit the room where the babies are kept. Their cots are lined up on the floor. They smile up at us, gurgling, innocent, seemingly ignorant of their fates. One of the helpers is changing a nappy. It looks to me like an old rag. Patricia blinks back tears.

'Oh, they're so sweet,' she coos, 'I almost want to adopt one myself.'

I want to summon tears too, but I can't. I'm just too nervous. I can't understand what's the matter with me – I don't normally get like this even before an audition. I am so used to being able to control my face and my emotions. Now they feel like a kite for which I have lost the string and they are racing all over the place. The sweet smell from the garlands is becoming increasingly sickly; I'm terrified I might even throw up. I'm not helped by the fact that every time I look at Mr Kaushal, he flashes an insanely optimistic smile at me, as though he fears I might flee at any moment.

Mrs Laxsmi says it's lunchtime. All the kids are back from the local school – we hear the buzz in the background.

'Now we go to see lunch and Devika,' Mrs Laxsmi beams. 'Then we eat together!'

I expect to be taken to a canteen, but instead we enter a corridor. At least this one looks clean. The children are all sitting with their backs to the walls in two lines, facing each other. Each has a small bowl of rice in front of them. When they see us, the volume of excitement rises several notches. They whisper and point and smile and laugh. Mrs Laxsmi touches them as she goes past, stroking a cheek, ruffling a head. She reaches down now and again, feeding them rice with her fingers. Then I see a girl at the end of the line jump to her feet. Mrs Laxsmi grabs my hand and takes me over to her.

'Devika! This is your Devika. Devika, this is Karina.'

Devika looks even more sweet and pretty than her photograph. Her black hair is tied back in a ponytail and her smile is positively superwatt. She says 'Hello' and does a little jig of excitement from foot to foot that provokes an 'Aw, cute' from Patricia. I smile at her, but something feels terribly wrong. I'm waiting for the wave of unconditional over-whelming love – but where is it? I don't feel anything; I just feel numb. Then I stare into her eyes and I see behind her smile. I see desperation. Complete and utter desperation. And desperation equals dependency. She thinks I am her saviour. Panic screams through me. I think she detects it because she springs forward and engulfs me in a hug, clinging on tight. Her emaciated elbows are bony, sharp against my shoulders. I bend down and hug her back, smiling hard, flashes all around us as the photographer snaps and snaps away.

6

Devika

Karina has just given me a hug when we hear the bell ringing. Everyone forgets me and runs about in a panic. The bell hangs outside the orphanage and when it rings it means someone has left a baby in the cot for us. I don't want Karina to see the baby. What if she sees it and decides she wants it instead of me?

I am very relieved when Mrs Laxsmi tells Karina the baby has to be taken straight to the doctor. She says I should show Karina round the orphanage once more. I am worried she might be hungry, so I pick up some rice from my bowl and hold it out to her, but she shakes her head, looking as though I have offered her a snake. I guess she doesn't like rice.

I take her hand and draw her out into the court-yard. I can't stop staring at her and thinking how beautiful she looks. From time to time, we've seen someone with a white face at the orphanage. When Mike first came, he looked white, but then the sun turned his face browner and browner until he looked like us. But Karina's face still looks so strange that I can't help staring up at it. Her skin is so white I can see the little threads of veins, like the colour of the sky seen through clouds. Her lips are like pretty pink flowers. But the most beautiful thing about her is her hair. It's so long and the colour of the sun when it's most angry and blazing. Every time she stares down at me, I want to reach up and stroke it. She holds my hand tightly and I feel as though I never want to let go. *This is my new mummy*, I keep thinking, *this is my new mummy*. I wish I didn't have to take her on another tour, I wish we could just get into a plane now and go to England before she can change her mind.

Then she says something to me. I stare at her face, trying to understand what she means. I look at her friend, but she just shrugs.

'Shoes,' Karina says. 'Shoes.'

Shoes? I've heard Mike say the word, but I can't remember what it means.

Then she points at my feet, and her feet.

'Shoes.' She taps the shoes she's wearing. They are very pretty and look as though they're made out of straw. Then she points at my feet. I wiggle my toes.

'No shoes.' I shake my head. I feel worried. None of us have any shoes. Did she expect me to have shoes?

But to my surprise, Karina crouches down in front of me and touches my face. She says something I don't understand. Then she says more slowly: 'You will have shoes.'

Just then, Mike comes into the yard and Karina waves and speaks to him in English. Mike grins at me and puts his thumbs up, which means this is my lucky day.

'Karina wants to take you shopping,' he says.

We go to see Mrs Laxsmi and she says it's okay for us to go shopping. I can't believe it; I'm so excited. I've only ever been to the market to help Mike buy batteries or vegetables and now for the first time in my life I'm going to have my own pair of shoes! But Karina tells Mike to tell me we're going to go all the way to New Delhi, where the rich people go shopping.

Karina wants her friends to come too. One of them is a woman with yellow hair who doesn't look as pretty as Karina. The other one is a man who keeps on staring at me through his camera, which makes me feel a bit funny.

I hail two rickshaws and I get into the first one. It's just me and my new mummy, on our own together. She reaches out and holds my hand and smiles at me. I think this is the happiest I have ever been in my whole life.

Karina makes me laugh on the rickshaw ride because every so often a cow passes us by or we drive round a hole in the road and she lets out a little gasp. I start to giggle but then she looks annoyed and I quickly stop.

As we pass by the slums, Karina forgets to be scared and stares at them with an open mouth. I stare at them too. They look the same as ever – shelters with plastic sheets covering sticks of wood and families living underneath. Some children are playing in a pothole and splashing each other. I smile and point at them, but Karina looks so sad I think she might cry. I guess they don't have poor people in England.

'Mummy, it okay,' I say. She jumps. 'Mummy. It okay,' I repeat.

I don't think she likes me calling her Mummy because she points to her chest and says, 'Karina. I am Karina.'

Then I feel sad because if she's going to be my new mummy, why can't I call her that? Maybe she is testing me and if I'm good she'll decide for sure that I am her daughter and *then* I will be able to call her Mummy.

Then we reach New Delhi and we get out and the rickshaw driver says to Karina: 'Fifty dollars!'

Karina gives another little gasp like we're still in the rickshaw and we've just missed a cow. Then she opens up her purse and starts to look for the money.

'No, no, no!' I cry. 'Not fifty dollars! Two hundred rupees!' I don't know to say 'two hundred' in English but I say it over and over to the driver.

'Forty dollars!' the rickshaw driver says, ignoring me and speaking only to Karina.

'Two hundred rupees!'

Karina looks from me to the driver as though she doesn't know who to believe. I feel angry with the driver because we both know it's not fifty dollars and he thinks she is a tourist and he can just take her money: Mike told me this happens all the time when white people come here.

Karina pulls a sad face and then *she gives him fifty dollars*. The rickshaw driver says, 'Thank you, thank you, thank you!' I can't help staring at the money. The notes are coloured green with a picture of the American president on them, just like Raji described. I have never seen so much money in my life. And she has just given it all away to a driver who is trying to trick her.

I think my new mummy needs me to teach her some lessons.

7

Karina

Shopping. Thank God for shopping! Our trip to New Delhi has totally and utterly saved me. I think I would have had hysterics if I'd stayed a minute longer in that hot, rat-ridden orphanage. But buying things for Devika has been so much fun. Now we're sitting in a rickshaw, on our way home, smothered in shopping bags. Devika keeps staring down at her new shoes, twisting her foot this way, that way. I think of the last time Clare took her older kid shopping for new shoes. Clare related that he had thrown a terrible tantrum in the middle of Clarks when she refused to buy him the most expensive pair, screaming, 'Mum, if you don't buy me those Nikes I'm going to DIE!' Just wait until I tell Clare about this trip, I think, unable to resist feeling smug. She'll wish she adopted too instead of suffering those awful twenty-four-hour labours.

I smile down at Devika, who grins back up at me. And though I'm not yet experiencing waves of unconditional love, I feel good. I feel confident. My panic attack is over. I know I can do this. Devika and I might have problems – not being able to exchange more than five words being the main difficulty. But Devika isn't going to be like a horrible typical British kid. She won't grow up suffering the usual adolescent trajectory: sex at the age of twelve, an abortion at thirteen, and a knife fight at fifteen. She won't be spoilt. She'll be so grateful for a proper childhood that she'll always behave. I'm so lucky, I think; I've found the easiest motherhood option anyone could possibly come across. From now on, every day is going to be a joy for both of us.

Of course, Fate must have overheard my smug thoughts in the rickshaw, because when we get back to the hotel things become rather challenging to say the least.

Back in the hotel room, Devika's eyes widen like moons. She keeps touching everything as though it's made of solid gold. As though she can't believe it's not about to vanish. The bed, the wardrobe, the rug, the mirror. I feel strangely self-conscious on my own with her, without the photographer or the shopkeepers as our audience. I point out the second bed and pat it, pointing at her.

'For you,' I say. My voice sounds high, unnatural, as though I'm trying to put on a motherly tone, and I try to normalise it: 'For you – tonight.'

Her eyes light up. Yet behind the light I notice a shadow of fear. Almost as though she can't quite believe she deserves all this. I pat her shoulder and repeat reassuringly: 'For you. Because you're worth it.'

I don't mean the slogan to pop out – it just does. I laugh and Devika laughs too. Even though she hasn't understood the joke, we still manage to share it.

Then she yawns and I realise how tired she must be.

'Lie down,' I say, making a pillow shape with her hands. 'Have a little rest. Now. I'm just going to run you a bath.'

I want to dress her in one of those lovely outfits before we go down to dinner, so she'll look her best for the photographer. But I can't help noticing she is rather grubby. Her palms are filthy and there are smears of dirt on her face and neck that I don't want to transfer on to her new clothes.

I leave her lying on the bed, humming to herself. It seems to be a habit of hers and I think it's rather sweet. In the bathroom, I run the bath quite deep and swish in some bubbles, breathing in their sweet almond scent, picturing how much she'll enjoy playing about in them. Clare's kids always grumble about bath time but Devika will no doubt feel she's in heaven.

I go back into the bedroom to find Devika standing in front of the wardrobe, staring at her reflection with a fierce, strange look in her eyes.

'Come on, it's bath time,' I say.

She looks up, confusion on her face.

'Come on.' I grab her little hand and draw her into the bathroom. She stares at the bath as though it's from another planet. I pull her pink top off. Her ribcage sticks out, bursting against the skin. I can't believe how thin she is; when we get home I'll have to give her millions of vitamins. I reach for her skirt, then pause. She keeps looking at the bath as though it's a dentist's chair.

'Bath time.' I swish my finger in the water, whirling up some bubbles. 'It's fun!'

She bursts into hysterical tears and runs from the room.

'What the . . .'

When I go back into the bedroom, she's vanished.

'Devika? Don't hide from Karina – from your m— Devika, where are you?'

How the hell can she disappear in the space of five seconds?

'Devika!'

A knock on the door. I open it breathlessly. It's Patricia. She's now wearing a cerise sari, which she has wound around herself like a mummy. She holds up the hem and wails: 'I still can't get the hang of it – can you help?' She peers past me into the bedroom. 'Is Devika okay?'

'She's fine,' I say briskly, pushing back my panic. I can't bear Patricia or anyone to see that I haven't got everything one hundred per cent under control. 'But she's sleeping, so I need to leave her in peace, really . . .'

'I can't see her on the bed,' Patricia says, sidling in.

'Oh, gosh,' I cry. 'She was just on the bed a minute ago and she was going to have a bath – she must be hiding from me. Naughty Devika. Devika! Where are you?'

Patricia and I both look around. I'm terrified she might have jumped out of the window and when I hear a noise from the wardrobe I nearly cry with relief. I open it up and Patricia stares over my shoulder. I'm aware how terrible the scene looks: my adopted child, half dressed, hiding in a wardrobe, weeping. I turn to Patricia, who looks as though she's ready to leap on her mobile and call the NSPCC. I realise that there's nothing I can do except be honest.

'I tried to give her a bath and she started crying and went crazy – it really freaked me out and then she hid and I just don't know what I did to upset her,' I blurt out in a rush.

To my relief, Patricia's face softens.

'I guess we can't imagine how strange this all is for her,' she says. 'All the things we're used to – running water, baths, beds – they're all new to you, aren't they, Devika?' She kneels down and comforts her, so easily, so naturally, that I feel almost jealous.

Patricia pulls Devika up out of the wardrobe and we both give her a hug in turn.

'We'll skip the bath,' I say to Devika. I point at the bathroom and I shake my head. 'It's okay – no bath,' I say. 'Just eat. Eat – you want to eat?' I mime putting rice into my mouth and she nods, smiling, looking much happier.

Later that night, after we have eaten and posed for a few more photos, we part company and I take Devika up to bed. I don't risk a bath, but I do wash her face gently and to my relief she doesn't cry. I also show her how to use a toothbrush, though she gags at the minty Colgate toothpaste.

I tuck her up in bed and say goodnight, but

Devika grabs the sleeve of my pyjamas, tugging gently. What now? Then I remember that when I was a kid I longed for my mother to read me a bedtime story. I'd beg for *Cinderella*, but she would always say firmly, 'There's no time for a story – we have to get our beauty sleep. We'll be up at five tomorrow for that audition and it's a long drive and you need to look your best.' I look at Devika and sense she'd like to hear *Cinderella*, but I doubt she'd understand a word of it. I guess I could draw her little accompanying pictures to explain – but then we'd be up all night. I already feel exhausted by the events of day – I just want to lie down and sleep.

Devika, however, seems to sense the complexities of the situation. She says something in Hindi, then opens her mouth and breaks into song. Instead of a story, we'll have a sing-song instead.

It's absolutely exquisite. With a voice like that, she could easily be in an all-girl band when she grows up – or even an Andrew Lloyd Webber musical.

I hear the words '*Krishna*' and '*Padma*' and sense it's a devotional song of some kind; I can hear passion in her voice, as though she's truly singing from the heart. I must try to get the hang of this Hindu stuff when we get home.

'Beautiful,' I cry. She looks almost tearful with delight.

Then she points at me and I realise it's my turn. What can I sing? I don't know any lullabies. I could sing her a Beppo song, but it's been years since the band and I made a point of forgetting the lyrics, putting the past behind me. Suddenly my mind is a blank. What can I sing, what can I sing? Then, without thinking, I burst into song.

Into Britney Spears's 'Hit Me Baby One More Time'.

Once I start, I feel like an idiot. But Devika beams and claps.

'That was Britney,' I say.

'Britney,' she echoes me, as though the name is sacred.

We smile and I wish Patricia was here to see us bonding like this. I lean over, brush an awkward kiss on her cheek and switch off the light.

My body is hungry for the relief of sleep, but my racing mind won't switch off. Worse, I feel as though I've been in such hyper mode that lying down and letting go brings release. Tears start stinging my throat. Images of the day spin before me – the rats, the babies, the market, Devika's hug, her smile, the shoes – and the pressure of tears grows stronger and deeper. All the feelings that I've been trying to repress all day come surging up. I'm scared. When we were sitting in the rickshaw and she called me Mummy it made every hair on my body stand on end. A shock moment that made me suddenly understand the reality of the situation. And, to ram it home, just behind Devika I could see the slums: dirty children with stick limbs running around in mud, mothers with gaunt cheeks hunched under houses made of old rags. I've seen the worst poverty I've ever encountered today and I want to take Devika away from it all, but I'm terrified I'm not up to this. But I can't back out now – I can just imagine the look on her face if I told her she had to go back to the orphanage. It would completely destroy her. But what if I can't do it? What if I can't be a good mother to her? What if I can't cope?

I don't want to wake her up with my crying so I allow a few tears to slip down my cheeks. I brush them away fiercely and force the rest back down my throat. I must concentrate on falling asleep: tomorrow there will be more photo opportunities, and a trip to collect Devika's new passport and some paperwork to finalise my guardianship; I'm a busy mother now.

I'm just dropping off when I feel the covers stir

and Devika slip into bed beside me. She snuggles up and falls asleep instantly. I want to curl up with her, for us to sleep nose to nose. But I feel irritated. Her head is heavy on my arm. The heat of our bodies is claustrophobic and I have to edge down the sheet. I try to ease my arm, inch by inch, away from her head, but she stirs and I'm afraid I'll wake her and then she'll cry, or we'll have to have another sing-song and I'll end up resorting to Westlife or worse. I close my eyes and I swear another hour passes and I can feel a high-pitched ringing in my ears that I get when I'm suffering from insomnia and I feel almost hysterical with tiredness.

What if she wants to do this night after night? I'll never get any sleep. I need my sleep. I love my sleep. I have to get at least eight hours a night or my skin looks sallow and old. Panic begins to spiral up again, along with tears of angry frustration. I quickly force them back down.

This is your first night together, I tell myself, so you can allow her this treat. Back home she can sleep in the room you've had decorated especially for her. Just take this one day at a time.

That feels reassuring. I keep repeating it over and over, like a mantra: just take it one day at a time, one day at a time, one day at a time . . . I feel much better, until I suddenly realise that this is the slogan recovering alkies tell themselves every morning. Then all the doubt comes rushing back. Oh God: can I do this? Am I really cut out to be a mother?

8

Devika

I've got my own passport to fly to England. Mummy Karina won't let me hold it, though, because she's afraid I might lose it or make it dirty. She worries about dirt a lot. She hasn't got me to have a bath yet, so she keeps making me wash my hands all day. It's as though she's trying to make up for the rest of me being dirty by making sure I have the cleanest hands in Delhi.

I've only ever seen a plane high in the sky, like a small flying car. When we get to the airport, I can't believe how big they are on the ground – like huge metal monsters. Every so often one of them goes shooting down the runaway and at the last moment it looks as though it will crash and then, like a miracle, the wind catches it and carries it into the sky.

It seems like we hang around for ever waiting for our plane to let us on. I sit and stare at my new shoes. One of them is hurting me and there's a pinky-brown bubble on my left ankle, but I don't want to tell Mummy Karina in case she takes them away and they cost so much I might not get another pair.

At last we get on to the plane and Mummy Karina shows me my seat – I am sitting by the window!

As soon as I sit down, Mummy Karina makes me get up. There are two grey floppy snakes attached to the seat. She pushes me so I sit back down again. Then she clicks the snakes over my stomach so I'm stuck to the seat. Mummy Karina says something to me. I hear the word 'afraid'. I know that word. Mike told me what it means. And she pulls a scared face and points at me. I nod a little. She smiles and holds my hand.

I sense Mummy Karina wants me to be afraid, just as she was scared when she went in the rick-shaw. It's my turn to be scared, it's her turn to comfort me. So I try to look very frightened and squeeze her hand very tight and she keeps stroking my hair.

But I am not really that scared, even when the plane screams into the sky. Not like I felt when she took me to the bathroom. When I saw the water, I couldn't believe she wanted me to get in. I thought she wanted to drown me, the way Sheetal's mother tried to drown her in a well when she was a little girl before she came to our orphanage. I felt stupid afterwards because I know my own mummy wouldn't want to drown me, but every time I see the water my stomach squeezes in fear. I feel like it's a horrible punishment; I wish I had my bucket to pour over me, but when I tried to ask Mummy Karina for one she didn't understand, even when I drew it.

'Look – clouds!' Mummy Karina points. I have never seen anything so amazing. Then, as we fly higher, the clouds fade away and I realise there isn't enough blue to go round the whole sky, for at the top is pure white. It's so amazing I want to stare and stare until my eyes hurt.

Then I notice a man walking down the aisle. He's very tall, with wild dark hair like he's just got out of bed and lost his comb. He is wearing a shiny black jacket and jeans and he looks like an American. He stops by Mummy Karina and says something. She doesn't seem to hear him, because she turns to me and smiles. I stare past her head to the man. He gives me a little wave. I wave back. There is something wicked in his eyes that makes me laugh. Then Mummy Karina turns back to him and says lots of things very quickly, in a very angry tone.

He shrugs and spreads open his hands. Then he walks away.

'Who's the man?' I asked Mummy Karina.

'Nobody.'

'Mis-ter Nobody,' I say, taking care to pronounce it correctly.

'No – not Mr Nobody.'

'No? I got wrong?'

She sighs and I am worried she's angry with me again.

'His name is Liam.'

'Lee-am.'

'That's right. Lee-am.'

Liam seems to have upset Mummy Karina because she seems angry for many hours to come. I am excited, though, because the nice lady in blue keeps bringing round things for us to eat. I have Coca-Cola! It's black and shiny and every time I sip it, it fizzes bubbles up in my nose. I keep wishing Raji was here so he could try some too. We could both fizz up our noses together and laugh like mad. I feel the bubbles popping and winking around my tummy and then I feel a bubble whoosh up my throat and explode in my mouth with a terrible noise.

'Devika!' Mummy Karina cries, but she is smiling.

I smile, and clap my hands over my mouth.

'I like Coca-Cola,' I say.

Her smile fades and she looks sad again. I want Mummy to be happy. I want her to be happy always. I think about what I can do to please her and then

I remember how much she liked my song. I turn to her and I begin singing it again, but I only sing one line before she shakes her head and makes a *shh* noise. Maybe she's got bored of the song. I try another one, but she shakes her head again. She makes a pillow shape with her hands to mean *sleep*.

But I can't sleep. I'm too happy and excited. I stare out of the window at the clouds and at the lady in the blue skirt and the man's head in front of me and drink some more Coca-Cola and I think there're so many things to look at and learn I'll never want to sleep again. I look at Mummy Karina and her eyes are closed. I feel worried because I need to go to the lavatory. I try to tug the two snakes away from my stomach, but their teeth are locked together and they won't let me out. It feels as though all the Coca-Cola I've drunk is pressing against me, dying to gush out between my legs and I clamp them together, terrified I'll wee on the seat and Mummy Karina will get angry. I tug harder and harder at the snakes. I can feel sweat on my head and I feel like I want to cry. Finally, I turn and I tug Mummy Karina's sleeve. Her eyes stay closed. I tug really, really hard. She wakes up.

'What?'

'Toilet,' I whisper. 'Please. Toilet.'

'Of course.' She unlocks my snake and we squeeze gently past the lady from the magazine who is sleeping. We go to the lavatory, but then we can't get in. Karina turns and looks to see if there's another one, but there are people waiting there too. She points at the little red light and shakes her head, so I think it means someone is using it and I wish they would hurry because my Coca-Cola wants to come out and I pray to keep it in, keep it in—

Then the door opens and Liam comes out.

And then the nice lady in the blue skirt who gave me Coca-Cola comes out too.

'My God!' Mummy Karina cries.

I think maybe Liam had trouble going to the toilet because his belt is undone and the nice lady reaches over and ties it back up for him. He laughs when she does it and then she gives him a kiss.

Liam ruffles my hair and grins at me and I laugh, but I can't wait any longer. I have to go and I run into the lavatory and pull down my knickers. For a moment I feel confused because I can't see the hole, where's the hole, and then I realise the lid is down and I push it back up and sit on the seat and all the Coca-Cola comes gushing out and I feel much better. I take some little bits of white paper from the paper thing, but I don't remember what to do with them so I put them in the hole too. Then I can't see the button to make it clean, so I put down the plastic lid and wash my hands using the little white soap which smells so pretty.

When I come out of the lavatory, Mummy Karina is still looking angry. And then Liam and the nice blue lady go back into the lavatory again. I want to tell them I didn't know how to make it clean, but they have already closed the door. I guess Liam has been drinking even more Coca-Cola than me. I wish I knew the English to explain this to Mummy Karina, but I can't think of the words, so we go back to our seats and put the snakes back on and sit in silence.

9

Karina

This cannot be a coincidence. Liam and I in the *same* country at the *same* time on the *same* flight home. Someone has set this up. Maybe it's *Elegance* magazine – although Patricia is sleeping soundly beside me and seems oblivious of the emotional fireworks exploding around her. Or, more likely, it's my agent – perhaps Liam's agent too – playing with us like puppets to generate some PR. Or maybe Liam himself found out I was on this flight home and deliberately decided to sabotage my adoption and hurt me – though why he would still want to hurt me after all this time I don't know.

I take a sip of white wine and try hard not to think about what Liam and the stewardess are doing back in that lavatory. It's not difficult, because

I remember too much too well. I picture him kissing her softly and running his fingers through her hair and shoving his knee between her thighs. Desire stabs through me. I watch another stewardess sashaying down the aisle, an amused smile on her lips, and I feel like shouting at her, 'Aren't you going to even try to stop your colleague? Aren't you going to fire her?'

In fact, she probably will be fired. But she'll be able to enjoy notoriety in the newspapers and maybe she'll feel it's worth it. Sex with Liam is not something you can ever forget. She'll be spoilt now; every man she's with will always seem grey and insipid in comparison.

I glance over at Devika, who is looking exhausted but too overexcited to sleep. I worry that my bad mood and this whole Liam charade might be upsetting her. I touch her shoulder. She smiles up at me. I smile back and make another sleep gesture. She nods obediently and closes her eyes. I sit back, wanting to sleep myself, but I'm just too mad. This flight back should have been filled with bliss – I should be focusing every drop of attention on my new daughter and now he's ruining everything.

I first met Liam nine years ago. I was twenty-five years old. Our all-girl band had split up and I was trying to become the next Catherine Zeta Jones.

My mum was still alive then, but she was in an old folk's home. When I went to visit her, she would quiz me sharply on how my career was progressing. I began exaggerating my success to keep her happy; I couldn't bear the look of disappointment on her face. Towards the end of my teens, I had begun to realise the sacrifices she had made to turn me into a 'child star' – holding down several jobs, skimping on new clothes for herself so she could afford them for my auditions, avoiding relationships in case they distracted her from our goal. I could sense that she was aware time was running out for her and she was anxious for me to have some success. But she wasn't easy to please. I was like the child who came home with A's and got berated for not having A pluses. I felt that nothing less than an Oscar and a worldwide number one hit would keep her happy.

So, I began to tell fibs. I told her I'd landed a part in a Hollywood film opposite Brad Pitt. Her eyes lit up and she said she'd love to come to the premiere. On the way home, I remember feeling sad that I had lied to her. That I couldn't truly satisfy her dreams. My agent was sending me up for audition after audition but I just wasn't getting the parts. The day before I'd been interviewed by a very sexy director and I'd really hoped I might get to lie across his casting couch. In my desperation (and lust) I had put my hand on his knee and he had looked appalled and cried, 'What are you doing! I'm a married man!' I blushed at the memory and then felt indignant – for goodness' sake, the casting couch was acting law and he ought to be following it. Then I began to sink into depression again, fearing that my mum might find out I was lying to her and pass away thinking I was a failure.

Later that evening I went out for drinks with Fran, who was having a depressingly successful time. Her solo single, 'Fly Girl', was at number two in the charts. We were interrupted by a call from my agent. He said he'd arranged for me to interview Liam Holt the following afternoon.

'Interview?' I cried, stung. 'What? What are you talking about? I want people to interview *me*.'

'It's a great slot for *The Sunday Times* where one celebrity interviews another celebrity and it was meant to be a Spice Girl doing it but she dropped out at the last minute. I had to work hard to get you in as a replacement – Liam complained that he didn't want to be interviewed by a fucking airhead from an all-girl pussy-band.'

My agent always forgot he was meant to butter up his clients.

'Did he?' I cried in outrage.

When I turned to Fran and told her, however, she nearly spat out her cocktail in shock.

'Oh *wow*! Liam is the sexiest sex god who ever ever lived! I'm so jealous, I'm so jealous!'

'You have a single at number two in the charts,' I appeased her.

'But Liam is even better – much much better.'

That night, I looked Liam up online. He was probably expecting me to sit and salivate over him, then ask inane questions. I decided to do my research. I was going to be smart and businesslike and cool as hell.

The following morning, I changed my outfit six times before I settled on jeans and a red top. I found a pair of glasses with clean frames that I'd bought for an audition for a part as a brain surgeon. I put them on and picked up my notebook, filled with carefully worded questions.

In the pub, I sat waiting for half an hour until my nerves turned into anger. I'd just phoned my agent and the newspaper to confirm I had the right place when Liam came sauntering in. He was wearing his usual rock god uniform – dirty grey T-shirt, black ripped jeans, leather jacket, designer stubble, D&G shades even though it was daytime. Despite my irritation, I had to admit that he was the definition of sexy.

But he wasn't alone. A group of people had tagged along with him. I recognised his drummer; there was also a cool black guy chewing gum, and a cute, petite blonde and a few other hangers-on. Immediately I felt cross and intimidated; if I'd known, I would have invited Fran along.

'Where's my interrogator?' he said loudly, looking round. Then he spotted me. 'Oh. You.'

'Yes, me,' I said.

He took his whisky, then came and grabbed a stool opposite me. His friends buzzed around, talking, drinking, stealing cigarettes off each other.

'Ooh,' he said, staring at my notepad, 'you're prepared. Go on then. Ask me what my favourite colour is. Ask me if my time in rehab fundamentally changed my attitude towards life, music and my inner values.'

I stared down at my pad, flushing scarlet. Obviously I hadn't been planning to ask the colour question . . . but the other one was rather close to the mark. His friends began to snigger. What a bully, I thought in outrage.

Then I looked up. He'd taken off his shades and pinned his dark eyes on me. There was a sparkle in them that said, *Don't take me too seriously, I'm only playing*.

'When did you lose your virginity?' I asked impulsively.

'Ooh!' his friends cheered and laughed.

Liam grinned. He seemed to like the question.

'When I was fourteen. She was my older brother's

girlfriend. He was in love, he wanted to propose to her, wanted to be her first – but I beat him to it. She was lovely.'

'And how many women have you had since then? A hundred? Two?'

Liam's grin vanished. Like a true womaniser, he didn't like the suggestion that he was a user, that he might be insincere.

'I like women,' he said, shrugging.

'But the liking only seems to last a night.'

'I don't break hearts. I don't pretend I'm interested in marriage. I'm always upfront about what I want.' He looked riled still. He took a Silk Cut from his packet, looking around for a light. The petite blonde obliged. He blew out a stream of smoke and stood up. I blinked. I'd been enjoying our banter, and I didn't realise then that Liam was a lot more sensitive than his tough act might suggest.

'Who's for a game of snooker?' he said.

'Wait – that's it?' I cried.

'Make the rest up – that's what journalists do, don't they?'

'I'm not a journalist, I'm an actress—' I began, but he was already picking up a cue. I felt I was losing control of the situation; what could I do now? I stood up and cried impetuously: 'I'll challenge you to a game!'

'You?' Liam gave me a scornful look. Then that

playful glint came into his eye again, only this time it was a little more dangerous. 'You can play with me, but I don't play normal snooker. I only play Strip.'

'Strip . . . *snooker*?'

Liam grinned at the riotous delight of his friends. I had an inkling he felt under pressure to keep transgressing, to keep them entertained. This sort of game wasn't my style at all – but I couldn't bear to lose, to back out and be a chicken. I put on a defiant expression and said: 'Sure. Prepare to end up naked.'

When Liam picked up his cue and potted the red, I thought uh oh. He grinned and brushed the tip of his cue against my sleeve.

'Take off your jacket.'

By now the pub was enthralled and a crowd had gathered around us.

Liam attempted to pot the brown and – thank God – missed.

'My turn,' I said. He deliberately pinned his laser gaze on me, trying to put me off. But I shut the crowd out and focused every drop of my concentration on to potting my red. I did it!

Now it was my turn to suggest he remove his jacket.

'Oh dear – you seem to be wearing fewer clothes than I am,' I said, with a sweet, sarcastic smile.

As he took off his jacket, I saw the ripple of his muscles under his grey T-shirt.

Naturally, I missed the next shot. I was much too distracted by those muscles. He then potted a red. I removed my shoes.

He potted a black. He pointed to my cardigan.

As he leant over the board, I thought in alarm: *if he gets this next one, it will either be my jeans or my top. Oh God, please let him miss.*

He potted it.

Everyone stared at me. Liam looked me up and down, smiling, then brushed his cue against my jeans. His eyes goaded me, as though he was expecting me to cry or play chicken and walk out.

I took them off. Everyone burst into whistles and cheers and I laughed, blushing. I saw Liam's eyes caress my legs. I blushed even more.

He turned back to the game and missed the pink. He was so wide off the mark I wondered if he'd missed on purpose, and felt a shiver of gratitude.

I potted the red and now it was my turn to point at him. He removed his T-shirt and every girl in the pub nearly fainted in delight.

I missed the pink. He potted a red. I winced. I really did not want to take off my top. And what if he potted another ball after that? How far was this going to go? I was just about to slip it off when he suddenly stepped in, drew me into his arms and gave me a big, grinning kiss. All around us, everyone cheered.

'I'm enjoying this game too much,' he said. 'Why don't you lose the rest at my place?'

And so, from that day on, we were a couple.

For the first time in my entire life, I was in love.

Some people have told me that falling in love is a state of serenity, deep peace and contentment. For me, it was a state of insanity. I did what I have allowed no other man to make me do – I surrendered myself. I let him take me over. I adopted his lifestyle completely; I allowed him to shape me like plasticine. If he wanted to go out partying until two a.m., I was by his side; if he drank, I drank; if he took drugs, I took drugs.

This was a shocking thing for me, Karina West, to do. My mother and my agent had always kept me squeaky clean. These days, Amy Winehouse's problems are considered cool. But a decade or so ago there was still the idea – which now seems quaint and old fashioned – that boy and girl bands ought to be good role models for their fans to look up to. So I was used to being a good girl. When we were Beppo, everyone told us what to do, what to say in interviews, what to wear; I was always billed as the blonde sweet one and perpetually dressed up in pink like a Barbie doll. Everyone always thought that being in a band must be lots of fun, but to be honest it was just very hard work. We were on a treadmill and so exhausted that we were in bed by ten most nights. We worked too hard to ever enjoy a drink – the luxury of a hangover was a forbidden pleasure, for we always had to be up to open a supermarket or be on breakfast telly or fly to Japan. I'd always been taught to be careful with the press and never let anything naughty slip out.

Liam's approach to the media was the complete reverse. He regularly got high and shared details of his sex life with the press. If they were in his way and he didn't feel like talking to them, his equivalent of no comment was a punch in the face. When someone snapped him taking cocaine, he just shrugged and said drugs were fun. He lived life without boundaries, doing whatever he liked when he liked. For me, this was complete anarchy. He made me break every rule I had been taught to obey and I loved every minute of it. I cut myself off from my mother and my friends and embraced the bad girl lifestyle, telling myself we were like Courtney Love and Kurt Cobain . . .

But the drugs became a problem. The paranoia, the shaking fits, the crying, the confusion. And they made Liam a different man. When he was sober, he was kind, funny and tender. After a few units and a few lines, he became cruel, unpredictable, sadistic, liable to burst into violence or randomly snog another girl. The first night we broke up – I had found him with his hand up the dress of a lingerie model – I wept until I felt sick. But the next morning he was on my doorstep, surrounded by photographers, apologising, and he swept me into his arms and the press flashed up and cheered. From then on, we were always breaking up and making up, until the press could hardly keep track.

Over time, I began to understand why he resorted to drugs. He wasn't necessarily trying to be cool or wild. He hadn't had the happiest of childhoods and he was a lot more vulnerable than he pretended to be. He told me that he was scared of the bubble bursting – of waking up and finding that his band was finished, or that his song-writing talent had drained away. And every time I thought he had pushed me to the limit and all my friends were screaming at me to dump him, he'd pull himself together, sober up and beg me to give him another chance.

'I want to be a brilliant boyfriend,' he told me one day, looking sad and confused, 'I just keep fucking up. I know, and I don't know why I do it, but I want to try to be better.'

I can't deny that our fame was a big aphrodisiac. Waking up and going to get the post and seeing a bevy of photographers outside the door just waiting to catch us. Sometimes Liam enjoyed turning it into a game. We'd sneak out of parties and hotels separately, racing off in cars to enjoy the thrill of their chase, keeping them guessing all the time. It made us feel that for all our acting, behind locked doors we shared something that nobody could ever understand or know or write about, that fame was just a private joke between us.

But after a while, he began to get tired of it. Once he caught me calling up the paps – I was only tipping them off that we were going to be dining at the Ivy that evening, so they would snap me wearing my new Versace.

'Why the fuck did you do that?' he raged. 'For God's sake, Karina, you're turning us into a bloody celebrity couple. We're not Posh and Becks, you know.'

I fell into a sulk and he put his arm round me, giving me a tender kiss.

'I'm just finding it a bit much, that's all,' he explained. 'I mean, it was okay in the past, but now they're bloody rummaging through our bins.'

I didn't get Liam's stressing; as far as I could see, our fame was turning us into the hottest, coolest couple in town. Soon everyone wanted to be seen with us. A-listers who would barely have spoken more than a few words to me in the past started asking us over for dinner. Sometimes we hung out with the Primose Hill gang, Sadie and Kate and Jude; on one amazing occasion Madonna invited us to join her for a yoga class.

And yes, I was the walking cliché. I thought that I was different. I thought that I'd be the woman to tame him. Fran and all my estranged friends tried to warn me I was delusional. They all told me I'd turned into someone they didn't recognise any more.

How I hate being proved wrong. After six months together, Liam broke my heart. It's too painful to go into the details even now. But it very nearly destroyed me.

When I had come out of rehab and recovered – that's when I became really ambitious and tried and failed to revive my career as a singer/actress. By then, the press had lost interest in me and Liam had moved on to his next blonde.

For years, I would open a magazine and see a picture of Liam nuzzling some girl and want to weep. From time to time, we'd bump into each other and it always started and ended the same way. We'd exchange frosty hellos, a few how-are-yous, the chemistry would start sparking between us and we'd end up having a drunken one-night stand.

But for the last two years I had undergone a Liam cold turkey. I had successfully given up on him, accepted we were never meant to be together, moved on. Even so, seeing him now on the flight home has cut me up.

Then I look over at Devika, who is now sleeping soundly. Her eyelashes, thick as moth's wings, brush the curve of her pretty cheek. She looks so sweet, so innocent. And I remember why I chose to adopt her. I don't want to find love with a man any more; I don't want to go through what I did with Liam ever again. I want to enjoy the pure, unconditional love of a mother and fill up every corner of my heart with that. Perhaps I have a hard journey ahead of me, but I have to do this – I have to try to succeed as a celebrity mother. I have to see this through.

10

Devika

I wake up and see Mummy Karina staring at me.

'England,' she says. 'England.'

We are home.

She gently unbuckles my snakes. I want to be excited but I feel so tired, I just want to curl up and sleep . . .

She shakes me again.

'Devika – we're home.'

She pulls me out of the seat and we leave the plane and enter a big building. We stand and watch suitcases dropping into a long moving black serpent. There's a boy who keeps trying to jump on to the serpent and pull the cases off. I keep waiting for his mummy to tell him off, but she just sighs and carries on talking to her friend.

The man from the plane, Liam, has disappeared.

It's very cold in England. When we go outside to get a taxi, we find it's daytime because all the hours got jumbled up in the clouds on the way over. The sky looks like the colour of dirty water in the tub after I've washed my clothes at the orphanage. My teeth start to chatter and little bumps shiver over my arms. I feel sick.

The taxi driver doesn't bring us any garlands to welcome us. He has a mean face and he smells of cars and smoke. We sit in the back. There are no pictures of Jesus in his car, even though Mike told me everyone in England is a Christian. Mummy Karina says 'Sleep' but now I am wide awake. England isn't how I imagined it in my dreams at night-time when I lay awake in the orphanage. Mike showed me some pictures of England. He showed me a castle and a big bridge and a tower. But there are no castles or bridges or rich people, just tall buildings that look old and sad, as though they are tired of the rain, and everywhere looks as though their god took a pail of grey and poured it over their colours. Then we drive on to some big roads, where all the cars go very slowly in neat lines, and there are no cows, for all the cows stand in green fields watching us. I see some pretty houses with smoke coming out of the roofs and they look as though rich people might live in them. Then we get to the city and it's more like Delhi because everyone toots their horns and tries to beat the other cars to be the fastest. This is London, my mummy tells me. Everything looks even greyer than ever and I want to see some colour. I feel sick again, as though all the grey is entering me and I want some colour like a medicine. I want to see a big Ganesh with yellow garlands or a pink sari or a stall with vegetables. At last we stop by a big house and get out and I'm sick.

I'm sick all over my beautiful sari and my new shoes and the driver cries out. I start to cry because I'm afraid Mummy Karina will be angry but she takes some white paper from her bag and wipes it off and smiles.

'It's okay,' she keeps saying. 'It's okay. It must be the Coca-Cola.'

'Bad Coca-Cola.'

'Very bad Coca-Cola. Look.' She points. 'Be happy. This is our new house.'

Our house is big and white and beautiful. We go inside and Mummy Karina drops the case as though she's been carrying an elephant. She takes a wet cloth and wipes my dress and my shoes all clean. It's very cold and I start shivering again, so she takes a coat and puts it on me. It's so big the sleeves come over my hands and the bottom bit touches my feet, which makes her laugh, and I feel warmer and better.

Then she takes my hand and shows me round the house. All the different rooms have their own names, but I keep forgetting them. I remember the name for the kitchen, which has a big white thing in it that opens up into a cold temple full of milk and food. Mummy Karina heats up some milk but I only have one sip and I feel sick again. She looks at me and says: 'You don't like? Don't drink. Don't drink.'

So I give my milk to her.

Then she takes me upstairs and shows me a bedroom and says, 'Yours.' I can't believe I have a whole room all to myself, with a bed and a mirror and a wardrobe. She points to the walls and says, 'Brown.' Then she points to my face and says, 'Brown. You match,' she says. That makes her look very happy, though I don't really see why. Then she shows me a statue in the corner. It's a statue of the Buddha. There are no statues of Ganesh or Shiva or Mahalaxsmi. She points to Buddha and says, 'Okay? Okay?' I don't know what to say because Mrs Laxsmi said I should never lie, but I don't want her to be upset, so I say, 'Okay.' And she smiles.

And then I lie down on the bed and I want to sing to her from the very depths of my heart to say thank you, to show how happy I am, but then I find my eyes are closing and I can't stay awake . . .

11

Karina

I wake up feeling as though I'm suffering from a terrible hangover. I reach out numbly for the emergency pack of paracetamol that I always leave lying on my bedside cabinet. Then my hand encounters something. Something warm. I blink awake – who did I come home with last night? Oh God, please let him be hot and not a dog with a tiny cock, let him be A-list and not some wanker presenter off children's BBC or a kid from an unknown boy band . . .

Then I see dark hair and a child's face and the present hits me with a sledgehammer. I sit up. I actually let out a sound that is close to a scream.

To my relief, Devika doesn't wake up.

Then I realise: I'm not hungover, I'm jet-lagged.

So dazed and exhausted that everything has jumbled in my brain. I sink back down into bed. Nine thirty-four a.m. We've been asleep since yesterday late afternoon. I'm a mother. A celebrity mother. I look at Devika's face. She must have crept into my bedroom during the night, but I was so shattered I didn't even stir. I feel a little comforted by this thought: maybe I can adjust to her nightly interruptions and still get my beauty sleep. My eyelids grow heavy. There is so much to organise but I could really do with a few more hours' kip – best to snatch it whilst I can.

Then, just as I'm drifting off, I remember: *photoshoot!*

'Okay, darling, we have two hours before the photographer from *Elegance* comes to photograph us settling in here. So we need to focus.' I've got into the habit of addressing her as though she speaks perfect English. Fortunately, she seems to get the gist of what I'm saying, for she nods and smiles, so we can at least pretend to be communicating.

'So – we need to have baths. Then get dressed. Then have breakfast.' I like making lists and I tick them off on my fingers. 'I think we can do that in two hours, don't you?'

She shakes her head. Oh. Perhaps she isn't getting

the gist of this at all. I nod my head at her. She nods back. I smile. She smiles. I realise she is just mirroring me in her confusion.

'And we'll get your English teacher sorted out right away,' I add hastily, feeling guilty. 'Now for a bath.'

Ah. Bath. I grab her hand and lead her into the bathroom, remembering just how popular our last few bath-time sessions have been. As we enter, her face pales and her grip tightens. I just don't understand why she's so terrified. I move to turn on the taps, but she squeezes my hand so hard I can't extract it. So I keep hold of her with one hand and use the other to push in the plug and run the water. I keep speaking to her all the while, softly assuring her that this is all fine and fun. Last night she fell asleep the moment I showed her her bed and I woke her to take off her sari and put her into a pair of gorgeous little M&S pyjamas. Now, as I lift up her pyjama top, I'm horrified by how grubby she is underneath. At this rate she'll get cholera. I reach for her pyjama bottoms, but then the tears start to come. This time she doesn't scream and shout. She just weeps silent tears, trying to push them back, but unable to do so – which feels worse than her previous hysteria. I lean over and kiss her on the nose to cheer her up. She manages a little smile, but her cheeks still tremble and she exhales a big, shaky breath.

'Oh, dear, what are we going to do?' I say, touching her cheek. 'You can't carry on being dirty.'

I make the mistake of letting go of her hand. She runs. Off into the bedroom, where she hides under the covers. I follow her and sit down on the bed. I really don't know what to do. Should I be firm, as my mother would have been? She would have just dragged me kicking and screaming into the water, ignoring my tears and telling me sharply to grow up. But Devika's had a much harsher life than me – who knows what sort of trauma she associates with baths, and it seems cruel to force her. What if I screw her up for life and she grows up being unable to ever look at a bath again? I begin to feel so het up I'm close to calling Clare to ask her for advice, but I can't bear to let her think I'm a bad mum who can't cope. I reach over and pull back the covers, exposing Devika's frightened face. Then I plunge my fingers into her ribcage and tickle her. She squeals with laughter and I laugh too, glad that she's happy, but feeling that I haven't quite solved the problem.

'Well, I at least am going to have a bath – we can't be the dirty twins. You stay here and sleep, okay?'

She nods. But there is fear in her eyes. I give her a little kiss on the cheek to show I'm not angry. She smiles and goes back to hiding under the covers. One day at a time, I tell myself, one day at a time.

Baths. Normally they're my favourite way of relaxing. I love sinking into a deep tub of sweet-smelling bubbles, music floating around me, closing my eyes and letting go. It's almost a meditation, and when I pull the plug an hour or so later it feels as though my cares drain away with the water.

But with Devika here, I can't relax. She isn't sleeping at all, for I can hear her padding around the flat. Every time I close my eyes I hear the floorboards creaking, or something being clattered, and my lids fly open. I can't help worrying that she's going to break something – I have visions of my treasured Tracey Emin sculpture in shards on the floor. Or worse, that she's going to do herself some harm – plug the iron in and electrocute herself, or trip over a teddy bear. And then Patricia from *Elegance* will turn up and she'll take one look at the chaos and call an ambulance and I'll be infamous as the worst celebrity mother who ever lived. I tell myself fiercely to just chill out – if I carry on worrying like this every minute of the day, I'll drive myself insane. How do parents do this, I wonder. How do they click off their childcare switch? Then I hear a noise. I sit up. Has she fallen?

'Devika,' I call. 'Devika.'

My heart starts to hammer. Then, to my relief, she appears in the doorway. She eyes up the bath uneasily and I smile, beckoning her. But she just sits in the doorway, watching me.

I decide my bath is over. I get up and towel myself off. Devika watches silently. I feel strangely self-conscious and suffer a flicker of exasperation: if she's not in the same room as me, I start to worry; if she's with me, I want to be alone in my own space.

We go into the kitchen for breakfast. I get out a bowl. Devika examines the flowery design in fascination.

'Bowl.' I point.

'Bowl,' she echoes me.

Then I give her a spoon and she learns another new word. I look at my Rice Krispies uncertainly, remembering how she was sick last night. But I have to give her something and there's no time to start looking up recipes for chapattis.

'Snap, crackle and pop.'

She looks blank. Then I pour the milk on and joy illuminates her face.

'Snap!' she cries, staring into her bowl. 'They snap! Snap snap snap!'

'Yes, snap!' I laugh, experiencing an unexpected wave of sheer delight. This is the wonderful thing about children, I realise – seeing the world afresh through their eyes. They make the mundane fascinating.

And then I feel a little confused, because only five minutes ago I was feeling irritated and wanting to be on my own. I seem to be yo-yoing between an array of emotions. I must ask Clare if this is normal.

Devika has a little trouble with her spoon – she keeps on putting it down and trying to eat the cereal with her fingers, which get very milky and messy. But I keep on showing her how to use it and she begins to get the knack.

After breakfast, we get dressed. I put another sari on and this time I dress Devika in an olive-green one. I start on my make-up and Devika watches in solemn silence. I teach her not only the names – mascara, lipstick, brush – but the brand names. I want her to grow up knowing the best products.

As I put on my make-up, I can't help feeling rather nervous. I hope Patricia is going to be kind to me in this article. Then again, *Elegance* doesn't seem the sort of magazine that makes a living from stitching people up.

I'm brushing Devika's hair when the doorbell

rings. I hurry over, smooth down my sari, take a deep breath and fling it open. To my amazement, instead of finding the team from *Elegance* on my doorstep, I discover—

'Fran!' I cry in shock.

Fran opens her arms wide and engulfs me in a huge hug. She draws back, crying, 'I know I was supposed to come in the afternoon but I just couldn't wait to see you.' Then: 'So where is she?'

I draw her over to Devika. 'Devika – this is my best friend, Fran.'

Devika holds out her hand.

'How do you do?' she asks solemnly.

'Oh, she's so cute,' Fran cries. She shakes her hand hard. 'I'm very well. So how do you like this horrible woman who's abducted you from your home country and plonked you in rainy England?'

Devika looks blank and smiles brightly.

I can see that under that smile Devika is nervous, as though Fran is a foreign creature she's frightened will bite. I take her hand and give it a reassuring squeeze. Fran intimidates everyone, including fully grown men, so it's no wonder a ten year old would be unnerved by her. She's six foot tall, with a lean figure and wild black curls. Today she's wearing skin-tight leather trousers and popping gum, and her eyes are covered by D&G shades.

'I was in the Met Bar last night. Oh, and Liam was there on his own and he left early. I've just heard it's over between him and Hayley after the air hostess scandal was in all the papers.'

'Really?' I pretend not to be interested.

'And I went back to Sadie's and had cocktails until five a.m. So I have a terrible hangover.' She smiles down at Devika. 'You'll soon learn the word hangover. Your new mum will use it often and you'll know you need to be quiet.'

Devika nods her head very carefully. Fran frowns and pulls off her sunglasses.

'Does she get a word I'm saying?' she cries.

I suddenly feel rather embarrassed. Why the hell didn't I think to learn some Hindi? I just assumed that Devika would already know a fair bit of English from her classes at the orphanage. To my relief, I am saved from Fran's piss-taking (and believe me, nobody can take the piss better than Fran) by the arrival of the *Elegance* team. There's a make-up girl, Gerry the photographer and his assistant, a sweet young blonde.

'No Patricia?' I ask.

'Not today – we're just here to shoot you and your child at home.'

Phew. That makes me feel relieved.

'Don't mind me,' Fran says. 'I'm just a gate-crasher.'

I give Fran a dark look. I'm sure she was dying to see me – but I suspect that she also couldn't resist the chance to squeeze into my photoshoot. I'm sure she approached the house envisioning glossy photos with the caption, *New celebrity mother Karina West, her child Devika and best friend Fran Stevens*. Honestly! Fran is currently the face of Parfum cosmetics *and* has released a successful solo album. After all this time, I've got my fifteen minutes of fame and now she's trying to steal five minutes of it.

But I love Fran too much to really mind – we've always shared everything. Her just being here makes me feel at ease. Since flying to India, life has taken on a surreal shade and now, with her, I feel more grounded, more myself again.

Gerry starts setting up the lighting in the living room, whilst the make-up artist and the assistant flutter over Devika – 'She is *so* adorable!' they cry, utterly charmed.

'She doesn't know much English,' I warn them.

'Much?' Fran grabs the opportunity to drag me into a corner. 'Your kid can't speak a word of English!' she hisses.

'That's because she's from India, Fran,' I retort in a sarcastic whisper.

'Well, it's nuts. You ought to have one that knows English – one that's already been trained.'

'We're not talking about getting a kitten that's been house-trained!'

Fran crosses her arms. 'So what are you going to call her?'

'It still sounds as though we're on the kitten theme. What d'you mean, what am I going to call her? She's got a name – she's called Devika. It means "little goddess" – I think it's lovely.'

'But Madonna's one is called David. That's not very African, is it? Surely she must have renamed him?'

'No, well . . . I'm not sure . . . actually, I think his name was David.'

'Oh, but Angelina definitely renamed her one. She called him Pax Thien Jolie – it's Latin for 'peaceful sky'. I read it in *Heat* so it must be true.'

'Hmm, well, yes . . .'

'If you want her to fit in as a true celebrity child, I think you should rename her. It's a sort of symbolic way of saying your kid has a new start. I think you should rename her Raspberry . . . or maybe Blackberry.' Fran giggles. 'Imagine – you can say, "I'm just picking up my BlackBerry." No – but seriously, Raspberry is so much better than Devika.'

'Hmm.' For a moment I am semi-convinced. It does have a real celebrity ring to it. I drift off, mentally flicking through fructuous possibilities, when the make-up artist calls over: 'I'm just going to put some make-up on her, is that okay?'

'Ah.' I hurry over to Devika. Although she seemed to enjoy watching me put mine on, I'm a little concerned – what if she reacts to make-up on her the way she does to baths?

I mime putting make-up on my face, then say, 'Revlon, mascara, blusher, Estée Lauder—'

'Estée Lauder!' Devika's face lights up in recognition.

'Good to know she's learning key English expressions,' Fran says.

I ignore Fran and kneel down next to Devika, holding her hand and reassuring her. 'It will be nice. You'll look lovely.'

When the make-up girl leans over to pat foundation on to her cheeks, Devika jumps and lets out a little gasp. Then a smile breaks across her face. She babbles something exuberantly in Hindi.

'What's she saying?' the make-up girl asks.

'Um . . .' I don't want to look an idiot in front of her and admit I don't even know what my own child is saying, 'she says she loves being made up!'

Fran shoots me a wry look and I pretend not to notice. Anyhow, I believe I did translate correctly, for Devika holds her face up to the girl as though she's enjoying a sunbathe. Then, when her hair is curled into black coils, she sits as still and radiant as an angel. When it's finished, the make-up artist gets her to stand up and give us a little twirl.

'She looks so beautiful!' Fran cries, with a touch of envy in her voice.

My heart swells with pride. This is my lovely new daughter. I love being a celebrity mother.

The photoshoot is great fun. We do a happy mother/daughter pose on the sofa, with Devika on my knee. For some reason, she seems to think she ought to be solemn rather than smiley and I have to tickle her to coax a giggling grin out of her. Then a pose by the fridge, its luminous glow highlighting our faces as I pass her an apple (do people keep apples in their fridge? I think not, but never mind). Then one with Fran – all of us sitting at the kitchen table, laughing. And I suddenly realise that I've been enjoying myself so much that I've forgotten to worry about whether my nose looks horrible and whether I'm being taken from the right angle. Which I think is the first time ever in a photoshoot.

Then they ask to take a couple of Devika on her own. They give her a teddy bear to hug and I notice she is struggling to hold back a yawn. It occurs to me that I ought to have delayed the photoshoot for a few days, to give her time to settle in – but when I set it up before India I just didn't think about it.

I'm about to ask them to wrap it up when my mobile beeps. A text. I check it and my heart stumbles.

'You okay?' Fran asks, seeing the look on my face.

It's from Liam: **I can't stop thinking about you – fancy a game of snooker? Lx**

12

Karina

I am feeling extremely annoyed. I'm standing in a designer clothing store that specialises in kid's wear. Devika is dressed in her pretty olive-green sari and we are trying to find practical outfits to wear. We were having fun – until I noticed the photographers outside.

'Oh God,' I sigh to the assistant, 'I think they're hounding us – it's such a pain.' Though I can't help biting back a secret, thrilled smile.

'Actually,' she muses, 'I think they're here for Amy Winehouse.'

'Oh. Really?' I peer out of the window. Sure enough, Amy exits a funky designer store and staggers down the street, her beehive defying the laws of gravity, not to mention her inebriated negotiation with the six-inch stilettos strapped to her feet.

I turn back to the clothes, but I can't help feeling ruffled. This is so unfair. How come they're more interested in Amy than me, the newest Celeb Mum in town?

'I like this.' Devika has drifted into the teen section and is innocently holding a T-shirt with a picture of the Mona Lisa smoking a joint on the front.

I quickly put it down and grab Devika's hand. Yanking her out of the shop, I fling myself in front of the photographers, weeping dramatically. When they notice and recognise me, I cover my face – which, of course, only lures them closer. I hear someone call my name and it ripples through the group. Their hackles rise like jackals who've been informed of fresh meat. My heart beams: *I've been recognised. My name has currency.* I turn away, shielding Devika.

'What's up with you, Karina, been dumped again?' one of them calls out.

I stare into my audience. Cameras click so hard I can't see any faces, just a mirage of light.

'I'm just sad because I just went into that shop,' I sob, 'and it brought back memories of sweatshops and India. I saved this child, Devika, from that kind of fate and it just breaks my heart to think of all the orphans back out there.'

They seem to like the story. I'm crying, that's the main thing, and nothing pleases the press more than a traumatised celebrity.

As we hurry away down the street, we pass Winehouse, who notices I've diluted her attention. I give her a superwatt smile and she returns it with a dirty scowl.

When we get home, I feel slightly foolish. I put the kettle on and then get a saucepan out to make some chai for Devika. And I wonder at myself: *what am I playing at?*

Devika has now been in England with me for ten days and I still feel stirred up; I'm waiting for my emotions to clear and settle. I keep waking in the mornings with a strange sense of anti-climax. *Elegance* printed an article about our Indian trip and it was superb – much more positive than I was expecting. It was strange, though, for when I read the article it was as though I was reading about someone else's life. I even felt envy for the Karina in the pictures, the Perfect Mother who looked so glossy and generous. I imagine readers all over the country must have felt the same thing. But it feels like a lie, somehow.

I thought that I would have slipped more easily into the role of motherhood by now. But to be honest it reminds me of being an actress. For example, even as I'm standing here making chai, I feel as though

I'm playing a role and a detached part of me is looking on in incredulity. There's also a feeling that that part of me is secretly waiting, expecting life to return to normal again, to revert to my pre-India existence. Which confuses and disturbs me, because that can never happen, can it?

'Mummy, what this?'

I smile down at her, charmed out of my worrying with a moment of pure heart. Her English is still awkward, bits and pieces of words stuck together, not yet strung on to the thread of sentences. But she's had a few lessons with an English tutor and she's improving day by day.

'This is surface,' I say.

'Surface.'

'Table.'

'I know, I know. Table.'

I point down.

'Ceiling,' she says.

'No – ceiling up,' I correct her.

She looks vexed and I smile and give her her chai. I watch her drink. I've begun to understand Devika a little better over the last ten days. I know she bites her lip when she's not sure of a word in English. I know she ducks her head when she's shy. I know she loves Rice Krispies and hates baths. But I'm also aware that she's much more complex than I ever imagined. Before India, I thought that a child would be a simple, straightforward creature and now when I look at her I realise how stupid I was, aware of the mysteries in her I've yet to discover.

The doorbell rings and Devika jumps.

'Don't worry,' I say in a high voice, swallowing. 'It's just the social worker, Angela. I'm sure she'll be really nice.'

As I hurry to the door, I feel nerves gathering in my stomach. At the moment, I'm legally only Devika's guardian. I've put in an adoption order at the local courts, but I can't officially become her mother for another six months – and in the meantime I have to endure regular visits from a social worker called Angela Hargreaves. She knows me quite well; I had to endure my 'home study' with her before I went to India, which was basically months of interviews and form-filling and checking I wasn't mad/terminally insolvent. Although she and the panel gave me the green light to adopt, she always makes me a teeny bit nervous, because I've never been a hundred per cent sure that she likes me.

I open the door. Angela shakes my hand and gives me a brisk smile. I'm pleased to see that she's followed my suggestion and had her brown bob highlighted. But, I'm sorry to say, she's also wearing a navy suit that I fear may have come from M&S.

'Hi,' I say.

'Hi. How was the trip?'

'Oh, it was just amazing!' Nerves overcome me and I joke, 'I expect you're here to check whether I'm trafficking Devika and about to sell her as a slave?'

I see Angela's smile tighten and think, *oops!* Okay. No more joking. Be serious.

In the kitchen, I try to introduce her to Devika, but she's so shy she hides behind my back.

Angela smiles earnestly at her and says, 'Do you like your new home?'

Devika stares at her curiously and then points around the kitchen. 'Table. Ceiling. Surface.'

Angela looks at me and we both laugh. Devika looks delighted.

'I can see she's learning English then,' Angela says, looking a bit more relaxed.

The interview goes really well – until the last five minutes. Angela and I are gossiping like old friends when she asks me if I have any worries as a new parent. I suddenly feel a burst of warmth towards her and decide to spill one of my biggest anxieties.

'I guess there is one thing . . .' I hesitate, wondering if she will understand.

'Yes?' Angela's eyes shine with sympathy. 'I do appreciate that being a parent can be tough.'

'Well, when I was dating Liam Holt a few years back, we were A-list celebs. And then I kind of slipped – I mean, I still hung out with Sadie and

Kate from time to time, but I pretty much ended up becoming a C. And I guess I thought when I adopted Devika, I'd become an A-lister again. I had this vision of Angelina calling me up and us holding a joint conference on adoption. And I thought I might get back in touch with Madonna again, but that hasn't panned out.'

'Madonna?' Angela asks, her eyes mooning.

'Yes,' I say, unable to resist name-dropping. 'You see, years ago, we did a yoga class together. I called her up, thinking we could bond – David could play with Devika. But her assistant said she was busy. I mean, since I've come back from India I feel as though I've gone up to a B-plus celeb, but I've still got a long way to go before I get to A again.'

There is a long, long silence. Angela looks at a loss for words.

'Well,' she says at last. 'Maybe Madonna was busy with her kids. You know, I think perhaps' – she pats my arm – 'it's probably best just to focus on Devika and not worry too much about fame. I mean, I guess the more you have, the more you want.'

Hmm, I think, and for a moment I nearly take her words on board. But I can't help noticing as she leaves that there is something surreptitiously sticking out of the corner of her briefcase: a copy of *Heat* magazine.

*   *   *

Later that evening, I keep replaying the interview and hoping it went okay. I can see Angela didn't get the fame issue – but then she isn't a celebrity, so she wouldn't. But other than that, it did go well. I think. I hope.

I try to focus on my laptop. *Concentrate!* I remind myself.

'Mummy Karina, what's this?'

I break off from my screen and look at where Devika's finger is pointing.

'A lamp,' I say.

'Lamp,' she repeats, then points again. 'Yellow.'

'Yes. It's yellow. Your English teacher is coming tomorrow. You'll learn lots of new words then.'

'What's this?' She points to the sofa.

'Sofa,' I sigh, then turn back to the screen. When I hear her voice behind me again, asking 'What's this?', I pretend not to hear her and carry on tapping away. Then I berate myself for being a bad mother. It's just that we've been playing this game all afternoon and evening. I feel as though I just want to put down my script and be alone for a bit. It's not that I'm tired of Devika; I just want some peace.

Besides which, I have a ton of work to do. I have to write a celebrity blog about being a Yummy Mummy for *The Times* website, not to mention my children's book, *The Celebrity Princess*, which my agent keeps harassing me for. How can I concentrate when she keeps on interrupting?

'Mummy Karina, what's this?' She points.

'The TV remote control. Look, I'll show you how to use it.'

Oh dear. I've been trying to stop myself all week but now I give in: I stick her in front of the corrupting, evil TV. I turn back to my screen, feeling guilty. Then I cast her another glance. When Clare's children watch TV, they look zombified but peaceful. But Devika leans forward, concentrating hard, eyes wide, as though *The Simpsons* is a complex documentary. I reassure myself that the TV is educational for her – it will help with her English and enrich her understanding of our culture. Or at least American culture. But anyway. I really *really* must finish my Yummy Mummy blog.

I've heard that in India there is a system of astrology called *Jyotish* which is apparently more complex than the Western one. I thought it might be a nice touch to weave this into my blog – work out Devika's Eastern star sign. Maybe I'm also hoping that if I know her star sign, I might learn a little more about her.

I am examining the handwritten notes that Mrs Laxsmi first sent me from the orphanage, which isn't easy, given her spidery scrawl, when I notice a little note scrawled under Devika's date of birth.

Birthday not known, date approx.

I've heard of parents who get to rename their children when they adopt, who even get a chance to change their date of birth. I can't help feeling this made up birthday, scribbled on a piece of paper, feels horribly random. I turn back to Devika.

'Devika,' I say, 'your birthday – birthday – understand?' She shakes her head, so I draw balloons and a cake, but she still looks blank. I realise she probably never celebrated her birthday properly in Delhi and I feel my heart pinch.

'Birthday – day you born, celebrate every year,' I say slowly.

Then her face lights up.

'Birthday,' she says. 'I'm ten, I'm ten.'

'But what about when you're eleven? You're meant to be eleven in a month's time, but I think it's unfair that someone made up your birthday for you. *You* should choose it. So then we make it special.'

She gazes at me, still confused but eager to please. I switch off the TV and turn to a pile of *Heat* magazines stashed in a corner and quickly spread them out over the rug. Devika sits beside me, still unsure, but gazing at the covers with interest. Suddenly she spots me on one of them and points, crying, 'Mummy Karina!'

I jump. Shit. It's the issue where Liam had just

dumped me and they photographed me looking wasted and covered in spots with a triumphant *Destined for rehab!* caption underneath. I quickly pull it away before Devika can start asking what rehab is. Finally, I find the issue I'm looking for: the June issue from last year. I turn to the horoscopes page, which lists the month's celebrity birthdays.

I spread out the pages before Devika.

'Now,' I say, 'you can share a birthday with Russell Brand. Or Howard French. Or Johnny Depp. You get to choose.'

Devika seems to have got the gist of what's going on. Her eyes flick from photo to photo in animation and finally she jabs Howard French.

'Howard. Hmm.' I once snogged French in the Met Bar . . . which means every year on Devika's birthday I'll wake up remembering our slurry tongues interlocking. Not a good association.

'How about Johnny Depp,' I suggest, pointing. 'He's much more A-list – and you're an A-list child.'

Devika nods, pointing. 'Johnny Depp,' she cries, and repeats his name several times in delight.

For a moment I have visions of bumping into Johnny in the Groucho or a film set or Cannes and introducing him to Devika, crying, 'It's such a coincidence – you have the same birthday!'

It's then that the idea hits me: an awesome, mind-blowing idea. If Devika's birthday is going to be next month, then . . .

'Party!' I cry. 'You have party! Presents, cakes, balloons.'

And, I think secretly, Madonna! Angelina! And every A-list yummy mummy in London with her kid in tow. I can already see the pictures in the glossies: a picnic spread out across my garden, Madonna's kid David walking hand in hand with Devika.

'Party!' Devika cries, looking excited. 'I can be a princess!'

Oh, gosh. Clare told me it was important to establish a routine for parenting and it's nearly ten o'clock; Devika was meant to be in bed by nine. But then something quite magical happens. I haven't yet got Devika into a bath, but I've been following some golden advice Clare suggested, just washing a little bit more of her body night by night. Tonight, I fill the bath and her eyes fill up with fear, but I succeed in getting her to sit on the edge and dip her feet into the water.

'Party!' she cries, suddenly forgetting her fear in her excitement and swishing her feet about. 'Party!'

'Yes!' I cry, and then a brainwave hits me. Perhaps rather than focusing on shushing and soothing Devika, which ultimately only reminds her of her fear, I should distract her. Talk about parties, schools – anything but baths, so she forgets she's even having one.

I'm just about to test this out when the phone rings and I tell Devika to sit still.

It's Fran, charged with gossip about her latest conquest, party and coke-fuelled orgy.

'Listen, Fran,' I cut in, in a rush, 'I really can't talk right now. Devika's having a bath and we're just at a crucial point—'

'Just chuck her into bed and talk to me!' Fran cries. 'I'm much more interesting.'

'Yes – but it's important. We're really making progress with her bath.'

There is a long sulky silence. Then Fran just hangs up on me. I stare at the phone in shock, thinking, *how rude!* Then I rush back to the bathroom to find Devika has already clambered quickly off the bath and is drying her feet. We were so close to making progress and now the moment has been lost. I curse Fran, and then feel guilty. I wish I could explain to her how hard it is to have time for anything outside Devika.

Like cleaning. It's only when I've put Devika to bed and look around my house that I notice what a complete tip it is. For the past few years I've not had a cleaner – after the celebrity routine my mum forced on me, I've enjoyed pulling on the Marigolds and getting stuck in myself. Now the house looks like a bombsite. But I just feel too exhausted. I think about calling Fran back and telling her all about my idea for the celebrity birthday party, but then I feel cross again – she can bloody well apologise to me. Honestly, Fran can be so selfish sometimes.

I pick up my phone, scrawling through my texts, making sure to avoid re-reading the one from Liam.

I must admit, as I sit there, feeling shattered and surrounded by chaos, that it does feel nice to have Devika in the house. To have company. I used to hate staying in for a single evening; the silence in the house would close in on me and every room would sigh with loneliness. Devika's essence, her smiles, her brightness, have cast a spell that sparkles in the air.

Come on, I tell myself, *time for bed*. But then I can't help it. I re-read it for the one hundredth millioneth time.

I can't stop thinking about you – fancy a game of snooker? Lx

Over the last week, I've translated that text into a whole range of amorous meanings. Sometimes I feel certain he was drunk when he wrote it and had forgotten it by the next morning. On other nights, like tonight, I feel he is really missing me and sitting at home wondering why I haven't replied. That he's realised we had something good and he was a fool to let it go; that, finally, he's realised I'm the One.

I ache to reply. Despite all we've been through, I still have a spark for Liam and it will never go out. But I know that getting involved with him will be like knocking an emotional domino, striking every area of my life. Right now, I need to focus on being a mother.

Even so, when I go to bed and lie under the covers, I can't help reading the text one last time. Then, with a burst of exasperation, I force myself to press DELETE. As the text disappears, my heart lets out a little wail, but I push it away and pull the duvet up over my head.

13

Devika

My English teacher only comes three times a week. When she's not here, I miss her. I feel as if English is a *rakshasa* I'm fighting with. It's as though all the words inside me can't come out. They sit in my heart but there's a big gap, like a hole in a road, so that they can't leap on to my tongue. And there's all these things I want to tell Mummy Karina but I can't and they build up in my heart until I feel it will burst.

When my teacher Mrs Raju comes, I find all my words pour out and out and out until finally she stops me talking and says, 'Devika, you must be quiet or I won't be able to teach you anything!'

I feel happy when she teaches me a new sentence or two that I can say to Mummy Karina to tell her what's in my heart. To say sorry I have not had a bath yet. To say I like my new clothes. To say I would like to go to the local temple here.

But I still hate English. It has words that look one way and sound another. It has words that make no sense and are stupid. And it has so many words, it feels as though it will take ten years to learn them all.

Today, I learn to write the word *though*. But I keep saying it wrong – I keep saying it the same as the word *toe*, which makes Mrs Raju laugh. She says no, toe is something that wriggles on the end of your foot. I also learn the different words for the colours of the rainbow. When I see and say the word *red*, I think of Mummy Karina. I think of her lipstick and nails and the warm redness of her heart.

Then at the end of the lesson, Mummy Karina comes in and says something very quickly in English to Mrs Raju, who then turns to me and says in Hindi: 'Today your mother is going to take you to meet her friend Clare. She has a son called Dominic whom you can make friends with.'

'I can't wait,' I cry back in Hindi, feeling excited. Dominic can be my first English friend.

Mrs Raju says our lesson has to end early and I feel a little disappointed, for I wanted to tell her all about my new birthday and Johnny Depp.

We get into the car and Mummy Karina ties the

buckle over my seat. As we drive out, I press the knob that opens the window and the wind carries London into the car. When I first came to England, I kept noticing how different it smells compared to India – it smells of rain and cold air and bricks and cars. But last night before I went to bed I pressed my nose against my skin, and it was starting to smell like England.

The house is big and white like our one. Dom's mummy opens the door. She has big brown eyes and a bright smile. I say, 'How do you do?' and hold out my hand, but she just laughs loudly and gives me a big hug. Even though the hug is nice, she makes me feel a bit stupid.

Mummy Karina talks very quickly and looks excited. I can tell they're talking about me but I don't know what they're saying, so I just smile. We take our coats off and then Dom's mummy points at my shoes so I take them off too.

Dom's mummy's house is different from ours. It is more old and there are lots of plants and it smells like a temple back home. Then a big furry cat, the colour of oranges, comes out of the kitchen.

'Cat!' I cry.

In Delhi I hardly ever saw a cat, though there was a skinny dog who used to run around our gate. He only had three legs so he walked with a funny sort of hop. In England, all the cats look fat and beautiful with fur like silk cloth. This cat rolls over and shows off her tummy and when I tickle it she purrs. English cats seem to like me.

Mummy Karina smiles and strokes the cat too and he purrs as though he can't believe how happy he is. Then we go into the dining room. There is a big table with gleaming plates. Mummy Karina shows me which chair to sit in.

I want to say hello to Dom, my new friend, but he seems to have disappeared.

Mummy Karina and Dom's mummy sit down and then Dom's mummy yells, 'DOM!' so loudly the cat's tail lifts up, as though it wants to fly away in shock.

Then there are footsteps and Dom comes in.

He doesn't look like I expected. I thought he would look like my old friend Raji, only with white skin. Raji was slender and had a cheeky face like a monkey. Dom is not slender and he looks like a mix between a hippo and a gorilla.

'This is Devika,' Mummy Karina says.

'Hello – how do you do?' I ask, jumping up and holding out my hand.

Dom looks at my hand and laughs just like his mum did. But he doesn't hug me and when I sit back down I feel stupid again.

I guess I will learn how to behave in England one day.

At least I don't have to talk during lunch – I can just fill my mouth up with food. There is a lot of food I haven't tried yet. There are green leaves which are called salad, and bits of a squishy purple thing that has a sharp taste, like a fruit, and little green dots which are sweet.

I don't like much English food yet. Mummy Karina has been trying different dishes on me. She is not very good at cooking rice and dahl, so yesterday she cooked me some cow. I know that to eat cow is a very wrong thing and that Lord Krishna would not like it. I kept saying, 'No, Mummy Karina, not in India.'

Mummy Karina went away to look at the Internet. Whenever she doesn't understand, she goes to ask the Internet and the Internet tells her what to do. Then she came back and cried, 'Hindus don't eat beef! I'm so sorry, I'm so sorry.' And then she threw my meat and *her* meat into the bin and pulled out a bowl and filled it to the brim with Rice Krispies, then sloshed on loads of milk. I hope she keeps serving me bad things by accident, then I can eat Rice Krispies all day.

During lunch, I have to speak once. Dom's mummy asks me if I like England. I mean to say yes but I forget the word. I get nervous and it pops out of my mind. So all I can do is nod. She turns away and I watch her carefully. I have learnt to look at

English faces so that I can understand the words their lips and cheeks and eyes say. English faces are not as bold as Indian ones and their emotions will run across their faces before hiding in their corners. When Dom's mummy looks at her son, her eyes speak love, but when she looks at me they seem uncertain.

After we have eaten, I feel happy when Dom's mummy says I should go upstairs to play with Dom. Now I will be able to try my English properly and make a new friend.

Dom's room is very messy. His clothes lie all over the floor as though they're sleeping. But he has a huge computer and a huge TV. He sits down on a big black chair and spins his back to me.

I wait for him to tell me where to sit, but he doesn't, so I stay standing up. I feel upset because it's obvious Dom doesn't think I'm good enough to be his friend.

He turns to me and says something and holds out a little black plastic thing that looks like a hunched-up spider with a tongue sticking out of it. Then my heart opens with happiness because he pats the chair next to him. I sit down and take the spider. Then he points to the TV screen. There is a woman with black hair wearing a green cloak and carrying a gun. He points to her and says: 'YOU!'

I feel confused because the woman on the screen

doesn't look like me at all. Then Dom waggles the tongue on my spider and says, 'PLAY!' in such a loud voice I feel scared because I don't really understand.

The screen changes. Suddenly next to the girl in the green cloak is a man with grey clanky bits on his body who is also carrying a gun. I wobble the tongue in my hands and the girl suddenly crouches low, then jumps up high. I feel excited, making her dance all over the screen, but Dom looks angry.

'Fire!' he keeps saying. 'Fire.'

I wiggle the tongue like mad, wondering if fire will leap out of her mouth, but nothing happens. Then, suddenly, the man on the screen shoots and blood spurts out of her chest and little pieces of red skin fly out and she slumps to the ground, blood pouring from her head. I scream and clamp my hands over my eyes, feeling really sick.

When I take my hands away, Dom is laughing like he thinks I'm even more stupid. He grabs the black spider out of my hands.

The woman on the screen is reincarnated in a green cloak again. But this time Dom won't let me play. I stare at his hands wriggling the tongues because I can't look at the screen. I don't want to see any more blood or I'll be sick. I think it's strange that English children should play a game like this because it means they pretend to be an evil *rakshasa* or a murderer.

I wait and listen to the nasty noises his game makes and I feel more and more upset and hot because now Dom will never be my friend.

Then I look up and suddenly notice a poster on his wall.

'Oh!' I cry, pointing.

'What?' says Dom.

'Johnny Depp.' I point. 'He's my new dad!'

'What?' Dom starts to laugh again.

'Dad – he's my new dad. Mummy Karina says so.'

Dom puts down his spider, turns to me and says very slowly: 'Moron.'

I don't understand what the word means but I know it isn't nice. I can feel tears in my eyes but I try to push them back down.

The door opens and the cat comes in. He stares around the room and sees me and then he seems to smile. He comes padding up to me and I rub his face. I wish I could be a cat too, so I didn't have to talk to anyone or learn English, just wag my tail and purr.

Then Dom suddenly bends down and hisses at the cat and he runs out, his tail bristling. I feel angry now when Dom laughs. I don't think Dom is very nice. Maybe it's a good thing that he doesn't like me.

'I go,' I say, getting up.

'No,' says Dom. 'You stay.'

I feel confused, but then happy as Dom pats the chair.

'I will teach you some English words,' he says, and for the first time that day he smiles at me.

14

Karina

I'm sitting on Clare's sofa, nursing a cup of coffee and enjoying a thoroughly good gossip. I've told her all about my plans for Devika's Celebrity Birthday Party next month and she thinks it's a great idea – 'and a lovely way for Devika to make new friends.' I'm debating telling her about Liam's text too but I have a feeling she'll just tell me Liam is a bastard not worth bothering with. Which is true, I guess. I thought deleting the text would unroot him from my heart but for some reason I keep thinking about him even more . . .

I'm quite pleased, however, that Devika and Dom seem to be getting on so well. I must admit, I felt a little apprehensive about Devika going up to his room, convinced that Dom's room is a den stashed with secret porn. I was half expecting Devika to coming running down within five minutes, but she's been up there with for him for ages now, which means Clare and I can have a great old gossip.

'Oh, I have to show you Dom's school report,' Clare says, suddenly putting down her cup.

'Cool!' I say.

You know, I used to find Clare phenomenally boring. Our friendship has survived the last decade mostly out of habit. Clare is a wonderful listener and if you ever have a problem, she is great at giving you a slice of her homemade carrot cake and a sympathetic response, even if it is delivered with a touch of piousness and a confident awareness of how great her own marriage/life/kids are. But Fran and I always used to agree that since having kids Clare has become the ultimate Mummy Bore.

'I went to Clare's yesterday,' Fran would often remark to me over a cocktail in Sanderson's. 'And God, she got out the holiday snaps of Dom on his adventure trek. I got to see Dom climbing down a hill, Dom running through a forest, Dom's canoe capsizing – I was praying she'd say he drowned!'

'Well, that's not as bad as what she did to me last week – I had to hear all about Molly's new allergy to peanuts . . . dust . . . leather . . . oxygen too, no doubt.'

'Well, at least you weren't fired as a godmother.'

Yes – Fran really was a godmother, until the christening, where she fell asleep in boredom with a surreptitious cigarette dangling out of one hand, and set alight to a pew. The blaze was thankfully quite small, but that was that for Fran.

Fran and I always used to feel a bit guilty, bitching about Clare. Deep down we knew we loved her, but we also longed for the days when Clare rebelled against our band management by dyeing her hair green and once had groupie sex with a boy fan.

Now, however, my attitude to Clare has suddenly changed. I feel a sort of fascinated reverence for her that I've never experienced before. I can't help seeing her as a sort of Buddha, whilst I am her pupil. I want to seek her wisdom, her years of learning. At the same time, I know Clare can be a bit annoying with all her advice-dispensing, so I'm trying to play it cool and let her gush out gems without asking too many questions.

'Yeah – this is Dom's school report.' Clare passes it over.

'Wow!' I say.

A's in history, English, maths. A-stars in biology, chemistry, physics.

'And look,' Clare says eagerly, 'look, look at this!'

She points to the paragraph that says: *Dom has shown exceptional aptitude for sciences this term;*

he is diligent, hard-working and has consistently achieved a high standard of progress.

Gosh, Dom is full of surprises. He always looks to me as though he'd have trouble spelling his name.

'Devika will be at school soon,' I muse, 'and I'll have to go through this . . .'

'Well, it'll be quite a thing for you, won't it?' Clare says. 'I mean – finding out what she's good at, bad at . . . who she is . . .' She goes back to the report, her face bright with pride. 'You see, he's inherited my knack for science,' she declares. 'Before I joined Beppo, I had plans to be a vet. I was predicted three A's for my A levels in science.'

I wince. Clare always talks about Beppo as though she was once a dustwoman. I still feel proud of all the hits we racked up.

'Molly, on the other hand, takes after Mark. She likes books already. But Dom takes after me – when he was born we always said he had my eyes, my face.'

I feel a sudden twinge of fascination . . . or even *envy*? Clare and Mark's genes have made love, entwined and merged and produced a blueprint for blue eyes and a slouch and a love of Bunsen burners. But I'm never going to be able to do this with Devika. Every achievement, failure or quirk will always possess an element of mystery; her past is as vague as a mist. And suddenly I feel irked. Clare is making me feel as though I have something that's second best.

'So have you decided where to send Devika yet?' Clare asks.

'I definitely want to go for a private school, I think. She's just so lovely and innocent – I don't want her corrupted by evil Brit kids.'

'Oh, Karina, why waste all that money? She's got to learn to integrate and be part of this country.'

'It's not a question of race, Clare,' I retort in a stung voice, 'it's because she's worth it. I mean, I may not have carried her in my womb for nine months but I love her just as much as if I had done.' Which may be an exaggeration, but I'm on the defensive.

'Okay, okay,' Clare says, looking alarmed. 'I didn't mean . . .'

'Sorry. Sorry. I know you didn't . . . it's just hard . . . I just feel a bit that because I've adopted Devika people don't take me seriously as a mother. I mean – like Fran. She doesn't get why I can't just come out drinking with her any more.'

'Oh, Fran!' Clare cries. 'I mean – come on, Fran is Fran. Look, it's something you have to come to terms with when you become a mum – your social circle changes. Birds of a feather stick together. Mums get on with mums, single people with single people – we're like two completely alien groups.'

She squeezes my hand. 'You're in the Mum Club with me now.'

'Well, thanks,' I say, but I can't help feeling a flicker of unease. What's next after the Mum Club . . . middle age, drooping tits and a pension, I guess.

We suddenly hear footsteps on the stairs and Dom comes slouching into the room, followed by Devika. I look at Devika and immediately intuit that something is wrong: there's an anxiety flashing in her eyes, a droop to her lips. But then I open my arms and she gives me a bright smile and climbs on to my lap.

'Dom taught me English words!' she cries.

I look up at Dom in surprise. There is something nasty about his smile, but Clare doesn't pick up on it.

'Oh, that's very kind of you, Dom,' she says, and turns to me, as though expecting me to acknowledge that we're in the presence of the second coming. 'Wasn't that kind?'

I quickly compete in the kind-children-with-impeccable-manners stakes: 'Say thank you, Devika.'

'Thank you,' she says.

'Well, let's see what words you've taught Devika,' Clare says eagerly.

'I have to do my homework,' Dom says. 'Mum, can I have another cookie?'

'Oh, Dom, it's dinner soon. Why don't you have some wheatgrass?'

'Because it tastes like green wee. I want a cookie. *Mum.*' Dom's voice is wheedling, but with a hint of steel in it. The balance of power between them has reached a critical point; there are faint wisps of a moustache sprouting on Dom's chin, a bullying confidence in his growing physique. Clare purses a face as though she's debating but it's obvious she's already lost and has been losing for some time.

'Okay,' she says. 'He needs the sugar for all that mental energy,' she explains as Dom pants down the hallway.

I pull Devika tight on to my lap and plant a kiss on her head. It's funny, for back in the clothing shop when the assistant was watching us, or here with Clare, I find it easier to put on my mummy role. An audience is somehow reassuring, makes me feel that I am getting it right. In turn, the role makes me connect with my emotions, twinges of real affection. Or maybe it's just the acting genes in me.

'So, Devika,' I coo, 'what words did you learn?'

She points to Clare and says very slowly: 'You . . . are . . . a . . . cunt.'

Then she beams, looking up at us for approval.

'Devika!' Clare and I cry in shock.

Then Devika turns to me and says: 'You have . . . a nice . . . nice . . . pussy.'

131

'Oh my God! Oh my God! No! No!' I clamp my hand over Devika's mouth and her eyes moon in shock as she registers my disgust.

'God!' Clare says. 'Where did she pick up such language? Have you been letting her watch TV?'

'Are you serious? Devika's never spoken a swear word in her life – she doesn't even know what one is! Your bloody son's taught her.'

'Oh, but Dom would never . . .' Clare flushes.

'Call him down!' I cry furiously. 'You get him down here and ask him to explain himself.'

Clare reluctantly goes out into the hallway, climbs halfway up the stairs and then, in the manner of Maria in *The Sound of Music*, cries up sweetly: 'Dom? Dommie darling?'

I look down at Devika, who is looking baffled and confused.

'Cunt,' she says again, quietly, as though unable to quite believe her nice new word is poison. 'Nice.'

'No.' I shake my head. 'No. No no no.'

'But Dom said nice.'

'No. Dom not nice.'

Devika, realising she has been the victim of a cruel joke, is on the verge of tears.

I hear Dom's door open and his footsteps trudging to the top of the stairs. But he refuses to come down and explain himself. I hear Clare coaxing him and then gently 'interrogating' him, which results in her coming back into the living room looking bright-eyed and giggly.

'My son! He has such a wicked sense of humour!'

'Well, I'm sorry,' I cry, setting Devika on her feet and standing up, 'but I don't happen to think this is very funny at all. Devika has spent the past few weeks learning all these new words and now Dom has completely shaken her confidence. And now – what fun – I have to go home and explain to her what the c-word means.' I break off as Devika starts to sob, and stroke her hair. 'There, there, darling, it's not your fault.'

'Oh, Karina, you're overreacting. Dom's an adolescent, he's growing, he's moody, he went too far but he didn't mean any harm—'

'So you're not even going to get him down here to apologise?'

'Well . . . I mean, he's just doing his homework and he said he was sorry . . .'

'Right. Fine.' And I drag out a sobbing Devika, ignoring Clare's belated and limp 'Sorry', and slam the door behind me.

Devika is subdued for the rest of the afternoon; every time I try to talk to her she just nods or shakes her head, her eyes downcast. Evening comes and I try to cheer her up with a treat. I order an Indian takeaway and we eat it on our laps in front of the TV, all cosied up together.

Before Devika, I hadn't a clue what was on TV on a Saturday night. I would always be out on the town with several drinks in my system. Now I'm quite hooked by Ant and Dec and the proliferation of various talent shows; tonight across the sweep of channels wannabes of all shapes, sizes, ages and degrees of lunacy are competing to be the best singer/dancer/choir, not to mention one show which just seems to celebrate random nutcase achievements – someone who can run down a street with an egg balanced on her nose or do the splits whilst delivering an operatic impression of Mariah Carey.

All the same, I can't help feeling a little downcast myself. A tiny voice inside me keeps wondering what Fran is doing. Normally Saturdays were always our nights together . . .

A middle-aged dinner lady from Brighton pops up on the screen to give a heart-rending performance of 'One More Time'. Suddenly Devika perks up. She starts to hum and then she can't resist – she starts to sing along, knowing the song is safe, the words vetted; finally able to release her emotions.

I look down and a smile of relief breaks across my face. Soon Devika is happy again and Dom is a shadow behind us. We call up and vote three times for the dinner lady.

And then a burst of inspiration hits me.

'Your mummy used to sing in a band,' I say. Devika looks blank, so I rummage through my DVD collection, finding the old videos stacked underneath. There. A video of 'The Only Guy For Me'. Our very first single. I shove it in the machine and Devika watches, transfixed, as me, Fran and Clare turn on a beach in bikinis, handsome young men in shorts flexing their dancing muscles around us.

Every time I see this video, I always feel a rosy nostalgia. But more often these days I also feel a sense of envy and fury for my former self. I wasted my teenage years worrying about tiny little body flaws, oblivious of the fact that twelve years later I'd look back and think: *I'd kill to have a figure like that*. Life is so unfair, I think sulkily, suddenly feeling old and ropy and wrinkled.

Devika, however, is overwhelmed by the video. The moment we finish, she cries, 'AGAIN!' And again. And again.

Then she suddenly jumps up and grabs a bottle of hand cream from the coffee table and starts singing into it. I'm amazed – she's picked up the lyrics amazingly quickly. Soon I am laughing and singing along too and teaching her our whole dance routine. I don't think I've ever had so much fun with Devika. This is something we can do without stumbling over the tripwires of language; finally, it feels as though we can communicate straight from the heart. To my delight, she even adds a few flourishes here and there to the routine and I clap my hands and cry, 'Genius!'

We're still bopping away when the doorbell rings. Fran. She is dressed in a leather miniskirt and a tank top. The last time we spoke she hung up on me, so there is a slight tension between us. But it quickly dissolves as she kisses my cheek; I can't be angry with Fran for long.

'Fran! Fran!' Devika cries. 'You have to see our show!'

'You have to see our show!' I echo Devika, swept away with zeal.

We sit a rather bemused Fran down on an armchair and then take possession of our stage: the brown leather sofa by the window. Devika takes her hairbrush, I grab my Volvic bottle, we're all miked up and we begin.

'*Oh baby can't you see you see you see,*' Devika sings.

'*That you, you, you are the only guy for me,*' I reply.

A smile tugs at Fran's lips as, no doubt, she remembers the old days. But it is soon replaced by a frown.

Devika and I only up the ante. We sing out hearts out, sashaying and swinging in synch. I can't stop thinking how proud I am of Devika; she really keeps up well, her face bright with concentration, following my moves with precision and panache. She really is a little star in the making!

We end the routine by climbing on to the sofa, me picking Devika up in my arms as we reach an operatic climax, then jumping off the sofa and splaying open our hands with a big '*Ta – da!*'

Panting, I stare at Fran. She looks at us as though the men in white coats will arrive to pick us up soon. Then, very slowly, she claps her hands.

'Oh, Fran, we're just having fun!' I snap.

'We sing "Dancing Queen"!' Devika cries. '"Dancing Queen"!' And she points to indicate she means all three of us together.

'Wow, that's such a great offer, thanks,' Fran says, 'but I want to go to the Victory Club. Once you've put Devika to bed, you can come,' she adds, as though Devika isn't there.

Devika's English might still be shaky but she's pretty sensitive to intonation. Her face crumples and I think, *God, that's the second time today: first Dom, now Fran.* I quickly grab hold of her hand and squeeze it tight and suddenly it's time to take sides – I feel both of their eyes on me, tearing me between them. I keep a firm hold of Devika's hand.

'Well, then,' says Fran. 'See you around.'

I show her firmly to the door and it feels as though I'm making a point. But as she walks away, I feel my heart wrench: Fran is my best friend, my partner in crime. Surely we're not about to throw away years of history? She turns as if to say something and I open my mouth, desperate to explain, but then she shakes her head and stalks off, her heels clicking like castanets.

I close the door with a self-righteous bang. Then I feel depressed again. I love Fran; I don't want to lose her; have I turned into Clare, a true Mummy Bore? Will I have any friends left by the end of the week?

'Let's do "Dancing Queen"!' Devika cries.

Oh, God. Suddenly the bubble bursts. I realise how stupid I must have looked to Fran. It's official: I have turned into a kid.

I think it's because of Fran that I decide to text Liam. Or maybe I'm just searching for a scapegoat. I put Devika to bed and sit down, feeling very odd, and then, without thinking, I pull out my mobile and write a reply.

Hey u. A game of snooker might be fun – but u r sure to lose. Kx

There, Fran! I say to myself, as though she's standing in the room, glowering disapproval. See. I've just texted my old lover boy rock god. I'm still interesting. I still have a life.

The moment I send the text I become almost hysterical with sexual excitement and flutters of confusion.

Liam always did have this effect on me. Five minutes pass and I keep picking up my mobile and checking there's reception; ten minutes pass and I start analysing my reply and groaning inwardly and wishing I'd thought of something more witty. Then, to my shock and delight, my mobile beeps.

Keep cool, I tell myself, *it's probably just Fran apologising*.

Then I scroll down and see it's from him and my heart stops.

You took your time, sweetie. So are you going to let me take you out for a drink next Sat night? Lx

15

Karina

'Karina – I cannot believe you are asking me to do this!'

I frown at the phone. I've just called Clare asking her for a small favour and she's behaving as though I've demanded she change her bloody will. Personally, given how her evil son treated my lovely Devika, I think it's jolly nice of me to call her at all and make peace. She could at least try to reciprocate.

'Look, I know the last time Devika came over, Dom and she didn't quite hit it off, but—'

'It's not about Dom, it's about Devika,' Clare interrupts. 'It's only been, what, three weeks now, and you're asking me to babysit her.'

'Yes. And?'

'It's just much too early. I didn't pass Dom over to a babysitter for a good three years after he was born.'

What does Clare want? An award for being the Perfect Mother? It's all right for her; she's married to Mr Wonderful Who Likes Changing Nappies.

'Clare, Devika is ten years old. She's not a screaming baby.'

'But she's in a fragile state. She's been dragged over to a country she doesn't know, you're still bonding—'

'She's settled in really quickly. I can't believe you're lecturing me. Clare, I have stayed in now for *three weeks*. Not one bar, not one club. Fran thinks I've become a nun.'

'Wow,' Clare says sarcastically.

'Come on, Clare, you're the best person to babysit her. She's met you. Otherwise it will have to be a stranger.'

'Oh, and what crucial event merits your passing Devika on to someone else? Don't tell me, there's a *Good Housekeeping* award for Glam Mother of the Year and you're going to win it?'

'No!' I cry, stung. 'God, Clare, I don't believe this – I thought you'd want to help. It's as though you're determined I'm a bad mother.'

There is a brief silence.

'Well, I don't mean to upset you,' Clare says in

a softer tone, 'I really don't. I'm sorry – I'm just really tired. Molly's got this infection and I've been up all night. But if I'm going to do this, then don't tell me you're just going out for a drink with Fran or something?'

'No, it's not Fran,' I say cautiously.

'Who, then?'

I think I'm going to have to tell the truth.

'Liam's asked me on a date. I have to go!' I blurt out.

There is a long silence. I instantly regret telling her. I should have known Clare wouldn't be impressed; she was never Liam's number one fan.

'So do you think Liam's ready to be a father?' she says in a terse, shaky voice.

'We're just going out for a drink, Clare!'

'Yes, but you know it will be more than that. You have to think about how Devika will feel if you have a man in your life. Can he handle being a stepdad?'

'This is crazy. I haven't been out with him for years. It's just a drink.' Though I have to admit it – silly as it sounds, over the last few days my imagination has been getting carried away with itself. I've been envisaging a black and white scene on a beach, like something out of a Calvin Klein ad, with Devika running in the sand and Liam looking moody in shades, the salty breeze blowing his hair back from his gorgeous cheekbones, and me looking like a bohemian yummy mummy in a flowery dress and a sunhat . . .

'You do know why he left Hayley Young, don't you?'

'Yes, because she's a silly airhead with fake boobs,' I cry, sounding like a total bitch – but Clare has put me on the defensive.

'No, not because of that.'

Silence.

'Oh, Clare, just tell me!'

'Because she wanted them to settle down and have kids. He was fine about the settling down – that's why he got engaged. But not the kids.'

I let out a nervous laugh.

'Well . . . well, Liam *must* know I've got a kid, I mean, it's in all the tabloids and he's still asked me out,' I cry breathlessly. 'And I don't want Liam's kids, I already have a kid of my own and she's enough, so if you don't want to help me babysit, then fine. Don't.'

'Fine. I won't.'

I put down the phone and glance over at Devika. She's watching the TV and sipping an Innocent smoothie and there is a delightfully earnest expression on her face.

I cannot believe Clare. For God's sake, my date will only last a few hours. Just a few drinks. There is *no way* I am going to be stupid enough to jump back into bed with Liam. Yet. If I'm honest, I'm feeling red hot with fantasies about him that no number of ice-cold showers would ever cure, but I've learnt my lessons over the years. I need to be cautious and clever. Reel him in slowly. Keep him waiting.

Besides, Devika will be fine. When she was at the orphanage in India, she was looked after by loads of different people. There was Mrs Laxsmi, and Mike, and all the various other helpers. Clare is only telling me off because her son is such a spoilt mummy's boy he has to be molly-coddled every minute of the day; she really doesn't know what she's talking about.

'Mummy looks beautiful,' Devika says, picking up my mascara and pulling out the wand, and beginning to apply a sticky layer to her lashes.

'Devika, give that back!' I cry, tugging it out of her hand. She looks sulky, as though she's about to cry, and I stroke her head quickly, impatiently. 'Look – you have your own make-up that Mummy bought for you. Play with that.'

I point to her bedroom and she sulks off. I feel like throwing up my hands in despair. I've been trying for the last two hours to make myself look beautiful for Liam, but it's been impossible. Devika, as though sensing my excitement, or because she's nervous about the babysitter, has been playing up like mad, insisting on sitting on my lap while I put on my make-up, staring at me intently and putting me off as I tried to apply it, tugging out the curls in my hair. Now I examine the results of my beauty harvest and all I can think is: *oh shit!*

My eyeliner is wobbly; I look as though I have two black eyes. My lipstick is a scarlet smudge. My foundation is all cakey because my skin is dry and tired after too many nights of being woken up by Devika. I look like a clown suffering from Tourette's syndrome.

This is a nightmare. I suddenly think longingly of my early dates with Liam, when I'd spend literally all day preparing, going to spa and beautician and covering my hair with serum and my body with butter and applying a thousand other sweet-smelling anti-ageing miracles. And I'd turn up glowing with beauty and health and he'd grin and say 'You look hot, babe' in that naïve way men do, as though it's entirely a gift of nature, with no idea of the efforts we make to create an illusion.

I am reaching for a tissue, about to smear it off and start again, when the doorbell rings.

The babysitter's here!

I hurry down the stairs, feeling nervous. It took quite a lot of effort to find one. I didn't want to use a sitter without a recommendation. In the end I used my problem as a chance to make up with Fran. I knew she'd be thrilled when she found out I was seeing Liam again; sure enough, the moment I called her up and told her, she screamed down the phone.

'That's more like it,' she said. 'I was getting worried you were going to be a spinster for life! Go out with him and then call me right away and tell me *all* about it. And then *we* have to go out drinking!'

So it was Fran who organised the sitter. She's called Adi and apparently she once babysat for Jude Law's kids. Naturally, Fran and I couldn't help giggling away and wondering whether Jude had had his wicked way with her.

'Ask her if he's any good in bed,' Fran insisted. She has had her eye on Law for some time.

'Fran, I can't do that!' I cried, appalled, but I know every time I look at her I will wonder.

I pause before opening the door, butterflies swirling in my stomach. I still can't help wishing Clare was doing this for me; Fran is not the most reliable of contacts. I'm afraid I will find a vamp on my step, chewing gum, headbanging to an iPod, smoking a fag.

I open the door and—

—sigh with relief.

She looks – normal. And very nice. She is a pretty black girl in her early twenties, with braided hair and big hoop earrings. She's wearing black jeans and a shiny blue top which shows off her gorgeous figure.

'Hi – I'm Adi,' she says, with a big, bright smile, shaking my hand with confidence and vigour. 'Wow, your house is lovely,' she adds as I invite her into the hallway.

'Thanks. Was . . . er . . . Jude Law's house nice?' I ask idly, wondering if I dare enquire as to what shades his bedroom was decorated in and whether he sleeps in boxers or the buff.

She looks flustered for a moment and I raise an eyebrow.

'I can't really discuss other clients,' she says, politely but firmly. 'I feel it's only fair.'

Of course, I only feel more tantalised. But before I can probe any further, I look up and see Devika sitting at the top of the stairs, holding on to a banister. She stares down at us.

'It's all right, Devika. I'm just here to be your friend for the next few hours,' Adi calls up.

I feel rather embarrassed, because even when I call her down, Devika just sits there. I feel a wave of guilty love; I hope I didn't upset her about the make-up.

'Look, I'll go up and introduce myself,' Adi suggests.

'Good idea,' I cry, leading her up the stairs. 'Come

on, Devika, say hello to Adi. She's going to babysit you for the evening. For three hours.' I hold up my fingers again to reassure her.

Adi holds out her hand to be shaken and I wait for Devika to shake it and say 'How do you do?' in her solemn British accent and Adi to be utterly charmed.

But, to my shock, Devika just stares at the hand and then pokes her tongue out at Adi.

'Devika!' I cry. I think it's the first time since we've been in England that I've seen her behave badly.

'It's okay,' Adi says. There is a kindness and firmness to her tone that reassures me and reminds me of Supernanny. 'I'm her first ever sitter. She's going to take a while to get used to me. But we'll be fine, won't we, Devika?'

Devika mutters something in Hindi that sounds ominous to me.

I can't help feeling worried in case I should sit down and explain it all again to her, but if I do that I'll be so late Liam will think I've stood him up.

'Don't worry,' Adi says, reading my thoughts, 'all I need now is your instructions.'

'Instructions?' I ask in confusion. Devika's not a DVD player – she doesn't have a manual.

'Normally parents like to give babysitters a set of guidelines,' she explains, 'you know – about bedtime, programmes they're allowed to watch, what they can eat, what they're allergic to.'

Now I flush with embarrassment. She must think I'm such a bad mother.

'She's always in bed by nine,' I lie. 'She'll have Rice Krispies for tea – of course, I wouldn't normally give that to her, it's just a treat for tonight. She always has a vitamin pill and a cod liver oil capsule. I think that's all . . .' I hear my taxi toot. 'Okay. Bye!'

I give Devika one last kiss, which she receives very grumpily, then rush out of the house and jump into the taxi and give him the address and let out a huge breath of relief. I sit in a daze for a few minutes. Then, on autopilot, I turn to my left, about to either pat or hug or speak to Devika. And I realise she isn't there. I'm alone. I'm free. I don't have to worry about whether I've got enough tissues in my handbag or if I've remembered to bring a bottle of water or an Innocent smoothie, or whether she's entertained or hungry or happy or sad. I realise how diluted, tugged at, I've felt over the last few weeks; now suddenly I feel rich and whole. I sit by the window and feel the speed of the taxi buffet wind through my hair and even though it will look like a bird's nest I don't care: I relish the caress, tasting freedom.

16

Karina

Liam is not alone. I spot him standing outside the pub in Soho along with all the smokers, accompanied by a large black Dobermann. I repress a smile: no doubt there will be some crazy story concerning the dog.

I'm about ten feet away when Liam spots me. Normally when I approach someone like this I always feel a little self-conscious, catching their eyes and looking away, impatient to bridge the gap. But Liam just stares straight at me and I stare back, so that it feels as though I'm being slowly sucked into his orbit. I walk up very close and stand still. We gaze at each other, savouring, remembering, comparing the present with the past. I didn't get a chance to really look at him on the plane back from

India; it's been nearly a year now since we last bumped into each other. Time has sprinkled laughter lines around his eyes and carved grooves at the corners of his mouth, but he still looks gorgeous. His hair is still dark and luscious; he still has the same fuzzy little sideburns that I used to love to stroke; his chin still has the roughness that used to make me happily complain about stubble rash after he'd been kissing me. He's wearing a diamond in one ear that would have looked adolescent on anyone else but looks cool on him. I'm also aware that all around us women are watching in envy and interest. It reminds me of the past, of the history of hurt between us, and as he leans in to kiss me hello I turn my face and force his lips to land on my cheek.

'Here,' he says, picking up a Baileys. 'I already ordered for you.'

'Thanks!'

He's remembered my favourite. He always had a good memory for detail, despite all the substances he took. I'm about to take a sip when he says: 'Hey, first I have to introduce you to my dog.'

'The dog belongs to you?'

'He sure does. Say hello to Rufus.'

I give him a cautious pat and Rufus licks my hand. I grin, for though Rufus looks scary he seems quite soppy really.

'So how are you?' I ask, as Liam picks up his beer. 'Been molesting any more air hostesses lately?' I meant to joke lightly, but my words sting the air.

In the press, Liam was quoted as saying the stewardess 'helped him to deal with his fear of flying – and took him to heights he'd never known existed'. But now he winces.

'I was pissed,' he says sheepishly, ruffling his hair boyishly.

I know he's manipulating me, and I don't respond. We're not going out, I remind myself; I have no right to lecture him on who he sleeps with.

'So what the fuck were you doing in India?' he asks, a little defensively.

'You haven't read about me in the tabloids?' I ask nervously.

'Eh? Me, read tabloids? Why, so I can imitate Kate's style or follow Posh's weight-loss tips?'

I laugh uneasily. Liam is one of the few celebs I know who doesn't care to read his clippings. I remember that he doesn't bother with the news at all.

'I . . .' The words are there, on the tip of my tongue. *I've adopted a girl from India.* But I can't quite get them out. And then, despite my own quiet inner horror, I find myself telling a blatant lie.

'I was just making a documentary. You know, about Indian kids being forced to work eighteen hours a day to make clothes we can buy for a few quid.'

'Really? That's a coincidence. Because I went out there to set up a sweatshop.'

His face is deadpan. I stare at him in momentary horror before he nudges me, then burst into giggles. I'd forgotten how much he could make me laugh.

As I laugh, he reaches out and touches my cheek. So tenderly. As his fingers brush my skin, he stares deep into my eyes. We just stare and stare at each other and then Liam smiles softly and I feel completely lost, drowning in desire and the ache of reignited love.

We break off, staring into our drinks, silent for a moment. I suddenly feel afraid and out of control.

'So who was that little kid with you on the plane?' Liam suddenly asks. 'Was that to do with your documentary?'

Shit. I'd forgotten that Devika had been sitting next to me. This is it: an open door. The perfect opportunity to confess and tell the truth. But then his eyes hold mine again and a pleasurable anticipation licks in my stomach. I can't bear to spoil the moment.

'Yes, we saved her from a sweatshop,' I improvise.

'She's going to be placed with a family in England – she'll be fostered, then adopted.'

'Wow – I'll have to start calling you Mother Teresa,' Liam says, but there is an affectionate admiration in his voice. I remember that Liam is a cynic: but, like all cynics, he is an idealist at heart.

Then he says: 'Aren't you going to answer that? I'm worried your mobile's going into cardiac arrest.'

I've been vaguely aware of my phone ringing, but when I pull it out to take a look I don't recognise the number. A faint unease comes over me. I didn't put Adi's number into my phone. It could be her. But hell, I've only been gone half an hour – what could possibly have happened in half an hour? It's probably some phone company offering me an upgrade. I quickly fling it back into my bag.

Liam raises an eyebrow.

'Someone you don't want to speak to,' he observes. 'Maybe you have a secret stalker?'

I give him a coy smile, thinking: if only my love life was that interesting.

Rufus bursts into a volley of barks at the sight of a poodle strutting down the opposite pavement. Liam ruffles his ears and I can't help seeing a paternal sweetness in the gesture. Surely the fact that Liam has got a dog is a sign of him being willing to take on responsibility? After all, pets are often substitute kids. Surely this is a good sign?

I feel my mobile vibrating in my bag again, shivering panic into my ribcage, but I firmly ignore it.

'So when did you get Rufus?' I ask.

'Oh, he wasn't my idea,' Liam says, his face darkening. 'He was the brainchild of my ex . . . Hayley.' He takes a gulp of beer, looking awkward.

'Oh right,' I say in a bright breezy voice, just to prove I don't give a toss. 'So did you get into a custody battle over him?'

'Fuck, if only,' Liam grumbles. 'She got me to buy her a dog and then when we split she didn't bloody want him. Of course, she was pretty mad at me cos I got her Rufus for her birthday and she had actually asked for one of those fluffy Pekinese things that would fit into her bag.'

'Oh, Liam!' I cry, giving him a reproving nudge and repressing a smile.

'Well, come on,' he says, 'she would have gone around looking like Paris fucking Hilton and I would have looked like a total dick. So I got her Rufus instead.'

I can't help bursting into laughter. This is such a classic Liam story.

'So now I'm stuck with him,' Liam sighs.

'Oh, don't you like him?'

'I do, I do, I do,' says Liam, giving the dog's ears another ruffle. 'But you know – it's all so much hassle. I quite like taking him for walks and having a good old think about everything – it's kind of like a meditation.'

I am surprised. Normally Liam's idea of meditation is sitting down with a joint.

'Yeah, I like that,' he goes on. 'But you know – it's the feeling of being tied down. I can't leave him on his own for too long. Sometimes I even have to get a bleeding dogsitter.'

I laugh out loud and very nearly say, 'But at least you don't have a kid—' and then catch myself.

'It's the responsibility,' Liam sighs. 'Knowing we're stuck together for years to come.'

'I know the feeling,' I say, taking a big gulp of Baileys.

My mobile starts vibrating and trilling yet again. I know I can't ignore it any longer.

'Excuse me,' I say to Liam. 'Just need the loo.'

'Cool. Can you get me some ciggies while you're there?'

Cigarettes! Liam momentarily sees the disapproval on my face and I quickly hurry away. In the past, I always used to crib Silk Cuts from him, but I was picturing Liam in my house, blowing smoke everywhere and turning Devika's lungs black overnight.

How is this ever going to work? I think. Then I keep reminding myself that I'm getting ahead of myself – this is just a drink. But it's more than that. I know it is. I've been aching for this for months, for years. By the end of the night, we're going to end up in bed together . . .

My mobile buzzes for attention yet again, but the bar is much too noisy. I hurry into the Ladies and switch it on. At first I can't hear properly, with the muted din of music and laughter. Then I realise it's Adi. Her voice is shrill with panic and there is a terrible screaming in the background that cuts right through me.

'Karina, Karina, Devika's really upset.' Her voice catches as though she's been crying. 'She's having hysterics and I can't calm her down and I'm freaked out – I tried to give her a bath and she just went *mad*—'

'A bath! Oh my God! Why did you do that? She can't have baths. You should never have tried to give her a bath!' I cry.

'Well, you never told me that in my instructions,' Adi shoots back.

So I didn't.

'Please, please can you come over? I'm scared—' She breaks off and in the background there is more screaming.

The noise tugs viciously at my maternal heart

strings. I feel tears prickling my eyes. 'Okay – I'll be right over.'

As the taxi swings into the road, I pull notes from my purse, dampening them with sweat. I fling them at the driver, telling him he can keep the change, then jump out and dash up the path, stabbing my key into the lock and flinging myself into the hallway. I'm expecting to be lambasted by screams; the silence is chilling. What if Devika went into some kind of panic-attack epileptic fit and then . . . what if she's . . .

I don't think I've ever been so frightened in my life. Not since that terrible moment when the doctors from the home called to say my mother had sunk into a coma. The memory of that panic segues into here and now, until I feel nearly faint with hysteria.

Then I hear Adi crying from upstairs: 'Your mum's back!' Footsteps clatter and Adi comes charging down the stairs, Devika in tow.

Devika is wearing her pyjama top and one sock. When she sees me, she holds out her arms and I bend down and she rockets into my embrace. I feel her small heart echoing the frantic beat of mine. Her breath shudders warm against my neck and I clutch her even tighter. She starts to sob and all my frustration at leaving Liam behind dissolves in an instant; I wonder how I could ever have left her at all.

'I'm really sorry,' Adi keeps saying, over and over.

'It's okay – I should have told you,' I say, over Devika's shoulder. 'She really doesn't like baths.'

'My first job.' Adi looks up at the ceiling, putting her hand to her forehead. 'I can't believe it – it's my first job and I totally mess it up.'

'*Your first job?*' I pull up sharply. Devika lets out a sob and I grab her hand. 'What? I thought you were Supernanny. I thought you looked after Jude Law's kids.'

'I did – kind of,' she says, looking panicked. 'Well, my friend was babysitting and I was there too to pick up tips – I told your friend Fran that I was new!'

I picture myself in the sky, hurling thunderbolts at Fran.

'I just wanted to be a celebrity nanny and have my own TV show,' Adi said. 'I thought I'd start with you and then maybe move on to Kate Winslet and then Jude. I am qualified and everything, honestly! But I am new . . . I'm really sorry.'

'It's okay,' I say, wincing at her distress. 'It's not your fault.'

'Really?' Relief shines out on her face. 'Oh wow, oh thanks, I swear if you hire me again, I'll be great, I swear.'

I nod and smile, but in my heart I have already decided never to leave Devika on her own again.

I lie in bed, staring up at the ceiling. Devika is sleeping too, cuddled up beside me, every patch of her bare skin connecting desperately to mine. Every so often she shifts in her sleep and her fingers claw at my top and I give her a little squeeze. I'm still feeling shocked, torn between emotions. The parent in me feels overwhelmed with guilt. Adi related to me that Devika actually *asked* to have a bath the moment I left. It was obviously her way of rebelling against her abandonment; she wanted to punish herself, or get my attention. Either way, leaving her for just a few hours made a much bigger impact than I could ever have envisaged. I feel frightened, for suddenly I'm reminded how important I am to her. I am the focal point, the root, the foundation of her world and her happiness. And, in turn, I feel a fierce protectiveness to live up to this, a desire to be a better parent and to keep her from harm always.

The child in me disagrees. Yes, it's there, although I want to ignore it. The child in me is throwing a tantrum and screaming, *why, why, why did you have to desert Liam?* The child is remembering Liam's face when I said a hasty goodbye, patted his dog and then ran off down the street yelling, 'TAXI!' The child in me is obsessed with checking my mobile for messages, but there are none; it sits by my bed, the green light winking forlornly. I'm convinced that right now, as I lie here with Devika, he is making love to another girl. He probably stood there, sipping his pint, wondering what the fuck I was playing at. Then he would have glanced around and seen a hundred admiring glances, women eager to step in and console him. Liam just isn't the type of man you can desert: he's too handsome and dangerous for that.

Perhaps I'll never see him again. Perhaps tonight he'll meet his Ms Right and go off happily into the sunset. Perhaps I've slept with a man for the last time. I try to remember the last orgasm I ever had. It was with Robbie Williams, I think, when we both got drunk at the *FHM* awards. And let's just say Williams wasn't on top form that night.

Imagine if that was my last ever orgasm! With Robbie Williams of all people! *Imagine!*

I think of the people back in the bar. People who are now smoking, drinking, having sex. People who are free. I picture them slotting keys into empty houses, drifting around, making coffee, kicking off their shoes, watching TV, sharing post-coital cigarettes, smiling lazily at each other, gossiping with girls, putting on a CD and swaying about. All those things I'll never do again.

Then I look at Devika and tenderness fills my heart. I switch off my mobile and try to get some sleep.

17

Devika

Today is the most exciting day of my life. It's my first day at school! Mummy Karina says I'm going to a special school where all the children have mummies who are rich or famous or princesses or celebrities. I will learn English and maths, which is adding up numbers, and geography, which is . . . I don't remember what geography is. But, best of all, I am going to make some nice new English friends.

Last week, Mummy Karina took me to a special shop to buy my uniform. It is very pretty, with a pink frilly thing round the edges which Mummy Karina says is called *braiding*. My uniform wasn't ready in time, so today I have to wear a sari. Mummy Karina has picked out my best green one with the sparkly gold bits. I keep thinking that all the other children will admire it and think I have a wonderful mummy.

Mummy Karina has also promised not to go away in the evenings and leave me with a babysitter ever again.

We drive to school. It has white gates and a big sign saying: WINTERSON'S PREPARATORY SCHOOL FOR GIRLS.

Mummy Karina takes me into the classroom. This is a very wealthy school, I can tell that at once, because none of the children are sitting on the floor. They all have their own desks and sit on chairs. There is also a big white board for the teacher to write on and plants and lots of books – there is so much luxury it makes my eyes hurt.

All the children look at me with big eyes and I want to smile at them but suddenly I feel shy and find myself staring at my feet.

Then I meet my teacher. She is called Mrs Something-beginning-with-H. I don't like to say that I didn't hear how to pronounce it, so in my head I call her Mrs H.

Mrs H is like a picture of an ostrich that I saw in my animal book. She is thin, with red hair that falls to her chin and big pink lips. She looks fierce but her eyes are kind.

She turns to the class and says: 'This Devika – she's come from India to join us here at

Winterson's, so I hope you will make her feel very comfortable.'

'Hello Devika,' they all say in one voice.

At the front of the class there is a girl with dark hair that shines as though the rain has polished it.

'Regina,' Mrs H says to the girl, 'you will look after Devika for the day.'

I smile at Regina but she doesn't smile back.

'Regina and Kelly – you'll both look after her.'

Kelly sits next to Regina. She has pretty blond hair that falls over her face. She tosses it back and gives me a smile before it falls back down again.

'Well, I should say goodbye now,' Mummy Karina says. She gives me a big hug and I see there are tears in her eyes. I touch her cheek, smiling. I want to say, *I'm the one who is going to school, not you*, but I feel so much love for her, I can only think in Hindi.

I sit down at my very own desk next to Regina. Mrs H gives me a notebook and tells me to write my name at the top. But I feel so excited, I can't remember how to spell it. I can feel Regina staring at me. Her eyes are brown and very clear, like pools of water, with long lashes that curl up and kiss her eyebrows.

'You have to write your name on it,' she whispers, miming with her pencil.

I quickly write *Devaikka*. But it looks wrong.

Then I see Regina looking too, frowning. She nudges her friend Kelly and points at it. They both giggle.

I smile too, but I feel a bit stupid. I decide to get so good at English I can spell anything. For the rest of the lesson, I use all my energy trying to work out what Mrs H is saying. But she talks very fast and by the time I've worked out one word she has gone on to the next sentence. By the time the bell rings, my head feels as though it is hurting from the effort.

Then I notice that the desks are even better than I thought they were. They are magic desks, which open up so you can put your books inside. I see that inside Regina's desk are lots of books and a fluffy toy cat, but when I reach across to stroke it she snaps the lid down.

'Sorry,' I say, feeling confused. Maybe I just did something really rude, but I was only trying to be friendly.

We go out into the playground. Regina and Kelly sit on a bench, making me sit in the middle. We open up our lunch boxes. But I can hardly take one bite of my sandwich because Regina and Kelly keep asking me questions.

'Is your mummy famous?' Regina asks. 'My mummy is a West End star. Do you understand what that is?'

I shake my head.

'It means she sings and dances on stage in London and she's very famous. Can your mummy do that?'

'Yes!' I cry and Regina looks surprised.

'No,' she says. 'She can't.'

'My mummy sings,' I cry. 'She sings.'

'How much money does she get when she sings?'

'Many pound coins,' I say. 'Lots and lots.'

Regina and Kelly laugh. I quickly take a bite of my sandwich, but it only makes me feel sick.

'Why are you wearing a piece of curtain?' Regina asks, tugging at the cloth.

'Sari,' I say. 'In India, they all wear.'

'Do you have any jeans?' Kelly asks.

'What are jeans?'

Regina and Kelly laugh a lot.

'Oh my God!' Kelly cries. 'You are so cute.'

Is 'cute' a nice word? Looking at Regina's face, I'd think it was horrible. Looking at Kelly's face, I'd think it was nice.

Back in the lesson, I give up on trying to understand what Mrs H is saying. I'm too tired and sad. I thought that everyone in England would want to be my friend. But Dom didn't like me and now Regina doesn't like me and I think Kelly would like me if she was allowed but Regina won't let her. Why don't they want to be my friend?

I think about all the friends I had back in the

orphanage. Suddenly I wish I was back in the courtyard, watching Raji dance, singing into his broom.

Mrs H keeps saying we should write things down, but I just pretend to – I scribble little pictures in my book so it looks like I'm working. Regina notices and she nudges Kelly. Then they give me a look as though I am very stupid.

I look out of the window and I suddenly notice Mummy Karina in the distance, waiting by the school gates. I give her a little wave but she's too far away so she doesn't see me. Then Mrs H says in a stern voice: 'Devika, please pay attention!'

I jump. I hear Regina laugh again. I feel bad that on my very first day I've been told off, even though Mrs H smiles at me. For the rest of the lesson, I keep my eyes pinned on her. I hardly even dare to blink.

Then the bell rings, so it's the end of class. I see Mummy Karina appear in the doorway. I want to rush up and give her a hug but the class is a river pouring out between us. Then I run to her and she holds me tight, but when I open my eyes I see Regina pointing at me with a horrible look and suddenly even my mummy's arms don't feel nice any more, just silly.

Mummy Karina talks to the teacher and they smile at me and I feel tired. I want to be magically transported back home, eating Rice Krispies and watching TV.

'You early,' I say to Mummy Karina as we leave the school.

'No,' she says. 'Not early – happy to see you.' Then a look comes over her face. I can't remember the word for it because my mind feels so tired. She stops in the middle of the side road and does a little jump up and down and then gives me another hug. 'You like school?'

She is smiling so brightly that I say, 'Yes.'

I don't tell her about the difficult words or Regina or my aching head because I don't want her to be upset with me.

When we get home Mrs Raju is there and tells me that Mummy Karina has got a special treat for me and I feel a bit better. Maybe Mummy Karina has bought me a pair of jeans or a fluffy toy cat.

We go into the living room and I want to sit on Mummy Karina's lap. But she looks annoyed and tells me I have to sit next to her. Mrs Raju says, 'It's okay, she can sit on me.'

Then Mummy Karina pulls out a big folder and puts it on her lap.

She says something to Mrs Raju and I hear the word 'story'. Oh. Well, stories are okay, I guess, but you can't take a story to school and show other children.

Then Mrs Raju tells me: 'Your mummy is very clever. She has written her own story which will be published in all the shops.'

Then I feel more excited. Imagine what Regina will say when she finds out my mummy is an author!

'The book is called *The Celebrity Princess*,' Mrs Raju says.

'Oh! Princess!' I cry in excitement.

'Yes! Princess!' Mummy Karina smiles and looks happy.

Then I feel more interested. Maybe you can't take a story to school, but you can fill your mind with nice and funny things. So far Mrs Raju has read me some really good stories. I love *Horrid Henry* which makes me laugh because Henry is so wicked. And I liked another book Mrs Raju read me about a boy called Charlie who finds a golden ticket in a chocolate bar and gets taken to a chocolate factory full of amazing sweeties like everlasting gobstoppers. I thought it was a real story, until Mrs Raju told me that if I bought a chocolate bar I wouldn't find any golden tickets. All night I dreamt that Mrs Raju was wrong and Willy Wonka had fooled all the grown-ups into thinking he was just a fairy tale, but really I would find a ticket and then my real parents would read about my prize in a newspaper and they would come to the chocolate factory and meet Mummy Karina to say

'How do you do'. Then I would have three parents and a lot of chocolate.

Mummy Karina reads her story out and Mrs Raju translates, line by line. I wonder if she is translating correctly, because it seems a very boring story to me. There are no special chocolates or naughty children or funny rude bits.

Every so often, Mummy Karina flashes her eyes at us. Then Mrs Raju quickly laughs or looks sad and then she flashes her eyes at me so I do the same. But I cannot help feeling disappointed. If Regina read this story, I do not think she would say it was very good.

At the end of the story, Mrs Raju claps her hands and I do the same. Mummy Karina looks so happy I am glad we pretended to like it.

Then Mummy Karina puts her story to one side and says something to Mrs Raju.

'Your mother wants to know why you don't like having baths.'

At the very word 'bath', I feel fear shiver through me. I want to explain but the words freeze up and all I can do is shake my head.

Mummy Karina looks sad and then I am miserable, feeling that I am not very good at English or baths or making friends. I feel better when she puts me to bed and sings to me, but after she has gone I slip out of bed and kneel down in front of my statue of Buddha. I wish it was a statue of Ganesh, but all I can do is close my eyes and pretend and hope Ganesh is listening.

'Please can I do well at school, please can Regina like me and please can I have some new jeans.'

18

Karina

Something's wrong with Devika. I thought she'd love school. But I'm beginning to suspect that it might not be her favourite place. This morning when I went to wake her up, she curled up in a tight ball under the covers and wailed that she felt sick. I was alarmed, worried that I exhausted her too much yesterday evening by dragging her along for a photoshoot with *Now* magazine. But when I checked her temperature it was normal, and her eyes look clear and her skin is shiny.

Now we're eating breakfast, the radio is playing in the background, and she's eating Rice Krispies, humming along merrily under her breath – I swear she's picked up every song in the charts.

It's too late for school, and I feel like an idiot for falling for her trick.

'How about we go to school at lunchtime?' I ask her.

I see a momentary panic cross her face. Then she screws up her nose and says, 'Don't understand, don't understand.'

Hmm: it seems as though Devika has learnt how to play the I-don't-know-English card. I see the fatal potential of this: excuses to avoid homework, baths, sleep, proper food.

'We. Go. To. School. Lunchtime,' I say, smiling firmly.

'No! No! Feel sick, feel sick,' Devika wails, shaking her head vigorously.

Hmm. Then I think to myself: *well, why not?* Skipping school for one day won't hurt. As I do the washing up, I decide that today is going to be special. It's going to be Devika's Day. A new start for both of us. She's still a little bit raw after I abandoned her for the date with Liam. The other night I popped out into the garden to sneak an illicit cigarette – I suddenly got gripped by a mad craving, as I do from time to time, and when I came back in Devika was hysterical; she thought I'd left her again and wouldn't be back for hours. Getting her to even wash, let alone have a bath, was impossible. I went to sleep tormented by guilt.

But today I will be the Perfect Mother.

When I tell Devika the day is hers to do whatever she likes, I wait for her to ask to go to the zoo, for she seems to love animals, especially cats, and is enchanted by the butterflies in the back garden.

But Devika tells me she wants to go shopping. She doesn't want to wear Indian clothes, she says sulkily, she hates her saris. She wants to wear *English* clothes. Jeans. T-shirts. '*Designer* clothes,' she says.

I can't help feeling a little uneasy at the vehemence behind her words. I wonder if she's suffering from some kind of peer pressure.

'Nice friends at school?' I say.

She nods quickly, but it's as though I've asked if she's been good.

Nevertheless, I cannot resist a good shopping trip. I cheer Devika up by reminding her that it's not long until her birthday, and as well as buying her some new clothes we stock up on goodies for the party.

Then we go into Selfridges. It is fun seeing Devika's reaction. It's as though we've just entered a temple made of gold. She keeps stopping and staring at things. And when we reach the jewellery department, she gazes into the cases of glittering beauties as though they are a rare and exotic species.

'Lollie, you mustn't touch that!' a mother shrieks

as her daughter's grubby fingers grab out for a diamond necklace.

'But why not?' she wails. 'It's nice.'

Devika watches them, wide-eyed. I can't help noticing how well behaved Devika is compared with other children. It was something I felt proud of a few weeks back, but now I'm not so sure. I remember how Dom, Clare's son, used to be before he degenerated into a sulky oaf: a cheeky, spoilt boy with scruffy brown hair and big blue eyes. Once we took him to the cinema and he kept yelling at the characters on the screen to run or shoot or look out, until people all around told us to shut up. He had the unselfconsciousness of a child who thinks the world revolves around him.

Devika, however, can never quite enjoy this cocoon. As we weave through Selfridges, admiring things we can't afford, I notice how nervy she is still, gazing at people, still happier to look rather than touch, drinking it all in as though England is a big school with rules and lessons she has yet to learn. Her self-consciousness gives her a slightly more adult air than the other children and I feel a little sad, feeling I've deprived her of some innocence she might have had back in India.

Then I remember the heat of Delhi, the flies and the shanty towns, and how thin she was back then. Her face is much fuller now, her hair more shiny, her eyes brighter . . .

I have been good with her, haven't I? Except for the bath thing. And that date with Liam.

To be honest, now I've calmed down, I feel almost relieved the date got cut short. Our meeting stirred up such strong feelings that I know I wouldn't have been able to resist him. Life is simpler without him.

However, when I see the bath section of the shop, a sudden thought strikes me and I cry, 'Hey – we should buy some goodies.'

'Goodies,' Devika says, smiling.

We enter an area rich in sweet flowery scents: lavender and vanilla and rose. I finger expensive talcs and body lotions and bubble baths. When I spot a rubber duck, I pick it up and show it to Devika and she falls in love with it instantly.

Then she makes me want to laugh.

'Miaow,' she says, waving it around, preoccupied with her cat obsession.

'Not miaow – quack,' I say, careful to conceal my mirth. 'Quack quack.'

'Miaow,' Devika insists, and I sigh and smile and we buy her miaowing duck.

We're just rummaging through the lipsticks when suddenly, through the crowds of women and haze of perfume mist, I spot Liam. But no: it can't be him. I smile at myself, waiting to catch another glimpse of the face and confirm I've superimposed his features on to a stranger. Then I freeze. I'm aware of Devika saying something and tugging my sleeve, but I can't hear her, because *I can't believe that it really is Liam heading towards me*. What the hell is he doing in Selfridges' beauty department? Then I remember that Liam is really rather vain and sometimes wears eyeliner.

I duck my head and quickly yank a lipstick out of Devika's hand.

'But Mummy Karina,' she protests sadly, 'I like it.'

'No, no, we have to go,' I say firmly. 'We have to get you some T-shirts.' I smile at the assistant. 'Sorry – it's an emergency. Something's come up.'

I spy the exit, past a maze of handbag stands and hat stands and beauty counters, and panic. But surely he won't spot us—

'KARINA!'

I look down at Devika and without thinking I drop her hand. She doesn't seem to mind, for she turns away and eagerly starts to examine perfumes.

'Liam – hi!' I cry. 'Oh God, it's so amazing to see you but I really have to dash—'

He silences me by grabbing hold of my shoulders, leaning in and giving me a passionate kiss. For a moment I'm so shocked that my lips don't move. Then I begin to kiss him back. Electricity sparkles from my lips and networks throughout my entire body. I hold him tight and kiss him and kiss him, releasing all my pent-up desire.

When I pull away, I am aware of Devika out of the corner of my eye, gaping up at us.

'I have to go,' I whisper, still stunned.

But he keeps his arms round my waist, his hands locked against the small of my back.

'Do you really?' he whispers back, his eyes sweet with passion and fondness. 'You always seem to be running away from me. Why didn't you call me back after our drink?'

'I . . . I don't know . . . I . . .' I drop my eyes.

'Will I see you again?' he whispers, his breath feathering my lips.

I look up at him and our eyes caress with ache.

'Can I have this eyeshadow?' a voice suddenly interrupts.

The bubble bursts. Liam pulls away, frowning.

'The Indian girl,' he says, looking down at Devika. 'Hey, you.' He ruffles her hair in a worringly doggy manner. 'We met on the plane, didn't we?'

I feel panic overwhelming me. I realise I can't go on like this; I'm going to have to meet him and sit him down and tell him the truth. But not here, now, like this.

'Will you be taking Karina to the toilet?' she asks.

Liam flushes and I resist the urge to laugh.

'I'm just helping out before the foster parents

take over,' I say quickly in a low voice. 'So anyway,' I say, putting the eyeshadow back firmly, 'I have to take her back now. I'll give you a call.'

Liam looks bewildered. I lean in and quickly kiss his cheek and he mutters, 'You'd better.'

I grab Devika's hand and hurry her off down the aisles. I can't resist glancing back several times. There is a very strange expression on Liam's face. I'm convinced he's put two and two together. I hurry Devika out into the fresh air and she stares back mournfully at the glamour and glitter of the shop.

Back home, my lips are still tingling with the memory of Liam's lips against mine. It's incredible what one kiss can do. It's as though a door has been opened inside me and feelings are pouring out, drowning my reason entirely. I stand in my bedroom, waiting for Devika to change, and stare at my face in the mirror. My eyes are dilated and sparkling; my cheeks are flushed; even my lips look bigger, as though stung by excitement. I'd thought this could never happen again; I looked into this same mirror many years ago and sternly told myself to give him up for good. But I'm hooked, I'm hooked, I'm hooked.

'Hey!'

Devika comes into the bedroom parading the new outfit we've bought her. I clap my hands as though she's a model in a fashion show. She smiles and does a twirl. Then I feel guilty again – what if she over-heard me telling Liam she didn't belong to me? What if she picked up the gist of what I was saying? I want to explain and excuse what just happened. But even without the language problem there are concepts I couldn't begin to try to explain about me and Liam. I don't want to even think about a birds and bees conversation with broken English and pictures. No, best save that for the time being.

Guilt, however, makes me utterly determined to round off Devika's Day with a wonderful conclu-sion. I go through a list of new words with her, make a homemade courgette soup for supper and then it's bath time.

When I tell Devika it's time for a bath, however, she looks moody.

'No – it's Devika's Day. Devika no bath.'

For a moment I consider indulging her. But then I look at the clock – it's only seven o'clock. There's plenty of time left before bed to do this. I'm still feeling terrible about the date with Liam and her bath trauma. Maybe I want to scrub out my own guilt, but either way I feel determined we must make some progress tonight.

'Bath is the best time of day,' I say.

I start to tug at her clothes, but she looks sulky. I notice her eyes flickering – she's spotted an escape route. She dives for the door but I get there first.

I slam it shut and pull the bolt across. She tries to stand on tiptoe to slide it back but it's too high for her to reach. She lets out a wail, tugging hard at the handle.

I quickly unwrap the bag of bath goodies and pull out the plastic duck she liked.

'Quack quack,' I call out, waving the duck. 'Quack quack.'

Devika turns, her eyes round and wet and swollen, and stares at it.

'Look, the duck isn't afraid to go into the bath. If he will, why not you?'

Devika blinks. She comes up and takes hold of the duck. I smile and stroke her hair. Then I spin round and turn on the taps: a mistake. She runs back to the door and crouches into a little ball with the duck, staring.

I watch her with exasperation and guilt. I keep wishing Mrs Raju was here so she could translate for us. But then Devika wouldn't tell her why she won't have a bath either. The only reason I can possibly think of is that she's scared she'll drown. Or maybe that's not it at all. I feel helpless, suddenly, with no idea of whether I'm being utterly cruel to keep her locked up in here or if we can make some progress.

Okay, I'll just try one last thing and if that doesn't work I'll give up and we'll just have to bath with a bucket every night from now on.

I take off my clothes, singing all the while. Devika half turns her head, watching me out of the corner of her eye. I get into the bath. She stares at me with moon eyes. I pour in some ivory bubble bath.

'Look,' I call. 'Come and look at the bubbles.'

She sits and faces me now, clutching the duck. She strokes the duck slowly, as though pretending it's all the duck's fault and he is the one that needs reassuring. Then, in the manner of a mother, she leans down and kisses its head and mutters something in Hindi. I feel my heart weep but I know I need to stay calm and steady, so I swallow hard and keep up my bright, happy act.

'Bubbles,' I cry. 'Lots of lovely bubbles.'

I blow a few across the room. Devika's head darts up in surprise. She reaches out as though aching to touch one, but fear holds her back and she sits back again, eyes glued on her duck.

I keep on singing casually. The warm water and bubbles are unravelling my tiredness. Maybe there is nothing I can do except let go now. Bubbles drift around me and Liam's face hovers before me and I retaste that kiss all over again . . .

Then I hear a noise. Devika is moving. She doesn't approach me, but gets up and wanders around the bathroom. I pretend not to notice or care, observing her surreptitiously. I'm suddenly reminded of being a kid and wanting to feed the birds, knowing the only way I might tempt them to venture up and peck from my open palm was to be as quiet and nonchalant as possible.

Devika potters about, picking things up and putting them down with her right hand, keeping a tight hold of the duck in her left all the while. She even straightens a few towels and I bite back a smile.

Then she sets her duck down on the sink and squeezes toothpaste on to her brush, cleaning her teeth. In the mirror, our eyes meet and hers flash anxiety. She carries on brushing, then wipes her mouth and briefly skips the brush across the duck's pursed yellow beak.

Then she stops and turns. Another bubble drifts across the air. She holds out the duck so the bubble kisses against him. When it pops, she lets out a gasp of delighted surprise.

Suddenly she's hooked. She whispers to the duck and he seems to agree it's a good idea to inspect the bath more closely. She comes up, step by step. I smile vaguely, though my heart is hammering. She stares into the bath, where the water is now entirely concealed by bubbles.

'Mummy Karina safe,' I say. 'Nice bath. Duck needs a bath.' I point.

A frown on her face, she curls her fist around the duck and lowers it into the water. When its yellow bottom hits the liquid, she tenses and lets out a gasp.

'It's okay,' I say, 'it's okay.'

She puts the duck into the water. One by one, her fingers uncurl. She keeps her palm still shielded round it, watching it bob on little waves.

'See?' I say. 'Happy duck. Now you come in.'

Devika stares into my eyes and I hold her gaze. She takes off her pyjamas and climbs in. Halfway through, she has a panic attack and freezes up, one foot in the bath, one out. I cup my hands round her waist, whispering over and over that she's safe, she's safe.

Another foot enters the bath and finally she sits down on the edge. I smile, but some determined part of me says this isn't enough. I've got her to sit on the edge before. I want her to go all the way tonight.

'Come in!' I coax.

She shakes her head.

'I die, I die,' she suddenly cries.

'No,' I say, relieved to understand, at last, what is going through her mind. 'No. You live. You live because Mummy Karina loves you.'

It's the first time I've used the word 'love'. It was one of the first English words she learnt. When I say it, her face softens with delight.

'Mummy Karina loves Devika,' I repeat, taking her hands gently from the edge. She giggles nervously as I pull her down into the bath.

Now she's in the water. She panics briefly, splashing about, but I curl my arms around her, holding on tight, creating a little warm cave of safety, kissing her on the head until finally, finally, she calms down.

There is a silence. She realises that she is in the bath and then, in the way that happens when someone passes a barrier, she forgets. Her fear becomes past. She starts to play with the bubbles. She skims her duck around, making it miaow.

I want to hug her and praise her and sing to the heavens. But I know if I make a big deal of it, she will only remember. And for her, forgetting is the best balm.

Later that night, I show my delight by singing her a song that shimmers with love and happiness. And before I turn out the light, she tells me that her duck loves me very much.

The next few days are euphoric. Liam and I text like mad. Every time I send one, I get a reply literally within thirty seconds. I have never been so busy or exhausted in my life, running around after Devika, organising the party, but Liam is always there, lingering in the backdrop of my mind like sunshine behind clouds. Sometimes I find myself stopping in the middle of something and I think of him and an irresistible smile breaks across my face.

I've agreed to see him the night after the Celebrity

Children's Birthday Party. Then I'll kiss him, sit him down and confess everything. *It will be okay*, I keep telling myself, *he'll understand . . . he's got to understand.*

At least, I hope so.

19

Karina

Everything is looking good; I think my Celebrity Children's Birthday Party is going to be a huge success.

I have to admit that over the last few weeks the party has become, erm, somewhat ambitious. For example, I was going to hire a clown, until Fran told me that this was ridiculously eighties and that the only 'in' entertainer for a children's party is a palm reader. I was quite surprised by this. Surely a bunch of ten years olds don't want to be told that they're going to meet a tall, dark, handsome stranger? They might all grow up thinking they're going to marry Daniel Radcliffe. Nevertheless, I couldn't bear to be retro, so I felt I had to hire him. Then: the cooking. That was going to be covered by a trip to M&S but Madonna's PA called and asked if the food was going to contain nuts. Then Samantha Willoughby from *Hollyoaks* got her nanny to call and find out if we were offering soya and wheat-free products. When Ms Halliwell's secretary then called to find out if we could cater for gluten allergies and a girl on a 'colour diet' (apparently each day of the week is a different colour and Saturday was her 'blue' day), I had to hire a chef to cook fancy treats to cover about thirty different dietary requirements.

I also felt I wanted a few traditional treats too, though. Pass the Parcel is a must. I've bought a paddling pool for them to splish about in, and some helium balloons with *Happy Birthday Devika* painted in silver. Lastly, Fran offered a horse. I was a little dubious at first, but she explained that her jockey friend Tamsin has a child-friendly horse she takes to kids' parties. Obviously there's no room for show jumping in my garden, but the children can sit on the horse and have their photo taken. Given Devika's current obsession with animals, I think it's a nice touch.

And then there are the goody bags.

'Can you help me with these?' I ask Clare, who has turned up early to help. Fran was meant to be here too, but she hasn't showed despite my texts. 'I need to get them into the garden, on the trestle near the back gate.'

'My God!' Clare cries, peering into one of the bags. 'What's in here?'

I freeze in alarm, my wrists laden with shiny gold handles.

'What? You don't think they're good enough?' I cry in alarm.

'No, I think they must have cost you a fortune. A *Gucci watch*? For an eleven year old?'

'Well, I was just going to put a little toy in, but Fran told me that at Honey's party the kids each got a Vivienne Westwood hairband and a pair of designer sunglasses. I have to keep up!' I feel a little foolish when Clare rolls her eyes at me. She always makes me feel so superficial. But these things *do* matter.

'Come on, Dom,' Clare says, her voice rising an octave with motherly affection. 'Help us with the bags.'

Dom has been slumped on the stairs looking shattered – perhaps he's spent all night fiddling with himself or his spots. He looks up and grunts. Then, with a huge sigh, he rises, lifts a meaty hand, picks up one single bag and carries it out into the garden as though completing an Olympic challenge.

I notice Devika shrinks away from him as he passes. I feel rather uncomfortable; I hinted to Clare that Dom might feel stupid being at a party with a load of kiddies but she insisted that he was dying to come and help his mummy.

Still, he and Devika don't need to spend any time together. All her new friends will be here soon. I have visions of her meeting Madonna's kid, David, and them playing kiss chase together. Imagine if they grew up as childhood sweethearts and then one day ended up with a wedding in *Hello!*

But I'm getting a little carried away with myself, I realise with a grin. I'm just glad that Devika is happy with the party. In fact, she seems a little overwhelmed. Last night she couldn't sleep; she kept on interrupting her story and crying, 'I'm going to be a princess tomorrow. I'm going to be a princess!'

Out in the garden, my nerves ease for a moment. Everything looks great. My garden isn't really that big, but I've planned carefully and cleverly to fit it all in. The paddling pool is to the left; the horse is nibbling my rhododendron bush.

'Are you sure he won't vault over the fence?' I ask Tamsin nervously.

'He'll be fine, he's very gentle,' she says, smiling. 'He's fifteen years old – he's retired from his show jumping career.'

Phew, I think. My next-door neighbour is a high court judge and I really wouldn't want to get on the wrong side of him.

The doorbell rings and I jump, terrified that

Madonna might have turned up early. But to my relief it's only Adi. I decided to give her a second chance, feeling she would like to help at the party and have a chance to network and offer her baby-sitting skills to all the celeb mums. She turns up looking gorgeous and gives me an ecstatic hug – 'Thanks so so much for letting me help!' she gushes.

A minute later, the doorbell rings again. It's the palm reader – and he gives me quite a surprise. I was expecting a plump, middle-aged man with a silly pointy grey beard and a purple cape. So when I see a dark, handsome man on my doorstep, at first I mistake him for a celebrity daddy. When he tells me he's the palm reader, I have to conceal my surprise. Clare catches sight of him and we exchange looks, biting back smiles and sharing the same thought: *He can read my palm any day!*

Finally, it's time. Clare, Dom, Devika, Adi and I stand in the garden.

The sky clouds over and I frown but then to my relief the sun comes out.

Bees buzz; the wind blows ripples across the paddling pool; the horse begins to chomp on another bush.

We wait for the doorbell . . .

We wait for the doorbell . . .

At ten past twelve there is a shrill and I jump up and down with shock.

I grab Devika's hand and we run to the door. We pause and then open it up.

'Hi!'

I don't recognise the woman standing on the door, clutching the hand of a small boy.

'This is Sven,' she says, in a thick Eastern European accent. 'I am Ludmila, his nanny, and ve are delighted to join you.'

My heart falters. Sven is the son of Pammy Rose, the latest star in *EastEnders*. She wasn't at the top of my guest list . . . but what if they've misunderstood? What if they all send nannies instead? The whole point of this party was to meet celebs!

Then behind her I see Liz Hurley getting out of a cab with her son Damien and a huge relief comes over me. I wave Ludmila on to the garden and hurry down the path to share air kisses with the lovely Liz, whom I haven't see for yonks.

After that, the door doesn't stop ringing. Now that the adoption has boosted my media profile, I'm back in with the top celebs; it's nearly as good as the day when I was dating Liam. Kate Winslet turns up, and Sadie Frost with her four children *and* Kate Moss, and Honey Kavanaugh from *Hollyoaks*, and eventually Fran, who apologises for being late and pretends she got the time wrong. However, there is still no sign of my most 'wanted' guest – Madonna with David and Lourdes. I had called up her PA several times, who assured me that Madonna 'might attend if she's in the UK at the time'. My agent also makes an appearance, dragging, to my amusement, his son. I'd never imagined he would ever stop thinking about contract negotiation long enough to have a son; I can't help imagining that the conception must have involved a conversation along the lines of: 'Well, I can let you have twenty per cent of my sperm but no higher . . .'

'Give Devika her present,' he says, and I feel rather exasperated as Devika tears it open. I wanted to save all the presents so when we wrote the thank-you letters we could be clear about who sent one, but she is too impatient.

Every time the doorbell rings I keep turning, hoping it will be Madonna. But mostly it's press and photographers now, all invited along by my agent. The various celebrity mummies look pleased and are photographed holding their kids in the air, or in their laps, or passing more presents to Devika. As for Devika – she still seems very shy in front of the cameras. I have to keep reminding her not to duck her head and lower her eyes as they snap her.

It all seems to be going swimmingly until the games start. The palm reader lasts about five minutes – none of the kids seem remotely interested or impressed. So we hurry on to Pass the Parcel. Clare cajoles a reluctant Dom into joining in. But somewhere along the unwrapping process, Damien misses his turn when Dom lunges in and grabs it first. Dom starts squabbling with his mum, the press begin to chuckle, and several kids get upset and start to sob.

'I think it's time for Karina to tell everyone a story,' my agent calls out. I flash him a trembling, grateful smile.

'That's a good idea!' I cry.

'Just here,' my agent says, ushering me over to the perfect photoshoot prop: my favourite white garden chair, decorated with ornate trellis, perched under the cherry tree, so that blossom will float about in a confetti haze.

Adi and Clare and my agent help to guide all the mums and kids on to the white tablecloth laid out on the grass. I sit down and open up my A4 file. This is the moment I've been waiting for, the finale of the party.

'Well, I'm pleased to say that today you are all going to enjoy an exclusive from me,' I say. 'My first children's book, *The Celebrity Princess*, will be published in a few months' time. There will be an amazing tie-in with a kids' clothing shop. But in the meantime, I'm going to read you all a sneak preview – aren't you lucky?'

The children look up at me uncertainly, but several mums start clapping and I smile, feeling my heart swell. My agent was right: this is a superb idea.

Then I catch sight of Devika, sitting in the front row. The party has been so crazy I keep forgetting about her and then remembering her with a jolt of guilt. There is a look on her face that truly touches me. She looks proud that I'm her mother.

I turn the first page and I'm about to begin when a photographer calls out: 'Bring the horse forward so it's in the background – that'll look nice.'

Tamsin dutifully pulls the horse forward so that he's just behind me. He gives the willow an uncertain nibble, then grazes peacefully. The perfect setting: I can just see how amazing this photo is going to look in the papers. I begin to read.

'Once upon a time there was a princess who was so beautiful even her own mirror was jealous of her.' I pause, waiting for the children to scream with laughter. But they just stare up at me.

I can't help feeling rather disappointed. Last night I was reading Devika a story that made her snigger and blush at every other word. What was it now? Some book by Jeremy Strong about an obnoxious lavatory. The humour was so crude I regretted even choosing it for her – but she begged me to, declaring all the other girls in her class loved it.

'Her mirror considered going on a diet to compete with the princess but in the end gave up for fear of becoming anorexic.'

Still no response.

Then I remind myself that Devika and her friends are a little old for a picture book. I couldn't do a book for older children because I'd have to write so many words and it would be exhausting; just coming up with a few per page was hard enough. I take another glance at the children and my heart sinks. Some are yawning. One is picking at the grass. Another is picking his nose.

But my agent gives me a warm and supportive smile and I continue.

I break off, hearing a sudden scream of laughter. Well, this wasn't actually meant to be a funny moment but hell, at least I no longer feel as though I'm addressing a group of zombies. Then I'm aware of warm breath against my ear, a presence behind me. I turn to see that the horse has my cardigan hem between his teeth and is having an experimental nibble.

'He's behind you!' one the children calls out and all the others take up the refrain too.

I smile and give Tasmin a very fierce look. She tugs the horse back, patting his mane, but I can see she's trying to hold back a giggle too.

'All the other princesses in the region were jealous, especially when princes kept writing rap songs for her,' I read. But the mood has been broken; I feel I've lost their attention. Then I feel a hot furry face by my neck again, and the sound of chomping. I stare in horror to see that the horse has bitten a chunk out of the corner of *The Celebrity Princess*!

'Tamsin!' I cry, unable to keep my voice down, '*Could you please control that horse!*'

Tamsin flushes. Behind me, the children are in fits, hysterical with merriment. Fluorescent lights flash as the photographers snap again and I just want to scream at them to stop.

The horse reacts badly to the lights and my fit of temper. He suddenly rears up at me and I hear a voice scream, 'MUMMY!' I stumble backwards in shock. Tamsin tries to soothe him, but he trots with a big splish-splash into the paddling pool. He neighs rudely, then starts to slurp up water. All the kids begin to laugh again but I can see the potential disaster and I yell, 'Get him out of there!'

It's too late. His hooves have punctured the plastic. There is a terrible hissing noise and a flood of water gushes across the grass. I shout at the children to move but they're too stunned, too slow, and within minutes thirty or so celebrity mummies are trying to calm their offspring, who react to their soggy bottoms with a mixture of amusement and distress.

This might have been bad enough, but I hear Dom turn to Devika and cry, 'Your birthday party is SO crap!'

Devika bursts into tears and runs to me. Suddenly in the midst of all the chaos I see an alternative birthday party, the one that should have been: something small and simple, indoors, with just a few select friends from her school, and homemade cakes and sandwiches. Something where I could have focused my love and attention on her and not felt torn in a thousand different directions. I quickly hold her tight and look over despairingly at Clare and my agent.

Clare, to my relief, turns into a total lifesaver.

'Okay,' she says, 'everyone to the bathroom. We'll sort them out there. We've got plenty of towels, haven't we, Karina?'

'Yes – we can all dry off there,' I agree, giving Clare a grateful smile. 'Come on, Devika,' I say, caressing her face, 'we're going to go and get you dry, okay? And,' I add, passing Tamsin, 'would you please get rid of that damned horse!'

'Okay,' says Tamsin with a pale face. And then I feel bad, because it really was a stupid idea of mine to invite a horse into a small back garden; I just got completely carried away.

All the celeb mummies seem glad to have a focal point to relieve their panic and lead their youngsters back to the house. Trying not to wince at all the damp footprints on the carpet, I weave through the queue, assuring everyone they'll soon be dry.

But when I try to open the bathroom door, it's

locked. I stand there, Devika in hand, and smile reassuringly.

'I'm sure they'll just be a sec.' I hammer lightly on the door. 'Erm – we're having a bit of an emergency out here . . .'

Honey Kavanaugh reaches breaking point. She hisses that she's had enough, grabs her kid Zach's hand and leaves. I notice Adi quickly intervenes and passes her a goody bag. Honey quickly checks what's inside and looks mollified, then turns to say a very gracious thank-you and goodbye. I give Adi a thankful smile and she gives me a surreptitious thumbs-up.

I knock once again on the bathroom door and a voice calls out, 'Won't be a sec.'

Hang on. I *know* that voice. It's Fran.

'Fran!' I hammer harder. 'What the hell are you doing in there?'

'Just hang on!'

Five minutes later, everyone is reaching breaking point when the door opens and out comes Fran. With the palm reader.

'Fran!' I explode.

'Really!' another celeb mummy cries. 'This is supposed to be a children's party!'

I quickly usher Devika in, grabbing any towel I can and giving Fran a vile look. She shrugs and drags the palm reader away. I am just rubbing

Devika's legs dry and organising everyone else when, through the chaos, I hear the doorbell ring.

I call for Adi to get it. And then a terrible premonition grips me. I have this feeling, this awful feeling, that Madonna is going to be behind that door, clutching David's hand. Maybe Madonna will find this fiasco funny. Maybe she'll start handing out paper towels and quoting soothing words from Kabala and we'll appear in the press with the caption: *A catastrophe at Karina West's party resulted in a bonding moment with her new friend Madonna.*

Or maybe not. I listen hard for her Anglo-American accent through the din, but all I can hear is Adi saying, 'I'm sorry but the party's over – it's probably best you don't come in.'

'What!'

I drop the towel, leapfrog over several mummies and hammer down the stairs, aware of Devika running behind me. I stop and grab her hand.

'Come on,' I cry, 'we're going to meet Madonna. Adi, what the hell did you think you were doing, turning Madonna away?'

And then I stop, because there on my doorstep is not Madonna . . . but Liam.

He has his hands in his pockets and he's chewing gum. He sees me holding Devika's hand and I nearly drop it; then I realise how awful that would be, and I hold it even more tightly, almost defiantly.

'I was chatting to Hayley and she said she'd heard on the grapevine that you'd organised a party for *your adopted child's eleventh birthday*,' he says. His voice is casual, but I can hear the angry undercurrent in the sharpness of his syllables. 'So hey, I thought I'd come and play the clown.'

'Liam – I'm sorry I didn't tell you. I just thought . . .'

'Fuck, I guess it just didn't cross your mind, did it? You probably just thought, well, went to India, got a bit of a tan, also happened to bring a kid back but didn't feel it was important enough to mention . . .'

I open my mouth to try to explain, but Liam turns on his heel and walks away.

I call after him, but he doesn't take any notice. I watch him go, feeling my heart claw and sob after him. Tears prickle my eyes. I am about to run after him when Adi calls me back and I remember I have over fifty guests who still need looking after.

We sort out the wet bottoms. The children play on. The goody bags are handed out. Devika goes to bed, smiling, surrounded by presents.

Clare offers to help clear up but I put on a bright smile and insist she goes home. Then, in the gloom, finally I can be alone and break down. I wander through the garden, picking up bits of sandwich crust and wrapping paper, sobbing so hard I can hardly see what I'm doing.

Back inside, I try calling him up but he doesn't reply.

20

Devika

Today is a horrible day. I hate England, I hate school, I hate everything.

I want to be back home in the orphanage. I want to be in the courtyard with Raji, singing and pretending to sweep my broom at him and laughing up at the clouds. I want to jump on to Mrs Laxsmi's lap and feel her give me a hug. I want to go into the little temple with the statue of Lord Ganesh in the gloom at the back where sometimes if you look hard but not too hard a smile flicks across his face. I want to give him a flower and say my prayers.

Mummy Karina walks me to school. All the way there, she is completely silent. She has never behaved like this with me before. I ask her to tell me what the word is for the red boxes where people put letters, but she won't reply. I point out a pretty white cat sitting on the wall of a garden, but she ignores me. When I stop to stroke its face, she just snaps, 'Come on!' When we get to the school gates, Regina is getting out of her mummy's big shiny white car. She turns and gives her mummy a big hug and a kiss. When I turn to hug Mummy Karina, she wriggles away. She shoves my lunch box into my hands and then turns and walks off.

I stare after her as she gets smaller and smaller. I feel a lump in my throat and I want to cry.

But I won't cry, because Regina is watching me. I shrug happily, wave after my mummy Karina and skip to the cloakroom.

My lunch box feels light and I pull open the corner to see what's inside. Mummy Karina has forgotten to put anything in it.

School is horrible. Regina is angry that she wasn't invited to my party. All through lunchtime, she and Kelly walk past me, arm in arm, Regina saying loudly, 'When I have *my* birthday in October, I'm going to get Justin Timberlake to perform. My mum says he's going to write a rap song just for me.'

Then, at the end of the day, I am the last one waiting at the gate. I feel scared because earlier I prayed to Lord Krishna to send me back home to India. Now maybe it will come true. *I want to stay here*, I pray to Krishna, *please let me stay here*.

My fear starts to get bigger and bigger. Mummy Karina isn't going to come because she's got bored with me and she's going to put me on a plane and send me home . . .

Then a car drives up and I see my mummy. I run and pull open the door and jump into the seat at the back. In the little mirror, I see she is wearing black glasses. She doesn't say anything, not even hello, how are you, did you like school?

The car rumbles through the roads and I stare out at people and cats and houses and I try to squeeze them all into my head because I'm afraid I won't see them again.

Back home, I go into the kitchen and see tissues screwed up like little fists all over the table. I am so hungry that I feel as though my stomach is going to scream so when Mummy Karina puts down a bowl of Rice Krispies I eat and eat and eat. Then my tummy hurts but I'm still so hungry I have to ask for more.

As I eat, she watches me and then gives me a sort of smile.

Then we go into the living room and watch TV. There's a programme on called *EastEnders* and I can't understand what they're saying, but everyone looks miserable and angry. Some people cry and some people shout and some people drink brown drinks and shout some more. I want to turn the

TV off because I think Mummy Karina will only get more sad, but I dare not move. I feel worried because the teacher gave me some word practice to do and I need to show it to Mummy K, but I dare not speak either. If I keep quiet and be good, then I think Mummy Karina's bad mood will end and I'll be allowed to stay after all.

Then all of a sudden Mummy Karina jumps up and goes to the kitchen and all the fear I told to go away runs back towards me. Is she calling an aeroplane to take me home?

She comes back in carrying a big shiny red bag. She opens it up and offers it to me. It's full of little chocolate balls.

I bite into one and it surprises me, because inside it tastes like a Rice Krispie.

Mummy Karina seems to like the chocolate balls. She keeps throwing them into her mouth so there will be no more room inside her for any sadness.

Then the doorbell rings.

I glance over at Mummy Karina to see if she will open it, but she just sits there, popping chocolate balls into her mouth.

The doorbell rings again. She doesn't move. I edge off the sofa and go to the living-room door. I stand still, waiting to see if she will tell me off, but she just stares at it.

I walk down the hallway, feeling a bit scared about who is at the door. Maybe it is Dom's mum; I hope she hasn't brought Dom. I stand on tiptoe and click open the door.

'Liam!' I cry in surprise. 'Hello!'

He is wearing jeans and a black T-shirt and there is a funny sort of smell on his breath, like apples. I like Liam but he also scares me a bit.

'Hey, kid,' he says, ruffling my hair. 'Is Karina in?'

'Yes,' I say. Then I look back to make sure she can't hear and I whisper, 'She's very very sad. She's eating chocolate balls.'

Liam looks surprised, but then he grins and suddenly I feel relief, because I have a feeling Mummy Karina won't be sad after she sees him.

Liam shuts the door and goes towards the living room. I hear Mummy Karina call out, 'Who is it?'

Liam crouches down and whispers something to me that I don't understand.

'Let's play a game,' he says. 'Here. You stay here – quiet.'

I sit down on the floor and pray to Lord Krishna that they will be nice to each other. I hear them speaking very quickly and Mummy Karina's voice suddenly rises to a shout. I'm scared Liam is hurting her and I pray like mad. Then everything goes silent. I hardly dare to look. I just sit there, too scared to move, praying. Then finally I manage to make my legs listen and I crawl to the edge of the door and peer round it.

I let out a gasp because Liam has pressed his lips to Mummy Karina's. I think he might be hurting her, because I see tears falling down her cheeks again.

I go up to her side and reach for her hand, but her arms are curled round Liam's waist, so I grab the edge of her dress and say to Liam, 'Nice, nice to Mummy Karina.'

He and Mummy Karina suddenly laugh and then they both put their arms round me. They keep laughing and I laugh too, thanking Krishna in relief that they are happy.

Mummy Karina says something to Liam about 'bed' and she grabs my hand and takes me upstairs. It feels as though a magic spell has been cast over her, a wonderful boon granted. Now she cannot stop smiling. She sings as she takes off my clothes and puts on my pyjamas. When I try to clean my teeth, she tickles me playfully and I spill paste on my pyjamas and she laughs and wipes it off. She combs my hair out for ages, stroking it as though I'm a princess. Then suddenly she grabs me in her arms and carries me into my bedroom. She pulls up the covers and tucks them in neatly, then leans down and gives me another hug and I'm so relieved that I cry: 'I stay here – I stay?'

'Yes. You like here.' She points to the bed.

'I stay in England. I stay with you.'

Mummy Karina's face breaks and she cries a little. I'm scared this means she wants me to go still but then she hugs me so tight I nearly end up in two pieces.

'You stay,' she says, 'you stay for ever.'

I don't know what *for ever* means. What if that is just a week?

'I stay long time,' I say.

'Yes! For ever!' she cries and she stretches out her hands as wide as they can go. That must mean more than a week, maybe even a year. She gives me a kiss on the forehead and turns out the light. *For ever*, I keep telling Lord Krishna, *she wants me to stay for ever. For ever is good. I think . . .*

The next morning I go down to breakfast and Mummy Karina is sitting on Liam's lap. Their lips are pressed together again.

Mummy Karina gets up and gives me a hug. Liam holds out his arms for a hug too but he seems so big and dark. Suddenly I feel shy and I hide behind Mummy Karina's back. She laughs and pushes me forwards, kissing my head.

'Liam is good,' she says. 'Liam good.'

I let Liam give me a hug. He smells strange, like strong metal and apples.

Then he pulls me on to his lap. I feel nervous I

will fall off but he bounces me up and down on his knee and I start to laugh.

Mummy Karina fills up my whole bowl to the brim with Rice Krispies and then sloshes in loads of milk. She tries to gently pull me from Liam's lap but he holds me on tight and I want to stay too.

When I pick up my spoon, Liam curls his hand on top of mine. He takes control of my hand and makes it dip into the bowl. As he carries it up to my lips, I am laughing so much I can't take it in, so he pulls it up and eats it himself!

'Liam!' Mummy Karina cries.

'Liam!' I cry too.

Finally he fills up the spoon and tips it into my mouth. I munch happily and the Rice Krispies have never tasted so good – they are like the ambrosia of the gods.

When I get to school I check my lunch box and find Mummy Karina has put in sandwiches *and* an Innocent smoothie *and* a chocolate bar *and* a pear *and* raisins. I won't go hungry today.

21

Karina

Oh, God. This is scary. Liam and I are about to have a Serious Talk.

I've been floating on waves of euphoria all morning. I've just dropped Devika off at school and now I'm driving back home. I find myself slowing down my speed to a crawl, until cars toot in a tantivy of impatience. Finally, I pull over a few streets away from home. I fold my arms across the steering wheel and bury my head in them, letting out a moan.

This morning was so heavenly. I replay it now, savouring every minute . . .

I woke up slowly, thinking the warm presence in my bed was Devika. Then I did a double take and a delicious jolt of shock shivered through me. And I remembered.

Liam's face was a few inches from mine on the pillow. He reached out and caressed my face, smiling. Last night came rushing back to me. Our row, our kisses.

Liam leaned in and gave me a kiss. I always used to love waking up beside him, breathing in the muskiness of his skin, feeling the bristle of his new stubble against my chin, floating in a hazy, half-awake bubble. His kisses became hungry. He pinned himself on top of me. I felt him hardening against me. His palms smoothed up my thighs. They reached my knickers. And paused. Then he broke off with a groan of frustration.

Fuck. Why oh why, last night of all nights, did I have to get my period? We were about to have phenomenal make-up and reunion sex all rolled into one – until I went to the loo.

Liam buried his face in the pillow and punched it. For a moment I thought he was seriously angry and indignation stirred. Then he lifted his face, laughing.

'I want to fuck you so badly,' he said, kissing me again. 'But I guess I'll have to wait.'

'Well, you can just hold me in your arms,' I sighed, sharing a private joke.

'When you look at me like that, it makes me feel

as though we'll be together for ever.' Liam played along.

'But will for ever be ours – or will fate separate us?' I said soulfully and we both burst into giggles.

About five years ago, I got a part in a movie adaptation of a historical romance by an author who made Barbara Cartland look like a Nobel Prize winner. I had to play a buxom maiden who kept accidentally spilling milk down her dress so that it clung becomingly to her curves, resulting in some seriously deep breathing every time her employer tried to wipe it off. It was perhaps the worst script I've ever come across and even my agent told me not to do it. But Liam insisted – 'This film is so awful, it will end up being brilliant in its sheer dreadfulness.' Liam was possibly wrong about that, as the film was probably the final nail in the coffin of my movie career. But the lingo became a private joke between us; we'd lie in bed and quote lines from it, giggling in between kisses, competing to be the most cheesy.

Remembering the joke brought a feeling of intimacy between us. We lay in peaceful silence for a while, just loving each other with our eyes, the sounds of birds and traffic outside seeming far away. His fingers slowly caressed the edge of my face. I know it sounds strange, but I felt quite relieved that we hadn't had sex. Just lying here with him made me feel as though I was falling, losing control. When we made love, Liam broke the seal on my soul. It was better that I hadn't let him in. Otherwise there would have been no going back.

I began to wonder what the time was, if Devika was up. Oh God, I was so mean to her yesterday. I still felt guilty.

I didn't want to get up and spoil the moment. There was still so much to discuss. Last night our row never reached a conclusion. We just shouted at each other. Liam had accused me of bring a liar and I'd kept yelling back that I'd lied because he was a womaniser who would obviously never want children. There was no winner; just a draw when we kissed. Then we collapsed into bed, exhausted.

We ought to have talked then, but in my cowardice I put it off. I told him we had to get Devika some breakfast. He didn't look sulky, as I'd expected; in fact, he was utterly lovely with Devika. But that might have been because Liam would also do anything to avoid a Talk.

Now I sit in the car and face reality: Liam is waiting for me back at the house and the Talk can no longer be avoided. And Liam's usual response to such a request is to put on heavy metal at top volume, or say, 'A talk? God, you sound like my bank manager.'

When it comes to Talks, Liam has all the depth of an eighteen-year-old boy.

The last time we did manage one was at the start of our last liaison. We agreed that we were both lousy at relationships so we might as well be fuck buddies. But somehow the sense of freedom only undermined the relationship. Acknowledging from the start that it couldn't work between us created a certain cynicism and flatness. It had soon fizzled out and I had ended up dumping him, but only because I felt I had to get in there before he dumped me. Now things were different; I was a different person and Liam had to understand that.

'I'm sorry, Liam, but last night was just a one-night stand,' I burst out, practically the moment I walk through the door and find him in the kitchen.

'Well, there's a twisted logic,' Liam says, putting his arms round my waist. 'Because a one-night stand should involve sex, which means you still owe me.'

'Liam! I just—' I step back. 'Look, I can't do . . . what we did before . . . the whole fuck buddies thing . . . that worked because we were both single and carefree. I just don't think it can now. You know, I need to be a good mother to Devika. I need to read her a bedtime story and be there to pick her up from school – I can't be spontaneous any more. It just . . .'

Silence. I bite my lip, watching his face, which is inscrutable.

'It seems to me,' he says, 'that you're making a lot of assumptions about me and what you think I want.'

Oh, great. So all he did want was a one-night stand; even fuck buddies is obviously too much commitment for Liam.

'As it happens, I want a lot more than just no-strings sex. I want us to . . . I mean, we're so good together, Karina . . . we've been going out and getting back together so many times . . . I think we should – you know . . .' He stumbles over his words, suddenly shy.

'What?'

'You know. Give it a go. Us. Properly.'

'You want to give us a go?' I ask in astonishment.

'I want', he says, with more confidence, 'to have a serious relationship. And I realise what you're saying. Anyone who has a relationship with you now is also in a relationship with Devika too. I get that, Karina.'

'So . . . you're saying you want to be a father to Devika?' I burst out in excitement.

'Well . . . I don't know if I can do that . . .'

Silence. I narrow my eyes. Is he just playing with words? Maybe he does just want intermittent casual sex, but is dressing it up to persuade me. Normally at times like this, I'd indulge him. Allow him to be vague and enigmatic. I'd shrug my shoulders, afraid if I pinned him down I'd scare him off; I'd declare I wanted my freedom too. Our whole game-playing revolved around neither of us ever quite knowing what the other wanted or thought. But now I need black and white.

'Well, what does that mean?' I demand. 'You're saying that *perhaps* you want me and Devika?'

'I'm saying – yes, I want you – but I'm also being honest,' Liam says, his voice rising a few notches. 'I want to be with you and I think Devika is adorable – but as for being a father to her, that's a real commitment and I think . . . I have to see how I go. I mean, I really want to be honest with you, Karina. There's no point in making promises I can't keep.'

This sounds like typical Liam: promising everything and nothing all at the same time.

And yet. When I look into his eyes, there is no cynicism there. Only sincerity and that nervous, slightly sheepish self-consciousness that auras around him when he lets his laddish guard down.

'Come on, Karina – it'll be the same with any guy. Nobody can really say if they can become a good father – it depends as much as anything on whether Devika takes to me. We've just got to take it one day at a time. But the point is, I do . . . I do care about you so much I want to make a go of it.'

His voice trembles slightly and then he swallows and grabs my hand, massaging it gently. He looks quite petrified now, as though he can hardly wait to get this talk over and done with.

Which means that he means it.

This is incredible. Happiness begins to dance inside me. I do actually believe he wants to make a go of it.

Except: 'Hayley!' I burst out. 'What about her? The whole kids thing was an issue there, wasn't it?'

'Eh?'

'You broke up with Hayley because she wanted kids and you didn't.'

'Where'd you hear that? Bollocks. Hayley didn't want kids – she was terrified it'd ruin her boobs. No, I'm serious. She did bring it up once, but along with calculations as to how much plastic surgery she'd have to have afterwards. Me, I just thought, what kind of mother would she make? Hayley and I split up because she was a stupid cow. And the honest truth is, half the time I was with her, I wished she was you . . . and that's happened a few times, Karina, with my last few dates. And look, I know in the past I was a bit of a shit boyfriend . . . I did treat you badly – though you gave me a hard time too.'

Yes, I think silently, *but only in retaliation: I felt I had to give as good as I got. To keep you interested. To keep the balance of power.*

'I mean, I can see that you're changing. You were always so obsessed with fame, but I can see Devika's bringing out your better side.'

'Well, being famous is part of my job,' I retort defensively, feeling stung.

'Karina, don't get mad. I'm actually paying you a compliment. When you're not worrying about being famous, you're one of the most lovely and genuine people in this industry – you're not like Hayley and those other airheads. That's what attracts me to you.'

'Well . . .' I say, feeling mollified.

'And . . . I also – I also feel – full of regret for some of the things I did, the way I've behaved. I mean, when I was on the plane and got off with that air hostess – I was pissed and I behaved like an idiot . . . and we went to bed and it wasn't that great and I woke up and thought, I could be doing this in ten years' time, just sleeping with random blondes, and where's the future in that?'

'Liam,' I say, with a wry smile, 'I don't think I'm the only one who's changing. It sounds as though you're growing up.'

Liam stops his confession, catching himself, and then smiles.

'Never,' he jokes. Then he looks serious again. 'I'll tell you something, Karina – and I never . . . I feel a bit . . . but my last single, well, that was about you.' He laughs awkwardly.

'What? Hang on? What was your last single?'

'You didn't hear it?' he asked. 'I thought you'd catch it somewhere and know it was about you. You know . . . it goes *I can't stop missing you, you're my minute, my hour, my day, my year*.' He sings a bit, then breaks off.

I do recognise the single – I've heard it in many a club and supermarket and awards event. But I used to grimace and pretend I couldn't make it out or sing along with sarcastic alternate lyrics inside, feeling sulky and cynical about all the girls listening to the song who were probably stupid enough to think it was about them.

'I was upset when we last broke up – when you went off with that kid from *Hollyoaks*. I was so fucked off – I really missed you.'

'I only did that because I thought you were flirting with Hayley!' I protest. I shake my head in wonder; he really wrote that for *me*?

There is a silence and Liam bites his lip, shoving his hands in his pockets.

'So you think you've changed, then?' I ask, eager for more: I don't think we've spoken with this sort of honesty before. But Liam has suddenly become self-conscious and I can sense he's snapped shut. He's allowed himself to be vulnerable and he can't manage any more. We've never talked with this degree of openness and honesty, ever.

So instead he leans in and gives me a long, deep kiss.

I melt against him . . . and then remember how I felt this morning in bed beside him: the resolution that had begun to crystallise in my mind. I break away from him and cross my arms uneasily.

'Liam,' I say, wondering how to word this so he doesn't take it the wrong way. 'There's just one thing . . . something which would really help . . . I mean, you don't know how you're going to take to being with me and Devika . . . so . . .'

'Yes?' Liam looks distracted; he's started to stroke the back of my neck.

'I can't have sex with you until . . .'

His fingers freeze. Then he smiles. 'Until we've achieved world peace and an end to global warming.'

'Liam – I'm not joking. Please try to understand – I just feel . . . it's just . . .'

'You just want to be *good friends*?' he spits out. 'Is that what you're saying?'

'No! No!' I lean in and kiss him. 'I'm dying to have sex with you – but I just – it's just that I want to see how things go before we . . . It's just so intimate – I want to see how you feel about things first . . . take it slowly . . . put off sex for a bit . . .'

I stare at him anxiously, worried I've blown it. Pushed him too far away. How can I explain that when we have sex, it never feels like sex. Liam always said that going to bed with me took him to a place he couldn't reach with anyone else. It was always so achingly intense for both of us, a passionate spiral of touch and taste and tenderness. Sharing gasps, him pinning his mouth on to mine as I came, swallowing my orgasm, spilling his down my throat too. He opens me up like a surgeon, peels me raw. And if he breaks my heart and I end up moping about the house, how will that affect Devika? I still feel appalled by how mean I was to her yesterday. I need to protect my heart, to keep it strong enough for her.

Then Liam's face changes. An unexpected sweetness comes over it.

'Okay,' he says. 'Sure. I'm happy. You see, Karina, it's all going to be different for us.' He takes my hands, swinging them exuberantly. 'A fresh start for both of us.'

Liam disappears, saying he needs to take Rufus for a walk. After he's gone, I walk around for a bit, dazed by this new turn of events.

Then I put that song on. I don't have his latest album – I deliberately didn't buy it – so I download the single from the Net.

When I hear his voice crooning with such emotion, I find tears in my eyes. Years ago, I used to secretly hope that Liam would one day grow up and settle down. I knew his womanising habits wouldn't be ended by his miraculously finding the One – it's my belief that the One only comes along when your heart is ready for it. When you've got enough love inside you to lavish on that special person who deserves it. Eventually I gave up on that idea, figuring that maybe some people just can't change. And now, just when I've given up on him for good – I've got him.

Devika *and* Liam. I feel as though I've won the love lottery.

Then a shadow of premonition falls over me. Surely life can't be this kind to me? Surely I can't have a wonderful daughter *and* a great partner? Everything has gone so wrong for so long, I can't quite believe there isn't a terrible catch.

22

Karina

Liam is true to his word.

He returns to the house later that day, an hour before I'm due to pick up Devika from school. And he even *looks* different.

He's still wearing black jeans, albeit a fresh pair, but his T-shirt has been replaced by a nice olive-green shirt. His cheeks are clean, not a speck of stubble to be seen; his messy hair is combed back neatly with a little gel. He looks great . . . though a perverse part of me can't help secretly feeling he looked more sexy the way he was. He looks more conventional, more ordinary, more *suburban* somehow.

Shut up, Karina, I tell myself, *just be grateful that he's making an effort.*

And I am grateful. Grateful and touched.

He has also brought Rufus along.

'Hey, I know Devika will love him,' he says.

I'm not quite so sure, and when I pick up Devika from school and tell her the news, she doesn't look that enthused.

'Don't like dogs – I like cats,' she cries eagerly, as we drive back home. 'Can I have a cat, Mummy Karina?'

'Erm . . . well . . . we'll see,' I say. 'Maybe.'

When we enter the house, there is a horrible explosion of savage barking. Devika looks quite scared and clutches my hand tightly. Then Liam brings Rufus out into the hallway and orders him to sit. Devika still looks nervous. Then Liam lifts up Rufus's paw and puts it into Devika's hand, saying gruffly, 'How do you do, Devika?'

Devika bursts into laughter. Then she puts her arms round Rufus and buries her face in his neck.

'Warm,' she says.

Liam and I catch eyes and smile. And then we glance away, feeling oddly self-conscious, aware that we are sharing something close to a parental bond. And hell, though we've shared everything before – from joints to baths to gigs – this is brand-new territory for us.

Then Liam – shock of the century – offers to cook dinner for us. Normally Liam's idea of a romantic meal is baked beans on toast. If he's working hard at song-writing or practising for a gig, he'll regularly resort to a McDonald's, and whenever we used to go out to fancy restaurants he always looked bored, and ever so slightly intimidated. Nevertheless, he comes up with a great dish, by sticking to something simple – pasta and veggies. I am not sure if Devika will like it, though. I've tried cooking pasta for her a few times and she's pulled a face and I've put out the Rice Krispies in defeat. But, to my delighted surprise, she gobbles it all up and beams at Liam, then sidles round the table to slip on to his lap.

'Devika,' I say, 'let Liam finish his food.'

'But I can help him, I can help him,' she cries, grabbing a pasta twirl and popping it into his mouth.

'Devika!' I cry, horrified at her manners, and then Liam and I burst into laughter. 'Come down, come on, come and sit on my lap.'

After dinner, I give Devika a quick bath and she doesn't even blink at the water; she just chatters away in Hindi to her duck and breaks off to ask me questions about Liam in English. How old is Liam? How tall is he? Does he love you?

'I – I don't know,' I say nervously. 'And don't you dare go asking Liam that question, okay?'

When I come downstairs, I expect to find Liam slouched out in front of the TV but *he is doing the washing up*. I actually feel slightly freaked out, as though my rock god boyfriend has been replaced by some Stepford Husband. There is just something inherently strange about Liam behaving like a new man; it's like Kylie trying not to be sexy.

'Let me take over,' I say. 'Really – it's fine. And hey, Devika wouldn't mind a bedtime story.'

'Cool,' he says, peeling off his gloves. He pauses, as though debating whether to kiss me; then, just as I am about to lean in and say a kiss is allowed, he backs off and hurries up the stairs.

I am even more shocked. I was expecting Liam to challenge my no-sex rule at every turn, in every room. I was expecting him to follow me into the bathroom or tug at my jeans belt in the living room or try to steal secret kisses in the bedroom. Now he has turned into not only a new man, but a monk.

And this is the man who once sang 'Enemy of the People' before stage-diving into the crowd and having a notorious coke-fuelled orgy with three groupies.

I wash up two cups before temptation tickles me. I want to see how Liam and Devika are alone together – if the warmth he shows her in front of me is really real.

I pull off my gloves and see Rufus sitting by the table, looking up at me. I'm worried he'll bark and press a finger to my lips. To my relief, he puts his head back on his paws. I tiptoe up the stairs, then pause near the top, listening hard.

'I sing for bedtime story,' Devika is saying. 'Mummy Karina sings.'

'Cool,' says Liam. Through the gaps in the banisters, I can see him: sitting by her bed, grinning down at her, his eyes sparkling. He looks as cute as those Athena postcards of a muscly man holding a baby – it's the tenderness in his eyes, the sensitivity in his voice. This is a side of Liam I haven't seen all that often. 'And what does Mummy Karina sing?'

'I sing it for you, I sing it for you!' Devika cries. Then she gives him an exquisite rendition of Britney Spears's 'Hit Me Baby One More Time'.

Silence.

'No!' Liam cries, putting his head in his hands. 'No. No. No *no* NO! I can't believe Mummy Karina taught you Britney. Now, repeat after me. Britney – bad, Razorlight – good. Mariah Carey – bad, the Kills – good.'

Devika, who was looking crestfallen at his response to her singing, breaks into a smile, enjoying the new game.

'Razor good,' she tries.

'Razorlight good,' he repeats, and she repeats it back.

'What is Razorlight?'

'They are men of great genius,' says Liam. 'I'm

going to make you a CD of educational songs. I think you really need it – we need to undo the terrible damage Karina's done to you, eh?' He tickles her and she laughs.

'You sing.' She points at him. 'You sing, you sing!'

He picks 'More Than Words'. As he croons, Devika's dark eyes widen and she looks enchanted; I am so touched, I feel a lump in my throat.

I creep back downstairs and continue with the washing up. I feel nervous again. I can see that Devika is falling in love with Liam. It seems to be the effect he has on all women, young or old, whether he is romantic or fatherly. And then I feel scared: what if it doesn't work out between us? Will Devika end up as heartbroken as me? I feel a moment of territorial protectiveness when I picture her eyes again: she is *my* daughter and I wanted to be a single mother and I felt certain that was all she needed. And now it looks as though having a father means just as much to her as having a mother, which makes me feel a tiny bit sidelined.

Then I hear Liam coming back down the stairs; Rufus barks in delight. He smiles at me and I feel any resentment in my heart melt away; this new Liam is becoming increasingly irresistible.

'She's off. I sang something decent to her.' He smiles at me, shakes his head. 'Britney, eh?'

I shrug, laughing. 'It was the first song that came into my mind.'

'Evidently. Anyway, I'd best be off now.'

I smile at him, my heart filled up to the brim with love. I turn my head, ready to feel his lips against mine. But he leans in and gives me a chaste kiss on the forehead.

I can't tell if he's teasing me for my no-sex enforcement, or if he's genuinely not in the mood now that he's testing out this new persona. When he leaves, taking Rufus with him, I can't help feeling infuriated. Why the hell did I come up with such a stupid rule? Why on earth did I think postponing sex would save me from my feelings? I spend all night in a state of euphoric frustration, burying my hot cheeks in my pillow, biting back smiles as I flit through fantasies, and then I realise abstinence is only making things worse: I want him more than ever.

23

Devika

When I first came to England, I thought that Johnny Depp was going to be my dad. But now I'm glad it's not Johnny because Liam Holt is surely the best, best, bestest dad anyone could have in the world.

I'm not actually allowed to call him *Dad*. I once said to Mummy Karina, without even thinking, 'Can Dad take me for a walk too with Rufus?' Mummy Karina looked a bit startled and said I mustn't use the word 'Dad'. She told me to call him Liam. But though my mouth says Liam, my heart whispers Dad.

The other night on TV we watched a film called *Four Weddings and a Funeral*. It made me wish that Mummy Karina and Liam would get married so I could wear a pretty white dress. Then I could know they would be together for ever and we would all be safe. I wish we could all live together and Liam could be my teacher and I could spend all day learning the lyrics of his songs and how to play the guitar instead of maths and English.

One morning Mummy Karina wakes up late and for the first time Liam drives me to school. We travel in silence. Liam hums under his breath and I feel excited, knowing that he must be thinking up a new song. But as we approach the school and I see the gates and the white sign and hear the roar from the playground, all the happiness flows out of my heart.

'D'you like school?' Liam asks suddenly.

I open my mouth to say yes but Liam looks into my eyes and sees my real answer.

He pulls the car up outside the school and switches off the engine. We sit in silence for a moment. I'm scared he's cross or thinks I don't like school because I'm stupid.

'Don't tell Mummy Karina!' I cry. 'Don't tell her I don't like school!'

Liam takes off his seat belt and turns to me. He holds out his arms and pulls me in for a big hug. Suddenly I find tears pouring out of my eyes.

'Hey, hey,' Liam says, pulling back. 'Is school *that* bad? What's wrong?'

Deborah Wright

I smear the tears away from my eyes. Through the window, I can see the playground, where everyone is playing before they go in for lessons. I search but there is no Regina. Then I see her mummy's car pull up. It is a sleek, black, shiny long car. Regina gets out. Today her hair is in two swinging bunches. I point at her.

'Her. She's mean to me.'

'Stupid cow,' Liam says. 'Next time just tell her to fuck off.'

I laugh and he laughs and then he says, 'Don't tell your mummy I said that.'

Then we get out of the car and I feel sad because I thought Liam was going to come up with an answer, explain how in England you make someone mean be nice to you. And now I have to get through another day where Regina will laugh at me for not knowing how to spell a long word or not having a pair of jeans that cost more than two hundred pounds or not knowing every song in *Cats*.

Then, as Liam gives me another hug goodbye, I catch sight of Kelly. Her mummy's car has just driven away and she stares at me with wide eyes. Then she walks up to us. I pray like mad to Lord Krishna, *oh please don't let her be nasty to me in front of Liam*.

But she gapes at Liam and says, 'Are you Liam

234

Holt? Oh wow! I have *all* your CDs, you are *so* cool. Can you sign my arm for me?'

Liam laughs. He gets a biro out of his pocket and Kelly rolls up her sleeve. He scrawls his name, then draws a little heart and a kiss next to it. Kelly watches him the whole time with a crimson face. When he finishes, she seems so happy, she can hardly stammer, 'Th-th-thank y-y-you.'

'Well, Kelly,' he says, 'I hope you're going to look after my Devika for me. She hasn't been in school long. I think she needs a bodyguard and it ought to be you.'

'Sure!' Kelly laughs and stammers, 'I'll be her bodyguard!'

Liam glances at me and gives me a wink, as if to say, 'See? School is okay after all!' I smile at him. As he drives away, Kelly waves like mad and he toots his horn. Then she stares at me, as though seeing me with new eyes.

Then my heart sinks as Regina comes up.

'Look,' Kelly screams, 'Oh my God – can you believe this – LIAM HOLT signed my arm!' She leans down and kisses the signature. 'I'll NEVER wash my arm again.'

Regina stares at us, her eyes narrowed.

'Is Liam your new dad then?' Kelly cries.

'Yes,' I say, my heart feeling big with pride.

Suddenly Kelly pulls me into a big hug.

'It's so nice being your friend, Devika!' she cries. Then she loops her arm through mine.

I look at Regina. She looks cross.

'Liam can't be her dad!' she cries. 'He can't!'

'Yes he is,' Kelly says. 'You're just jealous because you don't even have a dad.'

'Well, neither do you! Your dad ran off with someone from *Coronation Street*, how crap is that!' Regina bursts out.

Kelly glares at Regina and Regina glares at me. Suddenly I feel as though I'm torn between the two of them. Then Kelly tosses up her chin and says: 'Come on, Devika. Let's go.'

All through our lessons that afternoon, Kelly keeps turning and smiling at me. Sometimes if I look stuck on a word Mrs H is saying, Kelly leans over and repeats it slowly, in a whisper, which helps me so much. For the first time, I enjoy a lesson where I can understand everything that's going on.

I notice Regina watches us. First she gives me nasty looks. Then she starts to smile at me. At first it confuses me. Then I realise she is trying to make friends. Even though she has been nasty to me in the past, I feel my heart melt with forgiveness. Mrs Laxsmi always taught me that you should try to react to all nasty and horrible things with indifference. That way, your bad karma comes your way and it's gone, without you creating any more.

But in the lunch hour, everything goes weird. Kelly asks if we can eat together. We sit down on the bench and we're just opening our lunch boxes when Regina comes up. She sits down on the edge of the bench, looking a bit nervous.

'Let's go. There's a nasty smell around here,' says Kelly. I don't understand because I can't smell anything. But Kelly grabs my hand and drags me away. We sit on a new bench on the other side of the playground. Regina sits on her own. She stares down at her lap and plays with her sandwich. I feel sorry for her.

'Is Regina okay?' I ask Kelly.

'Who cares?' Kelly asks. 'Regina's pretty evil. She was always putting my mum down just because she's in *Holby City* and according to Regina *Holby City* is trash. She is such a snob. I was getting sick of her.'

All of a sudden, I feel as though a switch has been flicked. Kelly likes me! I feel so happy to have a new friend that I begin to forget how Regina must be feeling. Kelly plaits my hair and says she can't believe I don't have a mobile phone. She tells me I have to get my mum to buy me one and in the meantime I can borrow one of her old ones. She even says she'll teach me how to put make-up on.

But I feel nervous. Mummy Karina, Liam, Kelly, Regina: it seems as though one day they can be full of love and the next full of hate. Maybe this is just how people in England are.

24

Karina

Liam comes up behind me as I'm doing the washing up. He put his arms round my waist, pushing his hardness up against the small of my back, and then starts to kiss the back of my neck. His breathing becomes hoarse. I ignore him, carrying on scrubbing hard at a plate and tipping the milky remnants of a Rice Krispies bowl down the sink. He licks my ear. I start to hum as though nothing is happening. He whispers, 'I want you so badly, Karina.'

I whisper back, 'I don't think so!'

Liam pulls away with a loud, angry groan.

'Fine,' he says. 'Fine.'

He leaves the kitchen and I hear him storm out into the hallway. Then I hear Devika asking him if he will give her another guitar lesson and his tone changes, becomes warm and soft.

I feel desire shudder through me. And then guilt. I'm still playing the I'm-not-ready-for-sex-yet game and I'm not sure why I keep spinning it out when I want him so badly. We've grown so close in the last ten days; they've felt like a decade. Liam has stayed over here most nights. We've shared breakfasts together and gone for long walks with Rufus. We've taken it in turns to pick up Devika from school. We've all snuggled up on the sofa together watching DVDs. Yesterday, which was a Sunday, we even went on an old-fashioned outing to pick blackberries together and then made a pie which we gobbled down with cream. And yet I can't quite believe it. I keep having to pinch myself with the shock that we're behaving like a couple. More than that – a family.

Naturally, the press picked up on our reunion pretty quickly. My agent phoned me up to congratulate me on playing the publicity game, though he said, 'I'm not sure Liam *convinces* as a celebrity dad, Karina. I think you need to weave some details about him being a good father into your blog for *The Times*.' I gave him a curt reply, but I have to admit I did follow his advice. When Clare phoned up and had a go at me and I told her how good Liam was being with Devika, I could tell she didn't believe me. Even Fran, who's thrilled that we've got back together, said: 'Hey, just make sure Liam doesn't get your kid hooked on crack cocaine!' It made me mad to see everyone putting Liam in a box. And so I hammered out a passionate *Times* blog detailing how wonderful he was being and soon all the women's magazines starting sighing over the New Liam.

Of course, this has only made Liam more desirable. A few exes have come out of the woodwork – Hayley in particular. When questioned on how she felt about our renewed relationship, she played the nice girl card and said, 'I wish them well. I hope they're very happy together.'

Yeah, right. You can guarantee she's throwing knives at my photo and screaming her house down.

'Liam and I were quite close to having children,' she was also quoted as saying, 'and there are some secrets there which I will never disclose to the press.'

That was more mysterious. *Secrets?* What did she mean by that? When I asked Liam, he looked a bit shifty, and then got cross when I tried to push him. I figure Liam hates the press and Hayley is just trying to get attention.

Everything is perfect between us, except for the fact that we're not having sex. Liam's monkish resolve crumbled within days. I keep having to put him in the spare room at night and he sulks like mad. He can't understand why I'm holding him at bay.

Is it because I'm scared he'll lose interest? Perhaps I'm playing a game myself, though I never set out to do so. Maybe I'm just a bit scared that if we have perfect sex on top of everything else, our lives will be so perfect he'll get bored and then everything will go wrong.

A little later on, after Devika's guitar lesson is over, I come and sit next to Liam on the sofa and he curls his arms round me, which means I'm forgiven – for the moment. Even so, there is still a slightly touchy tension bristling between us.

'Janmashtami,' Liam says. 'Aren't you going to do something with Devika for Janmashtami?'

'Sorry?'

'Krishna's birthday.' He looks slightly dismayed. 'Don't tell me you've adopted an Indian kid and you haven't even heard of Janmashtami. Next you'll be saying you haven't heard of Diwali.'

'No!' I cry as he pulls away, sitting up and frowning at me. 'Of course I've heard of it. That's the one where they fast for a month, right?'

'That's Ramadan,' says Liam. 'Entirely different religion.'

'Oh, come on,' I cry, on the defensive now. 'We're

in a Christian country . . . I thought it would be better if Devika got into our culture . . .'

'Uh huh. Because you obviously take her to church every Sunday, right. Devika,' Liam calls out. 'Come here.' As she enters, I see delight on her face just to be called in by Liam and I can't help but smile, even though I'm furious that he's using my own daughter to gang up on me. 'Sing a hymn for us.'

'Hymn?' Devika frowns. 'What is hymn?'

'See!' Liam crows.

'Oh, fuck off, Liam,' I mutter quietly, seriously irked now. I grab a cushion and hold it to my chest, giving him a sulky glance. I know I'm overreacting, but I'm scared of falling into the past, of playing out roles we've acted many times before, repeating a pattern of hurt. Liam can be a real Jekyll and Hyde, one minute putting you up on a pedestal and the next making your ego shrivel to the size of a gnat.

'Janmashtami,' Liam says to Devika and her face lights up with joy.

'Krishna,' she says eagerly.

Liam turns to me and tries to kiss me, but I turn my face away. Then he tries to wrench the cushion from my chest, but I hold on to it tightly. Finally, he succeeds in dragging it away from me, then tickles me to force my sulky lips to dissolve into laughter. When I'm shrieking and vulnerable, he leans in and seizes a kiss. I make an 'urgh' noise and push him away.

Then we look at Devika, who stares at us as though we're two kids, rolling her eyes.

'Parents are *so* embarrassing,' she declares, before strolling out of the room.

For a moment we sit in silence. Devika's clearly reciting something she's heard someone say at school and her sweet, pompous admonishment makes me want to laugh. But that scary word also hovers in the air.

Parents.

We've only been together ten days and already she's pairing us off for good. Liam emits a slight cough. Then he turns to me and says: 'Come on, then, Karina. It's time you found out more about Devika's culture and religion. The other day she was singing me this gorgeous Hindi song – she told me it was about Lord Ganesh. She hasn't been to a temple once since she's been in England – it's about time we took her. We can start with Krishna's birthday.'

'Well, how come you're the expert now?'

'The Internet, innit?' he says sarcastically.

I poke him in the ribs and he tussles with me until I'm pinned down on the sofa, his knees on either side of my hips. I try to push him away but he grabs my hands. I struggle helplessly against him, thrilled by his strength, until I have no choice but to go limp and surrender. He stares down at me, with such a wicked look in his eyes that I squirm inside.

'I'm going to get you sooner or later,' he says, with a half-smile. 'You'll see, Karina West. You're not going to be able to keep this up.'

I have a feeling he might be right.

25

Karina

Right in the middle of the celebration, I suddenly feel like crying.

Crying because I'm so happy.

I had no idea Hindu festivals were so much fun. I followed Liam's advice and looked up Lord Krishna on the Internet. Yes, I'd looked up a few things before, like the no-beef rule, but I'd never gone into it properly. I guess I felt nervous, for it seemed such a strange religion. But, to my surprise, I discovered that Hinduism is not the worship of lots of gods. They only worship *one* god, but believe that the different *devas* are different embodiments of divine energy. Lord Ganesh, for example, is the great Remover of Obstacles, and a protector of women. Mother Divine is the embodiment of three different *devas* – Maha Durga, representing power and invincibility, Maha Saraswati, representing knowledge and the arts, and Maha Laxsmi, representing wealth, bliss and compassion.

I went out and bought a little book for Devika about the life of Lord Krishna and this morning we sat together on the sofa, reading and learning together. We read that Krishna was born to the royal family of Mathura, the eighth son of the princess Devaki and her husband Vasudeva. But the kingdom was ruled by a wicked man called King Kamsa and, afraid of a prophecy that the eighth son of Devaki would kill him, he put the couple in jail.

So Krishna was born in a cell and then was secretly smuggled out to live with foster parents.

'So you see,' I assured Devika, delighted by the resonance of the story, 'even divine beings can be adopted.' I gave her a kiss on the forehead and she smiled up at me.

There were lots of pictures of Krishna in the book, depicting different stages of his life. As a youth, Krishna was naughty and regularly indulged in mischievous pranks. Devika got excited and giggled when she read about how he used to steal butter, or how he once ate some mud and, when his chiding mother told him to open his mouth, he did so and displayed the entire universe to her there.

Then there were pictures of Krishna as a young

man, with blue skin and soft limbs, carrying a flute, surrounded by his beloved cows and doting *gopis*, the milkmaids. This Krishna, the book explained, who used to tease the *gopis* and enchant them with his flute, illustrates the *lila*, the play of life.

Later in life, Krishna is depicted as a wise and thoughtful seer. On the battlefield of the Kurushetra War, he gave each side the opportunity to have either his army or himself – though he would not fight in the war. Arjuna chose Krishna to be his charioteer, which was the right decision, for Krishna then gave Arjuna an entire discourse on the meaning and purpose of life, summarised in the *Bhagavad Gita*.

The very syllables of the name Krishna, the book concluded, have the power to destroy sin relating to the material, self and divine causes.

When Mrs Raju heard about the festival trip, she invited herself along too. Part of me wanted to say no and keep it a cosy threesome; Devika's English teacher is sweet but I've found her interfering at times. I have a feeling she wanted to make sure Liam was treating Devika well. She brought along a *dhoti kurta* for him to borrow and he gave her an ecstatic kiss on the cheek, telling her she was an angel. Mrs Raju blushed and watched fondly as Liam picked Devika up and spun her round, squealing with laughter. Within five minutes she was as charmed by Liam as everyone is.

Now we're all sitting in a temple together. Fun really is the only word to describe what we are having. I guess I'd always thought that religious festivals were serious affairs. But, packed into this temple, caught in ripples of laughter and chanting, the whole atmosphere is one of pure joy. In celebrating the birthday of Krishna, we are clearly celebrating life itself.

To be honest, I'm not entirely sure what's going on. We're sitting cross-legged on the floor, surrounded by Indians. At first I was slightly taken aback by the intimacy – there is no thought given to personal space. There are so many of us packed in tight together that elbows knock my knees and skin brushes mine. At first I had to resist the urge to shudder and curl into a ball, I felt so invaded. But then I noticed Liam was unfazed and realised I should just relax too.

The entire temple is decorated with flags, flowers, ribbons and garlands. At the front is a statue of baby Krishna, resting in a cradle, surrounded by sweets. Mrs Raju explains that because Krishna was born at midnight, the *puja* is starting very late. Once it is over, we will be able to break the fast we began at the start of the day and eat some yoghurt or some *barfi*.

Devika is sitting in front of me, her back against my crossed shins. She doesn't join in with all the chanting, doesn't know as much as I'd expected. I guess at the orphanage she wouldn't necessarily have been taught everything – I suspect Mrs Laxsmi just gave her a little knowledge here and there when she could.

As for Liam, well, Liam is a chameleon and he's blended his colours in perfectly. I can't believe how gorgeous he looks in a *dhoti kurta*. He's wearing eyeliner and there's a red dot on his forehead, and with his dark hair flopping over his face he looks like a cross between Puck and Lord Krishna himself.

The only thing that surprised me a little when we entered is that the men and women are separated, although only loosely, with the men on the right and the women on the left. We sat in the centre so we could all be together.

Tonight I feel as though we are celebrating the best of India. There is not a drop of negativity in this temple – only love and more love. As the celebration swells to a climax, I feel bliss surge through my heart. I turn to Liam and feel a wave of gratitude and I whisper in his ear, 'I wouldn't have come here tonight if not for you – thank you. Thank you.'

He smiles and touches my cheek.

* * *

When we get home, hours later, Devika is different. By taking her to the temple, by helping her discover an India within England, we have given her peace; there is a stillness in her face, a happiness starring her eyes.

Liam also seems on a high. He insists that he wants to tuck Devika into bed. I say good night to Mrs Raju, giving her a warm hug and feeling glad that she did join us. Then I collapse on the sofa, suddenly feeling exhausted. A peaceful happiness hazes through me. Given that it is now nearly two a.m., I would have thought that Devika would have gone straight to sleep, but I can hear her begging Liam for a short story because she doesn't want to miss out. I listen to Liam indulging her. The sound of his voice, cigarette-gravelly and sexy as hell, sounds incongruous with the innocent sentiments of a children's story. Liam's very good at accents and comic timing; he prompts more giggles, sighs and 'oh's' from Devika than I ever manage.

I feel my eyes closing and a smile breaking over my face as I savour moments of the evening. Today will definitely be one of those days that I will treasure always, I think. Then sleep draws me in softly, shushing me like a mother, and I gratefully surrender to her embrace.

When I look up, Liam is grinning over me.

'Sorry – have I been asleep long?' I cry, disorientated, but Liam puts a finger over my lips.

'Shh,' he whispers. 'You've only been out five minutes.' Then a wicked smile tugs his lips. 'I think you need a bedtime story too.'

I let out a gasp as he leans down and I feel his arms slip under my body. He picks me up and teasingly swings me round. I catch the hem of his *kurta* and giggle. My heart begins to hammer: I'm convinced we're heading for the bedroom.

But Liam is as unpredictable as ever. Instead he carries me to the back door, awkwardly tugs it open whilst keeping hold of me, and takes me into the garden.

It's beautiful outside. The sky is the deep, deep purple of pure night. Most of London is asleep and the traffic has quietened to a hum. There is a stillness to the plants and flowers; the cherry tree, pretty by day, has now acquired a magical hue, as though fairies might peep between the leaves. Liam carries me on to the grass and then sets me on my feet.

'Take off your shoes,' he says, still whispering, maintaining the bubble.

He kicks off his boots and I slip off my heels. The grass is soft and springy. I feel connected to the earth, alive and calm.

He grabs my hand and we walk towards the shade of the cherry tree. Then he turns to me. Moonlight glints in his hair and the sparkle of his eyes, making him look more like a mischievous Puck than ever. Then he takes my hands in his and pauses, stretching the moment out, teasing me, making me wait with ache, until he leans in and brushes his lips against mine.

The kiss is like some delicious nectar that trickles down my throat and fills my stomach with cool bliss.

We carry on kissing, on and on, until finally he pulls back. I let out a soft, shaky laugh and he says, 'What?'

'There's blossom in your hair,' I say, brushing it off gently.

He grabs my hand and kisses my palm, then takes my forefinger and pushes it between his lips, biting it very gently. I feel myself go taut with desire.

There is a question in his eyes.

I smile shyly and nod.

His eyes ignite.

'Let's go inside,' he says.

We tiptoe across the living room and up the stairs. On the landing, we pause, and I guide Liam up to the spare bedroom on the second floor where we will be less likely to wake Devika. Inside, we giggle and whisper, feeling oddly like a pair of teenagers; with all the responsibility I've taken on lately, it's fantastic to feel so childish and carefree.

We sink down on to the bed. In the semi-gloom, his eyes are glinting with desire, but behind the desire is a tenderness. The celebration has opened up something inside us. A special magic that can only be enjoyed once in a while.

When he kisses me, he does it so slowly, wanting to luxuriate in every moment of pleasure, draw it out throughout the night, that I almost feel like crying again. Then his hands curve downwards over my sari and he breaks off, a slight frown on his forehead.

'How the hell am I supposed to get this off with all these pins?' he asks.

I sit up, my hands shaking with excitement as I undo them, which only slows me down even more. Every so often, Liam gives me a little caress, on my arm or my breast or my thigh, making faint groans of impatience.

Finally, my sari is undone. I stand up and put the end of the cloth in his hands. Then, like something out of a movie, I twirl so that the cloth unwinds from my body. We both laugh quietly. Then he tugs at my underskirt and I pull that off too.

Now I'm just wearing a cropped T-shirt and my knickers.

'That's better,' Liam says, pulling me back down on the bed. He runs his hands over my bare stomach, then kisses it, pressing his cheek against it. He stares at me and something that I can't quite decipher clouds his eyes.

I tense up, suddenly feeling paranoid. It's been a few years now since we last made love. I've put on a bit of weight since then. Though I'm hardly wrinkly, my skin lacks the smooth, taut sheen it was once blessed with. But, as though reading my mind, he starts to caress me and whisper how beautiful he finds every part of my body. I relax, letting my limbs become liquid, desire flowing freely, a smile breaking on my lips. I feel beautiful; I feel wanted; I feel wonderful.

His hands tease the edge of my knickers. They stroke up and down my thighs until they burn against his palms. They edge open the lace hems an inch and then let them snap shut. I let out a sigh and he leans over me, his lips hovering a few inches from mine, my breath ragged against them. But when I reach up to kiss him, he darts away, shaking his head.

'D'you want me to touch you?' he whispers, licking my ear and making me shudder. 'D'you want to feel me inside you?'

'Yes, oh yes.'

'Are you sure?' His hands move over my knickers. Then, as I push up against him, craving more, they circle away. 'I don't know, maybe we should stick to your celibacy thingy.'

Now I understand. He's playing a game.

'You're punishing me,' I whisper in frustration.

'I am.' He lowers his lips to mine and then pulls back once more. I see that the cloudiness in his eyes is humiliation, built up after weeks of me pushing him away. 'You deserve it.'

'Please.' I squirm against him, reassuring him, letting him know how much I want him. 'Please, Liam.'

He finally leans down and presses his hot, sweet mouth against mine; at the same time, I feel the bare skin of his fingers slipping inside my knickers . . .

A few minutes later, we're tearing off the last of our clothes. Then he parts my thighs. He pauses, looking down at me, a faint question still marking his eyes. Then he thrusts forcefully inside me. He is both wild and controlled, drowning in his own desire but never losing the pace of mine. He's the only man I've ever been with who can take me all the way with him, who can make love with such sensitive attunement to my desire, holding back until we both break the same wave together, our mouths filled up with each other's cries of ecstasy. Then he rolls off and lies staring up at the ceiling. I look at him. He looks at me. I see happiness dancing in his eyes. I smile and touch his sweaty cheek. He flinches suddenly. In my raw state, I feel as though I've been slapped. I can't understand why he did that. Is he regretting this already? Will I wake up tomorrow to find an empty bed and Devika asking, 'Where's Liam gone?' I turn away, ready to get out of bed and pick up my clothes and storm out.

'Karina. *Karina.*' Liam reaches for me and pulls me back into bed. I try to fight him, but he uses all his force, turning me round to face him, my wrists locked into his fists. He showers kisses over my face and hair and lips. But I still can't quite forgive and forget.

'What is it?' I ask. 'Why did you do that?'

'I just . . . it was . . . I was just a bit scared. I was lying there, wondering what I'd done to deserve someone like you, and I was thinking, I'd better not fuck up, and then I just got scared that somehow I would . . .'

'You won't, you won't,' I cry, my heart melting in relief and forgiveness. 'Look – we're both fucked up, really, both of us . . . so it doesn't matter. We're going to fuck up together and it'll be great.' I smile and now it's my turn to give him a reassuring kiss.

I wait until Liam has fallen asleep, his face slack and boyish and at peace, before I allow myself to cry a little. I feel so overwhelmed with happiness I can't quite take it all in. Then I snuggle up against him, locking my cheek into the crook of his shoulder. Sleep begins to slip through my mind. A dream-bud blossoms, coloured with the evening's euphoria.

I'm back in the temple, with Liam, the chanting weaving around us, the candles forming a choir of light, and I reach out and touch his hand. He smiles at me, light glinting in his eyes and teeth, and I feel myself smiling just before sleep takes over.

26

Devika

Every time I wake up in the mornings, the first thing I see is a statue of Ganesh sitting on a table in the corner of my bedroom. He is very beautiful, his long trunk swirling out gracefully, his eyes kind and wise, his neck adorned with garlands. A little while ago, Liam asked me to tell him the story of Ganesh. I told him: 'Lord Ganesh was born from Parvati, Lord Shiva's consort. She was having a bath and she didn't want anyone to see her, and Lord Shiva was away at war so he couldn't guard the door. So she took her sandalwood paste and breathed life into it and that's how Ganesh was born. He stood at her door, guarding it. Then Lord Shiva came back from battle and he wanted to go into the bathroom, but Ganesh didn't realise who he was, so he didn't let him in.

Lord Shiva cut off his head and Parvati was very, very upset. So Lord Shiva sent his *ganas* out to find the first person or animal who was facing the wrong direction – and the first thing they found was an elephant sleeping to the north, so they cut off his head and gave it to Ganesh.'

Later that evening Liam came home and said he had a surprise for me. He opened up his jacket and pulled out the statue! I was so happy, I let out a big WHOOP, the way Kelly does when something good happens. Liam and Mummy Karina looked surprised, then they laughed.

But when I see the statue, I also feel a flicker of sadness in my heart. The same way I felt after we celebrated Lord Krishna's birthday. The celebration made me feel so happy, I felt as though I was floating with bliss. I could see Krishna in everything, everywhere. Krishna sang in the blue sky, Krishna burned in the bright sun, Krishna smiled in the autumn leaves that flew from the trees and teased around me like the notes of his flute. But when I tried to tell Kelly and Mrs H about how wonderful it was, they didn't understand. And then the feeling faded; I tried to hold on to it but it slipped away. And the sky became the sky again and the sun disappeared behind the trees and the leaves became soggy and died.

If I kneel down before the Ganesh statue in my

bedroom, if I half close my eyes and stare at his face, I can shut out the rest of the house. I can pretend the noise of cars is really the noise of rickshaws. I can pretend I'm sitting on a bare floor back in the orphanage. And then I feel happy again.

I don't know why I long for home sometimes. I love Mummy Karina and I love Liam. I have pretty things – even my own mobile phone, which Kelly gave to me. I like school now and I have a friend. So I don't know why I still miss India.

'Seven out of ten in your spelling test,' Mrs H says to me, laying it down on my desk. 'Very good, Devika. A *big* improvement.'

I smile, feeling pleased. When I first came to England, I used to get one out of ten. Or two, if I was lucky.

Later that day, I learn a new English word: o-pear.

After school, something exciting happens because for the first time I go back with Kelly to her house for tea. Her o-pear picks us up. An o-pear is a young woman with a funny accent who looks after kids and takes them home in a car.

Kelly's house is like ours, only a little bit bigger. We go into the kitchen where Kelly's mummy is. She is very pretty, with long yellow hair and blue eyes and very big breasts, so big they look as though they might fall off. She gives Kelly a hug and then she gives me one. Her bosom is not like Mummy Karina's, which is nice and soft, like a pillow. It is very hard, as though it is made of wood, and afterwards my cheek hurts a bit.

But Kelly's mummy is very nice.

'Devika!' she cries. 'You're so pretty! You are an Indian princess!'

We go into the kitchen and she gives us some milk and cookies.

'How is India?' She speaks slowly, so I can understand. 'Is everyone very poor?'

'Some,' I say. She looks sad and rubs my arm.

'Did you have to work as a child prostitute?'

I frown, not understanding, rolling this new word on my tongue. Mrs Raju has taught me I should break new or strange words down into pieces: *pross . . . tit . . . tute*. But I don't know what any of those pieces mean.

'Mum!' Kelly cries. 'You can't say that!'

'Sorry,' her mummy says.

She says something else too, and I hear the word 'honest'. I think she is saying she doesn't mind what happened to me in India. I think the word *prostitute* means beggar. So I say, 'Yes.'

'Really?'

I feel confused because now, having asked the question, she looks shocked, her mouth wide open.

'She doesn't know what the word means,' Kelly says, rolling her eyes. 'Come on, Devika, let's go to my room and do makeovers.'

'Thank you for cookies,' I say and Mummy Kelly looks as though she might hug me again so I hurry away because I know her bosom will hurt.

Kelly's room is like a big white teddy bear, full of cuddly and fluffy things. Her bed has little poles sticking up out of it with white veils and lots of cushions in the shape of hearts. On her wall is a picture of her mummy. She is wearing underwear and has no top on! I try not to look at it but my eyes seem to keep leaping back to it and every time my stomach is filled with shock. When I was in India, Raji once told me about a film that got banned because there was strong kissing in it. But in England there is lots of kissing in films and women take off their tops!

'Do you like it?' Kelly asks. 'She's cool, isn't she?' She rolls up her top too. 'When I grow up, I'm going to have a boob job.'

'What is boob job?'

'What?' Kelly cries. 'I love you, you are so funny!'

I love you is nice. *You are so funny* is not nice. But the way she says it, it's as though the *love you* feeling spreads through the whole sentence.

'A boob job is like this.' She puts her hands to her chest and then rolls them out. I get it: they will get bigger! And harder, with spiky bits on the end. I nod, even though I don't really understand how you make that happen. The word *job* must mean work is involved; maybe lots of studying and praying.

'Hold out your arm,' Kelly commands.

She grabs my arm and lines it up against hers. We look at our skin, mine brown and hers white with little freckles on. I cannot help feeling a bit ashamed, knowing that my dark skin was never popular in India. I always used to wish I was lighter-skinned; once I even tried to rub my white pillow against my arm, hoping the white would come off into my skin.

'I love your tan,' she sighs. 'How can I get a tan like yours? Hey, help me put it on.'

To my amazement, Kelly picks up a tube filled with something brown. As I help her rub it into her arms, I cannot help thinking how funny Raji would think this. In the orphanage people didn't want to adopt me because of my darker skin and in England everyone wants to be browner.

Then Kelly's mummy calls us down to dinner. When I look at her, I want to clap my hands over my eyes because I keep remembering the picture of her naked. But I know that would be rude, so I sit down and stare at my plate. I'm scared that we might get into trouble because of Kelly's brown arms. But her mummy is really nice. She looks pleased and then shows us her arms, which are all orangey.

'My tan is nice too, isn't it?'

'Yes,' we both say.

Kelly's mummy has not made us a very big tea. We have some soup, but it seems to be mostly made of water with little bits floating in it.

'I hope you don't mind. Kelly and I are on a diet,' Kelly's mummy explains.

Diet. I don't understand the word, even though Mummy Karina has explained it to me. In England, people have clean water and shops full of beautiful food, piles of fruit and vegetables and bread and cakes and Rice Krispies. And then they punish themselves by refusing to eat it. I keep thinking about all my friends at the orphanage who would love to swap dinners with the dieters of England.

'You see, Kelly has to look trim because she's up for an audition soon,' Kelly's mummy says.

'Hey, Devika, you should sign up for it too!' Kelly cries. 'It's for, like, a British version of *High School Musical*. Devika can actually sing really well, Mummy. I heard her!'

'Goodness, that's amazing!' Kelly's mum says, but in a voice that says she thinks I cannot possibly be as good as Kelly. Which makes me feel I want to stand up and sing and sing and show how good I can be.

Later, when we go back to Kelly's room, she frowns at my ears.

'If you're going to go for this audition, you are *seriously* going to need pierced ears,' she says. 'And some proper clothes. You need some cool jeans. Your ones are a bit out now. You need Victoria Beckham jeans.'

'Who's Victoria Beckham?' I ask. I've heard her name a lot and seen her pictures but sometimes I get muddled up between her and the one called Jordan.

Then, just as I remember who she is, Kelly cries: 'I love you, you are so funny! She's only the most famous and fashionable woman in the world.' She sighs. 'I wish I could be as thin as her. And have a boob job as nice as hers.'

So when Mummy Karina comes to pick me up later, I ask her if I can do the audition. She looks very excited and says she will phone her agent and get him to make it happen for me! Then I tell her that to look good for the part, I need a new pink mobile *and* a pair of Victoria Beckham jeans. Mummy Karina looks less excited. In fact, she looks a bit cross.

'Victoria Beckham jeans – what next!' she cries. 'You know, life isn't just about the things we buy, Devika. Don't start thinking like that. Money can't buy happiness.'

I smile at Mummy Karina and I know she's wrong. When you've lived in a slum in India, you know that money can buy happiness and life is very much about the things we buy.

'I love you,' I say, 'I think you're so funny.'

Mummy Karina gives me a strange look.

27

Karina

Liam and I are sitting in the back of a limo. We've been invited to the new James Bond premiere, proof that we're one of the hottest couples in town. But all my excitement about meeting Daniel Craig has been spoilt by a row that's simmering between us.

I pretend I haven't heard what Liam's just said and flip open my compact. I'm wearing a gorgeous Versace number my stylist picked out for me. It's so sheer I can't get away with wearing any underwear, but at least my dieting has paid off. The famous Lynda Taylor herself spent three hours making me up. My eyes look smoky and my lips are a luscious fuchsia; my hair is curled into a tight, glossy chignon. But whenever I'm heading out to public events like this, no matter how good I look, I can't help worrying about my dreaded nose. Paranoia digs its little hooks into me and it becomes a nervous obsessive compulsion: I have to dig out my compact every three seconds to check it. I feel like a female Pinocchio – every time I look at it I swear it gets bigger, as though it's feeding off my worries.

'Karina,' Liam repeats in a warning voice. 'I have to go tomorrow anyway, so why go on my own? Devika can come too.'

'Liam, I think your mum would prefer to see you on your own. Devika really needs to stay at home and practise for her audition.'

'For fuck's sake, we've been practising with her non-stop for the last seventy-two hours! You can practise in the car. You can practise at my mum's house. She won't care.'

'But why not wait until next month?' I ask, tilting the mirror at an awkward angle, convinced my nose is pretending it belongs on Captain Hook's wrist. *And by then*, I add silently, *hopefully she might have died. Which would be such a shame.*

Mean, I know. But if you had met Liam's mother, you'd understand. You'd help me pick out hymns for the funeral.

Liam whips the compact out of my hands and I let out a cry.

'Look,' he says angrily, 'for the last few months I have been bending over backwards to fit into your life. I've taken Devika to school, I've been a fucking new man, I've drunk hardly anything, haven't taken drugs. And now you won't do one small thing for me.'

'What?' I cry, feeling alarmed. 'You mean you did those things just to please me? I thought you cared about Devika!'

'I do. But you have to admit, I've had to make sacrifices. That's part of it. So now you have to make a sacrifice for me. Oh, fuck. Great. Now we're here.'

We both get out of the limo, bristling with tension. *Flash! Flash! Flash!* The photographers snap away as we walk on to the red carpet. But when I release Liam's hand, he drops mine lightly and approaches the wall of screaming girls; if it wasn't for the metal fence, I think they'd bury him under a ton of hair and lipstick and desperate nails. He oozes charm, asking a girl for a ciggie, getting a light off her friend, letting them snap him with his arms round them, scrawling his messy signature over their arms, kissing a girl's mum so she flushes bright red.

'Karina! Karina!' A few are calling out for me. I sign autographs, smiling brightly, but feeling close to tears inside. Liam and I have just had our first row since we've got back together; I hope this isn't the start of things falling apart between us.

Inside the cinema, however, we both calm down

a bit. Liam winds me up by muttering how gorgeous the Bond girl is, but then quietens down, engrossed by the car chases and casino sequence. By the time we get to the drinks party, and meet Daniel Craig, who is unbelievably sexy, we've both cheered up.

Then we start drinking. I promised myself before I came out that I wouldn't have any. But hell, Adi will have put Devika to bed by now. And these Bond-themed Martinis just look too sumptuous for words. I end up having five.

By the time Liam and I leave, Liam has to put his arm round me to keep me upright. The cold night air hits me but fails to sober me up. Dear me, the distance from the party to the limo seems a long, long way . . .

The photographers are waiting about in packs, looking excited. They know this is the moment when celebs forget how to behave.

'If you don't agree to come with me tomorrow to see Mum,' Liam whispers drunkenly in my ear, 'I'm going to lift up your skirt and make you do a Britney in front of that lot.' He giggles wickedly at the thought of it.

'Liam – noooo!' I cry in a slurred voice, feeling his fingers threaten my hem. 'That's so not fair.'

'I am, I am,' he whispers insistently, kissing my ear. 'You have to agree or else. Hey,' he calls to the photographers, 'come over here. Karina has something to show you!'

Oh, God. I think Liam is joking but there's that dangerous sing-song in his voice which suggests he might not be. He tries to tug up my dress, laughing as though this is the funniest game in the world. I hastily tug it back down.

'Okay, okay, I agree, I'll go with you to your mum's!' I cry, breaking away from him and running to the limo before he can try any more. He runs after me, both of us giggling like mad.

And then the kerb gets me. I pitch on to the seat, feeling the cold air on the back of my thighs. The blue flashes from the cameras light up the leather seats; I hear a photographer wolf-whistle. I hear Liam's laughter, then feel him collapsing on top of me. The driver slams the door shut behind us and we speed off.

'You just gave the photographers an eyeful,' Liam whispers, kissing the back of my neck, laughing as I groan. 'I think I need to get another look,' he adds, drawing up my dress, and then I feel his hands on my thighs and I gasp with tipsy pleasure and we make love on the back seat, giggling with heady euphoria.

And so the next morning I find myself in the back of Liam's car with Devika, who is begging to play I Spy, having been taught the game by Liam a few days ago. Adi has agreed to look after Rufus, and I had to get up to pack at seven o'clock, after just two hours' sleep. Bludgeoned by an evil thumping hangover, I flung anything into the cases. Liam is also suffering and he keeps shouting and swearing as he makes wrong turns. Devika laughs and I tell him not to swear in front of her. He gives me a foul look.

'Oh, because you're such a great mother,' he says.

Which makes me furious. Talk about putting the knife in.

My agent called me just as we were setting off to warn me about the pictures on the front page of the *Sun*. I've suffered shots like this in the past when Fran and I used to go out drinking and sometimes flash the photographers for fun. Back then, the headline always used to be *Saucy Karina!* Now it reads, *Bad Mother Karina Neglects Her Daughter to Party*.

I have stayed in for nearly three months and I go out for one night and I'm a Bad Mother. I can't help thinking about the fact that I have my first review with Angela from social services in a few weeks' time. It's an official goalpost on the way to fully adopting Devika. What if she's seen those photos?

Worse, what if Liam's mother has seen them?

Devika, as though sensing the tension, becomes antsy too. She keeps begging me to play I Spy, until

I feel as though I'm going to scream. I pull my jumper over my head and refuse to speak to anyone until we get there.

A pretty cottage in Kent, with roses climbing over the walls and lattice windows: it all looks so innocuous. As innocuous as the gingerbread house which concealed a witch inside.

Liam's mother appears behind the warped glass like a ghostly spectre. She stops to peer through her spyhole, then lets us in.

'Mum!' Liam gives her a hug and kisses her papery cheek. She smiles, then turns her milky eyes on me and Devika. Clutching the cross around her neck – as though we're potential vampires – she looks us up and down.

'Who's this, then?' she asks, eyeing Devika.

'She's mine,' I say.

Devika steps forward and says, 'How do you do.' But Liam's mother merely looks at her in astonishment and cries: 'She's brown!'

I grab Devika's hand quickly, trying to conceal my shock.

'She's Indian. I've adopted her.'

'Really? How much did you pay for her?' she asks, frowning. Then, sensing the topic of conversation isn't terribly popular, she sighs and says, 'Well, do come in. I've got the kettle on. You should have warned me you were bringing extra guests, Liam.'

'I did call you and try to tell you, Mum,' Liam says.

I try to catch Liam's eye to share my outrage, but he looks away. He's always different with his mother. Once upon a time he hated her, slagged her off in songs, told the media he'd never speak to her again after the childhood he suffered. But slowly he softened; recently he has even begun to dote on her. She's all the family I've got, he explained to me. He goes limp in her presence now, almost meek.

In the living room, Devika and I sit down on the sofa, leaning back against the tartan blanket. Dust motes hover in the air. Devika is looking nervous – she's used to adults being charmed by her. *How much did you pay for her?* keeps ringing in my mind, making my headache even worse. Was she being deliberately facetious, or just stupid? Oh, God, I wish I wasn't so hungover; I hope I don't throw up. We've only just got here and I can't wait to leave.

Liam's mother goes into the kitchen to make the tea.

'Cat!' Devika's face lights up as a fat ginger moggy waddles into the room.

I try to warn her that Liam's mother's cat is not like other pussies. Devika, however, is convinced all cats are angels with fur. She reaches out and strokes him. He lets out a yowl, then hisses and spits at her.

Devika recoils in shock.

'Bad cat,' I reassure her, watching him jump on to the windowsill and stare out at the world in a disdainful manner. 'Not nice cat.'

Liam's mother returns with a tray of cups and a pot of Earl Grey and a plate of Nice biscuits. I notice she doesn't bother to ask if Devika would prefer squash; luckily Devika likes tea. I offer Devika a biscuit and she shakes her head nervously. I offer one again and she gratefully accepts, curling her fingers tight round it and nibbling it like a squirrel. She keeps staring at the cat, still a bit shocked.

Liam's mother chatters on. About the weather. Her soaring heating bills (no wonder the house is so bloody cold). Her neighbour's fence. The decline of Britain – 'once the trains used to run on time and people used to be polite to each other'. I keep dreading that any minute she's going to start ranting about celebrities who forget to put their knickers on. Perhaps, I think, feeling quite hysterical in my hungover state, she's bought a pair of large horsehair knickers from M&S for me just to prove her point. But to my relief she doesn't bring it up. She can't have seen the papers. Thank God.

The miserable business of tea is finally over. Liam's mother is stooping down to pick up the tray when she cries sharply: 'You've got crumbs on my sofa!' Devika jumps, startled. With a loud 'Tsk!' the old bag leans forward, swipes the golden crumbs into her palm, gives Devika a fierce look and then picks up her tray.

By now, I feel close to punching her. Instead I smile at Devika brightly and pass her a cup left behind, telling her to take it into the kitchen, hoping it will make amends. Liam's mother, however, glares at her as though afraid she'll drop it.

I am sick and tired of this. I say I need to have a lie-down and take Devika upstairs to the spare bedroom. I'm expecting to find a double bed for me and Liam and a small camp bed for Devika. But there is just a double bed, made up with starched white sheets . . . and nothing else.

I gaze down at Devika. Her eyes are bright and her chin is wobbling hard. When I pull her in for a hug, the tears begin to flow. I feel so cross I am close to just going back home here and now.

Liam comes up to join us. He looks surprised and upset by Devika's tears. Kneeling down in front of her, he says, 'Hey, sorry, little one. My mum doesn't mean to be horrible – she's just old.'

Devika blinks, not really understanding, but she is cheered by Liam's concern. Then Liam gets out some old photos, showing Devika how his mum once looked. Devika looks amazed. The woman in the pictures has long, shiny dark hair down to her waist and wicked dark eyes ringed with kohl, and is wearing a miniskirt and a slashed T-shirt decorated with safety pins.

'See?' Liam says, grinning. 'She was once young and pretty, like you.'

Liam's mother. She's actually only sixty years old, though she looks and moves as though she's about a hundred. You might remember her if you're a fan of seventies music. She was a star for about five years. Famous for being a female equivalent of the Sex Pistols. She embraced feminism and notoriety. She swore for England and showed off her knickers and once even passed round drugs on stage at a concert. Women were always slagging her off in the press or the local pub, but men lusted after her as the ultimate bad girl.

Then she got pregnant with Liam. He was the love child of a drummer in a famous rock band. She dragged him around on tour with her. And then the eighties happened. Her style of music went out of fashion. Worse, she was still a drug addict and the various substances she was on ate away at her looks and talent like maggots. It's fine being a bad girl icon when you're shiny and young and beautiful. But when you're wrinkled and have a deviated septum and slur your words in interviews, suddenly you're not so cool any more. Liam was taken away from her and his grandmother brought him up. His mother was in and out of rehab for decades, until at the age of fifty she finally sorted herself out and found God. She hasn't touched a drop since. The trouble is, she behaves as though she's never touched a drop in her life. It's odd how the people who start off being the most liberal and transgressive can often end up being the most narrow and judgemental.

'Practise,' Devika keeps saying, worried about her audition on Wednesday. I have a feeling that if she bursts into song Liam's mother will come charging up and accuse us of enjoying heathen music. I tell her to be patient, saying it's only for one night. I guess I'm reminding myself.

Just get through dinner, I tell myself, *and then it'll all be over. You can go first thing tomorrow morning, insist Devika needs to prepare for her audition.*

We're just about to go down when Liam comes out of the bathroom and I can't help but notice that he wipes his nose. The gesture – which I've seen many times before – automatically fills me with a sense of dread.

'Having fun?' I ask lightly.

Liam grins and his expression looks so sweet that I wonder if I'm just being paranoid. It's not that I'd blame him, given that dinner with his mother isn't going to be the easiest thing to get through – and Liam does tend to turn to the coke in times of stress. But he *promised* me that whilst he was with me and Devika, he wouldn't touch so much as a grain of anything even remotely illegal.

And I know how one little bit of powder can lead to a lot more.

28

Karina

Lost in my own worries, I go down to dinner without really registering what's on the table.

We find the cat mooching by the radiator; he hisses as we enter. Devika sits down, eyeing him in shock, as though she can't quite believe this cruel place where even cats are mean to her.

But to give Liam's mother credit, she has made an effort: her best yellowing lace cloth, candlesticks and ancient cutlery. Devika sits beside me and Liam sits opposite and his mother takes her regal spot at the head of the table. She puts her hands together and begins to say grace. Devika looks confused and then mimics her, putting her hands together and muttering, no doubt to her own *devas*.

Under the table, I feel Liam's boot lightly press

against my foot. A little gesture to say: *we're both going to be okay, let's just do this.*

I smile at him.

'It smells lovely,' I say to Liam's mother, with sincerity. When I was a kid, every meal I ate was in a restaurant between auditions. I remember that I once went to a friend's house for Sunday lunch and could hardly believe how amazing a home-cooked roast tasted: my taste buds wept with pleasure. Since then, I've always associated a home roast with comfort.

Maybe this dinner will be okay after all.

I take a bite of cauliflower. It's been overcooked but it's oozing with sweet gravy. Then I take a bite of beef. It's a little bit chewy but quite nice . . .

'Oh!' In my shock, I spit the beef back on to the plate. It lands with a plop and flecks of gravy spew out over the treasured tablecloth.

I turn to Devika and see her tussling uneasily with the meat, a wince on her face.

'Devika can't eat beef,' I cry. 'I'm so sorry, but she really can't.'

'What do you mean Devika can't eat beef?' Liam's mother asks in an appalled voice.

'She's a Hindu. No beef is allowed.'

'She's a *Hindu*?' Liam's mother asks in a withering tone. 'But we're living in a Christian country now.'

'Actually, Mum,' Liam interjects in a diplomatic voice, 'we live in a multi-cultural country now, so . . .'

Devika stares at Liam's mother with frightened eyes. Then she looks at me. I give her a reassuring smile, then turn firmly to his mother, who is blinking in a distinctly reptilian way, her lips thinning until they nearly disappear.

'All right,' she says. 'But she can jolly well eat the rest of it. I won't have her wasting a good meal.'

I look down at Devika again.

'She can't,' I say. 'I mean, look – the beef's clearly got into the gravy and it'll be there, swirling around the whole dish. You can't make her eat it. Have you got any Rice Krispies?'

Liam's mother's eyes blaze. 'I spend three hours producing a nutritious home-cooked meal and you ask if you can feed your adopted child Rice Krispies because of some backward heathen notion?'

'Mum—' Liam tries to interject.

'If you ask me,' I say, 'Hinduism is a much more positive religion than Christianity. It doesn't celebrate suffering. It's about joy . . . and enlightenment . . . and Devika's just a child. I really don't see what's wrong with giving her Rice Krispies.'

'The girl,' Liam's mother turns to Devika, her face crimping in disgust, 'needs to go to Sunday school. I've changed my mind – you should eat up every morsel before you leave the table, or else I shall consider you a very bad-mannered child. As for Rice Krispies, there are none in the house.'

Devika looks frightened and quickly cuts a square of beef – until I grab her fork and fling it on to the floor.

'Don't you eat a thing!' I cry, grabbing Devika's hand and pulling her up from the table. Then I see Liam's face and I pause. There's a window – a tiny window – where I might still make amends. 'Look,' I say, 'I can get the Rice Krispies myself. I can go down to the shops and buy them.'

'What kind of mother', Liam's mother says, 'offers her child Rice Krispies? Well, I suppose I ought to have expected this from you. You flash your back-side in the paper, so it's no wonder you've no idea how to feed a child.'

I stand there, gaping in shock. So she did see the papers. She was just saving it up for an opportune moment to drop it into the conversation.

'I just hope', she concludes, 'you don't end up having any of your own with my son.'

'I can't believe that *you* of all people have the *nerve* to lecture me about being a good mother. At least I wasn't a drunk. At least I didn't abandon my kid.'

Liam's mother gasps and Liam swallows hard.

'Devika and I have had enough,' I cry in a shaky voice. 'We're going home.'

Liam's mother turns away from Liam and looks at me. There is a glint in her eye – one of almost gleeful triumph. *She's enjoying this*, I realise in horror, *she actually wanted to reach this point*. Maybe she even served the bloody beef on purpose.

'Karina!' Liam cries as I hurry up the stairs, Devika in tow. I grab our case, glad we didn't even bother to unpack. Then I get my mobile out and ring 118 118, who put me through to a local taxi service. Liam comes in just as I'm booking it.

'Karina – for fuck's sake, what are you doing?'

'Did you hear what your mum said at the table? I mean, how do you think Devika feels, being treated like that?'

'She's just old. You have to be patient.'

'You know, if Devika was my child, people would *never* speak about her like this!' I cry, so angry I'm forgetting that Devika's even there. 'People feel that because she's adopted they can say anything. It's as though she's an – an accessory they can comment on, like a new hair colour I'm trying out, or a necklace.'

I break off, seeing Devika's face. I don't know if she understood everything I said, but she got the gist. I clutch her tightly, bend down and whisper in her ear: 'I love you. We're going home. It's okay. It's okay.'

'You have to stay here,' Liam says roughly. 'You can't just go. I don't want you to leave.'

I stare up into his eyes; they are flushed bloodshot. I can hear the cocaine speaking through him.

'You said you'd give the white powder up.'

Liam is silent for a moment, then says quickly, 'What the fuck are you talking about? I won't be taking powder. I'm at my mum's.'

Down below, there is the toot of a taxi.

'You can't go,' Liam cries, grabbing the handle of my case. I try to wrench it back and we tussle. Then he grabs my arm, so tightly it hurts. I let out a scream and Devika mirrors it and Liam's mother hears and comes waddling up the stairs, demanding, 'What the hell is going on here?' and the room swirls with pain and chaos.

With a burst of angry adrenaline, I wrench the case from Liam, grab Devika and scythe out of the room and down the stairs.

Liam stands at the top and calls down softly: 'Oh, Karina. Come on.'

I ignore him, and am hurrying out of the front door and down the path when—

—lights flash around me. I realise the paps have been waiting in the front garden.

'Didn't Liam's mother approve of you then, Karina?' one of them calls out.

Reporters! How the hell do they have such a nose for these things?

Our taxi is only a minicab and when I say I want

to go all the way back to London he baulks – until I yank a sheaf of notes from my purse. Then his eyes light up and he sets off. The paps follow. Every so often, I see them in the mirror. The driver flicks several glances at me, realising that I must be famous.

'Hey, are you that girl from *Hollyoaks*?' he asks, screwing up his face.

'No,' I say abruptly. My mobile beeps. It's Liam. **Fuck off then, just fuck off for good.** Charming. But I know this isn't Liam's voice. I know that he's gone to the bathroom and had another line to cope and has wiped his nose and sent this text. And his stupid, stupid mother won't even notice his eyes or shaking hands, because Liam, of course, eats up his roast dinner and never asks for Rice Krispies, so how could he possibly take cocaine?

Oh God – why the hell has he started taking it again? I thought he'd given it up for good. But deep down I know why. I do understand. He wanted the dinner to go so well. He wanted me to be there, for us to be a happy hunky-dory family around the table; he wanted to try to re-create the childhood he missed out on. As it has for me, a roast dinner has a whiff of nostalgia for Liam, a reminder of lost normality. I remember a night, a few years ago, when he opened up to me. How he wept as I held him tight, how he told me he wanted to love his mother, to make up for the time they'd lost, but couldn't help hating her too, feeling full of anger and resentment about what happened. But I want it to be good between us before she goes, he explained. She's all I've got left.

For a moment I feel terrible for deserting Liam: right now, he really needs me. I nearly tell the driver to turn back. But then the memory of her spitting insults at Devika rears back up and something hardens inside. We're not going back. No way.

'Mummy, look,' Devika cries, pointing to a car which is veering dangerously close alongside us.

'I'm sorry,' I say to the driver. 'Please don't be intimidated by them – please just drive safely.'

'It's all right,' he says, sounding quite excited. 'I think I've worked out who you are now – you're in Girls Aloud!'

'That's right,' I lie, hoping that if the press speak to him, he'll sound like an idiot and they'll disregard anything he says.

At least, I hope they do. Oh, God. We're just pulling into my road now and I brace myself for the worst bit – that no-man's-land between the taxi and the front door. I keep thinking it through: just get the luggage, grab Devika tight, shield her, make sure she goes up first. I take my keys out of my bag, ready so I can thrust them straight into the lock. My stomach churns. Why do they have to follow us right up to the front door? Why can't they just be gentlemanly and stop at the end of the road? I realise then that I really am famous. This is what I've been craving, and now I've got it, all I can think of is that saying *Be careful what you wish for.* I'd forgotten that this is the downside of fame – once you've got it, you can't switch it off. You can't be anonymous for a day. The press lock you into a cage and you can't get out until they lose interest. Then one day they do and they chuck you the key and leave you to let yourself quietly out whilst they hurry off to trap someone else. And the sad thing is, the moment you get out, you feel regret, a longing to be back in.

Okay, here we go.

Into battle.

29

Devika

Tomorrow I am going for my audition for *English High School Musical*. I need to sleep. Mummy Karina says that sleep will keep me 'fresh' which means I will sing like an angel. But I can't stop staring at the ceiling and then tossing to my right and staring out of the window at the sky turning different shades of dark and tossing to my left and staring at my statue of Ganesh and praying to him that I will get a part.

I wish Liam was here. I missed him over the last few days when I was practising. When we practise together, it's fun. He plays a few notes and then passes the guitar to me and makes me play the notes. Or I sing and he strums along and weaves his voice with mine. When I get it right, he gives me a huge hug or punches the air and makes me laugh. But I never seem to get it right for Mummy Karina. I always seem to get it wrong, wrong, wrong. Over the last few days, Mummy Karina has made me practise on and on and on. She wrote out a timetable and pinned it to my door: *8–12 practice, lunch for one hour, 2–5 practice, dinner, 7–9 practice*. I haven't been to school. I haven't been allowed to read *Horrid Henry*. I haven't been allowed to watch *The Simpsons*. I've just had to sing until I felt my throat would bleed. And every time I hit one wrong note or pronounced my English wrong, Mummy Karina would frown and look cross, until I started to cry.

'Don't cry,' she said, hugging me, 'you will be a star. You have such talent. And we will beat Liam! We don't need Liam. We are two.'

But I liked it when we were three.

I need to go to the toilet. I peel back my covers and tiptoe into the hallway. I don't want to wake up Mummy Karina. I'm scared she'll come out and cry, 'You can't sleep? Then let's practise from midnight to five!'

But when I come out of the toilet, I hear a noise coming from her bedroom. And I realise Mummy Karina is crying.

I hurry downstairs quietly. I go to the kitchen and search in the cupboards. I find a bag filled with chocolate balls, like the ones she ate the night Liam made her upset. I take them and creep up to her bedroom.

'Oh!' she gasps, for I surprise her.

'Here!' I snuggle up in bed next to her and give her the chocolate balls. 'Make you better.'

'Oh, Devika!' she says. And then Mummy Karina laughs and cries and puts a kiss on my head and pulls me close. Then we each eat a chocolate ball.

I try to think of something to say to her that will bring Liam back. Finally, I say: 'I like beef. I eat beef every day now. I love beef.'

'Oh, Devika!' she says again, laughing. 'You don't ever have to eat beef.'

'But I like beef . . .' I trail off, sadly.

We sink down under the covers and soon Mummy Karina is asleep. I reach over quietly and take another chocolate ball, then suck it silently so she doesn't wake up. I keep worrying about the audition. I keep seeing myself getting up on stage and the people asking me to sing and when I try no sound comes out. But worst of all would be the look on Mummy Karina's face. I'm scared that if I fail, she won't love me any more. I feel I have to become famous so she will love me more and maybe then Liam will be allowed to come home.

30

Karina

In the taxi on the way to the audition, my mobile beeps as a text comes through. I feel a flare of indignation. It'll be Liam, sending another rude text, angry that I haven't taken his calls or answered the door when he's banged incessantly on it. But when I read it, I feel unexpectedly touched.

Good luck with the audition. Thinking of you. Lx

Oh, Liam. Suddenly I wish he was here with us, holding our hands.

But I can't call him now. I have to focus on this audition. Over the past few days, I've shut out all my pain by focusing on nothing but Devika. I've been tough with her in order to discipline and nurture her talent. Maybe it's because I feel Liam's mother was so insulting; I'm scared at how Devika must have felt. I'm scared she heard me say that people view her as my accessory. So I've pushed Liam away because I feel I owe Devika all my love and attention. I'm determined to make it up to her by making her feel special. To show her she's not some girl from India I've supposedly *bought* – she is a precious angel, a true star.

Inside the theatre, the corridors are bustling with anxious mothers fussing over their genius daughters, arranging their hair, tweaking their costumes, whispering inspiration in their ears. As we wait to be called, Devika holds my hand so tightly my palm begins to ache.

'You'll be fine,' I keep saying, feeling somewhat worried myself. I'd expected Devika to be nervous, but not quite this much.

Then I spot a familiar face in the queue: a little girl with glossy dark hair whom I've often seen outside Devika's school.

'Who's that? Isn't she one of your friends?' I hope Devika might cheer up at the thought of a friend by her side.

'Regina,' Devika whispers without enthusiasm. And when I wave Regina doesn't seem to notice.

We get closer and closer to the stage, watching girl after girl walk out into that circle of spotlight. Four girls to go . . . three . . . and then all at once it's our turn.

I stand in the wings and watch Devika walk out into no-man's-land. I can't believe how petrified I feel. This is far worse than any audition I ever endured. I realise this is how my mother must have felt when she sent me out on stage. I find myself praying for the first time in years.

'What's your name?' a woman sitting in the front row asks. She has grey hair and a pretty, wizened face; I suspect she was a musical star herself many decades ago. There are two men sitting beside her. One has a clipboard, the other has crossed arms and a slightly arrogant face, as though Celine Dion herself would fail to impress him.

'Devika West,' she says in a voice that is barely a whisper.

'What are you going to sing for us, Devika?'

'"Memory" from *Cats*.' Devika's voice shrinks even more.

'Well,' the woman says briskly, 'sing up.'

I have to fight to stop myself from running over and scooping her up in my arms. Devika is about to die on stage. The spotlight highlights the sweat on her brow, the fear flashing in her eyes. How could I have ever agreed to let her do this?

'*Memory . . .*' Devika begins in a cracked voice, then trails off.

There is a terrible silence.

'Try again, Devika,' the woman cajoles her.

'Come on, Devika,' I call from the wings.

Devika turns and stares at me. The look in her eyes breaks my heart. This is all too cruel. I open my mouth to call the whole thing off, and then Devika suddenly opens her mouth and bursts into song.

And the magic happens. She becomes a singing angel. The notes soar through the air and ripple down my spine and conjure tears in my eyes. Then, at the end of her act, she does a little dance with a triumphant whoop that makes me laugh out loud.

'Very good, Devika,' the woman calls out warmly and I know then, I can feel it in my heart, that we are through to the next round.

'You were so great, my darling,' I whisper for the tenth time, planting a kiss on Devika's head. 'Mummy's very proud of you.'

She grins up at me. We are sitting with a group of other parents and kids. Waiting for the verdict: who gets to stay and who gets to go. Those who are invited to stay will compete again this afternoon to go through to a final audition next week.

I know I have a tendency to get carried away, but I can't help it: I can see Devika's future unfurling like a red carpet. I just can't believe how radiantly she shone up there on the stage. The charisma she oozed. I was never that good at her age. If she gets this part, she is going to steal the show. She will be hailed as the new Sarah Brightman.

The woman with the grey hair comes out with her clipboard and the room falls silent. Parents grip their children tightly; hands are squeezed; a collective breath is drawn in.

'You all did tremendously well today,' she says kindly.

Get on with it, everyone screams silently, *just bloody tell us.*

'The names of the girls we'd like to see back this afternoon are Jamie McKinley, Penelope Sweet, Alexandria Strinkle, Ochre Harrington, Sienna James, Melissa Forrington-North . . .'

A pause. Devika and I lock panicked eyes. Then, to our relief, she carries on.

'Regina Perry and Lucy Sweeting.' She peers at us over her glasses. 'I'm so sorry to disappoint the rest of you. You are all very talented and you must all keep going.'

In the back of the taxi, I feel Devika reaching for my hand. She squeezes it hard but my response is limp; my hand slips out of her grip. I stare out of the window in a mild state of shock. I feel consumed with bewilderment and anger. Devika was just so brilliant. She was light years ahead of all the others. How could she not have been picked?

I turn back and look at Devika. Her expression is stoical and quiet. But I can sense that, on some level, a terrible and subtle damage has been done to her soul. A child's ego is such a fragile thing, I realise. Rejection must be one of the worst blows to a heart that is still forming, growing, finding its shape and identity. I was lucky; I passed my first ever audition and that turned me into a confident and rather spoilt star. Devika's rejection suddenly makes me see what my destiny might have been, a parallel universe I might have lived through. I feel like going back and shaking the judges. How dare they define her, how dare they put her in a box marked *Failure*.

I lean over and suddenly fling my arms round her. She starts and I shower kisses on her head.

'You were wonderful,' I cry. 'You were wonderful, wonderful, wonderful.'

A smile of warmth and relief comes over her face but I still sense that underneath she feels raw, is suspicious that I'm just being nice. I only feel even more cross: somehow, in the hierarchy of celebrity, their opinion counts for more than mine.

'You don't have to be a singer,' I say fiercely.

Back home, I find an encyclopaedia and keep thrusting pictures under her nose.

'You can be a doctor. You can be a teacher. You can be an artist. You can give singing lessons.'

Devika stares at the pictures, nodding, but none of them seem to grab her. I can't help feeling unhappy, feeling that, in some way, I am the one who has failed today.

The doorbell rings. Devika and I look at each other. Then we go to the door and open it. Liam is on the front path, wielding a branch.

'You just fuck off and leave us alone,' he shouts to the reporter who is ineffectually trying to hide behind the slim stems of a rose bush.

Seeing us, Liam dives forward and flings himself into the house, slamming the door behind him. He leans against it, sweat dancing on his forehead, and lets out a huge breath of relief. He looks down at the branch, which he's still holding in his shaking hand, and then drops it. We all look at each other, the silence electric. Then, suddenly, we burst into collective laughter.

'I've got a poker in the living room if that'd be useful,' I suggest and we all laugh some more.

I reach out to hold Liam, to say sorry, but Devika gets there first. She grabs him and he bends down, engulfing her in his arms. She sobs into his leather jacket.

'I didn't get the audition,' she weeps. 'I failed. I failed.'

Liam shoots me a glance and though there's no anger in it, I feel as if he's firing arrows of guilt into my heart. Oh, God. I pushed her too hard. I took all my stress and put it on to her, telling myself I was helping her. Why do I keep getting this whole motherhood thing so wrong?

'It's good that you failed,' Liam says, pulling back and catching her tears on his fingers. 'Good. Very good, Devika.'

'Good?' Devika asks.

'Yeah. Musicals are bollocks. Bands are good. You should be in a band.'

'Liam!' I cry, in laughing exasperation, suffering sudden visions of Devika being dragged through auditions in the manner of *Spinal Tap*.

'Or a vet,' says Liam gently. 'You would make a great vet, Devika.'

'A vet? What is vet?'

When Liam explains to Devika what a vet does, her eyes light up with euphoria. I realise he's hit on it. Of course: it's perfect for Devika. Then I suffer more guilt. After we've got Devika on the sofa with *The Simpsons* and gone into the bedroom for a private chat, the first thing I say is: 'Oh, God – why didn't I think of that? Why didn't I suggest she become a vet?'

Liam comes over to me and takes my arms, looking right into me. His eyes are raw with hurt. I realise he doesn't want to talk about Devika any more – he wants to talk about us.

'I'm sorry,' I say, waiting for a similar reply. But there isn't one. Liam can never bring himself to say sorry. Years of exasperation have taught me that. Instead, he gives me a rough kiss. There's an angry possessiveness to it that makes me feel cross and wanted and happy all at the same time. I put my hands up to my chest, pulling back. But he pushes my hands away, grabbing me close. I feel the strength of his arms, the passion in his grip and his kisses.

'You shut me out,' he says. 'Don't you ever do that to me again.'

'Well, you freaked me out. You have to make a promise,' I whisper, as he kisses my neck. 'Promise you won't do any more drugs. Devika's not mine yet – I have to behave. We have to behave.'

'I promise you, Karina,' Liam says. 'I'll never touch any more white powder . . . unless it's Persil automatic.'

I burst into laughter and he grins.

'Now,' he says, lightly pinching my waist. 'We get to have make up sex. I love make up sex.' And then he starts to whisper in my ear all the things that he's going to do to me, until my breath grows ragged.

'Stop it,' I cry. 'Devika has to go to bed first.'

Waiting around becomes part of the crescendo. Throughout dinner, our eyes caress each other; under the table, Liam's hand brushes my thigh. Devika goes to bed and later, after we've made love many times, I get up in the night and peer in to check she's okay. And I see the branch Liam left in the hall sitting at the foot of her bed, like some talisman to ward off evil.

31

Karina

Contrary to all the gossip flying about this week, I'd just like to set the record straight: Liam and I have not broken up and made up. We've been together for the last few months. As for all the hilarious press reports saying that Liam's mother and I don't get on and she disapproves of me – rubbish. I really respect Liam's mother after what she went through in her battle against alcohol.

I'm sitting at the computer, typing up my blog for *The Times*. It was meant to be my yummy mummy blog. I was planning to gush about how proud I am that Devika's English has become so good so quickly. But the editor emailed to remind me that readers want to know about me and Liam, not me and Devika.

> *At the moment, we're just like one big happy family. And despite all the press rumours about how we eat at the Wolseley for breakfast and Devika is driven to school by a chauffeur, I'd like to set the record straight: we're just an ordinary family.*

My agent has always emphasised how important it is in today's market to be down to earth, accessible. People don't want to put celebs on pedestals any more; they want them to have spots and trip up on escalators and suffer all those little things that everyone goes through. Which isn't hard; my life is far from perfect.

> *For example, at breakfast time we sit round the table together and serve ourselves (believe me, there is no housekeeper preparing it all for us). Liam always has Marmite on his toast, which I find disgusting. We had a hilarious moment at break-fast this morning, when Devika had her first taste of Marmite. Liam was convinced she'd love it; I was sure she'd hate it. She took a bite and instantly a look of pure disgust came over her face. But as she chewed some more, her disgust became euphoria.*

Now, after Rice Krispies, Marmite is Devika's
favourite food. So I lost my bet with Liam and in
return I had to make him happy dot dot dot

As I log off, I feel pensive for a moment. Of course,
I'd be the first to admit the blog is pure propaganda.
But it's not that I want to fool the public. I guess
in a way I'm writing the story of my life the way I
want it to be.

And all of the above is true (well, I guess the
line about Liam's mother is pushing it). But there
is a lot I've left out. I'm not letting the reader see
any of the cracks. At the moment they are spider-
thin, but they are there. Ever since our row over
his mum, Liam hasn't been quite the same. Liam
is . . . well, the only word to describe him is *rest-
less*. He's gone from new man back to his old self,
which is a relief. But he's also back to his rainbow
ways – flitting through a spectrum of moods, all
different colours at different hours of the day. In
the morning, he might be chasing me around the
house as I shriek and giggle until he pins me down
on the floor, tickling and kissing me. In the afternoon he might be slumped on the sofa, refusing
to talk to me, downing a beer. In the evening he
might take off and not even tell me where he's
gone, then come back at midnight to smother me
with guilty kisses.

Worse – I want to row with him but I feel I can't. I don't want Devika to hear us. So all my aggravation is being stored up inside me. I'm just smiling and going along with it and pretending everything is hunky-dory.

And it's not just Liam. Devika is different too, ever since she failed the audition.

I suddenly find myself opening up the laptop and pouring out a blog I know will never be published:

I feel so happy and proud because every day I can see Devika becoming more tightly knitted into our country. She's more confident. She surprises me with the range of her English. Her new favourite phrase is 'you're so funny', delivered with affection and a slightly patronising air, in a quasi-American accent. But as she gets stronger, I feel increasingly lost. She doesn't need me to explain what everything means or why the English sky is grey or why our postboxes are red. It's crazy, but I feel I'm losing her, that she's growing up and away from me . . .

And I don't even have her officially – not quite yet. Tomorrow Angela from social services is going to pop by for a meeting. She mentioned on the phone that if Liam is acting as a father figure for Devika, she'll need to interview him too. If it all goes well, I'll definitely be able to adopt Devika within a few months . . .

Hearing the doorbell ring, I quickly log off and jump up to get it.

32

Karina

'Darling!' Fran exclaims as she enters the house, giving me an ebullient air kiss. She is carrying a couple of newspapers and looking very excited. 'You are *so* famous. The press are going on about what you and Liam do together, how you eat, what sexual positions you like – there's this hilarious piece in the *Mirror* this morning about how you're both into tantric sex!'

'Shh!' I put a finger over her lips, scared Liam might hear.

I grab the newspapers from her, briefly admiring the headlines – it *is* fun to be famous – before hiding them behind the mixer in the kitchen. Then I draw Fran into the living room, where Liam is still watching TV.

'Hi, babe,' Fran says, air-kissing him too. Liam grins. He's always had a soft spot for Fran; in many ways they're two of a kind. 'Where's the Adopted Daughter?'

'She's next door in the living room, playing with her friend Kelly. She's teaching Devika how to put make-up on.'

'Fuck!' Fran cries, slumping on to the sofa next to Liam. 'When I was eleven, I played with My Little Ponies. Now when you're eleven, you learn to put on make-up. They grow up so fast,' she says in an ironic tone.

'I was eleven when I first wanked off,' Liam says in a deadpan voice. Fran giggles.

'D'you want anything to drink, Fran?' I ask. 'Cup of tea?'

'Cup of tea!' Liam snorts. 'What is this, an old people's home?'

'Well, what am I supposed to make her, a Sex On the Beach cocktail?' I cry. 'It's two in the afternoon and Angela's coming tomorrow – we have to prepare!'

Liam rolls his eyes and tugs a cushion to his chest. I let out a huffy sigh, annoyed that we're arguing in front of Fran, and go out into the kitchen. I make three cups of Earl Grey, savagely straining the tea bags and continuing my argument with Liam in my head.

When I re-enter the living room, I nearly drop the tea tray.

'What the fuck are you doing!' I cry.

'We're just – erm – nothing,' Fran quickly fluffs up her hair and adopts an innocent face. I notice her palm is curled into a suspicious fist. A little cellophane quiffs out of the top.

Liam, however, narrows his eyes at me coldly.

'We're snorting cocaine,' he says, with matter-of-fact firmness.

There is a long silence as I reel.

'You can't!' I cry, incensed. 'Devika's in the house! She's playing with Kelly in the bloody room next door!'

'Knowing Kelly, she's probably already got Devika to try it,' Liam laughs. He turns back to Fran and grabs her palm, trying to get his white packet back. Fran giggles and keeps her fist closed. He cuffs his hand round her wrists and stares into her eyes. I do not like his look at all. Fran stares back at him, giggles softly and then opens up her palm. He takes the packet and clears a space on the table.

I feel a hot sweat breaking out all over me. Tomorrow Angela will be here to check that I'm a worthy mother for Devika and *my boyfriend wants to snort cocaine off my living-room table*. And even if Devika is playing safely next door, I hate the person Liam becomes when he's on coke. He turns into a nasty, two-dimensional caricature of himself. I don't want Devika to see him like that. I can't believe this is happening. He promised, promised, promised me things would be different.

'Liam,' I say in a very quiet, intense voice, 'if you want to take that stuff, you can damn well get out of my house.'

Liam stares at me. I stare back. The look in his eyes is furious. Liam loathes rules. Or being told what to do. But what the hell else am I supposed to say?

Then his fingers curl round the packet and in a careless manner he flings it back into his pocket.

'Okay. Fine,' he says tersely. 'Fine.' He leans back on the sofa, folds his arms and stares at Fran. 'What shall we do now for entertainment? Maybe we should play Scrabble. Wouldn't that be fun!'

Fran emits a laugh, then sees my face and represses it. I can sense something dangerous crackling in the air, so I quickly laugh too, pretending everything is okay.

'So, Fran, how's your love life?' Liam asks. He reaches out and brushes back a stray hair from her cheek, staring at her intently.

I suddenly feel like a bartender, looking on as a sexy couple get it together.

'It's not bad,' Fran says, fluffing her hair, pulling a clump over one eye and then letting it spring back. 'I was dating Billy H for a bit.'

'Fuck. *Billy H?* I've heard his cock is even smaller than his music sales, and that's saying something.'

Fran lets out a scream of shocked laughter. Liam keeps staring at her. I am now positively bathed in a sweat of stress. I give Fran a stern look of betrayal.

'You know, Fran,' Liam says in a light voice, 'I think I need to use the toilet upstairs. I'm simply dying for a slash.' He jumps up.

'*Liam!*' I cry warningly.

'What?' He spreads out his hands, all boyish. 'I'm just going for a slash.'

And then he's gone. Fran explodes into nervous laughter.

'He's such a riot!' she cries. 'Oh, come on, Karina,' she says, seeing my prim face. 'Since when did you get so *boring*?'

'Since I became a mother,' I say, getting up, suddenly on the verge of tears. 'And because I care about what happens to her. In the meantime, I'd appreciate it if you didn't hit on my boyfriend.'

Fran gives me an offended glare, but I know it's only because she feels guilty. Unable to stand any more, I storm out.

Next door, Devika and Kelly are playing at makeovers. But I appear to be interrupting something, for the moment I enter they cry, 'Hide it! Hide it!' and then spin smiles at me.

'What's going on?' In my paranoia, I feel as though everyone I love is delighting in winding me up and hiding secrets from me. 'What are you hiding? Come on now. Give it here.'

Devika and Kelly stop giggling and look nervous. Then Kelly takes her hand from behind her back, still keeping it clenched shut. I'm terrified she's got something off Liam, but surely he wouldn't have been so crazy as to give eleven-year-old girls anything . . .

'Let me see!' I cry in a shrill voice.

She uncurls her hand. It's just—

—a lipstick. A silly old red lipstick. Oh, thank God.

'Why on earth did you hide it from me?' I say. 'Why?'

Devika and Kelly shrug, utterly mysterious in their childish logic. Then they exchange glances, as though I'm some annoying parent invading their girly bonding session. I feel tears prickling up again. Fran's voice rings in my ears. Have I become so utterly boring that even my own daughter finds me tedious and prudish now?

And I don't want to lose Liam. I really don't.

'Well, enjoy yourselves,' I say, making a swift departure.

I decide to go into the living room and suggest a compromise. Fran and Liam can go wild – well, within certain boundaries – but only after Devika has gone to bed and is definitely asleep.

Or is that still a terrible thing for a mother to agree to?

When I enter the living room, however, Fran too has disappeared. *What!* I feel furious. How dare they? I hurry up the stairs and hammer on the bathroom door. Then I hear surreptitious giggling.

'For fuck's sake – let me in!' I cry. 'Fran!' I appeal to her, knowing that she is slightly more reasonable than Liam in situations like this.

Finally, the door opens. Fran giggles and yanks me into a clingy hug, then draws me in. Liam is kneeling on the floor. A line has been laid out on the toilet seat – as though my bathroom belongs to some seedy bar! He turns, gives me an evil smile, as though he's even more turned on by defying me, then snorts his line. He wipes his nose, eyes watering. I feel ready to thump him. But then Fran goes over and lays out a line for me.

'Come on, Karina,' she teases me, her eyes wicked. 'Devika won't even know – she's safe down there for the next few hours.'

I stare at both of them, furious to be pressurised like some teenager. Then Liam sits on the edge of the bath, daring me with his eyes, and I feel something naughty flicker inside me. I can't help remembering the old days, when Liam and I were renowned for being the wildest ones at a party. The bad girl in me, who has been quiet for many months, suddenly wakes up. She whispers in my ear: 'Go on. You can't continue being boring for the rest of your life.' I'm feeling so coiled up with stress over Angela, I could do with an escape. Tomorrow will be different; tomorrow I'll be the perfect mother on her best behaviour. But for now . . .

I kneel down in resignation and Fran lets out a whoop: 'We're corrupting her! We're corrupting the yummy mummy!'

As I snort it in, memories of the past rush before me. Seedy bars; toilets; wild sex with Liam; rows with Liam; the paranoia; the depression; mood swings. There is a familiar red sting behind my eyes and then a hot white tingling in my mind.

I get up, feeling giddy, and Liam reaches out a hand to steady me. Then he pulls me on to his lap and stares into my eyes.

'That wasn't so bad, was it?' he says.

'No,' I reply girlishly, relieved to be forgiven.

He leans in and kisses me. Fran smiles and comes and sits on the bath next to us. She puts her arm round Liam, nuzzles her head against his shoulder and then steals a kiss from him too, whilst her hand strays to my thigh.

'Oh no!' I cry, getting up. 'We're not doing this here!'

Some years ago, when Liam and I were going through our most wild phase, we occasionally had threesomes with Fran, amongst other girls. Liam loved to experiment and push my boundaries. But that was a long time ago.

'Mummy Karina!' a voice calls through the bathroom door. 'Liam?'

We all jump. *Devika*. I go over and open the door and Devika peers in. Shame sweeps over my face. She sees Liam behind me.

'Is Liam helping you to go to the toilet?' she asks, though the question is no longer innocent – there's a gleam in her eye.

'Er, yes,' I say quickly, going out on to the landing. I smile down at her, trying to ignore the effects of the coke and the even greater shock of her make-up. Her faces shimmers with colours, cerises and blues and golds. She looks beautiful . . . adult . . . exotic . . . but let's be honest. My daughter looks like a slut. I want to grab a flannel and scrub it all off and see her lovely pure face again.

Everything is out of control. I can't stand any more of this madness. I'm going to tell everyone to get out of the house right this minute.

But then Liam comes out and picks Devika up and she squeals with joy. Even Kelly, ultra-cool Kelly, bursts into laughter.

Fran comes out of the loo too and Devika frowns, looking confused.

'So,' Fran says, trying to catch Liam's eye, 'are we going to hit the town now?'

But Liam is staring at Devika, his hard expression softening with a sudden affection.

'Actually,' he says abruptly, 'Karina and I are going to stay in and look after Devika. We're just going to have a quiet family evening. So maybe you'd better go.'

Oh, Liam. Suddenly he's mine again. I want to kiss him in relief.

And then my mobile rings.

'Hi, it's Angela here,' I hear a chirpy voice saying, punctuated by crackling. 'Just to let you know I'm going to be about twenty-five minutes late. Actually, make that thirty.'

'Er – late?' I ask, bewildered. 'For tomorrow?'

'What? No, Karina, our appointment is today, at three, remember? Is Liam there? I'm going to need to interview him too, remember?'

I gaze over at Liam. His bloodshot eyes are sparkling with drugs, his pupils narrow slits.

'Er – ah – right. Yeah, great. See you soon. That's fine. We're all ready for you. Fantastic,' I gush.

Then I switch my mobile off.

'What is it?' Fran asks.

I shake my head, speechless.

*　　*　　*

For the next five minutes, Liam and I argue like mad. I start screaming at him that he should never have taken anything, he yells back that he had no idea she was coming today and how the hell could I have got the date wrong. I call her up, about to ask if I can postpone, and then click off. This meeting is really important. I don't want to postpone. I want to be a wonderful mother. It will look really bad if I postpone, won't it? It'll be a black mark on my file and everything. Oh God, my brain feels addled and hyper from the coke and I just can't think straight.

Fran doesn't help at all. Perhaps because she's high or guilty, she starts cracking up. And then she just keeps on laughing and laughing.

Liam, however, can handle drugs a lot better than I can. All of a sudden, he seems to detach himself and sober up.

'Come on, Fran,' he says, 'you're going home. Now.'

He ushers her down the stairs, untangling her as she attempts to snog him goodbye, calls her a minicab and then dumps her in the living room whilst we wait for it to come. Then he turns to me and puts his hands on my shoulders. I try to speak but tears start spilling from my eyes.

'We're going to screw this up completely—' I break off, tears lacerating my voice.

'There's no time to cry,' he says very slowly, kissing each cheek in turn. 'If we're going to get through this, we have to get it together, okay? We can do this, Karina. We can do it.'

'Okay.' I breathe out deeply, sniffing. 'Okay.'

'Right.' Liam summons Devika and Kelly. 'We're going to play a game. It's called getting the house beautiful and spotless in twenty minutes. If you play, then you get a guitar lesson. Okay?'

'Cool!' Kelly says, her eyes shining.

'Okay,' Devika agrees, though she keeps looking at me with big eyes. She knows that Angela's meeting is important; I've been prepping her for the last few days, telling her to just be honest and relaxed.

'It's fine.' I pat her on the head.

For the next fifteen minutes, we all race around the house, packing stuff away, flinging armfuls of clothes and toys into cupboards and under beds. Liam's cigarettes are flung into the bin, along with several crumpled cans of beer. Kelly's make-up is hidden in the wine cabinet and Devika's face is scrubbed clean, despite a few feeble protests. Every so often, I hear Fran cackling away to herself in the living room. When the doorbell rings I jump, petrified that Angela might have got here before the minicab.

'Oh, thank God,' I breathe out, as Liam packs Fran off into the cab. Then, just as he starts heading back up the path, a blue Volvo pulls up and a woman wearing a crisp suit gets out.

Angela.

Liam shakes her hand heartily, introducing himself.

Nobody can fail to be charmed by Liam, I think, as I watch them. *Nobody can have their hand shaken by him and fail to smile and light up inside.*

Angela doesn't smile.

Liam turns back to the house and I see panic scurry through his eyes. He glances up at me, and in a moment of vulnerability his bravado dissolves and he mouths, 'I'm sorry.'

Oh, God. But no – *no* – I'm determined to be strong. Liam has given me enough confidence to feel we might just be able to pull this off.

Even if I can still feel cocaine fizzing and whizzing through my brain.

We all sit down together. I've asked Kelly to play by herself next door. Devika walks in, her hands folded together, looking meek and shy.

'So, Karina, how is everything?' Angela asks pleasantly.

'Great – we'll all doing really well.' I focus hard on keeping my voice steady and clear; when I'm on coke I know I have a tendency to talk faster and faster.

'Good.' She looks into my eyes and I'm paranoid that I see her do a quick double take. Do they look bloodshot?

Oh, God. This is a nightmare. I have to stop worrying or it'll only make it worse. I have to forget that I ever snorted that wretched line.

'So what's the situation with you and Liam?' she asks, nodding at us.

I look over at Liam but suddenly he seems to have lost his nerve; he stares shyly at his boots.

'We're – we're serious. We're both really committed to looking after her,' I say, smiling at Devika, who smiles back.

'Good,' says Angela. 'And what about you, Liam? Have you had any experience of bringing a child up before?'

'I have a dog,' Liam says, laughing.

Angela doesn't laugh.

'Um, maybe it's not the same thing,' I say quickly.

Liam's laughter fades and he scowls briefly. I can see Angela is working hard to resist his charm; something Liam just isn't used to.

'So . . . so,' says Angela, crossing her legs. 'The fact that Liam is living here some of the time does affect your application for adoption, Karina.'

'Right, right.' I can feel sweat on my cheeks. Do I look shiny? Is this going well, or badly – the drugs are blurring my judgement. I can't tell what's real paranoia and what's coke paranoia. Oh God, please let us just get through this, get it over and done with.

'So, what about—'

'I love Liam,' Devika suddenly bursts out. She goes over to his side and wriggles on to his lap. 'I love Liam lots and lots.' She leans up and gives him a kiss on the cheek. Liam grins and tickles her.

Angela watches them together and for the first time her face softens. She can tell they're not acting. There's no faking the sweetness between them. And then she looks at me and smiles.

I smile back, trembling with relief.

I think we might just get through this.

After Angela has left, I turn to Liam and let out a long breath. The knot in my stomach doesn't untie; the pain in my chest doesn't leave. It actually went well but I can't quite believe we got away with it. *We were on coke. We did Devika's assessment on Coke.* I reel. I let out a laugh. Then I give Liam a sharp slap on the face.

'I deserved that,' he agrees, rubbing his cheek. Then he looks at me. 'I'm sorry. But she liked me, Karina – she actually liked me. Come on, admit it. I actually think she fancied—'

'Liam, don't say it. Don't!'

For the rest of the day, Liam works like mad to make it up to me. He tells me to lie on the couch and gives me a foot massage to try to calm me down. He gives Kelly and Devika a guitar lesson. He hoovers the living room. He tells me to name any place that I want to go on holiday this year and assures me he'll start booking it. As the afternoon goes by, the tension in me starts to ease. Relief washes through me, lapping waves of happiness. We did it. We got through it. As Liam begins another massage, I lean down and give him a kiss on the lips.

'Am I forgiven?'

'No,' I assert. 'Not yet.'

We round the evening off by taking Devika and Kelly out for an Indian. Devika is disgusted by the meal, which she declares tastes nothing like Indian food. But Liam finds this hilarious and turns it into a big joke, cheering us all up. And I know then that Liam is a man who will never ever say he's sorry – but this is his way of showing it.

'My mummy says she read in the papers that you and Karina do tantric sex,' Kelly says.

Thank God Kelly wasn't allowed into the interview with Angela.

'Dear God!' I cry, then swallow. 'Kelly, your mother is quite mistaken.'

'No,' Liam says, 'let's not patronise them. Let's be honest – we do do tantric sex.'

'Really?' Kelly's eyes moon. 'My mum wants to try it. What do you do?'

'Karina and I lie in bed and count to a hundred whilst twirling our legs behind our ears,' says Liam. 'It's great fun.'

Kelly and Devika giggle like mad. They spend the rest of the evening staring at him in devoted adoration, laughing at his every witticism.

Later that night, however, I find myself lying awake in bed, unable to sleep. Liam slips out of bed and pads downstairs and I watch the moonlight streak lovingly across his broad back and naked buttocks. We've had such a lovely evening that it's hard to believe what happened this afternoon really took place. But it did, and I'm scared it might happen again. And then what do I do? How do I control a man like Liam? Maybe I shouldn't even try to cramp his free spirit; but that's who he is. How can I be a good mother and be with him?

As Liam comes back into the room I quickly close my eyes, pretending to be asleep. He slips under the covers and nuzzles against me, kissing my head drowsily, and soon I hear his sleep-heavy breath fluttering against my ear. I open my eyes and look. There on the bedside is a glass of water. That's all he went down to take. Just water.

It's going to be okay, I tell myself, *today was just a blip. Everything will go back to normal now.*

But it doesn't. In fact, things get much, much worse.

33

Karina

How do I keep him interested? *How* do I keep him hooked?

Since the infamous C incident a few days ago, everything has been all right, in the sense that nothing has happened. Devika's gone to school. Kelly's come over for tea. Liam and I have been photographed walking Rufus together. According to the *Daily Mail* we are the perfect domestic couple. According to *Heat* I am 'the woman who has tamed the untame-able man'. But. There is an underlying restlessness in the house, like dangerous clouds creeping up on the horizon.

Like this morning. Liam is up in the attic room, composing a song. He told me and Devika that he wanted to be left alone. Now Devika's curled up on the landing, at the bottom of the stairs, listening to him twanging and crooning. It's the first time Liam has shut her out and I can see the hurt she's struggling to conceal. I can't help feeling indignant. Liam seems to have gone through his phase of apologising and making it up to me.

I sit down next to her. We both listen to his composing: the jangled notes, the angry sighs. Then there is a long silence. We both turn and smile sadly at each other.

'Can I go to Liam?' Devika whispers.

'No, darling.' I kiss her head. 'Wait.'

She nods again, biting her lip, and I hug her close. I'm cross with Liam for upsetting her, though I realise I have to be understanding too. But I get the feeling that he's hiding himself away because the aftershocks of what happened are still trembling through him. It's his way of digesting the guilt.

I also get the feeling that having to face a social worker shocked him. Having to officially acknowledge that he's Devika's father and my partner. Commitment isn't easy for him. And Liam is a man with a low boredom threshold. I almost feel I have two children to keep entertained, and the trouble is, if I look after one, the other is neglected.

I am the woman who has tamed the untameable man, I assure myself, repeating *Heat*'s headline like a mantra. But the problem is, in order to prevent any more 'untamed' incidents and keep us on the straight and narrow, I need to keep Liam interested. Excited. On the edge. That's why the whole coke thing happened in the first place. In the past, whenever I sensed he seemed bored, I would organise a surprise. One night I told him I'd bought two tickets to Venice and we were leaving in an hour. Another night he came into the house to find the lights turned low and me dressed in black lace underwear, ready to perform a striptease for him. He always loved surprises.

But to do those things, I need to be spontaneous. I need to be single.

Liam starts up his song again, discordant notes clashing and screaming. Devika sighs and gets up and goes to her room.

Silence again. Oh, God, I don't want to lose him. What shall I do to keep him happy, what shall I do?

In the end, Fran comes up with a good idea. She calls me one afternoon to apologise for 'being a bad influence' and though her tone is slightly jokey I realise she genuinely is contrite. I tell her I'm afraid of losing Liam and spew out all my fears. She goes quiet and then suggests I tell Liam to go out for a drink on the town with the lads from his band. I end the call feeling euphoric, certain Fran's suggestion will solve everything.

When I suggest the idea to Liam, I expect him to look delighted at being let off the domestic leash. But he just shrugs.

'Yeah. I think I might stay in and watch TV,' he says.

'But I've arranged to go over and see Clare – you'll be on your own!' I cry.

He looks a little hurt, as though I'm deserting him, which only makes me feel more confused. I'd forgotten that there is no second-guessing Liam; he's always so bloody unpredictable.

'I just thought you'd enjoy the space,' I explain.

Liam smiles, reaches up and gives me a deep kiss.

'Hey, I'll be grand – you have a nice evening,' he says. 'I reckon I'll try a spot of song-writing.'

Devika begs to stay behind with Liam, declaring that she hates Dom. But I insist that she come along. A horde of paps follow us as we get into the car. She sits in the front with her arms folded, staring sulkily into the distance. As I glance down at her, I can't help suffering a sudden sadness. The sweet innocent Devika I brought over to England seems to be fading away. Is Devika becoming stronger and more integrated . . . or is she actually turning into a bit of a brat? Then I shake myself. Devika is my daughter. My lovely, lovely daughter. This whole media merry-go-round must be as hard for her as it is for me.

When we get to Clare's, thankfully the paps realise nothing more exciting than the consumption of carrot cake is going to happen and they don't bother hanging around.

Inside, Clare greets me with breathless delight. Dom comes down the stairs and gives Devika a sickly smile.

'Hi, Devika,' he says.

'Hi, Dom,' she says, matching the sarcasm in his tone and outdoing his grin.

Then, when I turn to hug Clare, I catch sight of Devika in the hall mirror, surreptitiously flicking Dom a V sign as she follows him up to his room.

I feel a little troubled – since when did Devika even know what a V sign was? But I forget it as I go into the living room with Clare, down a cup of tea, stuff myself miserably with carrot cake and then pour out the whole situation with Liam. When I tell her about the coke, she gasps and her eyes widen. When I finish, there is a silence.

'You think I have to dump him, don't you?' I ask, shoving the last bit of cake into my mouth.

'No,' she says. 'Not necessarily. I think that perhaps you *are* taming him. But you have to remember that it's not easy for him. A part of him is rebelling against it. It's the emotional equivalent of a man going crazy on his stag night, knowing he needs to have one last frenzy before he settles down.

I think Liam is just testing you and you have to be strong. Keep taming him. He'll break in the end, I think.'

'Really? Oh God, oh wow, I didn't see it like that,' I cry, relief gushing through me. 'Of course. Of course that's what's happening.'

'The question is whether he really can be tamed, though,' Clare says. 'And if not, then maybe you're going to have to make a choice between him and Devika. Who would you choose then?'

I hesitate for just one second and Clare looks horrified.

'Devika,' I say quickly. 'Of course it would be Devika.'

Upstairs, I am relieved and surprised to find that Dom and Devika are not trading swear words. They are utterly engrossed in playing a computer game. I guess PlayStations can bond across all creeds and cultures. When I tell Devika it's time to go home, she even lets out a wail and demands she finish. I wait patiently as she beats Dom to death on screen, wincing at how horribly violent it is. But when Dom gives a scream of defeat and Devika punches the air, I can't help smiling.

On the way home, Devika twirls the radio on in the car and hums along. I tell myself I feel better after speaking to Clare, but those words keep pulsing in my mind: *you're going to have to make a choice . . . you're going to have to make a choice . . .* When I look down at the steering wheel, I notice my knuckles are protruding like sticks of chalk.

As I turn into our street I hear the sound of music pumping through the air. I wonder if the ex-Bond villain who lives across the road is having a party.

Then, as I pull up, I find that I can't actually park my car outside my house. The kerb is packed with vehicles, so I have to circle down to the bottom of the street. As Devika and I approach the house, my heart starts to hammer. I've only been gone what, two hours? And this happens! It's a deliberate slap on the face; Liam is sticking up two fingers right at me. That's what hurts me the most. As though the silhouettes I can see dancing in the windows, the music that blasts into the pavement and spirals up my spine, is his way of saying *'I don't love you any more'.*

My eyes prickle as my anger intensifies. I'm going to march straight in there and call the police.

I look down at Devika and she gazes up at me with an expression of joy.

'Party!' she cries. 'Party!'

'Well, that's not such a good thing—' I break off as I am besieged by an angry neighbour, Mr Furtado (the High Court judge), and a horde of paps.

'Are you going to let Devika join the party?' one of them calls out.

'Karina, I have a case tomorrow and my three-year-old daughter is trying to sleep,' Mr Furtado cries.

'Absolutely not,' I cry to the press. 'Devika will be going to bed within the next half-hour.' I turn to Mr Furtado, and, seeing how flustered I am, his face softens. 'I'm so sorry. I'll sort all this out, I promise.'

When I turn back to Devika, to my horror I find her posing for the photographers, strutting up and down in front of them as though she's a supermodel.

'Devika!' I cry.

'I'm just having fun,' she sulks as I drag her away. 'My friends always pose if there're paps.'

'Well, I don't care what Kelly does,' I say, immediately translating the word *friends*, 'it's time for bed.'

I take a firm hold on Devika and march her into the house.

The hallway is full of people swigging from beer bottles. I recognise Brian, the drummer from Liam's band. He is wearing a brown leather jacket and looks completely out of it.

'What is this?' I demand. 'How the hell did everyone turn up at my house?'

Brian's drug-lazy eyes blink and he squirms with vague discomfort.

'Hey, chill, Karina. Liam sent a text round saying we could do some beers and have a jam. And then we figured our friends would like to hear us.'

'Where is he?' I cry. 'Where *is* he?'

'Uh – in the living room, man.'

Devika is now chatting to a random guest, boasting to him that she's a famous princess. I give him a severe look, grab her hand and take her into the living room.

The lights are turned down low. People are drinking and smoking. I march to the stereo and turn the music off. Someone has the nerve to mutter at me! Then I see Fran. I open my mouth to blast expletives in her face, but she leans in and gives me a drunken, clingy hug, smothering my cheeks with blurry kisses.

'Oh, Karina,' she cries, 'it's soooo good to see you!'

'Well, it is my house—' I begin. Then I am drowned out as someone puts the music back on.

Then the people part and I see him. He's sitting on the sofa, a bottle of beer in his lap. A girl is sitting on the arm. From the flow of blond hair down her back, her posed posture, her arched back and the polished fingers clamped round a cigarette, I can tell at once that she's Hayley. I watch, my heart skipping, as she shrieks at something Liam's said. Then she slips from the arm of the sofa on to his lap and leans in to kiss him.

That's it, I think dully. *It's over*.

But then, just as I'm about to confront him, I see him taking hold of Hayley's wrists and pushing her away. I catch a glimpse of his expression: it's sour. Once again, Hayley leans in. This time, he gives her a vehement shove, so hard she stumbles off his lap and on to the floor. She squeals, dishevelled hair hanging over her face, reaching for Liam to grab hold of her and help her to her feet. But he shakes his head and walks off.

For a few seconds, my anger vaporises. Liam is probably drunk and high and on God knows what, but he has still rejected an advance from a gorgeous ex.

That's something.

But it still doesn't make this party okay.

I break away from Fran and follow Liam out. I catch him, finally, halfway up the stairs, where a couple is sitting snogging.

'Karina!' He gives me an ecstatic hug. 'Hey, come on up. We're gonna do a gig in our bedroom – hope that's okay. It'll be just like the old days, before we got a record deal, when me and the band did gigs in the house and we let all our real friends come along and listen.'

Liam!' I cry, but he gives me a hard, alcohol-tainted kiss. I break away. 'Liam, what the hell is this?'

'What?' he cries. 'Fuck, Karina, you told me I should cheer up and get together with my friends. You told me to do it.'

'But I didn't mean—'

'Oh, sorry, so I was only meant to have fun within the little boundaries you've set for me?' he says, but his tone is light-hearted and he takes my hand, dragging me up the stairs and into the bedroom.

Our double bed has been pushed back against the wall. The windows are wide open. The band look at us expectantly, all revved up and ready to play.

'Liam, I just can't believe you organised this without my permission!'

'Look,' Liam says, grabbing my hands and hauling me over to the window.

Down below, I see a crowd has gathered in the road. I've no doubt that some of them are press and some of them are angry neighbours. But many of them are clearly fans, for when they catch sight of Liam they burst into cheers and wolf whistles. One girl even flings up a pair of knickers, crying, 'I love you, Liam!' though they only make it as far as the front garden before they catch on a rose bush.

Liam grabs the mike, sets it on a stand and calls out: 'Hey, guys, thanks for turning up. Tonight the set we're playing is dedicated exclusively to Karina – the love of my life.'

The crowds scream and cheer, though there are a few discernible boos from the females.

'Liam—' I try again, but he takes the mike and starts to sing, facing me and crooning: '*Since the day I first saw you, I knew it was love . . .*'

The rest of the band kicks in. The fans go crazy and begin to sing along. The words *love of my life* are echoing inside me. Feeling myself start to soften, I cross my arms sulkily, trying to maintain my outrage. But, I have to admit, it is hard when the love of *my* life is crooning at me, his eyes pouring out emotions I didn't know he was capable of.

Then Devika appears in the doorway. I'm scared she's upset and I'm about to go to her, insisting this all stop. But Devika comes up to the window and waves at the crowd. They cheer her and she blows them a few kisses. Liam grabs her hands and dances her round in a jig.

Okay. Now I'm had. I can't stop myself from breaking into a helpless smile. This is all crazy, but it is fun. And it's all so utterly Liam – nuts, spontaneous, unpredictable – some of the reasons I love him.

As the song draws to its final chorus, Liam lets go of Devika and grabs me. He holds me in his arms, singing with our lips just a few inches apart.

He doesn't even bother with the final line, punctuating it with a long, sweet kiss.

Down below, the fans go crazy. Devika claps her hands, grinning like mad. Liam pulls me in close and rubs his nose against mine in an Eskimo kiss.

'All my songs are for you,' he whispers. 'Always.'

'They'd better bloody be,' I say, having to joke because I feel so overwhelmed. This started out as a terrible evening and suddenly it's turning into the best night of my life.

And so the night goes on: dancing, singing, kissing. A bubble of bliss and euphoria. Soon the road is so packed out, the neighbours can't even get to the door to complain, and give up. It's not until two a.m. that the police finally arrive and break up the party.

34

Devika

There's something strange in my lunch box. Before we go into lessons, I take a peek at it, wondering what Liam has put inside. He brought me to school this morning. He said he had a hangover. I know in English this means 'Don't talk to me'. He wore black sunglasses and was silent all the way and when he dropped me off he didn't even give me a hug or a kiss.

'Hey!' Kelly says. 'Have you got something yummy in your lunch box?'

'It's just a sandwich,' I lie quickly.

Because what I've just found in my lunch box is what Kelly would call 'seriously weird'.

I have a feeling it's a bad thing. So I quickly put my lunch box back into my bag and hang it on my peg.

'Hey, guess what time I went bed last night,' I say to Kelly.

'Went *to* bed,' Kelly corrects me, rolling her eyes. 'Hey, when? Midnight?'

'No. Three o'clock in morning. Liam had a party at our house. Rock stars came!'

'Wow! That is *so* cool,' Kelly cries, looking impressed. 'All my mum did was moan because she's worried her breast implants might explode. Boring.'

'I went to bed at eight o'clock,' a voice cuts in behind us. We turn to see Regina smiling at us. 'I was practising for *English High School Musical*.'

'So? Who cares when you go to bed? You're just a bore.' Kelly laughs and I laugh too, though I know *bore* is a mean word. I feel a bit sad inside when I see the hurt on Regina's face. I think she wants us both to be her friend but it doesn't seem like threeway friendships can happen at school.

As we go into the class, Kelly asks me more about the party. I tell her about how I posed for the paps and she gets really excited. I tell her how amazing it was to stand by the window and look down to see hundreds of people cheering at me. But I don't tell her how I felt this morning in the car with Liam when I tried to sing to him and he ignored me. I know he had a hangover, but I was just trying to make him smile. He didn't even say goodbye to me. He seemed so cold, as though we were strangers.

I thought Liam would always love me and be my new daddy. But now and again I feel scared that he doesn't like me any more. And I don't know what I've done to lose his love. Maybe that's why he gave me such a strange lunch box today.

In the classroom, Mrs H starts to write numbers on the board. Maybe Liam will be proud of me if I get good marks and study hard. Especially now that he says I should be a vet. I love the idea of becoming an animal doctor. If cats came in with sad, drooping tails because they felt sick I would make them feel so good they would leave with their tails swirling up in happiness.

But Mrs H said people who want to be vets have to work very hard. So I need to concentrate.

I feel so tired, though. The music from the party has stayed in my head and keeps thumping its feet about. When I'm tired, I find it harder to understand Mrs H's English and her words begin to blur together into a stream of nonsense. My head starts to tip forward and my eyes close and her voice fades away . . .

I am in India. I am back in the orphanage, in the courtyard with the red flowers. The sun is an Indian sun, a real sun, burning bright and yellow on me. I'm afraid because I can't see Mummy Karina anywhere. I shout her name but she doesn't come. I start to panic, until two figures appear, shielding me from the sun. I start to cry tears of euphoria. They are *my parents*. We all hug each other. They tell me that whilst I was in England, they came to the orphanage. They were told I'd been taken away by Mummy Karina and they feared they'd lost me for ever. I jump up and down with joy, holding them tightly.

And then I see Mummy Karina. She is standing in the corner, looking sad, and I don't know what to say to her—

'Devika,' she calls out. 'Devika . . . wake up, Devika.'

Suddenly I hear laughter. My head springs up and I see Mrs H giving me a stern look. I expect her to tell me off and I cringe, waiting for her to shout. But she just says quietly, 'See me at the end of the lesson.'

'What did Mrs H say to you?' Kelly asks me, when I come out into the cloakroom for lunch break.

'She asked what time I go to bed,' I say. 'She was really nice and said I should take care.'

'Ooh, teacher's pet!' Kelly laughs. 'She would have told me off.'

As we reach for our lunch boxes, I remember the strange thing I saw inside my box. I think I'd better not show it to anyone except Kelly. I have a feeling that if Mrs H saw it, I'd be in even more trouble.

'Come into the toilets,' I whisper to Kelly. 'I've got something in my lunch box Liam gave me.'

Inside a cubicle, I open the box and show her. There is a piece of bread with no butter. And also a long, white thing. It looks like a cigarette, only it's a bit bigger. It smells a bit funny too – sweet, like a pretty herb from the garden.

'That is . . . cool,' Kelly says at last, because I think she doesn't know what else to say.

I feel confused. I know cigarettes are definitely bad but I also know herbs are good. I know Mummy Karina puts them in her cooking when she makes pasta. Maybe the herbs are good for me and they'll be cross if I don't eat it. I take a little flake from the end of the white stick and put it on my tongue and Kelly does the same.

'Ugh!' Kelly says, gagging. 'I think we're meant to smoke it, not eat it. Hey, I have a lighter in my bag. I stole it from my mum.'

Kelly lights the end of the cigarette and it flares red. She takes a puff and closes her mouth, then when she opens it smoke swirls out like the pictures of genies we had in yesterday's story.

'Here, you have a go,' she says.

I remember how Mummy Karina looked last night when she was dancing with Liam, smoking her cigarette and putting it in his mouth so he could take a puff. She looked so cool. I close my eyes and suck on the cigarette, but something nasty seems to pour down my throat. I burst into lots of coughs. My throat burns as though it has pieces of bitter ash in it. Kelly laughs at me.

'Haven't you smoked before?' she says, taking it back. 'Hey, I have – my mum made me try one to show how disgusting they are and make sure I never have one again.'

'Hey – what are you doing?'

We jump. Regina is staring over the top of the next cubicle.

'What's that?' she asks.

I quickly hide it behind my back. 'Nothing.'

'I'm going to tell a teacher.'

'Then I'll tell Liam you told a teacher,' I say.

'Teacher's pet!' Kelly calls up.

Regina pushes up her lips into a shape like my toy duck has.

'I won't tell anyone if you let me see it properly,' she says.

She disappears and then there is a bang on the door.

'Don't open it!' Kelly hisses.

I start to, but Kelly's hand springs on top of mine and stops it. Regina keeps banging. Kelly bites her lips together to stop laughter sailing out. I find I want to start laughing too. Suddenly everything seems really funny.

Then there is silence and Regina goes away. Kelly gives me the cigarette again and this time when I try it I don't choke or cough. I think maybe it tastes quite nice – not as good as Rice Krispies, but much better than beef.

Suddenly we hear a door swinging open and the click of footsteps.

'Oh shit!' Kelly cries.

And that's when we know we're in big trouble.

Kelly and I sit in the headmistress's office. We look at each other. Kelly's eyes are scared. I feel scared. The white cigarette thing, which she took away from us, is sitting in the middle of her desk. She has called up our parents, which is Very Serious.

Kelly's mum arrives first. When she enters, she makes a really weird, really scary noise. It sounds like a vampire in the film Kelly showed me the other night, when it gets a piece of wood through its heart.

Then she runs forward and pulls Kelly against her chest, squeezing her hard, her hair hanging over Kelly's face in a yellow cave as though it wants to protect her. The headmistress keeps saying, 'Please, if we could just *discuss* this,' but Kelly's mum doesn't take any notice. They just stand there, holding each other tight.

Then Kelly's mum steps back and yells, so that even the headmistress jumps: 'What the hell was my daughter doing, smoking a joint in your school?'

A joint. I puzzle over the word for a minute. I thought a joint was a bit in your body. But there are lots of words in English that mean two things. This one must also have a dark side.

Next to me, Kelly starts to cry.

'It wasn't me,' she sobs, 'it was Devika's fault!'

'Hey!' I say. 'I didn't ... I ...'

Kelly's mum gives me a look that makes me feel close to tears. I want my mummy Karina to be here, to tell them that she put it in my lunch box because she thought it would be good for me.

I get so scared that when the headmistress says something to me I can't translate it, so I just cry out: 'I'm sorry, I'm sorry, I'm sorry.'

Kelly's mum goes bright red. Then she says: 'Sorry isn't good enough.' She starts to rant and I lower my head, watching tears plop into my lap, praying to Lord Krishna for everyone to stop being so mad at me.

Then, suddenly, there is a knock at the door. It's Liam!

He comes in and I run to him and he grabs me and picks me up, holding me tight. Then he puts me down on the chair and looks around.

'Everything all right?'

All of a sudden, Kelly's mum changes her voice. It becomes soft and pinky.

'It's all a mistake.' And she swings her hair back over her shoulder and smiles at Liam, as though he is a naughty boy she is telling off but still loves in her heart.

'A very big mistake,' the headmistress says in a cross voice. 'Will you kindly explain why Devika had *this* in her lunch box this morning?'

Liam stares at the white cigarette. We all stare at him. I ache for him to explain. I don't know why he's here and not Mummy Karina. I have a feeling Mummy Karina would explain better.

Then Liam starts to laugh. It seems wrong, but I'm so scared I start to giggle too and it makes me feel a bit better.

But nobody else laughs.

The headmistress looks very angry and I quickly swallow my giggles down my throat.

'I do not find this amusing,' she says. 'Do you regularly give joints to Devika?'

'Hell, no, we couldn't afford it,' Liam says, still giggling. 'Really, it'd be far too expensive to have a kid with a drug habit. I mean, she might advance to crack cocaine and imagine the rehab bills!' He breaks off, laughter taking hold of him.

'Well,' the headmistress's voice rises to a terrifying pitch, 'will you explain why this was in her lunch box?'

There is a long silence. Even Liam stops laughing and looks a bit scared.

'Em . . . er . . . erm . . . I don't know,' he says quietly. 'It was just a mistake.'

'That's not good enough,' says the headmistress.

But Liam isn't listening. He is smiling at Kelly's mum. There is something strange in his smile, as though he doesn't quite own it, as though something naughty and a little bit evil has painted it on his face.

'I like your boob job,' he says.

Kelly's mum smiles and frowns at the same time. Then Liam starts to giggle again. I stare at him, willing him to stop being silly. But instead he picks the joint up from the table, sticks it into his mouth and lights it with his lighter.

The sound that the headmistress makes is so frightening that Liam grabs my hand and drags me out of the room. At first I try to resist, because I'm afraid I will be excluded. But he tugs me down the corridor and I cry, 'Sorry, sorry, sorry,' back towards the headmistress. Then we are out in the playground, running, running for the gates, and out of the school.

35

Oh my God. Oh my God oh my God oh my God.

All morning, the phone hasn't stopped ringing.

'Karina,' my agent cries, 'I'm doing my best to contain this – I'm saying Devika found the cigarette just outside the school premises and tried to pick it up because she felt littering was a bad thing, but it is *not* easy . . .'

'I know I'm not supposed to say this,' say Fran, 'but you have to admit, it *is* funny . . . I mean, it's just so terrible, you have to laugh . . .'

'Karina, this has gone far enough,' says Clare. 'You have to get Liam out of that house *now*.'

'I am just calling to check that Devika's okay,' Mrs Raju cries.

'Karina,' my agent calls again, 'the papers have

349

bought the story that it was all a misunderstanding and I'm booking you a supermarket opening for Save the Children to clean up our profile. But Jesus, you had better dump Liam. You cannot sustain your celebrity couple status any longer – you are now celebrity poison . . .'

'Are you going to dump him?' Fran asks. 'I mean, I guess you'll have to . . .'

I put the phone down and it rings again and I scream, 'SHUT UP!' at it. Because I can't take any more. My throat is hoarse and my heart is beating with a perpetual hammer of shock. Then I hear the message playing out. 'Hi, Karina, it's Angela here from social services – I've just seen the press and I wanted to, ahem, make sure everything is all right.' Oh, God. I can't listen to any more. I hurry up the stairs to Devika's bedroom again. She is sitting clutching a teddy, pulling at his ear, looking quiet. The worst thing is that I know she feels she is in some way to blame. And it's not her fault, not her fault at all – it's all mine. I am officially the world's worst mother.

But how the *fuck* was I supposed to know Liam was going to *put a joint in her lunch box*?

I keep rewinding the moment. After the concert, Liam and I woke up yesterday morning on the floor of my bedroom. We looked at each other and groaned. As we sat up, smoothing our rumpled and torn clothes, a beer can rolled across the floor. Then I felt a weight on my foot and realised the guitarist had fallen asleep with his head sprawled over my ankle. I gently kicked him away.

Then Devika crept into the room. To my guilty amazement, she had got up and dressed herself in her school uniform. She came over and gave me an excited kiss; I could see she was still fired up from the concert.

'Mummy – I need to go now,' she said. 'I'm going to be late. And I need my lunch box.'

'I'll go,' Liam said.

'Oh, you don't have to,' I protested feebly.

'No, I'll go,' he said, giving me a dazed kiss. I remember he pulled away, his eyes bloodshot but tender. I remember thinking, *oh my God, I can't believe how lucky I am – my partner is a wild rock star who will also volunteer to take the kids to school when I have a thumping hangover.*

If only I had insisted. If only I had packed it; if only I had gone. If only, if only, if only.

I wasn't in yesterday when Devika was at school. I'd popped out to get a Starbucks in the hope that it might ease my headache. I was tired and my hair smelt of smoke and my temples were pounding but I was still on a high. I found myself tipping the waiter, hazily humming songs from the concert, replaying moments of our dancing and kissing in front of the crowd. Every so often, I took a sip of my coffee and a smile would break over my face.

I left the coffee shop. Autumn had finally arrived, stinging the air and smoking the sky. I thought how enjoyable it would be to share my first autumn with Devika. Liam and I could take her looking for conkers, and then there would be bonfire night – maybe we could even have our own firework display in the back garden. I pulled my coat tight about myself, joyfully breathing in the cold air, and drifted through some vintage shops. I bought a pale pink dress covered in beautiful winking beads, my head filled with romantic dreams of some forties-themed event that Liam and I would be invited to. I would wear this dress and he'd wear an old-fashioned suit and we'd waltz together across a misty dance floor. Smiling, I wandered back home. I even had a grin for the paps loitering outside the house.

The moment I got in, I realised something was wrong.

'Why is Devika home so early?' I asked, taking off my coat.

'Er, you'd better ask Devika about that,' Liam muttered. 'I'm just, er, popping out for a bit.'

The expression on his face. I can't forget it. It was one of pure guilt. It shocked me to the core. I just stood there numbly as he left the house, tugging Rufus after him. I knew then he'd done something terrible. At that point I was convinced he had another woman, that maybe he was planning to leave me for Hayley after all. It was a few minutes before I could struggle past the dread in my heart and ask Devika herself why she was home early.

That was only yesterday afternoon. Less than twenty-four hours ago. And now it's Friday morning and my life has changed for ever.

A few hours later, Angela from social services comes over for an emergency meeting. Before she arrives, I tell Devika over and over, 'You didn't have a joint in your lunch box, okay? You didn't have one.' Devika nods, wide-eyed, looking scared. Then I practise speeches in front of the mirror, adopting a light-hearted, brisk Mary Poppins tone: 'There's no truth in the rumours – it was just the press as usual. Devika and I are going to make butterfly cakes now and then we'll read a story together.'

The doorbell rings and I let Angela in, giving the press foul looks as they snap us.

'Hi.' I beam a superwatt smile at her. 'Come in. D'you want some camomile tea? I know it's your favourite.' I hastily pour a cup for her in the kitchen. 'And would you like a biscuit? Here, Devika, give Angela a biscuit.'

'Karina, calm down,' Angela says gently. 'Just tell

me the truth, okay?' She opens up her folder and clicks her biro, ready to write an official report.

'Er – nothing happened,' I say brightly. 'I have no idea what the press were on about.'

'Oh, thank goodness.' Angela looks relieved. 'I was worried for a moment.' She makes some notes in her neat script. 'Of course, I will have to speak to the headmistress of the school and just check everything is fine.'

'Oh,' I say in a small voice.

'Oh?' Angela echoes me, raising an eyebrow.

Suddenly I feel exhausted with keeping up this insane act.

'Oh, God,' I say, my voice breaking. 'The story's true – but it's not nearly as bad as they're saying. Yes, Devika found a joint in her lunch box but Liam put it there and she took it straight to the teacher – nothing happened.'

Angela looks white with shock. She takes a huge gulp of camomile tea. Then another one. I keep on ranting, spewing explanations, apologies, excuses. Devika looks scared, sensing that things aren't going well. I put my arm round her and hold her tight. She nuzzles against me and says sorry for the fiftieth time and for the fiftieth time I tell her it's not her fault.

'Will I have to go back to India?' she asks, looking sad.

'No, of course not,' I insist, squeezing her tight.

Angela stares at us and sees the look on my face. My terror that I might lose Devika; the thought fills me with so much pain I can barely stand it. She bites her lip, her expression softening.

'Look,' she says to me, 'I'll be honest – this isn't good. But I can write you a more favourable report if you assure me that Liam is no longer going to be a part of Devika's life. It's clear that whilst you care for her very much, Liam doesn't.'

'I love Liam,' Devika interjects, her eyes filling with tears.

Angela looks surprised, then shakes her head.

'Karina?' she asks me in a warning voice. I hold Devika's hand tightly and nod my head.

'I swear to you that he won't go near her again.'

I have to get through this. I have to keep my daughter. I have to make my choice.

I pick up the phone to call Liam.

I've tried a few times over the weekend and he hasn't replied; I know he's hiding away in shame. When he finally picks up, I feel surprised and my heart turns over.

There is a silence.

'D'you want to come over for a chat?' I ask quietly.

*   *   *

Oh, God. I don't want to do this. I watch Liam get out of his car. He scythes through the press, his face shielded by sunglasses, his face set. Every time I see him, I remember how much I love him. The ruthless bravery that he manages to muster as he holds his head high despite the jeers of the press cuts my heart. *He put a joint in your daughter's lunch box*, I keep repeating sternly. *Toughen up, Karina*. I run to the front door and open it. Liam kicks away a photographer who's actually trying to barge into the hallway. Then he turns to me. The angry speech I've been rehearsing disappears instantly. Without even thinking, we fall into each other's arms and hold each other tight. I try to draw away several times, but Liam holds on, pulling me back in, his chin jutting hard into my shoulder.

Finally, he lets me go. I smile at him sadly and he gives me a gruff smile back.

'How's Devika?'

'She's back at school,' I say. 'She's not going to be excluded, thank God.'

The look of relief on his face is unbearably touching. Then I remind myself: *toughen up*.

'After all, it wasn't her fault. The head and the teachers were more concerned about us.'

The relief on his face turns to guilt again. His eyes harden.

'It's over, isn't it?' he bursts out. 'Your agent and all

your friends have told you to dump me, haven't they?'

'Well—' I break off, seeing the letterbox open as a sly reporter slips a mike in. I grab Liam's hand and lead him up the stairs to my bedroom. I yank the curtains closed and then we sit down on the floor, by the bed, our legs out in front of us. I've been in such a state of shock, I still haven't cleared up fully since the party. There are still some rumpled beer cans lying in the corners; a reminder of that fatal night.

We sit in silence for a moment and then he says: 'It was an accident – you know that, don't you?'

'I realised that.' I squeeze his hand gently.

'I mean – I keep going over and over it in my mind. Seriously, Karina. I was in the kitchen and I saw that one of the guys in the band had rolled a joint at some point in the party and left it right in the middle of the kitchen table. I mean – here's the fucking irony – I thought, fuck, what if Devika got hold of that? So I picked it up and in a kind of panic I just put the stupid fucking thing in the fridge. So then I make Devika breakfast . . . and once she's had her Rice Krispies, she reminds me about her lunch box. I go back to the fridge but there's nothing to put in her sandwich. I get the joint out, thinking I can't leave it there, and I've got an Innocent smoothie in one hand and the joint in the other . . . I can just see myself standing in the kitchen – and I put one in my pocket and one in her lunch box. I mean – fuck.'

As I picture the moment, my heart seizes up. But then I remind myself that we have to be honest with ourselves. Really, this was no accident.

'There shouldn't have been a party here in the first place,' I say firmly. 'If there hadn't been, there wouldn't have been any joints, and we wouldn't have had hangovers.'

'Devika was dancing!' Liam shoots back. 'She was enjoying herself! I mean, God, it's better than those fucked-up school kids who go to private schools and have nannies and play chess at weekends and vomit up encyclopaedias for their exams.'

Exasperation fills me. Can't he see that those kids aren't going to school with drugs in their lunch boxes, in danger of being excluded?

'But Liam, we made an agreement,' I cry fiercely. 'I said things had to change between us. You didn't change at all. We have just carried on like the old days. I can't do this with you, don't you see that? And it's too late for you to say you'll change – you won't—'

'I can, I will—'

'I know you won't, Liam. I mean, you – you . . .' my voice is laced with tears, 'I actually don't want you to change. You are you and you are wonderful. You should just stay you. But it won't work for us.'

I try to draw my hand away but he holds on tightly.

'You say you don't think I can change – but I don't believe you can either, Karina,' he says passionately. 'You're not some suburban yummy mummy either. If you were, we'd never have got together. You can't change either—'

'That's not true,' I reply angrily. 'I *can* change, because Devika needs me to and I love her.'

'But what about me?'

I shake my head, biting my lip, unable to say the words.

'So you're saying it's over?'

'The thing is, Liam – you've forgotten that I'm not Devika's mum yet. I'm her guardian. We had that assessment, which you nearly ruined by being high on coke, and I saw Angela on Friday and she was *not* happy – she says I have to keep you away from Devika. I've got the police coming over later to interview me as well and I'm going to have to bullshit like mad. And you – you cannot be here. I have to tell them you've gone for good. Can't you see that I could lose her? And that would break my heart.'

'I'm sorry,' Liam says. 'I'm so sorry.'

'You've got to leave,' I say, with more conviction. 'You've got to.'

Liam stares at me, his eyes liquid with tears of remorse. Tears begin to slip down my cheeks too.

Then I hear my mobile shrill. I tear my hand away from his. It could be the police, my agent, Angela. Ignoring Liam's howl of rage, I answer it.

'You are fucking joking!' Liam cries.

'Karina,' my agent says in a deep, excited voice, 'I've arranged something for you that is going to solve *everything* – I've negotiated for you to have your own reality TV show, right in your home, showing just how well you and Devika bond together—'

'Reality TV?' My head is now spinning. 'Well, I'm not really sure—'

'Reality TV?' Liam shouts. He grabs the phone, swears at my agent, then throws it across the room. 'No!' he cries, as I go after it. 'Leave it there. Karina. Please. We just have to forget this circus for a moment and talk, okay? We—'

He is interrupted by the shrill of the doorbell. I go over to the curtains and peel them back a centimetre. The throng of reporters is now spilling out into the road. A neighbour toots his horn angrily as he has to swerve round them to park his car.

'Come over here,' Liam says in an intense voice. He grabs my hands and pulls me over to him, looking deep into my eyes. 'We have to forget them and focus on us. What matters. I know I've been shit. I know this is my fault. But I love you. I love you so much.'

I feel stunned. In all these years, this is the first time he has ever said those three words. Yes, he's come close before. I've been the love of his life, his angel, his inspiration. He's told me he loves being with me, loves having sex with me. But never those words.

'Oh, Liam,' I cry, 'I don't know, I . . .'

He leans in, resting his forehead against mine, his breath warm and urgent on my salty lips.

'Look. I know what we do,' he whispers fiercely. 'We tell your agent, all your friends, everyone, that we've broken up for good. And I'll go away – I'll go to rehab. There. You know how much I hate that fucking shithole. But I'll do it for you. I'll go away and clean up and come back so squeaky clean I won't even touch a fag. And then maybe they'll see me differently. And whilst I'm there, we can still speak, we can text, Jesus, we can even write like some old-fashioned fucking Romeo and Juliet. We can be together in secret. Until they're ready for us again.'

'I don't know.' I gulp back tears. 'I just don't know.'

'Come on, Karina,' he says urgently. 'Come on. We can't break up. We're meant to be together.'

I look up into his eyes, blinking hard. 'You promise you'll change? You promise you'll go to rehab?'

His eyes declare his devotion. I smile, bite it back, smile again. Crying with relief, Liam folds me into his arms and squeezes me tightly. Then he kisses me, and we taste each other's tears, whispering promises, concocting the lies we will tell everyone . . .

36

Karina

What the hell am I doing here?

I'm sitting in a white room, wearing a gown, about to go under anaesthetic. I feel as though I'm floating about in a mad bubble and any minute now it will break and someone will appear and cry, 'It was all a dream!'

My mobile rings; it's Devika. She's staying with Clare for one day and night whilst I'm here. She wanted to be with Kelly, but I told her it wasn't a good idea. I couldn't bear to tell Devika that Kelly's mother has called me and said our daughters must never mix again.

'Mummy Karina?' she asks. 'You won't die, will you?'

'Don't be silly, darling,' I say. 'I'll see you tomorrow.

Your mummy will look pretty. And then we'll be home together.'

'Okay. I miss you.'

'I miss you, my darling.'

'I miss Liam. And Rufus.'

'Don't worry, darling, Adi's looking after Rufus,' I say. I don't mention his owner.

We chat a little longer and she tells me that Clare let her have Rice Krispies for lunch on the condition that she drank a glass of wheatgerm juice.

'She thought I drank the juice,' Devika confides, 'but I poured it in her plant. Now her plant is happy.'

I burst into laughter and Devika laughs too. For a moment it's as though all the bad things are forgotten and we laugh and laugh in glorious euphoria. Then a nurse appears in the doorway, beckoning me forward. As I say goodbye to Devika and stand up, I can't help wanting to tear off my gown and run out of this place, into the Kent countryside and the sunshine and normal life. It's weird: I've been wanting to do this for five years, putting it off, pondering it, saving up, and now, now that I'm finally doing it, I just feel empty.

In two weeks' time, you see, my reality TV show will begin. A team of men will already have invaded the house and started wiring cameras into every sodding room – except the bathroom. The show will be called *A Modern Mum* and it will show just how wonderful Devika and I can be together.

I had severe doubts about it all, but my agent kept calling me night and day to tell me I should go for it. And when I saw the piece in the *Daily Mail* entitled *Is Karina the Worst Mum in England?*, along with a phone line for readers to call and vote, I decided I had no choice. But ever since I've agreed to it, I've been fraught with neuroses. You can't imagine how terrifying the thought of the public seeing into every corner of your house is. I've had cleaners in to scrub it from top to bottom. I've taken down my black and white photos of Liam and me on the beach at Brighton and replaced them with tasteful Monet reproductions. And it's not just the house. It's the thought of people seeing me in my dressing gown. Or catching close-ups of my cellulite. I've already realised I'll never be able to take my make-up off – I'll have to keep it on every night, which'll be bloody bad for my pores. And, worst of all, my nose.

I lay awake nearly all last night picturing it. The camera zooming in from the left, the right, above, below, capturing my awful beaky, crooked, bent, horrible, deformed nose. And that was when I realised that before the reality show started, I had to transform.

My new nose would symbolise a fresh start.

'You are insane,' Clare told me, when I asked her

to look after Devika. 'You're just madly stressed – God, if I was going through what you are, I'd probably be having a nervous breakdown. But really – a new nose!'

At the time, it felt as though a new nose would somehow solve all my problems. I'd go under the knife and emerge with a brand-new face, and I'd feel confident and beautiful, and shine and shimmer before the cameras.

But in truth, as I walk down the corridors towards the operating theatre, I just wish Devika and Liam were here.

Liam. Over the past few weeks, he's showered me with texts and calls, even a postcard. It made me laugh – it was a picture of his rehab centre, over which he had scrawled in biro *Wish You Were Here*. But I've felt myself see-sawing between my heart and my head. Sometimes when I've thought about the tearful promises we made to each other, they seem silly and impractical and I've ignored his texts, feeling it can never work between us. And then sometimes I've found myself missing him really badly and I've pictured him in a bare room, puking into a bucket, curling up in a shaking ball, feeling I've deserted him in the most difficult time of his life. I've reminded myself that he's going through his hell for me and I've called him up or texted him. I've been scared my hot/cold behaviour might unsettle him but he seems grateful for any contact I make, for any drop of love I give him.

I think of him as I lie down on the operating table, as the gas pumps through me and the face of the surgeon above me begins to blur. I picture him, sitting in a room in a gown just like me, feeling lonely and confused and a bit foolish. All the crazy events of the last few weeks splinter into kaleidoscope pieces that dance in my mind: Devika, the joint, the parties, the press, the fights, the madness. I think about his sweet kisses, the way he once sang to me and told me I was the love of his life . . . and then black roses fill my mind and I'm lost to the world.

It's a relief to escape it.

When I meet Devika the next day, I'm not quite prepared for how strong her reaction is.

I think she was probably expecting that I would pick her up from Clare's with a nice fresh straight nose, easy as buying a new dress and putting it on. She probably didn't envisage the bruises or the bandages or my tired, weak face.

Naturally, the paps did and as we pull up outside Clare's house I tug a jumper over my face. The trouble with hiding from paps, though, is that it's quite hard to actually see when you're wearing dark glasses and a jumper on top of them. I collide with the edge of

Clare's garden wall, stumble up the path and then collapse against her door, banging hard and shouting, 'Let me in, let me in!'

Clare lets me in and tries to hug me, but gets so nervous about knocking my bandages that we have to resort to air-kissing.

Then I kneel down, ready to give Devika a hug as she comes down the stairs. We've only been apart a day but I've missed her so much!

When she sees me, however, she stops short and stares with moon eyes. Horror fills her face. She bursts into noisy sobs.

'What is it?' I cry, hurrying up the stairs to her side. 'What is it, darling?'

'Mummy's had her nose taken away. Mummy lost her nose,' she weeps.

Clare begins to giggle, until I shoot her a look.

'Take them off,' Devika cries, reaching up for the plaster.

'No!' I say vehemently, swatting her hand away, scared my nose really might come off with it. I hear Clare smothering more laughter and my cheeks burn.

Then I have a brainwave. I remember the book they gave me in my goodbye 'care' pack when I left the clinic.

I open up my suitcase and rummage about inside to pull it out. It's called *My Beautiful Mommy*, by a man called Dr Michael Salzhauer, who felt he needed to help the Hollywood mummies who were perpetually going under the knife. It explains, in simple language for children, the steps of Mummy's magical transformation from an ugly caterpillar who emerges from her cocoon of bandages to become a beautiful butterfly.

When we get to the final page, Devika looks at the picture, then at me, her swollen eyes flitting back and forth.

'You promise you're going to be a butterfly?' she asks.

'I promise,' I assure her, putting my arm round her and giving her a squeeze. 'A butterfly with the nicest nose in the world.'

Devika and I take refuge in Clare's house that night. I tell her it's because I want to hide from the paps. But the real reason is that whilst I was in the clinic the team from Channel 4 was given free access to my house in order to wire in the cameras. The thought of them sitting in my home, their muted eyes ready to switch on and watch me, makes me feel uneasy; I'm scared they might turn them on early for the mileage of filming me taking off my bandages and proving that I've had a nose job.

Because if you're a celebrity and anyone ever asks you if you've had plastic surgery, you have to say no. Really. It's just part of the shame. It's bad enough admitting to yourself that you've had to pay several thousand quid for someone to take a scalpel to your face, let alone the public.

So I decide I will stay at Clare's until my nose is ready.

Later that evening, when I'm sitting up in bed with Devika, reading to her, trying to ignore the pain in my septum, a sense of unease comes over me. There was a story in the newspapers this morning about how Devika was buried alive when she was a baby. Even though Devika's been with me for four months now, we've never discussed this. Early on, Mrs Raju warned me that Devika thinks she was buried because her parents mistakenly thought she was dead, not because they wanted to murder her. I've felt that to bring it up would be too traumatic. And I'm reluctant to now, except that if every newspaper in the country is covering my TV show, what if one of her friends picks up on the story? How dreadful it would be for Devika to learn the truth via playground gossip.

I see Devika's yawning and decide to try to broach the subject before she nods off.

'Devika,' I say delicately. 'I want to talk to you about how you were born.'

'I know how babies are born,' she scoffs. 'People have sex. You don't need to tell me a birds and bees story.'

Now I'm taken aback. How come Devika knows

about sex? I had no idea about sex when I was eleven . . . I didn't find out until I was at least twenty. Well, nearly, anyway.

Devika grins up at me and suddenly I can't bear to tell her. I don't want to ruin her happiness and her innocence. She has blossomed since coming to England, despite all the disasters at school and the mess with Liam; I don't want her heart to wither with the shock. Later, I tell myself, much later I'll tell her, and in the meantime I'll just have to protect her from the press.

Well, here I am.

Tonight is the night.

The night over ten million viewers will switch on their TV sets and see me and Devika. My house is spotless; I've laid the table; I've cooked up a gorgeous meal of rice and dhal and I'm about to prove to the world just what a wonderful mother I can be. I let out a deep breath and my eyes flit to the clock. Six o'clock. It's time. There are no Big Brother-style loudspeaker warnings telling us when the cameras are on or setting any rules. We just have to be entertaining and funny and perfect – and completely natural, of course.

Devika sits down at the table. She pulls a faint grimace when she sees the rice. I know she would prefer rice that comes out of a cereal box with a snap, crackle and pop but I've explained to her that we need to have proper food whilst we're being filmed. Which I actually think is a good thing – it might encourage us both to eat more healthily.

'Hmm, isn't this good?' I say, chewing discreetly.

'Yeah, I guess,' Devika says in a quiet voice. Her eyes keep flitting to the camera and I give her a little signal not to stare at it too obviously, or we won't look natural.

'I think it's delicious.'

'Yeah.'

'I mean, rice is just so healthy. It's good for us to sit down together as a family every evening and eat it.'

Devika is now looking at me as though I'm from another planet.

'Don't forget your cod liver oil capsules. And we've got yummy rice pudding for dessert.'

'Wow,' Devika says in a flat voice.

'Devika!' I whisper under my breath.

And then she gets nervous. She drops her knife and – Sod's law – instead of landing on the floor and making a yellow splatter, it has to go and ladder her school tights and slice her leg.

'Mummy!' Devika lets out a scream.

Oh my God. Oh my God. We've only been on camera for thirty seconds and already my daughter is welling up blood! What if someone turns on the TV right now and this is all they see?

'Okay, it's okay,' I cry, kneeling down in front of her and trying to obscure the cut from the cameras. 'It's tiny.' I dab it with a piece of kitchen cloth and the flower of blood that wells through panics me.

'Plaster, plaster,' Devika pants.

'Plasters! Okay, I'll get the plasters.'

Shit. Do I have any plasters? Oh God, please let me have plasters in the house. Yes, I do, I do – in the bathroom cabinet. I run up the stairs, tripping a few times, fling open the cabinet, yank out the plasters and bandages and then tumble back down the staircase. When I reach Devika, the blood is dribbling down her leg and she's still crying.

'It won't stop bleeding, Mummy.'

'It's all right – sometimes a small cut can bleed a lot but it won't do any harm, I promise.' I clean it up and seal a plaster over it.

And, thank God, it looks all right.

Of course, by then our meal has gone cold and Devika doesn't want to eat it. As I shovel it into the bin, I can picture the accusations: *Karina is encouraging her daughter to become anorexic . . .*

For the rest of the evening, I act as though her cut is cancer. I pamper her and fuss over her and make her hot drinks and shower her with kisses.

Devika enjoys all the attention, though even she begins to look a little tired of it after a while. Do I look as though I'm spoiling her? But I want to spoil her in front of the world, to show how much I love her.

When I check my mobile later that evening, I see a flood of texts.

Stop behaving like a Stepford mother! Fran has texted.

Blood nice touch – good drama – suggest more bloody incidents? – my agent.

I miss you, K. Why aren't u replying to my texts? – **Liam.**

I stare at his text, my heart aching. Then I suddenly panic. What if one of the cameras zooms in on it? I quickly delete it and don't dare to reply.

37

Devika

I run into the bathroom and lock the door behind me. I can hear Mummy K – Mum – banging on it, but I ignore her. She promised me there are no cameras in the bathroom, otherwise I would have to go to the toilet or bath with all my clothes on. This is the one safe place in the house.

I hate our reality TV show. I hate it, I hate it, I HATE IT.

I have decided that I will stay in the bathroom and not come out. Mrs Raju once told me a story about Gandhi. He stopped the British being mean and violent to the Indians by telling everyone to practise *passive resistance*, which is a way of saying no without having to fight with your fists. Well, I will do the same. I will stay here until all the camera eyes have been smashed and they cannot see me any more.

I sit on the floor and open up my school bag. I open my exercise book and try to start on my homework. We have been given lots of different numbers to add up.

17 + 43 = ?

I try to make the numbers click together, but I can't stop all the voices from school filling up my mind. I hear the other children the first day after the reality TV show started. All the girls were crying things like: 'Can I be your friend, Devika?' 'Can I come to tea at your house, so we can be on TV together?' 'Can I sit next to you in class?'

Then I hear the voices that came a week later. Kelly and Regina laughing at me for calling my mum 'Mummy Karina'. They kept teasing me and calling me 'Mummy Devika' until the name spread like fire and everyone in the class started calling me that. Then I hear Mrs H saying to me, 'I didn't realise how much your mother helps you with your homework. It should be *your* work, Devika, not hers.' I tried to tell her that Mummy Karina – Mum – doesn't normally help that much, she was just acting like that to look extra special and caring on TV. But Mrs H didn't believe me. Then she got even more angry when some men with cameras sneaked into the playground and tried to film our class through the window.

'Film me! Film me!' Regina cried, standing up on her chair. Then Kelly did the same and they both wriggled in a little dance.

'Regina! Kelly! Sit down right this instant!' Mrs H shouted and then she went to tell the cameramen off. They looked quite scared, as though they'd just been told they were excluded.

Then when Mrs H came back into the classroom she gave me a look, as though I'd asked them to come. But they must have followed me. Now every time I walk anywhere I'm scared they will suddenly turn up and I'll get into trouble.

17 + 43 = ?

Now I really need to do my homework but I don't want to sit at the table downstairs. If I do, Mum will come over and try to help me. She'll look good for the cameras but I'll look stupid. And if I tell her not to do it, she looks upset. Now that she's made Liam go, she seems sad and lonely. She keeps making me hug her, but she holds on tight as though I'm her mummy and she wants me to make her feel better. And sometimes she holds me so tight I just want to push her away and run and run out of the house.

I try to focus on my numbers but my tummy starts to cry out. I want to go to the kitchen, but all I will be given to eat is a piece of celery, which tastes like green water, or a piece of carrot, which takes like red wood.

I'm not allowed Rice Krispies any more. Mummy says the newspapers don't like them because they aren't proper food and she looks like a bad mummy. She acts as though the newspapers are God.

I feel a tear beginning to squeeze out of one eye, but I push it back in. Even though there are no cameras in here, I'm scared one might be secretly peering through the window. I don't understand why we have to do this. I don't understand why Mummy Karina can't make them all go away.

17 + 43 = ?

I feel as though the white walls of the bathroom are closing in on me. I see my rubber duck sitting on the edge of the bath. I feel as if he's laughing at me. I don't know if he likes me or not. I don't know if Kelly likes me any more or not; one day she's nice to me, the next she's on Regina's side. I don't know if the other girls like me or if they just want to be on TV, if Mrs H likes me or will throw me out of school, if Liam loves me still or will never come to see us again. I don't know who I am or what I should do to make the newspapers happy with us. I pick up the duck as though someone is seizing hold of my arm and then I throw him across the room.

He hits the wall and falls to the floor with a quack.

Then I feel mean and horrible. I jump up, planning

to go and make him feel better, and notice that the cabinet over the sink is open a little bit. I open it fully and stare inside. I feel the same force trying to take hold of my arm and bring everything smashing and crashing to the floor, the bottles of shampoo and the hairbands and the little razors and the twiddly things you use to clean your ears. But I bunch up my fists and tell it to stop.

Then I see a box. I take it out of the cabinet and read the label.

Super Blonde.

I have seen Mummy K – Mum – put this on her hair. I always thought her hair grew gold, like the sun. Then I saw some photographs of her when she was a little girl. I know her real hair is the colour of mud and she puts this on to make men like her. She told me once that Liam didn't like her with hair the colour of mud.

Maybe people would like me if I had hair like sunshine.

I open the bottle and nearly drop it. It smells sharp, like lemons. It also smells of something nasty. I stare at my hair in the mirror. Mummy Karina is always brushing it out and plaiting it and telling me how beautiful it is. I think of how angry she would be if I turned it yellow and I get a funny, happy feeling in my tummy. Maybe my hair will look horrible but then maybe the cameras will stop.

I look at the bottle and try to read the instructions, but I don't get them all. So I just try to remember what Mummy Karina does. I know she makes her hair wet, then she puts it on, then she leaves it a while, then she washes it off.

I run water over my hair and then I squeeze the bottle on to it. A big whitey blob comes out. I wince again – it smells so gross, as Kelly would say. But I keep putting it on until there are whitey blobs all over my hair. Then I push it behind my back and sit down and do my sums. I find I have suddenly stopped worrying and I do them really quickly. Or maybe they make me feel better because when I have to think about the numbers I don't have to think about how my hair will look.

'Devika!' Mum bangs on the door again. 'Devika, are you okay?'

Silence. I'm scared she might break the door down.

'I'm okay,' I say back.

'Will you come out and have some tea?'

'Soon,' I say.

Silence. I can feel her waiting by the door, I can feel her unhappiness swirling through in waves. Then I hear her footsteps as she goes away.

I jump up and pour water into the sink. I put my head into it and swirl the water through. But when I look in the mirror, I don't look right. My hair is still wet, but some bits look dark and some bits look white.

I get another scared feeling in my tummy, but I can't stop giggling. Mummy Karina is going to be so mad at me.

I open the bathroom door and step out on to the landing.

'Mummy Karina?' I call down to her. My voice sounds weak, I'm so nervous.

'Devika?' She stands at the bottom of the stairs. Then her face goes white and her voice turns angry. 'What the *hell* have you done to your hair?'

I stand firm as she runs up the stairs, even though I feel like crying. I stare up at her and say in a fierce voice: 'It's called passive resistance.'

38

Karina

Passive resistance. *Passive resistance*. What Devika doesn't understand is that we're in this war together. In my heart of hearts, I'm on her side. I know that signing up for this stupid show was a mistake. And yes, what I'd really like to do is go round smashing every camera in the house. But the situation just isn't that simple.

I did try calling my agent. I dropped Devika off at school and then speeded away to Clare's house. The camera team followed me and tried to come in too. Clare, however, was wonderful and fierce. She told them where she'd stuff her carrot cake if they so much as dared to cross the threshold. Her tone was convincing. They stayed in their cars.

Clare's house has become my safe house. I can't

tell you what a relief it was to collapse on to her sofa. To know that nobody was watching me. To be able to burp and fart and curse and sigh. To allow expressions to flit across my face. Over the past few weeks I've controlled my expressions with such care, I've had newspaper columnists declare that I must be having Botox injections. But I'm scared of frowning at the wrong moment and looking as if I'm scolding Devika.

Clare immediately leaps on her cordless phone and thrusts it into my hand.

'Call your agent *now*! Tell him to put an end to this madness, Karina.'

'But I need the public to see I'm a good mother,' I recite in a pale parrot voice.

'Karina!' she snaps.

I cave in in relief, desperately glad that she is forcing me to do what I've lacked the courage to do myself.

'I need to get out of this show,' I beg my agent. 'I need it all to stop. *Please.*'

He replies in a surprisingly gentle tone. 'I know this is harder than you thought it would be. And by the way, I do think your new nose looks just great. It was a fantastic move . . .'

'Yes, but—'

'There's just the issue of your contract.'

Contract. That's the word he keeps bringing up,

with more force each time. He binds it round my neck like a noose. If I stop now, they will sue me. Probably for millions. I might even lose my house. And then where would Devika and I end up?

'Come on, Karina,' he cajoles me. 'The show is a huge ratings success.'

'A ratings success! But people hate me. They're turning on to pick on every little thing I do so they can then leap on it and declare what a bad mother I am. Everyone's just put me in that box and *you* said this show would change everything but it's just made it worse. If I help Devika with her home-work, they say I'm interfering. If I teach her English words, all the bloody multicultural columnists say I'm patronising her – God, there was even a *Guardian* column implying I was somehow racist. If I tell her off, I'm evil. If I don't, I'm letting her get away with murder.'

'But don't you see,' my agent interrupts glee-fully, 'this is why it's all so brilliant! This is pure zeitgeist stuff. You've come along at a particular moment in time when society is hysterical about children being overprotected or violent or ill-educated. Everyone is asking how children can be brought up better. And you, Karina, are at the centre of that debate! You're not just being discussed in *Heat*, you're even going to be on *Newsnight Review*!'

'Oh no. Please, no!' I cry, close to tears.

I can already picture it: Germaine Greer, her face pinched in disapproval, crying, 'This Karina West woman – she's just pathetic, isn't she? Pathetic. *Pathetic.*'

And then they'd dissect my behaviour according to current feminist literary post-modern theory and decide that I was a perfect example of the terrible modern working celebrity-driven single-but-confused-in-love mother.

'The only thing I'm not sure about,' my agent cuts in, 'are those pink streaks. The nose job was great, like I said. But the pink streaks . . . I think they're a no-no.'

My agent is right. The pink streaks I sprayed into my hair are dreadful. But when I saw what Devika had done to hers, I actually cried. Her natural hair was so beautiful – long and dark, soft as silk. The dye had blotted badly and left her with yellowy blotches and stripes like some kind of skunk. I told her that we must dye it back black at once. But she said no. She said she would only dye it black when the cameras were turned off.

I felt anger and love storm through my heart. I couldn't believe that she was trying to manipulate me in this way, but I could also see that the show was making her unhappy. With a burst of determination, I went out to the shops and bought a load of black dyes, convinced that after a day of teasing at school Devika would change her mind and beg me to turn it back.

That was when I saw the pink sprays and acted on impulse.

When Devika came home and saw the pink streaks in my hair, she did actually laugh. And then she looked sulky. And then she laughed some more.

'Mum, you look silly.'

But the tactic did work. By copying her, I wrong-footed the press and the public. It diffused the impact of Devika's rebellion. Suddenly it looked as though we were both behaving like teenagers and conducting mad hair experiments on our hair together. As though it was all intentional.

'I think the strategy is insane,' Clare told me. 'I mean, what happens if Devika starts rebelling in all sorts of ways? What if . . . say . . . what if she goes and shoplifts a pencil – are you going to go and shoplift a skirt to follow suit?'

Clare isn't impressed either when I tell her my agent can't annul my contract. She just shakes her head and looks sorry for me. On the way back home, I feel an increasing sense of dread with every mile.

When we talked on the phone, my agent also reminded me that my contract states that I should be on film for at least eighty per cent of my waking day. So much as I'd love to just sneak off and go shopping in Covent Garden, or wander around a gallery, or spend an afternoon shopping with Fran, I have to either take a camera crew with me, or return to my prison. It's like being under bloody house arrest.

As I unlock the door and walk down the hallway, I feel slightly sick. My home is not my home any more. I make myself a cup of camomile tea and then sit down, closing my eyes. At least the one place they can't get into is my mind.

I can't help feeling that if Liam were here, none of this would have happened. For a start, he would never have let me agree to a reality TV show. Mind you, I was pretty determined about the idea. But even if I had forced him into it, I can't imagine that Devika would have ended up dyeing her hair. Liam would have diffused the tension by doing silly things on camera, turned it into a joke.

And it strikes me then that although Liam has been labelled as a terrible father and the joint fiasco was as scary as hell, he is actually really very paternal in many ways.

I realise that perhaps I'm not enough for Devika. Perhaps she needs both of us.

The thought makes me feel uncomfortable. I did send Liam a text or two, composed under my covers so the cameras couldn't see, to ask how rehab was going. But he didn't reply. I guess he hasn't forgiven me for cutting him off; I guess he never will.

I suddenly hear something bang against the window and I jump in fear. Is someone out there? A stalker? Some crazy nut who's seen the show and thinks I deserve a brick through my window? I recall uneasily the last words my agent spoke to me before we said goodbye today: 'We need a bit more drama in the show. We need to keep it coming. Night after night. I think I've got a little surprise which might jazz things up . . .'

It wouldn't surprise me if he has arranged for some stalker just to spice things up. But when I peer out of the French windows, the garden looks empty.

Devika and I eat dinner in silence. I ask her how her blond hair is going down at school and she shrugs. I ask her if she's got lots of homework to do and she shrugs.

Oh, God. I have to get out of this show. She could end up holding a grudge against me for life for this. There are only ten days more to go but they feel like ten years, stretching out before us . . .

We finish eating. She goes into the dining room to work and I do the washing up, wearing a smile on my face like a label on a bottle even though I feel like crying. I decide to log online. Every day the show's producers forward the hundreds and hundreds of emails I'm getting. They're meant to filter them so I only get the best (and the worst) ones.

Hi Karina, I'm a 33-year-old mother of four from Wolverhampton and I would like to say how brave I think you are for going on TV and showing everyone how hard it is to be a mum. All my life I have wanted to be on TV and escape my boring life (I work as a cleaner in Asda). I didn't get through the X Factor auditions or Big Brother, but I was just cleaning today when a brill idea struck me. Maybe you and I should do a life swap and you should come and live my boring life and I should come down and look after your Indian kid and live the life of a celebrity . . .

Hi Karina, I have greatly enjoyed watching your show. I don't know why it is but every time you put the rubbish out I watch the wind flapping through your dressing gown and I get an erection. I was wondering if you might be interested in going out to dinner. I am only a civilian, as they say, not a celebrity, but I assure you I have never taken drugs.

Dear Karina, We are writing to say we think you are a totally stupid cow and evil bitch. How can you let your daughter eat fish in the evenings? Don't you know that eating animals, even fish, is cruel and disgusting? We are revolted by your behaviour and we want you to STOP and think about the little fish and their feelings when you make your daughter eat them and corrupt her into thinking everyone in England does this.

Dear Karina, I seriously think you are putting the health of your child at risk by allowing her to wear manmade fibres. Several medical studies indicate that they can cause disease . . .

Oh. God, I want this show to end.

'Mummy,' I suddenly hear Devika calling, 'the doorbell rang.'

Did it? I was so engrossed that I didn't even hear it. I log off quickly, not wanting Devika to see any of the emails by accident.

'Mummy Karina!'

'Okay, I'm coming, I'm coming!'

I head down the hallway, wondering whether I will be able to face replying to any of them and what kind of benign, vague sentences I can muster up (*Thank you for your fascinating email. I was greatly interested in the points you made, but . . .*).

Then I open the front door, frowning. An elderly Indian man is standing on my doorstep.

'Hello,' he says, very slowly, struggling with his English. 'I am Devika's father.'

39

Karina

I stare at the man standing on my doorstep. He's quite elderly – in fact, he looks far too old to be the father of an eleven-year-old girl. He is wearing British clothes: olive-green trousers and a flowing striped shirt that doesn't match them. His back is slightly hunched. His face is wizened and blotted like an old brown apple; his dark eyes peer out from under folded lids, full of unexpected sweetness. For a minute, I suffer a strange jolt of recognition, for it's as though I'm staring into Devika's eyes.

Then I realise I'm searching for Devika in his face.

'I Mr Charduri. I Devika's father.'

I stare at him. What can I say? Is this a joke? A stunt that my agent has organised? (If so, he's fired.) My producers? Is this a hoax? Someone looking for fifteen minutes of fame and money? Capitalising on our success?

Beyond him I see a familiar car. Mrs Raju is sitting behind the wheel. My frown deepens. What the hell is she doing here? I can see her looking over, through the window, though I can't make out her expression. She seems to be gesturing.

Then Devika comes into the hallway.

I see Mr Charduri's face light up and a jealous anger suddenly grips me. What the hell are these people doing, playing around with my daughter's emotions? I shut the door quickly and turn to Devika.

'Who's he?' Devika asks.

I collapse on to the bottom of the stairs.

'Devika,' I say in a high voice, 'I need you to do me a favour. I need you to go up to your room and just wait for me there. Is that okay?' I tuck a strand of yellowy black hair behind her ear.

She nods her head slowly. I listen to her footsteps travel up the stairs. Then I hear her hovering on the landing.

'Devika,' I call up. 'Go to your room please, darling.'

A sulky sigh; then the click of her bedroom door shutting.

I open the front door again. Mr Charduri is still standing there, patient and still as my Buddha statue. I see Mrs Raju get out of her car and come up to the house.

'The producers asked me to come,' she says. 'So I can translate.'

I stare at both of them. Then I turn away from them and call my agent.

'Just what is going on?'

'Isn't this *so* exciting?' he cries. 'You see! I told you I had a surprise for you! And he's the real thing. We checked him out. His story adds up.'

'Well, how exactly did you check him out?'

'Karina, I think it will make much better television if you speak to him yourself.' And he hangs up.

I turn back to them.

'Okay,' I say. 'You can come in for twenty minutes. That's all. And then I never want to see you again. And please don't think you're going to see Devika. Don't call out her name or try anything.'

Mrs Raju looks startled by the vehemence in my voice. She translates rapidly to Mr Charduri. I feel a knot of tension in my stomach, and wait for him to shout at me or throw a tantrum. But he blinks. Nods. Remains calm.

Which somehow unsettles me even more.

The moment he comes into the house, I feel a sense of deep regret and unease, as though a dark cloud has drifted in and is now dispersing through the rooms.

In the living room, we all sit down. Mr Charduri

gathers together several cushions and bundles them behind his back.

There is a silence.

'Look,' I say. 'Even if you *are* Devika's father, how can you expect me to be glad to see you? You buried my daughter alive. You tried to kill her. By turning up here, you are basically handing yourself in as a child murderer.' I hear my voice rising helplessly. 'I mean, I could go and call the police.'

Mrs Raju translates nervously. Mr Charduri raises an eyebrow. He replies to her in slow Hindi.

'Mr Charduri has a request. He would like to explain everything in full. He'd like to tell you his life story.'

'All right,' I say, sitting down. 'All right. Tell me your story.'

Mr Charduri begins to speak in a low, mumbling voice. Every so often, he lifts his eyes to my face, assessing my reaction. Mrs Raju translates.

'Mr Charduri would like you to know that when Devika was born, he was delighted to have been given a beautiful little girl by the gods. Yes, he and his wife, Abha, had prayed for a boy. But Devika was their first child and they were so happy when she arrived. The rest of their household was not so happy, however. They lived all together, twelve Charduris, grandmother and grandfather, uncles and aunts and nephews, crammed into one small house in Shahpur Jat – one of the most deprived areas of Delhi. And Mr Charduri's brother was particularly angry when Devika came along. His brother blamed Mr Charduri for the collapse of his business, for bad advice and for encouraging him to take out a loan he could not afford to pay back. He was now working as a rickshaw driver and he was exhausted by the long hours and his health was at risk. He had a strong appetite and he was always hungry. He saw the arrival of Devika as the last straw. She would be another mouth to feed, which meant less food for the rest of them. The rage burning inside him erupted. He took her one night without permission. He took her out into the fields and buried her alive and when he came back he said that he had done what was right.'

I swallow, stunned by this turn of events. All these months, I've secretly hated Devika's father, pictured him as some grotesque man who tried to kill his baby. And now I'm hearing a completely different version of events.

If this is the truth. Perhaps it's just a good story.

'Mr Charduri and his wife Abha wept and wept when they heard the news. They screamed and shouted and threatened to go to the police. They ordered him to bring her back. But when they all went out to the fields to look for her, she had gone. They searched around the neighbourhood and the local orphanage but nobody had seen her. The man who found Devika must have lived outside Shahpur Jat, and taken her out into another part of Delhi.

'After the loss of Devika, Abha fell ill with tuberculolis. It was a terrible thing. She began spitting up blood and weeping. She told Mr Charduri that she felt she was being punished for not waking when her daughter was being stolen from her. Mr Charduri, however, feels she died of a broken heart. For within six months of losing his baby, he also lost his wife.'

I look into Mr Charduri's eyes and I can't help it; I feel tears welling up inside.

'Since then, Mr Charduri has lived an empty life. He has not married again. He worked as rickshaw driver for some time, until one day, by chance, a distant cousin came to Delhi and looked him up. His cousin had emigrated to London and enjoyed success setting up a packaging company. He offered Mr Charduri a chance to come over and see a new culture, a new country.

'Imagine his surprise when one day he turns on the TV and looks into Devika's eyes. He says that he recognised her at once, by her eyes. He knew for certain that he was watching his daughter on screen. He thought it was a miracle. And then he told himself it was impossible – for how could his lost daughter, buried alive in the fields of New Delhi, suddenly turn up alive and well in England?

'But he has this photo. And when he looked at the screen and the photo, he kept telling himself that there could be no doubt. It was her.'

Mr Charduri takes the photograph out of his pocket with a shaking hand and passes it over to me. I let out a gasp. My heart starts to stutter. I can't deny the similarity: The same dark eyes, innocent and beautiful, almond-shaped, fringed with thick lashes. Those dimples, those ears that stick out slightly, those full lips.

Then, seeing Mr Charduri watching me closely, I hide my reaction quickly and frown.

'What about some other proof?' I ask. 'A birth certificate, for example?'

Mr Charduri shakes his head, spreading his hands.

'She was born at home; he couldn't afford a hospital,' Mrs Raju explains. 'There are thousands of children born in India without a birth certificate. Mr Charduri says he doesn't even have one himself.'

'Yet he had enough money to buy a camera to take a photo?'

Mrs Raju frowns at me, as though I am being unreasonable to keep asking so many questions.

'He says that one of his uncle's nephews stole the camera from a Western tourist,' she explains.

There is a silence. I stare at the photo again: the similarity seems more striking every time I look at it.

'Mr Charduri understands that this is a big shock to you – he can hardly believe it himself. He understands that you have saved her from a terrible life and he is overwhelmed with gratitude.'

I smile as Mr Charduri nods respectfully at me. Then he smiles. There is something a little spidery about that smile – it flits across his lips in a creepy fashion. But then, he's obviously nervous and shell-shocked himself.

'He just asks,' Mrs Raju concludes, 'that he might see his daughter. Just once. Just once.'

'I . . .' I don't know what to say.

I suddenly hear a noise from the hallway and start. I run to the door and see that Devika has been standing outside for goodness knows how long. She has clearly heard too much, for her face is pale and her eyes are brimming with tears.

'Oh, Devika,' I say. I brought her to England to escape her past, to shield her from tragedy. I feel horrified that she is now being dragged through it all again. Overwhelmed with protective love, I try to draw her in for a hug, but she pulls back fiercely.

'Is my daddy in there?'

'I don't . . . I don't know—' I break off helplessly.

'Let me see him.'

'Next time,' I say quickly. 'Next time would be better—'

'No.' Devika shoves past me and bursts into the living room. She stops short, staring at the man sitting in the armchair. He stares back at her. His eyes turn liquid with emotion. Then a noise emerges from his lips. Like a wail of sadness and a moan of delight.

I've never heard a noise cut through with such deep emotion before.

And then they hug. I watch them clinging to each other and I find tears springing to my own eyes. In that moment all my doubts and suspicions disappear. It's just beautiful, watching them come together. Watching them find each other.

They start talking rapidly in Hindi and I collapse back down on to the chair, feeling stunned. I wonder if he's telling her his story, but then I remember that Devika doesn't know she was ever buried alive; she was always protected from that.

They chat some more and then, as though they're too exhausted to speak any more, they both fall silent and just stare at each other in wonder.

Then Mr Charduri stands up.

'He feels he has disturbed you enough,' Mrs Raju says. 'He feels he must leave you alone.'

'No, don't go!' Devika cries. 'Don't go. Daddy, no, no, no!'

Mr Charduri speaks to her again in Hindi, hugs her and then gently disentangles himself.

'He suggests that he come back again,' Mrs Raju says to me. 'For Devika's happiness.'

'I . . .' I pinch my lips. This is all happening so quickly. The photo does look like her, but a photo can be faked, can't it? Then I look over at Devika in confusion. Perhaps that kind of connection can't be faked. But Devika has always wanted to find her father. What if this is all a game, a trick, and we're both being sucked in?

'Yes,' I say at last. 'Okay.'

I figure that I can always change my mind later.

Mr Charduri shakes my hand and says goodbye. He gives Devika another hug, their tears mingling. I watch as Devika runs to the dining room, yanking back the net curtain to watch him go. I watch her waving desperately, whispering, 'Daddy, Daddy.' And I wonder if this is the best or the worst thing that's ever happened to us.

40

Devika

Karina pushes my head forward into the sink. I used to be scared of having my head under water but now I like it. All the noises fade and everything seems faraway, like being in a dream. I open my eyes. The sink is greeny-blue, like the inside of a mermaid's cave, and little bubbles float from my mouth and bob about.

Karina is turning me into an Indian again. She is dyeing my hair black so that I will look like my real self. My daddy doesn't like my hair. He says it looks ugly and that Karina is trying to westernise me. Karina laughed and told him that nobody would have hair with black and white blobs out of choice, but he didn't understand. You are westernising my daughter too much, he said. Then Karina went pale and her lips looked tight. And I felt horrible inside, because I don't think Karina and my daddy like each other very much.

Karina squeezes stuff which looks like black mousse out of the bottle on to her palm. Then we both stare into the mirror as she smooths it into my hair.

'You will look like a princess,' she says.

'But I can't be a princess, my daddy's not a king,' I say, because we learnt all about the royal family at school.

'I mean that you'll look beautiful.'

'Hey, you're getting it in my eyes, Karina!' I cry as a bit dribbles down.

Karina frowns. And then she looks very sad.

'I'm not Karina, I'm Mummy. You can call me Mummy or Mummy Karina,' she says. 'You're my daughter, after all.'

'Sorry,' I say quickly and I wish she would plunge my head back into the sink so I can hide my face from her.

But Mummy Karina says we have to wait twenty minutes for the dye to work.

I sit on a chair and Mummy Karina wraps a towel round my shoulders. Then she puts a plasticky thing over my head so I don't get black stuff over my clothes. Mummy Karina starts to clean the bath. She hums and I can tell the song is Britney. I don't like Britney any more.

I stare into the mirror and remember the photo of my real mummy that Daddy showed me. She had long black hair and dark eyes and Daddy says I got my dark skin from her, for he is more pale. I like holding my arm out in the light to see how dark it is and it feels as though Mummy is there inside me, whispering through my skin. At night-time, I can sense her up in heaven, looking down on me. Daddy says that souls go to heaven to have a rest before they reincarnate. I know she's going to wait so that she's born at the right time so I can be reborn as a seed in her belly. And next time things will be different and she won't die when I'm a little baby. And then we'll sing songs together and go to the temple and go shopping for jeans – we'll be like best friends.

Mummy Karina comes up behind me and suddenly she says something really horrible.

'I don't think you should see Mr Charduri any more.'

'No!' I cry. 'I want to see my daddy.'

'But we don't know for sure that he is your daddy,' Mummy Karina says. She has an angry tone to her voice, the way she does when she's asking if I've done my homework.

'He is my daddy, he is, he is!' I cry. 'You're just jealous.'

Now Mummy Karina looks even more cross. She

kneels down in front of me and I stare down at her. I can feel my eyes growing wet, I'm so upset. I know he's my daddy. I prayed to Lord Krishna and the *devas* for him to come back for me. I always knew in the orphanage, when I used to stand at the gates and call out for him, I knew deep in my heart that somehow my voice would carry on the wind and enter his heart and he'd find a way to find me again.

'Look,' Mummy Karina says, 'I want you to be happy. I made a mistake, letting you see so much of him. I just want to check again that he really is your daddy and be sure.' She touches my cheek and I feel cross, because she's trying to pretend that she's being nice when really she's doing something mean.

'If you stop me from seeing my daddy, I'll run away and find him,' I burst out.

Mummy Karina's eyes become big and I know I've said something really bad. I wish I hadn't said it because now she'll watch me and if I do try to run she won't let me.

'I have a story to tell you about your daddy,' she says. 'He was a murderer. He didn't bury you because he thought you were dead. He buried you because he was poor and he didn't want you. And I will tell you this, Devika. No matter how poor I was, if I had you, I'd never do such a terrible thing.'

'You're lying,' I say, for I know this could not be true. My daddy would never do such a thing.

'He was very poor and you were a girl. You know it happens – you were in the orphanage. You know that sometimes mummies and daddies can't afford to pay for girls to have dowries. That was why he tried to kill you. I'm so sorry,' she says, tears pouring out of her eyes, 'I wanted to protect you but this is the truth.'

'You're lying, you're lying!' I put my hands over my ears so she can't tell me any more lies, but she only speaks more loudly.

'When your daddy comes tomorrow, you can ask him.'

'No!' I get up and run to the door. I want to run away right now and never speak to her again.

'Devika!' Now her voice is soft. She comes up behind me and puts her hands on my shoulders. Her hands are warm. I suddenly want her to give me a hug.

But she doesn't. She tells me that my hair will look silly if we don't clean the dye off. She sits me down on the chair and fills up the sink with water. I stare at her but she doesn't look at me. She just keeps sniffing a lot. She tips my head forward and suddenly I feel scared. What if she's so angry that she decides to drown me? But then she brings out the shower attachment which is like a long white snake and lets the water run over my head. All the black stuff pours off my hair like paint. I remember how at school Regina once said, 'You were buried alive. I read about it in the newspapers. Your daddy tried to murder you.' I thought Regina must be lying but how come she and Mummy Karina both think the same story? Maybe Mummy Karina is really horrible and she told the newspaper people a lie. Or maybe it is true. The water keeps going in my eyes and making them hurt but it means I can cry without Mummy Karina noticing.

41

Karina

He can't be her father. He just can't be.

When he first turned up on the doorstep, I was so overwhelmed by his story I felt he could be telling the truth. But I've had a few days now to put the whole thing into perspective. To think it through. And I don't think I believe in Mr Charduri.

I remember that five months ago, when I visited the orphanage, Mrs Laxsmi warned me this could happen. To be fair to Mr Charduri, I can understand how desperate he is. I can see the true story, beneath the story he told us. After his farming business failed, he's been living in the slums of Delhi for several years when one day a relative flies back to India and gets in touch. He turns out to be a long-lost cousin who is now doing well, running his own newsagent in London. He treats Mr Charduri to a plane ticket and offers to let him stay for a month. So Mr Charduri comes to London and drinks in a glamour and luxury he hasn't ever tasted before. He starts watching TV. Adverts torment him. They promise shiny cars and beautiful clothes and big houses. Suddenly it feels as though all the things that seemed like dreams when he was in the slums might actually become real. Possibilities whisper to him; hope brushes against his heart; ambitions fill his skull. How might he stay in England, how might he change his life? He thinks of the slums back in Delhi, where he drank and washed in dirty water; he lies in his luxurious English bath and shudders at the thought of ever going back. And then, one afternoon, he switches on the TV. He sees me. And then Devika.

Maybe she reminds him of a daughter he did once lose. Or maybe there was never a daughter at all. Maybe he's just spent his whole life longing for a princess as beautiful and special and sweet as Devika.

Or maybe – and this is my deepest suspicion – maybe he smells the scent of fame and money. He sees how nice this house is; he wonders how much he might be able to get. And even if we realise he's a fraud, maybe he figures he'll earn enough in TV deals and newspaper interviews to make it worth his while.

He is a desperate man. I have to keep reminding myself of that.

Especially when he's testing my patience. Here I am, sitting in my living room, with Devika beside me and Mrs Raju on the other side, ready to translate. Mr Charduri sits by the window, in the armchair.

I don't think I have ever seen anyone sit in my Conran armchair with such discomfort. He wriggles; he sits on the edge; he pushes himself back as deep as he can go; and every so often he pats his arms against its flowery sides as though he is reassuring a pet.

When I watch him squirm like this, I do feel a brief sympathy for him. He's obviously acutely conscious that we're on TV. In fact, this is the last day of filming. I woke this morning with a smile on my face and a sense of lightness in my heart. But also a sense of determination.

Over the past few days, I've indulged Mr Charduri. I've invited him over for a few meals and listened to his stories. I've allowed him to spend some time on his own with Devika, which I now regret; he has filled her mind with rosy fantasies about her mother which I think have brought her more disquiet than peace of mind.

And I still don't know for sure that he *is* her father. I called up Angela from social services, who came over to give me some advice. She seemed pleased that Devika's real father had turned up and I couldn't help feeling paranoid that she was secretly thinking, *I've always felt that fame-mad Karina would never be the best mother for her. She'll be much better off with her real dad.* When I started to get jumpy and defensive, Angela quickly soothed me and said, 'Look – for the sake of your sanity and Devika's, you have to clear this up for good. Mr Charduri seems the real thing to me, but the only way to sort it out is to organise a paternity test.'

A paternity test. Hmm. Just seeing Mr Charduri's response to such a suggestion might be a test in itself. If he looked uncomfortable and tried to wriggle out of it, then I'd know . . .

But, now that I'm sitting here with him, I've had a change of heart. If I suggest a test, how long is that going to take? Days, weeks? And in the meantime, he can just keep playing his little game and stringing it all out. I can't take any more of this. Whoever the man is, I don't need him. Devika doesn't need him. He let her go and she has a new life now. I want to wrap this up, on camera, so that the public knows the story is closed. I don't want the next few months to be full of comings and goings and rows and discussions and newspaper articles every other day discussing who Devika ought to belong to.

This morning, for example, the *Daily Mail* ran a feature with the headline *Tug of Love*. The *Express*'s headline was even less diplomatic: *Give Her Back, Karina*.

As if Devika is some toy I can just hand over. Don't they understand that she's my *daughter*?

What I'd really like to do is just scream and shout at him to leave the house. But since I'm on camera, I have to be polite but firm. I have to show him I'm not prepared to play this game any more.

'Look,' Mr Charduri says, for he came in with a newspaper folded under his arm.

'What?'

He passes it over to me, that creepy smile twitching across his lips. His gnarled finger jabs the story.

In our poll, 64 per cent of readers felt that Devika belonged with her father, despite the allegations that he buried her alive (which he now denies). Public sympathy seems to be growing for Mr Charduri, who said, 'I have spent years and years praying every day for the return of my daughter. To discover her again is a miracle.'

I fold up the newspaper and stare at Mr Charduri, who keeps smiling away at me. What does he want me to do, give him a medal? Oh, God, I just wish he would stop smiling. I just want to shout at him: 'STOP PLAYING THESE GAMES! STOP TRYING TO PRETEND TO BE NICE!'

Once again, I force myself to calm down. He's just a harmless old man. He can't hurt us.

'What does it say?' Devika asks, pointing at the newspaper.

'Nothing,' I say, smiling at her, stroking her hair. Ever since he's turned up, I've found I need to keep touching her arm or giving her a hug, or stroking her hair until sometimes she seems quite fed up and I realise I'm going over the top. I just need to keep feeling the warmth of her skin connect with mine.

Then Mr Charduri does something I hate. He starts talking to her rapidly in Hindi. She talks back eagerly. I sit there, frozen, without a clue what they're saying.

And then suddenly all three of them – Mrs Raju included – burst into laughter. I force a vague smile, as though I'm in on the joke too.

Then I give Mrs Raju a testing look. She frowns, looking a bit sheepish. Paranoia flickers inside me. The reason I've made sure Mrs Raju comes to every meeting is so that he can't start telling Devika any more lies and Mrs Raju can pick up on anything dodgy. But what if they all share a cultural bond; what if she's on *his* side?

Then I look down at Devika. She is staring at

Mr Charduri with an expression of sheer awe. The fear in my heart deepens into panic.

'Mrs Raju,' I say, 'can you ask Mr Charduri to tell me exactly what he'd like from us? He's been here a week now and we've met often. And now I think he needs to be clear about what he wants to achieve.'

Mrs Raju's face grows serious and she nods at me. I feel a sense of relief, a sense that yes, I can trust her. She repeats my request to Mr Charduri. He blinks and then replies. Mrs Raju translates: 'He wants to see your beloved daughter . . . and also, he would appreciate your help. Back in Delhi, he has some members of his family in the slums.'

A-ha! I knew it. I can't prevent a smile from breaking across my face. Then, seeing Mrs Raju's disapproval, I quickly wipe it off.

But I knew it, I knew it – what Mr Charduri sniffed when he saw us on TV was the scent of money. He knew that I'd want to look like a philanthropist on TV and repair my reputation. I can see the bargain he's trying to strike.

I get up and go over to the cabinet and pull out my chequebook and pen. Then I sit back down on the sofa and begin to write out his name. Devika watches with wide eyes and I give her a reassuring smile.

'Please ask Mr Charduri how much he wants,' I say to Mrs Raju.

Mrs Raju looks slightly shocked and then smiles. She repeats my question to Mr Charduri.

To my surprise, he doesn't smile his creepy smile. He starts. He sits up. Then he stands. He comes over and peers at my chequebook. Then he looks into my eyes. And then he wraps his arms around me, pulling me up into a hug.

I hug him back, feeling rather taken aback, and then draw away. I sit back down briskly.

'I'd like to help his family. How much?' I repeat.

Mrs Raju translates his answer: 'Mr Charduri would be happy with whatever amount you would like to donate.'

A poker player's response.

'Well . . .' Shall I come out and say it? I may as well. 'How much do I have to give him so that he will leave us in peace?'

Mrs Raju frowns and asks me to repeat what I've just said. I say it again and she bites her lip and passes it on to Mr Charduri. Immediately, he stops smiling.

'He doesn't understand what you're saying,' Mrs Raju translates. 'He doesn't understand why you want to be left in peace.'

Oh, God. How hard is he going to make this?

'Look, I feel that for Devika's sake – er – look – a thousand pounds, okay?' I know this is a huge sum of money in India; I know it can change a life for ever. I scrawl out the cheque and pass it over to Mr Charduri with a tight smile.

'Is that enough, then?' I ask.

Mrs Raju posits my question to Mr Charduri, who keeps threading my cheque through his fingers.

'He is worried,' she says. 'He appreciates your help but he is also keen to see his daughter.'

'Yes, I want to see Daddy,' Devika chimes in and I turn on her, exasperated, and give her a strong look. She lowers her eyes and purses her lips, looking cross. How many times do I have to explain to her that he is most unlikely to be her daddy?

That is why this has to stop now.

'It's not fair on Devika,' I say. 'He takes the money – and then he goes. I don't want to see him in this house again. I don't want him to see Devika again. I want him to leave us in peace and I wish him well.'

There is a long silence and then Mrs Raju repeats my words to Mr Charduri. Mr Charduri looks aghast. He stares down at his cheque, his hands trembling. He moves as though to rip it up and then stops himself. He can't bear to part with so much money.

Then he shakes his head and starts talking quickly to Devika. She lets out a cry and jumps up into his lap. He holds her tight, the cheque still flapping out of his fingers, tears pouring down his face.

'Okay, that's enough!' I cry, jumping up. 'You say goodbye now and that's it!'

'No, no goodbye!' Devika cries.

'Devika . . . *Devika* . . . we'll talk about this after he's gone . . .' My head is spinning. It wasn't supposed to go like this. He was meant to take the money and leave. Did I not offer him enough? Are those tears for real? Or is he just a really good actor?

Mr Charduri shakes his head and stands up. Devika throws a tantrum, clinging to his leg, demanding that he stay. I try to coax her away and she lashes out at me. I stand up, folding my arms, breathing hard, looking away. I can feel Mr Charduri's beseeching gaze on me as he leaves the room. Devika tries to follow but Mrs Raju takes a firm grip on her. Then I hear the click of the front door as he goes.

And there is silence, except for Devika's screams. Now I feel like crying too.

'Come here,' I say, holding my arms open, desperate to hold her tight, but she pushes past me and I hear the tumble of her feet up to her room. 'Oh, God.'

I hear the phone ring and I pick it up.

'What are you doing?' It's my agent. 'Don't you realise how badly you just came across? It's the last day of the show. The cameras are going off in half an hour. You have to call him back!'

'What! I can't . . . I mean, what d'you expect me to do?'

'You tried to buy him off and he loves his daughter! You tried to *bribe him*!'

'I'm just trying . . . I just feel Devika's completely screwed up and I'm sorry if it looked bad but this is about more than a TV show – it's about my daughter's happiness.'

I put the phone down and wheel round in a circle. I sit down on the sofa. I breathe out. I swear I am doing the right thing. I know everyone thinks I'm being harsh but I just know, I feel it in my heart, that Mr Charduri isn't for real. Then I decide to call up Clare.

'Karina,' she says, 'I know it's hard. Devika's been all yours up until now . . . but you've got to learn to share her. I think you have to. Or you're going to lose her.'

'I can't lose her! She's my daughter!' I cry. But even as I repeat the words, I keep remembering something Mr Charduri asked me a few days ago. He asked if I was her legal parent and I had to admit I was only her guardian. That I had to be her guardian for six months before I could legally adopt her.

Suddenly everything feels so fragile.

'I'm afraid I'm going to lose her,' I say. 'And I just have this feeling about him.'

'Karina,' she says warningly. 'Listen to me. You have to do the right thing. Like Angela said, you really need to organise this paternity test. *Then* you can decide.'

I switch off the phone and stare down at it. Then I grimace up at the cameras. How did I get into this mess? Am I merely jealous? Am I just being petty and trying to demonise Mr Charduri? Am I simply afraid of losing her?

I pick up the phone, swallowing hard, and call Mr Charduri. I ask him to come back.

Ten minutes later, there is a tentative ring of the doorbell and I invite him in.

'Look – I owe you an apology,' I say, lacing my hands together. 'I . . . I'm just scared. I admit it – I'm scared you're going to take her away. And maybe a bit jealous too. I feel threatened . . . but only because I love her.'

I expect Mr Charduri to be moved by my confession. It took a lot to say it. I thought he'd hug me and say we were both her parents. Instead, he sits down, that slightly creepy smile on his face, and a dark look comes into his eyes. He sits up straight in my armchair as though he is a king on his throne and says slowly: 'I am her father.'

'Look,' I say, swallowing, 'there's something I'd like to suggest.'

And I realise why I've been holding back: because

I'm terrified that a positive result will be so final, so absolute.

'I'd like to suggest a paternity test,' I say shakily. 'That will definitely prove, beyond all doubt, that you're her father.'

I gauge his reaction closely and he nods firmly.

'Very good,' he says. 'Very good.'

42

Karina

Have I made a mistake? I think I have. I think I should be with my daughter right now. Today is Diwali, the most important festival in the Indian calendar. I ought to be sitting in a temple with her, chanting, enjoying the celebrations. Instead, I'm sitting in a limo, wearing Galliano, my publicist on one side of me, my agent on the other. They are both talking into their mobiles. I stare past them, seeing vignettes of London through the tinted glass. Drizzle spiders over the window. Red and blue neon bleed like shimmering poster paints. Devika is with Mr Charduri. Of course, Mr Charduri looked very smug when I said I couldn't go. He was able to assume the moral high ground, behave as though I'm too busy to bother. But it's okay for him. He doesn't have to worry about what the public think about him. He lives a normal life; he's *free*. He doesn't get invited to events run by *New Woman*. He doesn't have an agent who twists his arm and *insists* he attends.

I can't work out if the readers of *New Woman* are being sincere or taking the piss. I can't quite believe it: I've actually been nominated for Celebrity Mother of the Year. I'm up against Kate Moss, Geri Halliwell and Posh Spice.

My agent fiddles about with the TV set and flicks through the channels until he reaches some satellite channel which is actually covering the awards event. There are crowds of people waiting outside – autograph hunters and the usual herd of paparazzi.

Then Davina McCall pops up on screen, brandishing her mike and welcoming viewers to 'the *New Woman* awards – it's become *the* celebrity awards event of the year. Every actress, every presenter, every girl band – you name it, they're all hoping and praying they walk away with something tonight.'

I wonder what Devika is doing. I felt uneasy about Mr Charduri taking her off on his own. But what choice do I have?

He came over yesterday with the results of the test. For the first twenty minutes or so, he just sat in my armchair with the envelope balanced on his knee, smiling and waiting for me to ask. I refused to let him see how wound up I was and I played it cool, smiling back and serving him tea. Finally, I couldn't bear it any longer.

'So?' I cried, my voice trembling. 'What's the result?'

He passed over the envelope. I opened it with damp fingers. Even as I drew out the results, I knew what they were going to be. I stared at the paper blankly.

'That's great . . . amazing . . .'

'I am her father,' he asserted firmly, nodding his head.

He got a little angry when I said that I wasn't happy about letting him take Devika off on his own. So he is her father, but I still don't really know him. I still have a responsibility, as her guardian, to make sure she's kept safe and protected. So I insisted Mrs Raju had to accompany them.

And despite all my pain, I have to admit that his presence has made a huge impact on Devika. Since he appeared on my doorstep, she's become a different person. Finding her father has given her an anchor. There is a peaceful quality about her, a sense of having been found and having found what her heart has been searching for since she was born. Yet I can also feel her moving away from me and I have to keep fighting my jealousy. I figure that Mr Charduri will stay in England and I'm going to have to accept his continuing presence in our lives. So I've tried to make more of an effort to be nice to him and he, in turn, has responded warmly. Yesterday I was touched and surprised when he brought me a present, a small Indian silk scarf woven with gold patterns. It was as though the gift symbolised a silent agreement between us – we both agree to at least *try* to get on for Devika's sake.

And who knows, maybe gradually we will even grow to like each other.

'Look.' My agent nudges me.

'What?'

On the small TV screen Davina is asking the crowds for their opinion on the hot topic of the minute: me.

'So what do *you* think?' she asks a middle-aged woman. 'Should Karina West give her adopted child back to her real father?'

'I think she has to give her back,' she says. 'I mean, Devika is an Indian girl. She ought to have an Indian upbringing.'

My jaw drops.

'How about you?' Davina addresses a blonde twenty-something.

'I think Devika should be with her real father. He's her flesh and blood. He deserves to have his daughter back.'

What! What the fuck do these people know about me and my daughter?

'They haven't even met me!' I howl. 'All they've done is watch five minutes of my stupid TV show. Right. Turn it off.'

Just as my agent reaches out and switches if off, I see Hayley, Liam's ex, pop up on the screen.

'Turn it on!' I cry. 'Turn it on!'

My agent and my publicist exchange oh-god-what-a-diva! glances.

I miss the first half of Hayley's verdict on me, but judging by her patronising expression, it's not kind. *Bitch, bitch, bitch*. And then she drops her bombshell.

'But I do think Karina is probably better off now that she's split from Liam,' she says, with a pained look. 'When I was with Liam I got pregnant and he made me have an abortion. I can't tell you how much it hurt me that he didn't want me to keep our baby. But I'm strong and I came through it and here I am, nominated for Babe of the Year. If I win tonight, I feel I can be an inspiration to young women every-where who have been pressurised by their partners to give up their babies.'

'She's been saving that up,' my agent remarks. 'Saving it for maximum impact. Clever.'

An *abortion*? Is that the truth? Liam never, never mentioned that. I feel quite shocked. I can't quite take it in; all I experience is a flood of ache at the mention of Liam's name. It's been so long now since I last saw him. I guess I hardly have a right to be angry, either, when we're no longer together. But he ought to have told me.

As we get out of the limo, I'm lambasted by two separate waves of energy. The first is from the press, who flash away exuberantly.

The second is from the crowds. To my shock and horror, they start booing me.

'Give her back!' someone yells. 'Give Devika back!'

'Come on, quickly now.' My agent hurries me through, his eyes narrowed.

As we speed down the red carpet, something flies through the air and lands by my feet. It's a crushed tin of baby food. I gape over at a woman who is brandishing another tin. Security hurry over to stop her before she can chuck it. Her face is red and furious. How can she be so angry with me when she doesn't even bloody know me? I'm completely shell-shocked. It's only at events like this that you get to connect with the public, to see past the white-washed reassurances of your publicist and agent, to recognise the truth.

And the truth is that I'm not that popular any more.

I can't tell you how relieved I feel to step from

harsh reality into the fantasy bubble of the awards ceremony.

'Come on, Karina,' my agent cajoles me. 'You're up for Mother of the Year.'

'Yeah, as though I'm going to get it,' I say sulkily.

As we enter the main room, which is filled with tables and celebrities, I feel a cloud of depression come over me. I've been to these events before and I always suffer the same fate. Normally I come along not because I've been nominated but because my agent has got me an invite after a lot of last-minute wrangling. Normally I end up sitting at my table and looking around at all the other tables, analysing the hierarchy of the room. I stare out and see a table with Kate Moss and all her chums and another one with the Sugababes and Girls Aloud and another with Kelly Osbourne and the Geldof brigade. And then I look around my table, which is normally me, Jodie from the *Sun*, a *Big Brother* winner and some kids' TV presenter, and I know how badly I'm doing.

So tonight I'm more than a little taken aback when I'm escorted to a table right near the stage. When I see that Cheryl Cole and Liz Hurley are also at the table, my agent gives me a look as though to say, *see, it's not so bad*.

Booing one minute; a table with A-listers the next. I guess you could say I'm the ultimate love/hate figure at the moment.

The awards begin and the winners are fairly predictable. Girls Aloud win Best Girl Group and Kylie is Best Female Star. And then it's time for my one. Cheryl Cole grins at me and Liz Hurley whispers, 'Good luck!' and my heart lifts a little.

For some crazy reason, they have got Russell Brand (since when did he epitomise all that is great about motherhood?) to present the award. He gets up on stage looking as if he might have had a few drinks, wickedness glinting in his brown eyes.

'The lucky winner of tonight's Celebrity Mother of the Year award is going to be the delighted recipient of a kiss from me. And they'll also get this stupid statue thingy too.'

Everyone laughs, both excited and uneasy, knowing that with Russell Brand on stage anything might happen.

'And since a snog is involved now, I'm just praying that Victoria Beckham doesn't win.'

A few cheers, a few boos. Victoria handles the teasing well and manages a good-humoured smile. My agent looks as if he's positively salivating at the prospect of such a good photo op.

Russell opens the envelope. Even though I know I definitely can't win against Posh or Geri, even though there is *no* possibility that it can be me, my heart beats wildly all the same.

'And the winner is . . .' Russell draws out the

suspense, frowning sexily, 'is . . . well, this *is* a surprise. Apparently if you put joints in your kid's lunch box, that makes you the best mum of the year. So let's all stock up on our supply of crack cocaine to pass round in the playground. Yes – it's Karina West.'

Me? *Me!* Shit. Fuck. I sit there like a lemon, whilst people smile and congratulate me. But there are some discernible boos of disapproval flying about too.

My agent drags me into a hug. Then he rubs my arm gently, gesturing that I should go up. Finally, when I still sit there numbly, he gives me a shove.

I stagger across the floor, weaving through tables. Geri Halliwell gives me a sunny smile; Posh gives me the thumbs-up; Moss is too busy snogging her beau to notice me.

As I climb the steps, feeling utterly dazed, I trip slightly and for one scary, shaky moment it looks as though I might go flying. But I manage to stay upright and glide up on to the stage to face Russell. It all feels so surreal, as though I'm watching myself from above. I've always dreamt of snogging Russell Brand, but not in front of five hundred people with cameras flashing.

Russell leans in and suddenly I feel all shy. I duck my head. Unperturbed, he plants a kiss on my left cheek, then my right . . . and then ducks down and secures his lips against mine. He's a good kisser . . .

a very good kisser. Cheers and wolf whistles fill my ears. Russell finally releases me and I stagger over to the mike, my face brilliant red, clutching my trophy.

'So, Karina, let's address the forbidden topic that we're all dying to know about,' he says. 'Are you going to do the decent thing and give your daughter back to her rightful owner?'

All the sweetness of his kiss leaks away. I give him a furious glance and then turn to the audience, trying to think of what to say. How can I show them the true colour of my heart? How can I make them see who I really am? Out of the corner of my eye, I see my agent gesturing, keen that I don't forget to mention him.

But I don't want to do a Paltrow and gush thanks everywhere.

Suddenly I know what to say.

'I'd like to dedicate this award to my daughter Devika,' I say. Just saying her name out loud fills up my heart with love. 'This award really is for her. Since I adopted her five months ago, we've had our ups and downs and I'm sure everyone here knows about them. But every day has still been magical and wonderful. Devika – I love you lots.' I kiss the trophy and smile.

And then my smile fades. Everyone is clapping. But the audience looks glazed. I can tell they didn't digest a word of my speech. They just thought I was another celeb using pretty words, saying the right thing. I slink off stage, suffering the downswing of anticlimax.

As I make my way back to my table, I discover that despite the blank reaction to my speech everyone has clearly decided that I am somebody. It takes me a long time to reach my seat as I handle an obstacle course of kisses and handshakes and congratulations.

By the time I get to the table, I feel weary, as though all the fakery has brushed on to me, soiling my skin. I sink down into my seat. My agent gives me another hug. I draw back. I think of Devika. I think of the last time we went to the temple: me, Liam and Devika. Sitting together in our bubble of bliss.

But – I check my watch – it's too late now. Even if I did jump up and order my driver to take me over to Neasden, we would still have missed the celebrations. Maybe Devika is on her way home right now. Frowning, I try calling her mobile, but there is no reply. Maybe she's even in bed. I gave Mrs Raju strict instructions to make sure Mr Charduri didn't enter the house; I organised Adi to wait at home and take over as babysitter and read Devika her bedtime story. When I call up Adi, however, she says Devika isn't back yet.

'I need a drink,' I tell my agent sulkily.

'I can get them to bring you anything you like,' he says with an expansive smile. 'You're Celebrity Mother of the Year!'

I order a cocktail with a silly name. The waiter brings it before the next award starts. It has a mint tint and about five different liqueurs in it. I down it quickly and catch my agent watching me with a nervous smile. He doesn't dare tell me off, though.

Up on stage, Hayley pops up to present the next award. In her gold dress held together by safety pins, she looks like a Christmas tree on a budget.

'And the winner of the Celebrity Dad of the Year award is . . . the proud father of three wonderful children . . . let's give it up for David Beckham! Yah!'

Becks smiles and strolls up on to the stage wearing a suit. He blows a kiss at Victoria, who beams up at him. Hayley quickly yanks him in for a hug and he looks rather uncomfortable.

'Well . . . this is great . . . I'd like to thank you all . . .'

My eyes travel round the room. Is it my imagination, or is that a familiar dark head at the back? Looking over at me? I squint at him, my heart leaping. But before I can ascertain if it's really him, he makes a swift exit.

No. It can't possibly be Liam.

Liam is in rehab. Locked up in a room with a bucket.

I order another cocktail.

This one has five liqueurs in it and a strawberry flavour.

I knock it back and then decide I need some air. David Beckham's finished speaking, so I grab the opportunity to scoot across the room and outside into the stinging cold. Here, at the back, there are no crowds or paps; it's a safe place for celebrities to have a smoke and a quick break. That said, there are always journalists prowling, hoping for a titbit of gossip.

'Karina?'

A familiar voice makes me shiver. Surely . . . it can't be?

And there he is. Leaning against the wall. Smiling a smile that is shy and possessive and sexy all at once.

'Liam—'

He interrupts me by pulling me in for a long, deep kiss. It's been so long. The moment our lips touch I realise how hungry I've been for him. We kiss each other's faces and lips and necks greedily, our breaths shallow with excitement and pleasure. After weeks of feeling on edge, I sink into his embrace like a warm bath. He feels so warm, so wonderful – so *real*.

Finally, we pause and look at each other.

'You look . . . you look great,' I whisper. 'You look so – *healthy*.' His eye whites are clear and his skin is shiny and translucent. Without that shadowy, slightly sour look the drugs give him, he looks years younger, boyish rather than manly. But he also seems more fragile, for he's lost weight and his leather jacket is slack round his shoulders.

'I've missed you,' he says. 'Why did you cut me off? We made a promise we'd carry on in secret. Were you just too busy with your TV show?'

Despite the fact that I'm fairly drunk, the mention of the TV show evokes flutters of panic inside. Okay, so I have been booed, but winning Mother of the Year will surely salvage my reputation somewhat, and I don't want that stupid TV show to have been for nothing. If anyone sees Liam and me together like this, I'm ruined.

Liam, however, seems to read my mind. He grabs my hand and leads me over to some large black bins. We crouch down behind them. At least, I try to crouch down; my dress is too tight and in my drunken state I end up with it riding up round my thighs.

'I'm sorry I didn't . . . I thought you were better left alone to heal,' I improvise guiltily.

'No,' he says angrily, grabbing my arms. 'You thought I might ruin your stupid TV show and your precious image. I watched it whilst I was in rehab. All the time.'

'Did you?' I flush. 'Did you like it?'

'You came across as a complete cock. I guess the new nose isn't bad, though.'

'Well,' I retort angrily, 'I wouldn't have had to do the stupid show if you hadn't bloody put a joint in Devika's lunch box!'

'True. But two wrongs don't make a right. Devika wasn't happy. Are you going to let her dad take her back?'

'Of course I'm not!'

'But what if he has the right?'

'I . . . he won't do that. Devika won't go,' I assert. That is one thing I feel completely sure of. Devika loves me and will stay with me; that I know. 'We've accepted each other. We're going to share her.'

He stares into my eyes, cupping my face in his palms.

'You didn't tell me about Hayley and the abortion,' I burst out.

'You never asked,' Liam says, lowering his eyes.

I feel tears welling up in my eyes. This isn't a conversation we should be having when I've got this much alcohol in my system. But something inside me, still raw from the past, drives me on to keep asking.

'Why?'

'She just . . . it seemed the right thing to do. We weren't right together and bringing a kid into the world didn't seem fair, not when it was obvious we were never going to be there to look after him—' Liam breaks off as the tears start to stream down my face. He curls his arm round me and says, 'Shh, shh, it's all right – what happened with her is all in the past, you know that . . .'

'But I lost my baby . . . your baby,' I hear my slurred voice saying. Beneath the haze of my inebriation, a horrified voice is telling me to *shut up, shut up!* But I can't stop the words from flowing out. I've had to hold them inside for so long. Years ago, I would lie in bed with Liam, in the tender aura of a post-coital chat, and be so, so close to blurting them out: *Liam, I'm pregnant with your child . . . it was an accident . . . you know, that night we went out for a drive and we got excited and we didn't have any protection . . .*

Liam's soft voice suddenly becomes icy.

'You did *what*?'

'Nothing.'

'*Karina.*'

'I'm sorry . . .' I lift my face, trying to smile. The sky spins. 'I didn't tell you because I thought you'd hate me, you were always so anti-commitment, so I just did what I thought you'd want me to do . . . it was all so crazy and I was . . . you know . . . we were taking a lot of drugs . . . I was scared it might have been harmed.'

'So you're saying you were pregnant – with my kid?'

'Yes.'

'When? When exactly? What, five years ago?'

'About seven.'

'And you never told me?'

'We were just having a fling at the time . . . I thought you'd dump me. I thought you'd go mad,' I cry. 'You were always saying you never wanted kids.'

Liam is silent. He scrapes his fingers against the gravel, grey splinters filling up his nails.

'And the worst thing is,' I start to sob again, 'is that I lost our baby. At the time I thought I didn't want kids either, thought I could wait for the future . . . but now because of that abortion the doctor says I'm messed up . . . I don't know if I'll ever be able to have them and all I have is Devika . . . she's all I've got and now her father's turned up and he wants her too, I can tell he does, but she's *mine*. She's all I've got.'

'And what about us?' Liam asks. 'We might have had that kid together. You just went and – God, you just decided for us, you just made an assumption that I'd tell you to have an abortion. You always fucking assume! You think you know me so well, you just go ahead and—'

I put my face in my hands. I don't want his ranting and his rage. I want him to hold me tight and tell me everything will be okay. That I will keep Devika and that we'll find a way to be together. But he just keeps shouting and swearing at me.

'Oh, for God's sake,' I burst out savagely, unable to take any more, 'if we had had a baby, then what? You could have a put a joint in their lunch box too.'

'Oh, hilarious.' Liam stands up, kicks the gravel and walks off.

'Liam,' I call out faintly. 'Liam . . . Liam . . .'

But he walks away and I'm left crouched behind the bin, tears coursing down my cheeks, still clutching my Mother of the Year trophy.

43

Devika

Today is a very special day. It is the birthday of Maha Laxsmi, my favourite goddess. And my daddy is taking me to the temple to celebrate.

Mrs Raju takes us in her car. It's not like Karina's car, which drives smoothly, like a happy cat. Mrs Raju's car is red and rusty and growls like an angry dog. My daddy and I sit in the back. Every so often, he looks over at me and smiles and I smile back.

I heard Karina telling someone that my daddy doesn't smile much. But with me he is always smiling. I often wondered how it would feel to find my real daddy and I never imagined how special the connection would be. His body made me from his hair and skin and eyes and teeth and hands. There is a part of him in every strand of my hair and every cell of my skin. It feels as though our hearts and faces are Siamese twins. When he smiles, I have to smile, and when he's happy I feel the same emotion beating in my heart.

'I like your sari,' Daddy says, nodding and looking pleased. 'You look like my pretty daughter now. I don't like you in jeans. They're too westernised.'

'I like it too,' I say, beaming. My daddy just said I was pretty!

I love the way we can talk in the same language. My daddy says he's amazed how good my English is. But when I speak English, I can never speak fully from the heart. My head always has to step in and work out which word to use. It's so nice to be able to speak Hindi, to let my feelings flow out through my lips like a river.

My daddy and I have talked about so many things over the past few weeks. He has made me tell him every detail of the orphanage, about Mrs Laxsmi and my old friend Raji who is still there, saving up to become an American. I told him about the mat I used to sleep on and how we would sit on the floor and eat rice from bowls. I told him how I used to go to the gates and call out for him every night. He cried when I told him that.

'But Karina hasn't bothered to come tonight,' Daddy says.

'No, she's getting a special prize,' I say. Sometimes

when Daddy is mean about Karina I start to be mean too and it's like a horrible secret between us. Sometimes when she's talking he gives me a look, or says a rude remark in Hindi that she doesn't understand. It makes me feel nervous and want to laugh out loud. But then I feel bad too, because Karina is my mummy, even if she's not a proper one.

When we get to the temple my daddy tells Mrs Raju that we will walk around before the celebrations begin. Karina told Mrs Raju that she had to be with us at all times. But she doesn't tell us off. She just smiles and pinches my cheek, telling us to enjoy.

The temple is big and white; Daddy says it's in a place called Neesden. We walk around, looking at the *devas*, who are displayed behind glass cases. We look at the books on sale and the packets of incense and the pictures of Ganesh and Laxsmi. I feel a bit strange because it's the first time I am on my own with my daddy without Mrs Raju. Suddenly I can't think of anything to say and I keep picking things up from the stall and putting them back in the wrong places and my cheeks get hot.

'When I go back to India, my cousin has said that he will lend me some money, so that I can buy my own farm,' he says.

'You will go back to India?' I cry.

Suddenly the best night of my life is becoming the most horrible night of my life. I thought my daddy would come and live in London with us. I thought he would buy a house on the same street. I thought we would go to the temple every day and I would visit him after school and show him my homework and sing him each new song I learnt. He promised that we would visit all the famous places in London, that I could show him the Tower of London and the Houses of Parliament and the palace where the Queen lives and royal guards ride on horses. He promised he'd stay. He told me that he was very happy to have found me and that he never wanted to leave me again.

And now he is going back to India.

'Why won't you stay here?' I ask, my chin wobbling.

'Because I don't like England,' he says. 'In India, we put our religion first, but here they put money first. They worship the god of money – but it isn't Maha Laxsmi. We know that Laxsmi represents bliss, whether it is spiritual bliss or the comfort of material wealth or the warmth of love in a parent's heart. The god the British worship gives them money and then makes them miserable. Their god is laughing at them, but he keeps on feeding them and living off their misery. They think they are better than India, they think the West is more enlightened, but it is not the case. We have higher values. In India children do not go on to the streets and play with knives and guns. Even our poor children do not do that.'

I can't listen to what he's saying. I can't understand it. I have only just found my daddy and now he's going to desert me. I try to pull my hand away from his to wipe my eyes so he doesn't see my tears. But he holds on tightly.

Maybe he doesn't love me. I stare into the crowds and wish I could run into them and hide amongst all the colours and faces. Daddy says Karina doesn't really love me, or she'd come to the temple with us tonight. He says if she loved me she'd let me wear saris and not try to make me be like her and wear jeans. I said that I liked wearing jeans, but he said that was only because she'd taught me to. He said she is filling my head with bad ideas. Because she doesn't really love me.

But if she doesn't love me and he doesn't love me . . . who will? Maybe I'm just ugly and stupid. Maybe I can't be truly English or Indian. Maybe I just don't belong anywhere.

Then my daddy stops. I can feel him staring down at me. It makes me look up at him. His eyes are sparkling.

'Would you like to come and live with your daddy on his farm in India?' he asks.

'You mean I could come and visit?' I ask in relief – my daddy does want me, he does want me!

443

'Even better. You could come for a long time – a very long time.'

'Wow!' I cry in English. Then I say in Hindi: 'Could I come in the summer holidays?'

He says something but there is a noise from the crowds. He leans down and says into my ear: 'You could come and stay for ever.'

'For ever?' I remember how Karina once used the words for ever. She said I could be with her in England for ever.

'Yes.' He beams. 'Would you like that?'

'Yes!' I cry in excitement. My prayers have been answered. I could be with my daddy all the time. But then I think about Kelly and school. I wouldn't ever go there again. Mrs H would never tell me off in class for not concentrating. I would never be able to go into the back garden and play under the bushes. I would never eat Rice Krispies or English chocolate again. I wouldn't have baths with my duck or hear Karina read me a story or tell me I should do my homework.

'Would Karina be able to come and stay with us?' I ask, feeling scared, because I know my daddy doesn't think Karina is a very good mummy.

'Of course,' he says. 'We'd have our own farm, we could invite whoever we liked to stay with us. But Karina might not want to come. She prefers England, I think.'

'She likes to wear saris,' I say.

'She likes clothes,' he snorts.

We are silent. I gaze up at a picture of Maha Laxsmi on the wall. I stare at her dark, flowing hair and beautiful eyes. I wish she could clear my heart and tell me if this is the right thing.

'Could . . .' I try to ask, but my daddy is gazing into the crowds and he doesn't hear me. I look at Laxsmi again. I feel as though she is whispering that I should listen to my heart, to the sadness inside it at the thought of not seeing Karina again.

'Could Karina come for the whole of the summer holidays?' I ask.

Suddenly Daddy looks annoyed.

'What do you care if she comes?' he asks. 'She is a liar. She tried to poison your mind. She told you that I tried to kill you and bury you alive. We know that is an utter lie.'

Daddy got very angry last week when I told him Mummy Karina had said that.

'But maybe she just got the story wrong,' I say. 'I mean, sometimes she gets my bedtime story wrong if she's tired and she doesn't read it properly.'

'Karina would not care if you left. She only cares for herself. She likes you now, but she will not like you for ever. In a few year's time she will ask you to leave anyway.'

'No! She wouldn't . . . I don't think . . .' Suddenly I feel confused. Maybe Karina has told him she only wants me to be with her for a little while. But she told me she wanted me *for ever*.

We stop by a stall and Daddy buys me a packet of incense. I press it to my nose and he laughs. I breathe it in. It doesn't have that funny smell like the ones Karina buys for me, that stink like bubble bath. It smells of sweet sandalwood. It smells like home. I can smell India; I can smell the sun and the temples, the markets and the flowers.

Then we see people flowing into the main room. The celebrations are about to begin.

'You mustn't tell Karina about our plan to go to India,' he says. 'We must keep quiet, or she will be angry. We will tell her when the time is right.'

I feel scared because suddenly it all seems decided. It feels as though I have no choice now. But then I look at my daddy and see how happy he is, and I feel happy too.

'Will you keep it a secret?' he asks.

'Yes,' I promise.

44

Karina

I am standing in the middle of Selfridges when I suddenly realise I have to buy a pair of Victoria Beckham jeans.

I've never been a big fan of Posh, so I can't help feeling a faint blush creeping across my face when I ask the assistant whether her much-hyped children's line has come into the shops yet. I can tell from the way she looks at me that she recognises my face, but she is professional enough just to smile and be polite.

When I see her wrapping the jeans up in tissue paper, however, and I punch my pin into the machine, euphoria sparkles through my heart. I picture the look on Devika's face when I pass her the Selfridges bag. I picture her tearing off the tissue paper, her big eyes, and her gasp of joy when she sees what I've bought her.

Oh, God. I miss her *so* much. I've been without her for a whole day and I still have one night, one morning and one afternoon to go before I see her again.

I leave the shop, planning to head back, but somehow I don't feel like going home yet. I wonder what other presents Devika might like. I find that I can't help going into shop after shop, pulled by the tug of my heart. I mull over lipsticks, trying to find a shade that I feel is demure enough for an eleven year old to wear. Finally I settle on a pleasant shade of dusky pink that I know will look beautiful with her hair. Then I buy her a new pair of slippers, and a new teddy bear with a goofy grin, and five different packets of incense in different shades of sweetness.

Back home, I lay out all the presents on her bed and put the incense packets by the statue of Ganesh.

Then I decide that after so much tiring shopping, I really need a good bath. I sink in, watching the little rubber duck bob around between the bubbles.

'Devika will be back tomorrow,' I tell him.

Then I feel a bit mad, realising I am talking to her duck.

The reason Devika isn't with me is because she is with her father. A week ago, Mr Charduri suddenly announced that he would shortly be returning to Delhi. Of course, my first feeling was one of elation. I'd have Devika to myself – maybe for good. For Mr Charduri confessed, with that creepy smile flickering across his face, that he wasn't sure if he'd ever visit England again.

'England is not my place,' he said. 'It is not our home.'

I told Devika the news and she reacted strangely. She fell very quiet and hugged her teddy bear, her lips pressed tight together.

And then she put her bear aside and reached up and gave me a huge hug. I couldn't help feeling sad for her. One minute Mr Charduri's playing the loving father role and the next he's bored and hurrying off home (with my cheque). Despite myself, I can't help feeling rather disappointed in him. Devika deserves better.

Then Mr Charduri dropped his bombshell.

'I'd like to spend the next five days with my daughter,' he requested. 'Just me and my daughter.'

When Mrs Raju translated this to me, my smile disappeared.

'Once I have spent those five days with her,' he said. 'I will leave you in peace.'

'I'm sorry,' I laughed incredulously, 'but we don't

do that in this country. I can't give my daughter over to some strange man ... well, sorry,' I corrected myself hastily, 'you're not some strange man, you're her father. But ... I still feel ... uncomfortable.'

Mrs Raju looked disapproving.

'I will supervise,' she said to me, without translating my grievance back to Mr Charduri. 'I will be there all the time to make sure Devika is okay.'

'How can you possibly be there all the time for five days?' I demanded crossly. 'How can I know he won't try to kidnap her the moment your back is turned? No, I'm not agreeing to this. No, no, no.'

But, of course, Mr Charduri went and told Devika that I'd said no. And she threw tantrums. She begged me to let her spend some time with her father. Mrs Raju came back to me and suggested that she and Devika could stay with Mr Charduri and his cousin for just one night. She encouraged me to go and visit the house and see where they would sleep.

'Okay,' I said. 'One night and one night only. Devika can be picked up in the morning and she can come back the next afternoon.'

Was I wrong? I felt if I said no, he might hang around. I admit it: I couldn't help feeling that it was the perfect opportunity to get rid of him. To go back to simply being just me and Devika.

I felt very panicky when I said goodbye to her; I very nearly cancelled the visit altogether. I asked Devika if her daddy treated her well, if she was *sure* she would be happy to stay with him, and she assured me that he was a good man. She promised she would text and call me. Since then I've spoken to her a few times and she does seem okay. But I'll still be glad when she's back tomorrow.

As I slip into bed, I suddenly catch sight of a camera glinting in the corner of the room. One they forget to remove. I assume it's been switched off . . . but you never know . . .

I hurry downstairs and rummage in the cupboard under the stairs, yanking out a hammer. I wield it with relish and enjoy the satisfying sound of splintered glass, letting out a whoop. As I clear up the splinters with a dustpan and brush, I recall with regret the madness I put Devika through with that TV show. When she gets back, though, I'm going to make it up to her. I'm going to shower her with presents. And there'll be no more gimmicks, no more TV shows, no more photoshoots, no more interviews. I've realised that motherhood and fame don't mix. And I know which one I prefer.

When I look back and remember how I used to be, before I got Devika, it makes me wince. I can hardly believe that was me. I remember that every Saturday night I used to get dressed up with Fran, fretting over my appearance, worried that we'd go out and *nobody would photograph us*. We'd sit in bars with other famous folk and wannabes and Fran and I would be pretending to talk to each other when really we were glancing around the room to see if anyone was looking at us. If I woke up the next morning and I wasn't mentioned in the gossip columns, I'd feel hollow inside. Rejected. As though the press and the public were some parental figures who'd said they didn't want me any more.

I was looking for fulfilment from my fame but it was only ever a sickly sweet satisfaction, a binge that never really nourished me.

That's been the biggest relief about having Devika: being so worried about her that I don't have to worry about myself and those column inches. When I got that stupid nose job, it really drove things home. It didn't make me feel much better; I realised that nobody particularly cared if my nose was straighter and it certainly wasn't going to change my life.

It's the people you love who change your life.

I lie back down on the bed and remember all those years back, when I was pregnant with Liam's baby. I had no idea what a gift I'd been given. I was terrified that I was about to lose my freedom. I felt no connection to the creature inside me, just a horrified panicky loathing. I had no regrets when I had the abortion – until later when I was told I probably couldn't have any more children. Now that I have Devika, however, I feel another sense of sorrow, knowing what I missed out on. I wish I had chosen a better time to tell Liam, rather than in a drumken state at some awards ceremony.

But I also feel that that baby was never meant to be, for then I would never have found Devika, and she is without a doubt the best thing that's ever happened to me.

The next day Mr Charduri brings Devika back ten minutes later than we agreed. Those ten minutes feel like ten hours. When I open the door and see he has brought her back safely, I nearly weep. I fling open my arms and scoop her up and shower her with kisses, crying, 'Did you miss me, did you miss your mummy, mmm, did you miss me?'

I ask Mr Charduri if he wants a cup of tea. He says no. And then I feel the slightest unease. There's a funny look on his face. And Mrs Raju also looks rather pinched. In fact, she can hardly look me in the eye.

'What?' I ask in alarm. 'Did anything happen to Devika?'

'We have something to tell you – there is no easy way of putting this,' says Mrs Raju. She looks at

Mr Charduri and he nods solemnly, indicating that she can translate. 'Mr Chaduri says: "I have spoken to my daughter and she has decided to return home with me."'

I hear myself let out a faint laugh.

I look at Devika, who looks up at me with big, frightened eyes. Mr Charduri's face darkens and he speaks once again to Mrs Raju.

'"Devika has agreed,"' Mrs Raju translates. '"I am her father. She belongs with me."'

Is he *serious*? I feel panic tearing through my stomach. A day ago I was buying her pressies and now I'm about to say goodbye for ever.

'Devika,' I say softly. She keeps her eyes downcast, avoiding mine. Then, finally, she looks up and nods.

'I'm going with my daddy,' she says. He reaches for her hand and she clutches it tightly.

I narrow my eyes. This is insane; this is impossible. Oh, God, I've been tricked! *He tricked me!* He said he just wanted to see her one last time. He told me he was going to go to India. He must have known all along that he wanted her to go with him. And I fell for it. I let him persuade her. Oh, God!

'I need to speak to Devika on her own,' I say in a very loud, very fierce voice.

'Devika has made her decision,' Mr Charduri says quickly, speaking in English.

'Oh, I'm sure she has made *her* decision. I don't know what you've said to manipulate or pressurise her, but I won't accept it! I won't!'

Mr Charduri responds angrily, raising his voice, and Mrs Raju translates for him in a polite tone that is utterly at odds with the words he speaks.

'"How can I manipulate her? How can I manipulate a child who wants to be with her father? We are related by blood!"'

'You have to let me speak to her. You *will* let me speak to her. I'm not going to stand for this. I am her mother. I've fed her and loved her and cared for her—'

I break off as Devika bursts into tears.

'Stop arguing,' she weeps.

'Now you see? You've upset her.' Mr Charduri pulls Devika close to his side. He strokes her hair and the gesture shoots an arrow of raw, jealous pain through me.

But I refuse to accept this. I don't believe, can't believe, that Devika loves her father more than me.

'Please. I have a right to discuss this with her – a legal right and a moral right,' I say, making a huge effort to control my voice. 'I am her guardian,' I play along with him, 'and even if she is planning to go, then I'd at least like to say goodbye alone.'

Mr Charduri struggles with himself. Then he says: 'Okay.'

He leaves the room and closes the door behind him. Mrs Raju gives me an apologetic glance and follows him. A heavy silence fills the vacuum. I gaze over at Devika. I feel as I did when I first approached her in the Delhi orphanage: delicate and nervous. Her brief fit of tears is over and her face looks puffy and tired. I sit down on the sofa near her, trying to find the right words. I remember how she looked on that day in the orphanage: her brittle bones and skinny face and desperate eyes and bare feet. Now she looks enchantingly pretty, with plump cheeks and soft eyes and expensive shoes. I've given her so much; I have so much more to give her. Or maybe this is merely a selfish justification because I need her; I just can't imagine life with her.

And I still can't believe she would want to leave me.

'Devika,' I say softly. 'Come here.'

She comes over and I hold both her hands in mine. I try to look her in the eye but she hangs her head. I feel confused again – what on earth has he said to her?

'Devika – you know that you can trust me? You know that you can tell me anything?'

Her eyes flick up to mine, then back down again.

She nods. I feel as though we are strangers; I'm desperate to tear down the wall between us. How can we lose five months of intimacy in just two days?

But I guess I'm being naïve. I've been trying to deny it over the last few weeks, but it's been happening – I lost Devika the moment he knocked on my door.

'Devika – do you really want to go and live with your father?'

'Yes.'

'But why? What has he said to you?'

'Because I love him,' she says simply. 'He's my daddy. My *real* daddy.' The way she emphasises the word makes my heart clench.

'Okay,' I say, struggling to keep back my emotions. 'But don't you like living with me, your mummy, in England? D'you really want to go back? You're happy here, aren't you? You like school now?' I shake her hands, harder than I intend to.

'I want to be with my real dad in my real home.' She hesitates, then looks into my eyes and blurts out: 'I always prayed that my real mum and dad would find me and I'd live in my real home. I've lost my mum but I still have my dad. I prayed for him and now he's here. He's a gift.'

I realise then that Mr Charduri is right. He hasn't

manipulated Devika. The reason she's being so sheepish and ducking her head is because she feels guilty. She doesn't want to let me down. I stare down at her hands, entwined in mine, and I feel tears well up and slip out of my eyes. I take a deep, shaky breath and force a smile.

'It's up to you,' I say. 'And if you feel you must be with your real dad, I understand—'

I break off, unable to speak any more, as my voice shatters into tears. Grief engulfs me. She leans in and hugs me tightly and I clasp her close, crying into her hair. She holds me as though I am her daughter and she's my mother. When she pulls back, however, her eyes are shiny with sadness too.

'Please don't cry, Karina,' she says, touching my cheek, her chin wobbling. 'Please don't be angry.'

'I'm not angry. I do love you. I love you very much. I want you to be happy, always. I'll come and visit you in India, or you can come and visit me, and we'll still be friends, won't we, Devika? Won't we?'

She nods her head vigorously.

'I love you,' she says. 'You are my friend, always.' Then she leans in and gently rubs her nose against mine in an Eskimo kiss. I feel as though my heart will break and I pull her close to me for one last hug, breathing in her scent and bottling it inside me: the sweet smell of her skin and the silk of her hair.

An hour later, the rage hits me. I call up Mr Charduri and scream down the phone that he's never going to take her away from me. He doesn't understand a word I'm saying, but I think he gets the gist. He just keeps repeating over and over, 'I'm her father, I'm her father.'

Then I call up social services and rant at Angela. I point out that I've put in a court order to adopt Devika, everything is under way and in less than one month's time it will all be official.

Angela goes quiet.

'It's a shame you didn't originally go through an adoption agency that was recognised by CARA,' she says. 'Then the adoption would have happened there and then, instead of you having to go through the process here.'

'But – but – the reason I went for that agency was because they speeded everything up! I didn't want to wait years. I mean, God, I've even heard of one couple who took *eight* years to adopt. Are you saying I don't have any rights? I mean, I am her guardian.' But even as I say the word, it sounds lame and weak.

'I can put you in touch with someone who can give you legal advice,' Angela says quickly, soothing me. 'I'll give you the number now. But the issue you really might want to think about here is Devika. Does she want to be with you, or with her father?'

'She wants—' I break off. 'I . . .'

'You see, if she really wants to be with her father, then the kindest thing might be for you to withdraw your adoption order and let her go. You've had a very bumpy time over the last few months, Karina, what with Liam and the . . . er . . . school incident. I can't even guarantee that adoption will be granted – the panel will have to assess it and your case is . . . well . . . whatever you feel is best, Karina. I'm here to help you.'

'Right.' I swallow. 'Thank you, Angela.'

'I didn't mean – I can put you in touch with a lawyer . . .'

'It's fine. You're right. I need to speak to Devika. This is her decision.'

The rage turns to tears and I spend hours sitting in my bedroom, weeping and weeping. I don't go to Devika, I don't beg her to stay with me, I don't put any pressure on her. It feels wrong to do so, to tear her apart too, but finally I can't bear it any more. I go into her room. She is sitting there, looking terrified and tense. I know she's heard me crying and she's been too afraid to come to me.

I sit down on the bed next to her and say, 'Did

you like all your presents? I can see you've opened them. Did you like your jeans?'

And, very slowly, her face taut with guilt, Devika nods her head.

45

Karina

'Honey, will you *please* put the chocolate biscuits down!'

I'm standing in the local organic supermarket, looking at breakfast cereals, when the woman's voice shrills right through me.

I turn to look at her. Her daughter is blonde and looks about ten years old. And she is throwing the world's worst tantrum.

'No, Honey,' her mother cries, grabbing the biscuits out of her hand and flinging them back on to the shelf. 'You *can't* have them.'

Honey starts to weep. I turn away, trying to shut the noise out. I try to focus on the supermarket sounds around me: the happy-dappy tinkle of music, the chatter of Thursday evening shoppers, the

voiceover of the manager advising us all that broc-
coli is on special offer. But I can't help it. Honey's
sobs magnify and penetrate every cell in my body.
An hour ago, I was sitting in my room, weeping,
and I knew that I had to get a grip and get out
of the house. I told myself to shop, because there
was nothing but mouldy milk in the fridge and
shopping was a good, practical thing to do. I told
myself that getting out would clear my mind. That
it would make me stop replaying the moment,
over and over, when I said goodbye to Devika at
the airport and we both wept. I held her close
and her sobs wetted my ear. It's as though my ear
has become a shell, holding her goodbye like the
shush of the sea, a sound that will echo inside me
for ever.

I turn to look at Honey. Her red eyes widen nervously, as if she's worried that another adult is going
to tell her off. I give her a surreptitious, reassuring
smile. She blinks and smiles back. Then, her confidence boosted, she waits for her mother's back to
turn, then reaches out and takes the chocolate
biscuits off the shelf again. Then she gives me an
impish little grin, as though the biscuits are our
secret. I am starting to shake my head when Honey's
mother turns back.

'HONEY!' As she grabs the packet, it breaks.
Crumbs and chunks shower and scatter over the floor.

'Oh, God.' Her voice is quiet now, a voice of utter despair and exhaustion.

Without thinking, I pitch in to help, picking up bits of biscuit from the floor, gathering them into a handkerchief.

'Oh, thank you,' she says, 'that's so kind – but really, you don't have to – oh, thank you, thank you.' She turns to her daughter. 'You *stupid* girl – I've just about had it up to here with you!'

Her harsh tone makes my heart weep.

'Don't shout at her!' I cry. 'She only wants biscuits.'

'I—' The woman looks faintly startled. Her eyes flash, the gratitude fading, replaced by suspicion.

'I mean, what kind of mother are you,' I burst out, 'shouting at your daughter just because she wants a few biscuits? Does it really matter?'

'How I treat *my* daughter is none of *your* business,' she snaps fiercely. She grabs Honey's hand and drags her away, leaving the shattered remains of the biscuits on the floor.

Well, I guess at least I succeeded in getting her to stop shouting at her daughter.

I turn back to the breakfast cereals, my heart pounding hard. That was a bloody stupid thing to do, a voice inside berates me. If she'd recognised you and gone to the press, the headlines would have been outrageous: *Screwy Celebrity Mum Karina Accosts Innocent Mother in Supermarket.*

But I didn't mean to have a go at her. My heart feels tight with frustrated emotions. I only meant to say please don't waste precious minutes shouting at your daughter. Because you never know what's going to happen. Life can take the people we love away from us at any moment. And being a mother is the best gift in the world. Don't take out your tiredness on your daughter – leave it behind at work. Save up your best for her. Treasure her. Do wonderful things together. Love her, always.

That's all I really meant to say.

Back home, I notice there are only two paps outside my door. That's down from the twenty there were three weeks ago, just after Devika left, and ten last week. They both look cold and bored. I ignore them, my dark glasses rendering my face expressionless.

'Cup of tea?' one calls out.

I close the door and put the shopping down. The house seems cold and silent. I put the shopping in the fridge, the Rice Krispies in the cupboard. There are already five boxes in there – I'm building up quite a collection. I watch TV, eating lukewarm baked beans on toast.

Just before I go to bed, I go up into Devika's room. This is my nightly ritual.

I've left everything as it was just before she left. She took most of her clothes with her, but there

465

wasn't room in the case for all of them – there were a few left behind. Her Ganesh statue still sits in the corner. Her bed is spread with the mermaids duvet that covered her on her last night at home. I sit on the edge of the bed and remember how I sang her one last song goodbye that night. How I struggled with myself, trying not to make her feel guilty, yet silently, helplessly wishing the song would bond us, make her change her mind, make her stay.

I take out my pen and pad. I do this every night. I write a love letter. Most of them I don't bother to send. They start off well and become a gush of emotion.

Dear Devika,

I pause, almost afraid to begin, feeling a prickling behind my eyes. Will I sit here for ever, writing letters night after night? I can't ever imagine stopping.

I want you to know that I will never forget you. I don't understand why this has happened to me. I don't know why life gave you to me, such a wonderful gift, and then took you away. Maybe I wasn't good enough for you, maybe I didn't deserve you, and that's why I lost you.

But I will always treasure all the times we spent together. I'm already looking forward to your birthday. It's many months away. But I'm always going to remember that day. I'll bake you a cake here. I'll send you a card. I'll light a candle and think about how you're doing. One year you'll be starting a new school. Another you'll be with your first boyfriend. Then you'll be at university. You'll be tall and graceful and beautiful then. You'll be the top of your class. Then you'll be working. I think you will become a vet, though I'm not sure if there's much call for them in India. Maybe you will come back to England then. Maybe one day on the street I'll bump into you and you'll be shoving a pushchair about and your husband will be carrying shopping and we'll look at each other and smile. You'll remember I was the crazy woman who gave you Rice Krispies and forced you to be on TV.

Maybe I made mistakes with Liam and the TV and everything. But I was only trying to do what I thought was best. That's all you can ever do as a parent. I've realised that. You start off with the best intentions, thinking you'll be perfect. But you mess it up, over and over. You stumble around, learning all the time, hoping one day you will get it right. I used to think it was imperative that you became famous. I feel ashamed of that now. But that was before

I fell in love with you and I realise now that all I want is for you to be happy. Then I can feel proud that I was a good parent. Except you have your own father now, and that pride will belong to him . . .

I am crying too hard to finish. I put it down and stare at Ganesh. I want to scream at the world, WHY? I want a divine explanation. I want to know why I have to go through this. Maybe there really is such a thing as karma and I did something truly terrible in a past life. I don't know; I don't understand.

I sit and cry until there are no tears left inside me.

I sit and wait.

The house is silent.

Out of the window, I see the distant flashing gems of a plane passing through the sky. Then it fades away and the night turns to black.

The next morning I get up, on tenterhooks as I wait for the post to come.

At eleven o'clock there is the slap of the letterbox. I dash over, my heart beating. I pick up the envelopes. Mostly logos: *Barclaycard . . . Dial A Flight . . . Pizza Hut . . .*

Nothing with an Indian postmark.

I go back into the kitchen.

The phone rings. I don't answer – just let it go to voicemail. Then I press PLAY. It's my agent, asking me if I want a guest slot on a TV breakfast show.

I go to the window and take a surreptitious peep, wondering how many paps there are today.

Just one.

He's already looking bored, as though he might take off soon. I know he won't be there tomorrow. The thought makes me feel depressed, as though once he's gone it's a definitive proof that my story is over. That Devika is gone for good.

The next morning, I hear a knock at the door. As usual, I ignore it. I climbed into bed yesterday afternoon and I haven't got up since. A large bag of Maltesers is spooled over my beside table. Screwed-up balls of paper dance in the creases in the covers.

Dear Devika. I try to begin again, *I'm worried about you. I had a dream last night and in it you were crying for me. But I'm sure it's just me being silly. I miss you I hope you are happy. I hope I might visit you soon . . .*

Another knock at the door. I pause.

I get up and creep across the landing and into Devika's bedroom. For one wistful moment, I hope Liam might be on my doorstep. When I slip back the curtain, I see it's Fran and Clare.

For a moment I hesitate, wondering whether to answer or hurry back to the cocoon of my bed. Then Fran glances up and spots me. I quickly let the curtain fall back.

'DON'T TRY TO HIDE,' Fran yells up at me. 'WE'RE GOING TO STAY HERE UNTIL YOU LET US IN.'

I let out a cross sigh, then trudge down the stairs in my dressing gown. Before I open the door, I gather myself. I mustn't snap at them, I tell myself miserably. I do hate people's sympathy. They all say the same things: *let it all out and move on . . . you'll see her again one day . . . you'll pull through*. As though Devika is a passing loss, like a spate of bad weather, or mislaying a handbag. They think that because she's not my real child, not from my womb, the grief doesn't cut as deep. That I can just forget her, replace her with someone else. Or, the classic consolation line, tentatively expressed: *well, surely you can have one of your own*. Nobody understands.

I open the door and they stare at me, then exchange concerned glances.

Behind them, there is a flash as the final photographer, who is clearly made of sterner stuff than I suspected, feeling he may as well have a go, has a go.

'Quick!' Fran cries, looking me up and down, 'you look like total shit – quick – get in!'

They bundle me into the hallway. I notice vaguely that Clare is carrying a large cardboard box.

'Well,' says Fran. 'How are you?'

I don't reply.

'Fran,' Clare hisses. 'Don't ask stupid questions.'

'Sorry.'

I feel a moment of angry hate for my friends. I can see Fran hiding a nervous, hysterical smile. I feel like shouting at them to leave.

Then Clare presses her chin against her box and looks at me with her clear eyes.

'Let's go into the kitchen,' she says in a steady voice. 'We'll have a cup of tea and then if you want to get rid of us, you can just tell us to go and we won't be offended.'

'We'll make the tea,' Fran adds desperately.

'Okay.'

They look pleased, as though we've all held hands and jumped over a hurdle together. Do they really think a cup of tea is a triumph? That a shot of Earl Grey and sugar is a sign that I'm better? No; they just want to make themselves feel better. Play at being token friends so they can go back to their lives without feeling guilty. Fran can drink and snort coke and Clare can go back to her kids. She can hold them close and breathe in their beautiful scent. She can think of me and thank God she hasn't had to go through the same.

I drag myself into the kitchen and slump into a chair. My eyes flit to the clock. I decide I'll give them ten minutes.

I realise that Fran and Clare are gazing around the kitchen with taken aback expressions. I guess it is a mess. Piles of washing up clutter and tower in the sink. The bin is overflowing and because I couldn't be bothered to empty it I've started using an M&S carrier bag and dumping rubbish into that. I blink, slightly surprised, when Fran pulls on a pair of rubber gloves. I don't think Fran has ever done any washing up in her life before. Clare puts down her box on the table and then changes the bin for me, huffing as she drags it out from under the sink. As she opens the door, a few crisp autumn leaves swirl into the room. I frown, breathing in the bright, fresh air. The air in here is stale with grief; I only realise that when I taste the contrast.

Then Clare makes the tea. I'm actually grateful for the big box in the middle of the table. It means I don't have to look at them. I still can't work out if I feel relieved or resentful that they're here. I keep wanting to tell them to go, but then I feel I'll miss them.

I realise I'm going to have to humour them and ask the question sooner or later.

'So what's in the box?'

Clare and Fran exchange excited glances.

'You open it.'

'No, you,' says Fran. 'Then if she doesn't like it, it can be all your fault.'

They look at me, smiling. I shrug at them impatiently. Their smiles fade.

Clare opens up the box.

'She's from both of us. We thought she might cheer you up.'

And out of the box jumps a little kitten. She's white, with ginger patches and big bright mischievous green eyes.

'Oh!' I cry in shock, not quite sure whether to laugh or cry.

'Here! Bond, woman, bond.' Fran picks the kitten up and plonks her into my lap. I touch her uneasily. Her fur is pure fluff, like the soft teddy Devika used to cuddle. She starts to purr.

'Oh, Devika would have loved her so much!' I cry. My mouth sags. 'She wanted a kitten and I didn't get her one. I should have got her one.'

Fran and Clare exchange glances.

'I told you it was a shit present,' says Fran. 'I told you we should have got her a dog.'

'No,' Clare cries. 'Dogs are smelly.'

Suddenly, for the first time in days, my cold heart thaws and a trickle of warmth comes out. I realise how wonderful and kind my friends are being. I realise that even though something has been ripped out of me, perhaps this might be the start of a healing. I hug the kitten close and cry, 'I'll call her Sophie. That was Devika's favourite character – from *The BFG*.'

Fran and Clare stop arguing and look pleased.

'See,' Clare says, 'she'll keep you company, cheer you up. I mean, I know it's not the same as . . . but . . .' she trails off awkwardly.

They both smile tentatively.

Suddenly I feel like opening up to them. Suddenly I feel they might understand.

'I had a dream about her last night,' I say. 'I had this dream that she was crying out for me. She was in a dark place and she was calling my name. I think I need to go over to India. Just to make sure she's okay . . .'

Fran and Clare look at each other. My anger returns. They think I'm crazy.

'I am her mother!' I cry. 'I have to be sure!'

'You have to let go,' Clare says. 'Yes, you should visit, but wait a few months. Wait until you've dealt with your grief a little more. For your sake, Karina. You could go over there and reopen so much pain. I think you need to just go through this for a while. And we'll be here for you. You can call us any time. You can come and stay with me for a while, if you like.'

I shake my head, forcing a smile.

'She doesn't answer my letters,' I say. 'I write to her and she was writing back and then the letters stopped.'

'Well, the postal service over there is pretty crazy. And Devika's probably busy at school. Would you rather she wrote you letters or did her schoolwork?' Clare asks.

'Okay, that's it!' I say, jumping up. 'Thank you for the kitten, but I really think you should go now.'

'We're only trying to help,' Fran cries defensively.

But Clare is more stoical. She washes up the cups and then takes a few more things out of the box: a little dish and a packet of cat food. I thank her politely and nod my head and wait for her to go.

Later that evening, I go up into Devika's bedroom. I've been sitting there for a while, my pen in my hand, my pad on my lap, when the door suddenly pushes open and the kitten comes in. For a moment I want to put it out, feeling my sacred space is being invaded. But then it comes and jumps up on to my lap, so benign and innocent, and I feel it can't do any harm. It purrs and claws my jumper, reaching up to rub its whiskers against my cheek. My tears plop into its fur and I rub back, feeling consoled and despairing at the same time.

'They're right, aren't they?' I say. 'I have to let

her go. If I love her, I have to let her get on with her life back in her own country. It's best for her.'

I take the sheet of paper and scrumple into a ball. Then I sit on the bed, stroking the kitten, making a new resolution. Clare is right. I won't get in touch with her or worry about her for at least another month. I have to let her be; I have to let her live her life.

46

Devika

I'm scared. I want my mummy Karina. It's so dark
in here and I'm so tired. When the men look at me
like that, I think they might kill me. *Oh, Krishna,
I want my mummy Karina. Please help me.*

47

Karina

A week later, I am woken by an insistent paw thumping against my cheek. My kitten Sophie stares down at me with beseeching green eyes, wondering why I'm sleeping when her tummy is rumbling for crunchies.

I get up and feed her, smiling fondly as she munches away. Then my smile fades. I see the ghost of a girl in the kitchen, crouching down to stroke Sophie, gently tugging her tail, laughing in delight as the kitten miaows.

My eyes flit to the clock. I jump. Thank God Sophie woke me up, or I would have been late for my TV slot.

I've got just enough time to change before the doorbell rings and the car from the studio picks me up.

I take off my pyjamas and they puddle on the floor. I've been wearing the same pair all week and it feels like shedding an old skin. I get into the shower and feel the water kiss my head; I soap in shampoo, massaging gently. My eyes wander over to the bath and I see a dark girl splashing and playing in the bubbles, making miaow noises at her duck. I shut my eyes quickly, letting the spray sluice over my face. The new clothes I put on feel crisp and clean against my skin and when I go outside the air tastes fresh as apples. I notice how beautiful the winter trees look, stark against the sky. But every pleasure is laced with guilt. I feel as though I've rejected life and it's trying to seduce me back to normality. But to succumb feels like a betrayal. I feel I ought to stay in bed for ever. To show Devika – even though she's halfway across the world and probably never thinks of me – that I still love her.

I push through the guilt and get into the back of the car.

Over the past few weeks, my agent has called me repeatedly with mammoth offers for magazine and newspaper and TV interviews. The *Daily Mail* topped them all with a ten-thousand-pound offer for an exclusive on *My Heartache: Living Without My Daughter*. It's extraordinary, really, how much they were prepared to pay for a piece of my grief; I suggested sarcastically to my agent that they might like to make an offer on a tear by tear basis. When I turned them all down, he got decidedly cross.

'I don't know what's the matter with you, Karina,' he complained. 'Earlier this year, you were begging me for any bloody inch in any magazine you could get.'

Earlier this year, I was a different person.

In the end, though, I felt nervous that he might drop me. And I realised that feeling nervous was a good thing. It meant that underneath the grief a part of me wanted to get up and get out and get on with my life.

So I said yes to the mid-morning TV show. Because they don't want me to break down on TV. They want me to talk about dieting and fashion: reassuringly trivial stuff.

When I get to the studio, I'm taken off for make-up. Susie plasters my face with product and chatters away merrily. When I look at my reflection, I'm startled to see that I look like my old self again (if a little orange). I begin to chatter back. I realise I'm actually enjoying myself.

I step out into the TV set and settle down on the blue sofa. We're off air whilst the ads are running so I say hi to the presenters, Lottie and Mark. And then I meet the other guest on the programme. My smile freezes. Oh, great. Guess what, it's Hayley. My agent neglected to tell me about *that* little detail.

'Hi, Karina!' Hayley cries, air-kissing me as though we're the best of friends. Lottie and Mark smile, clearly thinking we're all going to have a jolly time together.

'So let's just have a quick run through,' Lottie says. 'We'll talk about diets first – just a relaxed chat about what ones have worked for you, which you think are fads. Then we're looking at clothes on a budget – okay?'

Before we go on air, Hayley turns to me and says lightly, 'Hey, I saw Liam last night. We had a drink together. Your name came up. He said he hadn't seen you for ages.'

And she smiles, a smiling dripping with rich triumph, a smile that says, *I've won. I've got him in the end.*

I shrug to suggest that I don't care a bit. But I do. She has just thrust the knife into my heart, already raw from the loss of Devika. During my period of mourning, I sometimes used to hope that Liam might get in touch, that we might one day repair things, that even if I was never going to be a mother, I might still have him. But he never did and I never had the guts to call him. And now he's back with Hayley. So I've lost not only my precious daughter but the love of my life. I sit there on the sofa, surrounded by lights and cameras and voices, and suddenly I feel very alone.

'Hi, welcome back from the break,' Lottie greets the camera. 'And today we're joined by guests Hayley Young and Karina West who are here to discuss the hot topic in the news today – dieting. On the one hand, we're all being criticised for high obesity levels and on the other we've got a continuing problem with size-zero models in the fashion world. Are diets just a fad or are they a healthy thing? What do you think, Hayley?'

Hayley tosses back a waterfall of blond hair and says, 'Oh God, I *never* diet, never. I think it sets a bad example to young girls who might be suffering from anorexia.'

Bollocks, total bollocks. I know for a fact from Liam that Hayley tries every diet under the sun, even a bizarre one where she only ate twelve peas for each meal.

'What about you, Karina?'

'I used to diet,' I reply honestly, 'but when I became a mother I stopped worrying. I only cared about what my daughter was eating.'

There is an awkward silence and I dread that Lottie might push me, but she doesn't want any controversy at ten thirty in the morning when house-wives and mums are watching; she might have to bring up the joint-in-the-lunch-box debacle. So she gives me a delicate smile and after another ten minutes talking aimlessly about how dieting is a waste of time but actually might be a good thing, we get on to the subject of the credit crunch. A shopping 'expert' pops up and lays out a series of outfits for us to see what Christmas bargains we might buy on a budget.

'See – I put together this outfit for just twelve pounds. This skirt was just three pounds on the high street. This top came at a bargain price of only five pounds—'

'Wow, that's *gorgeous*,' Lottie gushes. 'Those beads are just exquisite. They give it a really authentic handmade look.'

We all coo over the turquoise top, which is decorated with pink and purple beading. But I can barely summon the energy to look excited. My depression is beginning to tiptoe back. I'm starting to feel detached, to wonder what the point of all this is.

'How about you, Hayley? D'you shop on a budget?' Lottie asks.

'Oh, absolutely – don't we all?' Hayley cries. 'Even us celebrities have to budget too. I like to mix vintage with designer with sales bargains. I'll buy a T-shirt in a supermarket for a few quid one day but then the next I might splash out seventy-five pounds, as I did yesterday, on a *Stop Breast Cancer* one.'

'That's a very important point, Hayley,' Lottie agrees.

At last the show is over. I've barely said two words but nobody seems to care. I thought the experience might offer some form of redemption, but I just feel rather tired.

'D'you fancy breakfast?' Hayley asks. 'We can have a catch up.'

'What, so you can spend an hour rubbing it in that you've won Liam?' I laugh. 'Really, I'm fine. I'm going home.'

It's in the car on the way home that I make the decision. Actually, it doesn't even feel like an intellectual choice. It feels as though it makes itself.

I feel a rush of crazy exhilaration. But underneath there is a cool, clear calmness, an anchor that convinces me this is the right thing.

When I get home, I'm careful not to stop and think, in case I lose my nerve.

First of all, I hurry to the cupboard and take out my passport. I check my Indian visa. I got an annual, multiple-entry one. And yes – I still have several months left before it expires.

Then I pick up the phone, call Dial A Flight, and book a ticket to India. They manage to get me for tomorrow afternoon.

When I give them my credit card details and it's all confirmed, I suffer a shaky moment of doubt and

I hear Fran's and Clare's voices crying, 'What are you doing?'

But I'm doing the right thing. I know I am.

I go upstairs and start to pack. As I do, I realise I've been repressing my feelings for the past week, without knowing how tightly I'd packed down the lid.

I laugh at the thought of seeing her again. Then I cry with the fear of how hard it will be to say goodbye again. Then I do a dance of excitement at the craziness of it all.

The kitten comes into the bedroom and jumps into the case, gazing up at me with wide eyes. I stroke her chin and assure her that she won't be left on her own; Clare can take care of feeding her. I'll have to make up some lie about going on holiday.

'When I come back, maybe you'll even have a new owner,' I say.

For, in a moment of sheer hope and madness, I have booked two return tickets back from India: one adult, one child.

48

Karina

What am I doing here? *What am I doing here?*

I pull my T-shirt back on and yank my suitcase back on to the bed. This is crazy, I tell myself, bundling up socks and saris, you're behaving like a nutty child stalker. I decide to call the airport, change my flight, check out early and just go home. I'll pretend I never came here and seriously thought about doing this. Nobody will ever know.

Then, just as I'm about to zip up the case, I stop. I arrived in Delhi at three this morning; I've only slept for four hours. I'm completely exhausted and I'll have to endure another eighteen-hour journey back to England. I'm here now. I may as well try to see her. I mean, I don't have to talk to her. I don't have to disturb her existence, unsettle her life. I've got her address so I can just creep up, potter about, maybe catch a few glimpses of her. I picture myself sidling up behind a bush and watching her in the field with her father. I picture them digging together, hot and tired but satisfied with their simple life; I picture him giving her a kiss and scooping her up in the air as a reward for her hard work. Or maybe I'll catch a glimpse of them in their farmhouse kitchen, Devika sitting at the table, golden lamp-light glowing around her, her father leaning over her as he helps her with her homework. And then I'll carry her back home in my heart; I'll probably cry throughout the flight but they will be tears of peace.

Then I'll be able to get on with my life.

I decide to put my sari back on. That way if I do encounter Mr Charduri he can't complain that I look too *westernised*. The sari is a mess, though, because my hands are shaking and I can't focus on getting the pins in the right places. I just keep thinking: *in half an hour I'm going to see Devika.* Will she be different? Oh God, I don't think I will be able to just watch her. I'll end up calling out her name, saying something. I know I will. I keep warning myself that I must prepare for the worst. She might well turn her nose up at me, declare she's happy; she might have forgotten me, even. But Devika is much too loving for that. I can't imagine anything other than being greeted with a hug.

I am just about to leave my hotel room when suddenly I'm thrown off balance by the arrival of a text from Liam.

Hi u. How r u? Lx

If only you knew, I thought, laughing out loud with nerves and fear. I haven't heard from Liam in ages now and perhaps if I wasn't in India, feeling so lonely and disorientated, I might have spent hours debating whether to reply. But I'm so grateful for contact with a friend, I immediately text back.

L, I'm in India. I've done something crazy. Back for Dev. Kx

I want him to reply instantly, to reassure me that I'm doing the right thing. But there is a silence. I guess he does think I'm crazy. I shove my mobile in my bag and forget about him. All I care about now is finding Devika again.

Downstairs, a line of rickshaws is waiting outside the hotel. I hail one and give him the address. The driver is tall and wears a baseball cap; his limbs look thin but strong, as though they're made of wire. Then I remember what Devika taught me on my last trip here: I need to set an agreed price before we leave.

'Two hundred rupees,' he insists, waving my piece of paper. 'Long way, long way!'

Then I wonder why I'm even haggling. All that matters is Devika – I'm prepared to pay any money in the world. I give him a twenty-dollar bill and his eyes moon. He kisses it and I laugh in joy.

'Let's go!' I cry, clapping my hands.

The rickshaw passes through New Delhi and into Old, heading in the direction of Shahpur Jat. Gradually the glamour of New Delhi's stylish sari and sweet shops is replaced by increasing grime, and houses start to squat or lose doors or windows. We pass by the Shani Bazaar, rainbow stands piled high with fruits and vegetables, flies fighting customers to be the first to feast. Spices sweeten the dusty air, hazing over stalls sprawling cloths in swirls of ochre and green and pink, not to mention the statues of the *devas*; a beautiful Ganesh smiles at me as though reassuring me I will find her in the end.

My senses feel battered from every direction, for every face might be her face. Every time I see a young girl with dark hair, my heart leaps . . . and sinks in disappointment. The rickshaw slows to a halt and I think we must be here, but the driver shouts something and starts to padal again. I realise we're doing a U-turn in the road. We narrowly miss a car.

'Are we there yet?' I call out. I feel confused. I was expecting us to head to a rural area, to be travelling through fields. But we're still in the heart of the city.

'Okay, we find, okay,' he cries back.

I knit my fingers in my lap. Frustration and uncertainty plait inside me. For all I know, he could be taking me anywhere.

He cycles a few more blocks, swerves, then drops me next to a crumbling building. The bottom windows and doors are just holes; a rat comes running out of one.

'Here?' I ask.

'Yes, here very good. Now ten dollars more,' he says, holding out his hand.

'But . . . *here*?' I look at the building. 'No – farm. *Kheta*.'

'Yes. Here. No *kheta*,' he insists. He gives me back my piece of paper and jabs it. 'Ten dollars.'

'Okay, okay,' I cry, dazed, passing him another ten.

As he cycles quickly away, I stare at the building.

So Devika's father hasn't bought his farm yet. Was he lying when he said that was his dream? Or did he change his mind? Or have I just been conned and found myself in the wrong place?

I venture into the building, but it appears to be deserted. I wrinkle up my nose as a horrible smell of sewage pierces my nostrils. The walls look slimy and scaly. I reach the bottom of a staircase which winds upwards – but there is a large gap halfway up it, so getting to the next floor is impossible. I stand still, listening. I can't hear any human voices. Just a faint scratching noise . . . and then I see them. More rats.

I hurry out quickly, into the scorching sun. Market cries blare around me. Despair fills me up. Where the hell is she? A small boy who is selling statues gestures to me.

'You buy statue?'

'No . . . can you help me?' I show him the piece of paper, tapping the name. 'Mr Charduri – you know?'

The boy nods eagerly. But then he shakes his head and holds up three fingers.

'What?' Sweat drips into my eyes and I mop my forehead.

'Mr Charduri . . . three.' He points to a rotund man who is selling clothes on his stall.

'Oh – you know three Mr Charduris,' I twig. 'Yes, of course . . . I mean the Mr Charduri who has a girl, Devika.'

'Devika!' He makes a gesture of small height with his hand.

'Yes! Yes!' I cry. 'Can you take me to Mr Charduri and Devika?'

'Yes! Yes!' He grins. 'I will show you.'

He leads me towards the shanty towns. I can't

help feeling a shudder of horror as we enter them, knowing they must be rife with diseases, knowing I am about to see some terrible things.

It is terrible: people living under bits of cloth held up by pieces of wood; children covered with dirt, with stick limbs, playing in pools of polluted water; eyes staring out at me from weathered, withered faces. There is an atmosphere of claustrophobia and camaraderie amongst them. Unfortunately, this sense of collusion quickly focuses on me; a whisper ripples through the camp and soon every child is surrounding me, tugging at my clothes, begging. When I spill coins at them, it only increases their hunger. The boy turns and shouts at them. They take little notice. He drags a few of the children roughly away, then grabs my hands and pulls me through. They continue to give chase, weaving after me as I struggle and stoop under the makeshift roof.

There is no privacy in this place; we look into people's lives and see them all laid bare. An elderly man lying on the floor, dribbling. A mother breast-feeding her baby, her nipples looking painfully dry and pinched. By now, my clothes are caked in sweat and I feel dazed with the horror of it all. I can't believe that this is where Devika has been living for the last two months. Why the hell didn't I get out here sooner?

Newspaper soundbites flash before me: *Karina*

should never have dragged a child from her home country . . . she would have been better off being brought up in her natural habitat . . . cruel to take her out of her culture . . . How the fuck could any reporter, any campaign, any cynic declare that blood and genes and culture justify taking a girl out of a comfortable, happy British home, with three meals a day and a bedtime song every night – to end here up? Even the joint incident with Liam feels trivial by comparison. Hell, I was put on trial as a mother before the adoption agency, the press, the public; the slightest thing I did wrong provoked a tantivy of protest. But here, *here*, Devika will be lucky if she even gets clean water and food. Can't everyone see that it's not a question of culture, or country, or place? There are millions of wealthy, loving families in India who could have looked after Devika wonderfully. But I'm pretty certain the Charduri family isn't one of them.

When I find her, I have to be calm. I'm terrified that the moment I set eyes on her I won't be able to stop myself from picking her up and running out. But I have to control myself; if I do that, they'll accuse me of kidnapping her and maybe I'll never get her back. That's if she's in a fit state to even say hello to me. Hysterical what ifs are rising inside me. What if she's fallen sick? What if her immune system has become weakened by being in England and now she's feverish with typhoid?

What if, what if, what if.

The boy leads me out into a small clearing, where there are three or four wooden shacks. He points to the first one, then bangs on the door, crying, 'Mr Charduri, Mr Charduri.' Then he turns to me and splays out his palm. I give him ten rupees and his eyes shine.

Then he runs off.

'Wait – hang on!' I groan, dreading that I've been conned again. I knock gently on the door of the shack. No reply. I push at the door and it creaks open.

It's quite dim inside, for the only light comes from a little lamp with a candle in it. Mr Charduri is lying on a blanket on the floor, staring at the ceiling. There is a small pile of fruit and food in the corner, some folded-up clothes, and very little else.

No Devika.

Mr Charduri gets up and cries out something in Hindi. I start and tense up, wondering if he's going to throw me out. As his arms fly up, I recoil, anticipating a blow. Instead, he draws me into his arms and hugs me as though he's a lost little boy and I'm his mother.

'Karina, Karina,' he cries. When he pulls back, his eyes frighten me. He looks as though he's been lost in the depths of despair and I have trickled hope into his life.

I seize up inside, so frightened that I hardly dare ask where she is. The shadows from the lamp twist and dance over his face. He lets out a deep, shaky breath, his hand spidering against his chest.

'Mr Charduri, are you okay?' I ask in alarm.

He nods again, then suddenly grabs a banana from his tiny supply of food and offers it to me. I feel momentarily touched.

And then angry. This is no place for Devika to live. And is this tiny little pyramid of food meant to feed her too? And where the hell *is* she?

'Devika,' I insist. 'I want to see Devika.'

'Devika . . .' When he frowns, his forehead pulls his whole face into corrugations of deep worry. He makes a gesture, like a pen moving across a pad.

'School?' I ask, half relieved.

He hesitates, then nods quickly, but something inside tells me he's lying.

'School . . . work?' I ask.

He nods again. He mimes a needle being sewn into a cloth. Then, as though anticipating my rage, he offers me the banana again, with a shaky smile.

'What does that mean?' I ask, mimicking his needle gesture. 'Devika should be at school. She should be learning to read and write . . . and why the hell is *she* working? You were going to buy a farm.

You were going to look after her properly. You promised me; you promised her. Why is *she* working, why not you?'

He taps his eyes and I frown, unable to see what's wrong with them in the light. He can't be blind, for he's able to see me – is he *going* blind? He starts talking in Hindi again and offers me the banana once more, in a manner that is almost pleading.

'No!' I shout. I want to throw the banana to the floor. I felt that something bad was going on, but I didn't think it was going to be as bad as this. For all his moral stance in Britain, I just knew it was wrong to let him take Devika. He failed her once; no reason to think he wouldn't fail her again.

'Well,' I say, managing to control my voice, 'Devika will be here soon, won't she?' I point round the shack and he looks blank. 'Devika – back here?' I tap my watch. 'One hour? Two?'

Mr Charduri stares at my watch and then traces a trembling forefinger around the circumference of its face.

'Devika no home. Devika working. Devika home Saturday,' he says.

'Saturday? What d'you mean, *Saturday*? Devika's working until *Saturday*? What is she?' I splutter hysterically. 'A hedge fund manager? Now, you tell me where she is. Tell me!'

'I see Devika Saturday. I miss Devika,' he says sadly.

I feel as though I'm reaching screaming point.

'Where? Where?' I ask and then realise it's futile. Nobody in Delhi can tell me where bloody anything is. 'Take me. Take me to where she works.'

Mr Charduri looks alarmed and says something in rapid Hindi.

'You have to take me!' I cry. In my anger, I grab hold of his arm, shaking it, and he roars back at me.

I stumble backwards, my head pounding. I stare into his eyes and see the fear. I realise that my panic is only fuelling his.

'Take me,' I say quietly. 'It's okay, it's okay. Just take me.'

Mr Charduri sighs and looks sad. Then he nods agreement.

We have to navigate a difficult path back through the camp. There are so many children it's difficult to move at times; my clothing is tugged and torn. I'm so desperate to see Devika that impatience and fear overwhelm me and I shout at them, but they seem undeterred.

Finally we leave the camp and I shower coins behind me, shaking them off as they fight to pick them up. Mr Charduri leads me through a maze of back streets. The sun feels violently hot; my sari clings to me with a film of sweat. I ask Mr Charduri what happened to his farm. He spreads out his hands and then stops.

'What? Where is she?' I ask. I'm exhausted. If this is another wild goose chase, I shall go insane.

Mr Charduri points nervously to a building. I can't even see a door, just a series of small steps leading down to some sort of basement.

'Down there?' I frown. 'But . . .'

Mr Charduri starts to back off.

'You go . . . you go . . .'

'Me? But . . .'

Mr Charduri smiles and nods.

I turn back. Is this just some trick to get rid of me? Well, if she isn't here, then I will damn well go back to his shack and scream at him until we find her.

I walk down the street. A couple of teenage boys who are sitting by the steps stop talking and stare at me with a curious, unnerving gaze. I pause by the steps, swallowing. Despite the fierce sun, deep shadow veils their depth and purpose; this feels like something out of Dante's *Inferno*. I have started to venture down when out of the darkness comes a cry in angry Hindi. Suddenly, below me, a man appears. As he ventures up the steps I see him fully: a tall, thickset man with a rotund face, a bristly moustache and beady black eyes.

'I go in?' I beg him.

He looks me up and down in confusion and then shakes his head and points upwards.

'No. You see, my daughter—'

He makes an angry noise and gives me a shove. I trip backwards and yank myself on to my feet, swearing angrily. He grabs my arm and drags me back up the steps, then pushes me back on to the street. I smooth down my sari furiously, yelling at him that I want my daughter. He turns and retreats down the steps, disappearing into the gloom.

'Careful,' a man with a British accent warns me.

I turn in hazy shock. He looks Indian but his accent is pure home counties. He is tall, in his thirties, with floppy black hair, and he's wearing smart trousers and an open-necked shirt. I am so relieved to find someone with my own accent that I reach out and clutch his arm, clinging to the warmth of his skin. Seeing my distress, he gently leads me away from the bouncers and guides me quickly down a street. I keep looking back and he hisses at me not to. Another side street; I wonder where he's taking me. The sun glowers down over us. Am I being abducted? I break away from his grip, shaking, telling him to leave me alone.

'Look,' he says sternly, 'if you're doing a story, you have to be a bit more subtle about it.'

'I—'

'Someone from *The Times* was here a few weeks ago and he was pretty insistent about getting down there and he got beaten up. These people don't mess around. They're running a business, as far as they're concerned.'

'I'm not – I'm not from *The Times*. I – what is it?' I burst out. 'What's down there?'

'It's a sweatshop,' he says, looking amazed at my ignorance. 'Are you from a charity?'

'No – no. My daughter's down there.' I feel ashamed as I say the words.

'She's British?'

'No, I – I adopted her. She's Indian.' Another wave of dizziness passes over me and I feel as though I might faint.

'God,' the journalist says, looking shocked.

He is silent for a moment. Then he looks into my eyes and says, 'Where are you staying?'

It turns out that we are both staying at the same hotel.

'I think we should head back there now and you can tell me what your situation is. I might be able to help you. I can't promise anything, but I might. I'm Arvind Vishwanathan, by the way. I'm from London too – I'm here doing a piece for the *Telegraph*. You're Karina West, aren't you? I thought I recognised you. Dear God, this is the last place I expected to bump into a celebrity.'

'I'm not a celebrity, I'm a mother,' I reply automatically.

Back at the hotel, I nearly collapse in the lobby.

Arvind goes to reception and organises for a cup of chai to be brought up. He sits down next to me, pressing the hot drink into my hands.

'Drink it,' he urges me. 'It's sweet; it'll be good for the shock.'

What Arvind doesn't realise is how the creamy, spicy taste is laced with the poison of memories. Of my first trip to India, the first time I tasted chai. Of my first day at the orphanage; of my first glimpse of Devika, when she was skinny and bony and had a nervous, goofy grin and was afraid to have a bath. Tears begin to press against my eyes but I push them back.

'I need to know everything. How many children are in there? How do I get my daughter out?'

'There are about a hundred down there,' Arvind says. 'There are sweatshops like this all over India. About twenty per cent of their economy actually relies on child labour. Not all of them are as bad as this one. In many the children begin work at about seven and go home at about midnight. I think this is probably one of the worst because, from what I can see, the children aren't going home. They're being set to work every minute of the day and then sleeping on mats down there in some sort of communal facility. I've heard they're only getting one meal a day and it's dark, too, so there's potential for severe damage to their eyesight. And of course there's no proper sanitation.'

'So . . . you're saying . . .' I can hardly keep my voice steady, 'she's not going to be out on Saturday? I thought Saturday was their day off.'

'Saturday?' he asks, looking puzzled. 'This isn't the kind of place where children get a day off.'

'I mean – it's just her father – Mr Charduri – said she'd be out on Saturday. I don't understand what this is all about. She's mine – I should never have let her come back to India. I don't – I—'

'Did Mr Charduri say how much he sold her for?'

'Sold her? He's *sold* her?' I spit out.

'Many of the children in there have been sold. They grow up in rural areas, there's no work for them, so their parents send them here thinking it's actually a better opportunity for them.'

'I don't believe this. I don't believe it. He brought my daughter back and then he *sold* her? How can these places exist? How can this be allowed in this day and age?'

'You might argue that they ought to be closed down, but it's not as simple as that. In cases where that's happened, the children have been left jobless. They've ended up as child prostitutes,' he says in a matter-of-fact voice.

I am silent with shock.

'Those poor children—' I break off, my voice snagging with tears. 'But – how can I get her back? I just want my daughter back!'

'We might be able to help you. The fact of the matter is, the police and various reps may conduct a raid on the place and get the children out. It's a huge source of embarrassment to the clothing store that this has happened – so they too want the place closed down so that they can be seen as heroes.'

'What clothing store?'

When he tells me the name, I shiver. It's one of the biggest chains in the UK, renowned for their upmarket, quality clothing.

'But they can't be involved in this.' I want to curl up in embarrassment. I can't bear to admit that this very chain has been involved in helping to promote my children's book *The Celebrity Princess* in its stores. There was even an offer – buy a book, get a kid's sweatshirt half price. 'I mean, I've actually bought Devika clothing from there.'

He smiles at the bitter irony of it.

'But they don't sell clothes for two quid or anything like that,' I cry. 'I thought it was just the cheapie places that were involved in this.'

'Fuck it, loads of them are,' he says. 'It's just that this one makes a bigger profit margin. And to be fair, they argue that they don't know about it because they sub-contract. And their sub-contractors sub-contract and so on until they lose track of the chain.'

'But . . . but . . . I . . .' I can barely ask the question, but I have to. 'If they don't do a raid – if this goes on – can I buy her back? Is that possible? I mean, I just want her back now. I want her back today.'

Arvind doesn't look shocked.

'It may be a possibility. Look, I'm going to continue with this story for the next week. I promise I'll do what I can to help you, okay? Just don't get silly and go over there and try to break in. I'm telling you, journalists trying to uncover this story have been beaten up. I'm playing it low myself.'

'Thank you,' I say, unable to still quite absorb it all. 'I . . . I think I'd better take a rest now.'

Arvind looks at me, curiosity in his eyes.

'I—' I turn back to him. 'I don't really want the press involved in this, if that's okay. I mean – I don't want anything reported that could harm my chances of getting her out. Will you promise to keep this quiet?'

Arvind holds up his hands.

'Look, I'm here for a factual story, not celebrity gossip.' He breaks off as I wince, looking awkward. 'I didn't mean that to sound as it did. I think you should take a rest, Karina. And look, you can trust me. I will help you and I won't report on it, okay? Here's my card. My mobile number's at the bottom.'

I take the card, thank him and go slowly up the marble stairs to my room. I remember how, just a few hours ago, I made the journey down, taking care not to trip over my sari, my head filled with rosy visions of Devika's farm. I was even wondering if they might grow pomegranates, my favourite fruit, and if I could take some back to England. In the space of just three hours my whole life has changed. I get into my room and sink down on the bed. My mobile beeps. I pull it out blankly and lie down, curling into a ball, staring at the screen.

K – where are u staying? I'm coming to India. Don't say no. Think u need me. Liam

49

Karina

'I want my little girl back. I want to kill them. I want her back,' I sob.

The moment Liam turned up at the hotel, I broke down. I felt I couldn't cry until he got here; I felt I had to carry the weight of what I'd learnt, that I had to stay strong for Devika, focus all my energies on getting her back. But the moment Liam came through the door and I opened my mouth to tell him what had happened, the dam inside me broke. I couldn't hold out any longer; I had to share my pain with him. I collapsed on the bed and began to sob like a child. He dumped his bag on the floor and came over and put his arms round me.

And now I can't stop. I cry and cry against his

chest. Grief tears through me, racking through my ribs and stomach. He holds on tightly, rocking and shushing me patiently. Every so often, I try to speak, to explain what's happened, but all I can manage to stammer is, 'I want my girl back. I want Devika back. Oh God, I want her back.'

Eventually my tears dry up. I feel hollow, exhausted. I lie down on the bed with Liam, his arms wrapped tight around me. I don't want to sleep; it feels selfish to do so when I should be spending every second worrying about her. But the jet lag and shock of the past forty-eight hours overwhelm me. I give in, sink against him, knowing I am safe in his arms . . .

When I wake up Liam is looking at me with worried, tender eyes. He kisses me gently on the nose.

'Tell me everything,' he says. 'If you can bear to.'

I have to be concise and stick to the facts.

'Devika's father – he sold her. I don't know why. He didn't buy his farm, he just – got her working in a sweatshop. And she's there now and it's guarded and I can't get her out.'

Liam turns white. 'Well, we'll fucking well get her out.'

'It's not as easy as that. It's heavily guarded and I met a journalist who told me that a colleague had been beaten up for just reporting on the story.'

Liam gets up. He storms around the room, ranting and swearing, saying he wants to go and knock their heads off and pummel them to the ground.

He calls up the journalist and we meet up again and discuss what we can do to get her back. Then we go to visit Mr Charduri. Liam manages to contain himself from socking him and we find out the full story of what happened to him and Devika when they came back to India.

We both agree that we can't bear to wait. That if we hang about hoping that the police raid will take place, it might be weeks. That Devika is in too much danger. We decide on a plan for tomorrow. But even waiting one more night feels as though it's too long.

It might be too late, a voice whispers inside me, hissing and insidious, *it might be too late already, she might already be—*

I shake my head frantically, shutting it out. I have to be positive. I have to be strong. We will get her out.

We have a quiet, early dinner downstairs in the hotel. We're so tired and nervous we can barely eat, as we talk over our plan again and again.

'D'you think it will definitely work? Offering to buy her back?' I ask. I bury my face in my hands and then look up at him. 'It just feels so disgusting – having to *buy* my own daughter back. I mean, when I first brought her to England, people like your mother asked *how much did I pay* and I felt so angry and now – now we really are having to.'

'Well, it's what we have to do, so we do it. This is a different country, a different culture. Remember what Arvind said – think of it more as a bribe.'

'Is it even legal? Can I even take her back out of the country if we've . . .'

'She's ours now. She's ours.'

'I can call Angela and ask her for advice . . .'

We eat in silence.

'We just get her out,' Liam says. 'That's the most important thing.'

'What if they say no? What if they want more than—'

Liam put his hand on mine. 'We're going to get her back, okay? We're going to get her back.'

I stare at him.

'I haven't even asked you anything about what's happened to you,' I say. 'About rehab, and how you got back with Hayley—'

'What? I'm not with Hayley. We had a drink together, a quick catch up. I've no doubt the press reported some reunion, but that was all.'

Hayley reported it, I say silently.

'As for rehab – well, I've been clean a few weeks.

I want it to last.' Liam shakes his head. 'We can't talk about this. None of my crap matters. I can't focus on anything but Devika and neither can you.'

Silence.

'Thank you,' I say at last. 'Thank you for coming. Nobody else would have come – nobody else understood . . . and you came right out for me. Thank you.'

Liam smiles briefly.

We pay the bill. It's still early and upstairs in my room twilight has crept in and spread its soft blue over the bed. Liam suddenly steps back, tentative.

'I've booked another room. I can stay there.'

'No. No. I don't want to be on my own tonight,' I say. 'Please be with me. I want you to hold me.'

Because if you go, that voice might come back, whispering possibilities, warning me that she might be . . .

Liam comes up and pulls me into his embrace, kissing me. I break off and shake my head, wanting to say no, I can't do this right now. But then I look up into his eyes and realise he's offering me an escape: the relief of oblivion. I reach up and kiss him back, with a fierce desperation, our teeth clashing. I pull off his T-shirt and he wraps his arms around me, crushing me against him. I press my cheek against the hardness of his chest. The thump of his heartbeat reverberates in my ear. I can see her, in a dark place, weeping, breathing her last gasps . . . Liam reaches down and twists my face back up to his, planting his lips against mine and forcing me to forget again. He unwinds my sari, removes my top and underskirt, caressing me tenderly but insistently, then pushes me down on the bed. I close my eyes as I feel him push inside me. Pleasure flows through me and I cry out for him. But as it builds and laps against me it feels false, a betrayal, and the pleasure ebbs away and I see her, in darkness, praying and hoping that I haven't forgotten her, and tears start to trickle out of my eyes and my breaths become a muddle of desire and grief. He stops, gasping down at me, his eyes wide and afraid. 'D'you want me to stop?' he whispers. I shake my head, kissing him back, asking him to go all the way, and then I close my eyes and arch against him, searching for brief snatches of paradise.

Afterwards I cry some more and so does he.

I realise then that he is feeling as scared as me, underneath his show of strength.

'In some ways this is all my fault,' he says. 'I put that stupid joint in her lunch box and that fucked everything up and then . . . it all went on from there.'

I tell him not to be so stupid. I tell him if it's

511

anyone's fault, it's mine, for letting her go, for listening to everyone else who was telling me I had to give her up instead of fighting for her. Everyone wanted to turn our story into an Issue, simplify it into a tale of East versus West, Nature versus Nurture, when it was never really about that at all. I wouldn't have cared what country Mr Charduri was from if he'd been a good father; I let everyone blur my judgement and persuade me to ignore my intuition.

I kiss him and tell him that when Devika gets out, she's going to need both of us. He nods, breathing shakily, and we hold each other and then whisper our plan again. What we're going to do, how we're going to play it if anything goes wrong. Then Liam whispers how I'm going to feel when I see her and hold her and I have to tell him to stop. It's too unbearable to even think about it.

And I don't tell him how I'm also scared of seeing her, scared of how she might be, scared that if she's damaged I might not be enough to heal her, scared she will never forgive me . . .

Liam falls into a deep sleep and I lie awake as twilight bruises to black. I think of Mr Charduri with a sense of deep shame. I remember how on the plane out here I was half hoping he might have screwed up in some way, that Devika might confide in me that he wasn't the best father in the world after all. But I thought he might just neglect her homework or fail to buy her a new pair of shoes. I thought she might miss Western music or her jeans or her mobile. I never imagined it would be like this. I play over our meeting earlier in the day, when Liam and I went back to find him and discover the full story. Arvind translated for us as Mr Charduri wept and explained through his tears that a few days before their return to India, his cousin let him down. The loan he'd promised fell through because of the credit crunch and the problems his cousin was having with his own business. Mr Charduri felt too proud to back out; he couldn't bear to let Devika come back to me, fearing he'd lose her for ever. So they came out to India and Mr Charduri worked in the market, selling clothes, until one day a thief stole everything from his shack and he found himself owing money to a supplier. He fell into a terrible depression and Devika had to find food for both of them by stealing from the market and begging tourists for change. He said that when the men from the sari factory offered to give him money for her, he thought he'd be able to work again and get her back, that it would only be for a while and that it was the best thing for her, for at least she'd be fed twice a day. I can't tell any more what is the truth and what is lies when it comes to Mr Charduri. I'm not sure even he knows. His heart is good, I think, but his mind is muddled. I felt sorry for him; he seemed a broken man. But I also hated him, and a part of me always will.

I close my eyes, telling myself that I need to get my sleep to be strong and bright tomorrow. But all I can see is Devika, and what she might be doing, right at this minute, and I try to feel her, to find some connection, some intuition that might tell me if she's sleeping or waking or praying, but there is only blankness.

And that terrible voice: *she might not be able to hear you because she might be—*

I look at Liam. I'm glad he came. Whatever happens, I'll know from now on that he was the one person I could depend on. We're going to be together now, no matter what the press or my friends or anyone thinks. We're going to be a family.

And if we don't get her tomorrow, we'll get her the next day. Or the next.

We won't leave this place until we find her.

At two a.m. I suddenly find myself crawling out of bed in a haze of desperate exhaustion, collapsing on to my knees before a picture of Lord Krishna and praying that we find her. I feel an unexpected sweet peace, a sense that everything might be all right, before the fear comes back and I crawl back into bed and pray and pray until the night turns to dawn.

50

Devika

There is a snake crawling up my skin. It's an itchy
red snake and at night it wakes up me because I
can feel myself scratching. I can't see it properly
because it's always dark down here so I trace my
fingers over the wriggly shape of it. There's another
one starting to crawl up my left arm and little patches
of itchy stuff on my legs and feet.

It's dark. I can hear snoring and breathing. This
is how it used to be in the orphanage. But there I
could wake up in the night and creep out into the
courtyard. I could see the moon painting the trees
silver and dancing across the stones and playing with
the fountain. Here, there is nowhere you can go at
night-time. There are no gates to stand by and stare
through hoping someone might recognise you.

Everyone in this room is snoring with miserable and tired and sick breaths that fight in the air and form a thick layer that presses down over us.

I want to go to sleep so much. We only have six hours to sleep each night. My whole body wants to sleep – my feet are moaning and my stomach is screaming for food like it always does and my head is hurting and wants to switch off like a TV set. But my eyes keep opening even though they are burning too. I lift up my finger. It is red and little bits of skin are peeling around the edge of the nail. I hold it out and look at it. It is dark but I can see it. I hold it out a bit further but it gets blurry. I bring it closer and it becomes sharp again. Every night it gets more blurry. I cup my hands over my eyes and pray to Krishna, *please let me keep my eyes, please can Daddy change his mind and make the men give me back to him, please let me keep my eyes.*

Last week, Nesreen went blind and was thrown out of the factory. Then Vikram said he wanted to lose his eyes so that he could escape too. But I want to keep my eyes even if it means staying here a little longer. I will escape one day. Lord Krishna will answer my prayers. And I want with all my heart to come out of the darkness and see the light. I want to see the blue sky and the bright sun, the markets and the saris and the garlands. I want all the colours to pour into my eyes and fill me up with love.

Oh, Krishna, please can that day come soon. Please, dear Krishna.

I close my eyes and try and try and try to sleep but all I can see is Mummy Karina. Then, just as I am slipping down, the itchy snake flicks his tail across my arm. I reach down to scratch it and then it's too late, I'm awake. And then I lie awake some more and suddenly the night is over and our boss storms into the room yelling, 'WAKE UP! WAKE UP! TIME FOR WORK!'

We all get up, rubbing our eyes. There are two little rooms next to our bedroom. One for girls and one for boys. We wash with some water in a bucket. It is quite dark and we all look like shapes cut out from black cardboard. Then I find the hole for the toilet. I hate going because it is dirty and smelly and there is no toilet paper here.

Then we have to start work.

Our work room has rows of tables in it. We sit in line on little benches. We pick up our needles. My fingers have lots of little red dots from all the prickles when I missed the cloth. We take the blue tops that ladies will one day wear in England. We take the little pink and purple beads and sew them on, one by one, in the pattern drawn on the top. I sew slowly because my arm is already aching.

Normally it takes until the end of the day for it to ache, not the start. My back is aching too and my head feels heavy, as though it might fall off. If we were in England Mummy Karina would give me the magic medicine, the paracetamol, and then she'd tuck me into bed and sing me a song. I try to work out how many hours we have to go before we can sleep again. Fourteen hours.

At eleven o'clock, we have a fifteen-minute break for food. The man passes us little bowls of rice. It is sticky and cold and badly cooked, with hard bits, the way Mummy Karina used to cook it because she was bad at rice.

'I used to eat something called Rice Krispies,' I tell Leena. 'You put them in a bowl and pour milk over them and they bounce around making crackly noises.'

'Really?' Leena asks.

Kishun gives me a glare.

I am always telling Leena about England. I told her how they have big red buses and white houses, only they're really cold because they never heat them, and hollow chairs you go to the toilet in and roads with no holes, where cars can travel smoothly, and cows in fields and lipsticks and jeans and Britney Spears and *The Simpsons*.

'Rice . . . crisps?' she asks in wonder.

'Rice Krispies.'

Kishun looks angry.

'You're lying,' he says. 'You keep telling us these lies and I told you to shut up.'

'I'm not lying, I lived there with Mummy Karina. She was English. She adopted me,' I cry.

'Liar!' Kishun stops, rubbing his eyes, as though he can hardly find the energy to keep being angry. But then he bursts out: 'You want to pretend you're better than us, but you're not! You belong in this factory like all of us. This is your *dharma* too! Your English mummy isn't going to come and get you; you're going to stay here like the rest of us.'

'I'm not, I'm not.'

'You will, you will.' Kishun leans over and grabs my rice.

I cry out and try to grab it back but he takes a big handful and crams it into his mouth. All the other boys and girls quickly eat the rest of their rice, scared he might steal theirs too.

I feel myself go cold. I still have a bruise from last week because I didn't eat my rice. I gave it to Leena because she was so hungry, and then I fainted at the work table and the guard beat me.

'GIVE IT BACK!' I shout. 'GIVE ME BACK MY RICE!'

'What is going on here?' The guard comes into the room.

'She stole my rice so I stole hers back,' Kishun cries before I can say anything.

The guard grabs my arm and yanks me out of the room. I keep yelling and screaming that it wasn't me, but he doesn't listen. He drags me into another small room where there are bags and bags of tops wrapped up in plastic, ready to go to England. I stand very still and stare at the floor. I know this guard likes to hit; he always seems excited to be able to tell us off. If I scream loudly, he will be satisfied and stop faster. I close my eyes and set my teeth together. I need to make myself go hard inside so that it won't hurt so much.

I saw my daddy go hard inside when he said goodbye to me. I was upset that I had to come and work at the factory but he said it would just be for a holiday. We hadn't eaten for three days and he didn't want me to keep having to steal. He cried and held me tight against him, saying he would pray for me every night and I must never forget him. But then he hardened. He brought me to the factory and I saw the men and the dark place where I would work and I didn't like it. I clung to him, crying, but he shook his head, his eyes blank, and pushed me away, saying, 'Go, go, you have to go.'

I see the shadow of the guard raising his hand to strike me—

—when someone else enters the room. The guard

barks, angry at having his fun interrupted. But then he lets out a gasp and makes a few apologies.

I look up. I have only ever seen this man once before – the day that Daddy brought me. He is big, with a moustache and a round belly. He looked me up and down and turned me round and round and opened my eyes wide with his fat fingers, to make sure he was buying a good product.

Now he points at me.

'This one's coming with me,' he says.

The guard looks disappointed but he nods quickly and pushes me forward.

What's happening? Where am I going?

The big man beckons that I have to follow him. I want to run. What if he is going to punish me really badly? He sees me hanging back and crouches down in front of me, squeezing my face between his thumb and fingers, and spits out: 'You are coming with me, okay?'

I nod quickly but my heart is beating. I think they are going to kill me. And it wasn't even my fault, I didn't steal any rice. *Oh, Krishna, please don't let them kill me.*

The man pulls me up towards the big steps.

Then I realise we are going outside.

We go up and up and the door opens and we walk out into the light and I am praying so hard I am weeping and a voice says: 'Devika?'

But I can't see. I can feel wet in my eyes. I can feel arms around me. I can feel someone holding me tight but I don't know who it is because all I can see is white. I feel someone kissing my face and rubbing their cheek against mine and I cry, 'My eyes, my eyes!' and I try to push them away.

'Devika, it's Karina!'

I recognise her voice. It's my mummy Karina, come back for me. I hang on to her tightly, my eyes streaming with tears, and she is soft and warm and she says I'm okay, she won't let me go, everything will be all right now.

But all I can see is dazzling bright white.

Then she pulls back and I see her: a dark outline, moving in the white, and another man with her, hovering like two angels.

I take her hand and close my eyes and I feel my heart breaking with happiness. But I'm scared it might all be a dream or maybe the man did kill me and I'm in heaven. Then I feel her breath on my ear and I know she is real and then I feel too happy, so happy I don't think my heart can take it, and everything spins and the white turns black and I find I am falling, falling into softness . . .

51

Karina

I wake up. Unfamiliar sounds trickle into my consciousness: the moo of cows, the toot of horns, a babble of foreign voices, the winding melody of a *saringi*. I blink, staring up at the circling arc of the fan overhead. There is a terrible pain in my heart, a raw sense of devastating guilt . . .

And then I remember.

I roll over and see her lying on the other side of the bed. For a moment I can hardly believe she's here with me. She's sleeping soundly. I want to hug her to bits but I just manage to restrain myself in time. After all she went through yesterday, my darling Devika needs to sleep. I stare at her face anxiously, noticing the gauntness of her cheeks, the tired circles under her eyes, the faint bruise on her forehead and the little sliver of dried blood.

Anger seizes me up as I remember the way we fled yesterday. I remember the cold look in the man's eyes as we passed over the money, the flicker of doubt as we took Devika away, fearful that he might be losing a better profit. I damn well wish I had punched him; I was close, but Liam whispered in my ear, 'Stay cool, stay cool.' I glance across at a picture of Lord Krishna on the wall opposite and spontaneous prayers of thanks are welling up inside me when—

—*she wakes up*.

A look of horror comes over her face. She thinks she's still in the factory; she fears she's overslept, or she's dreading another day spent in slavery. Then her eyes widen as she remembers. She turns and sees me.

She lets out a small cry of sheer delight. Spontaneously, we move towards each other and hug each other tight.

Then I feel her body start to shudder as tears overwhelm her.

'It's okay,' I keep saying, kissing her fiercely, 'it's okay.' Then I look into her eyes. Last night she woke up, rubbing them, screaming that she couldn't see. But I switched on a light and she looked around and I held my breath anxiously. And then I saw something light up in her eyes; saw that she was not blind, just shocked by the brightness after weeks of being shut underground.

'See,' I say, staring at her pupils. 'You can see. Your eyes look good, don't they, darling? You can see okay, can't you?'

'Don't want to go back,' she says, sniffing. 'Don't want to go back.'

'You don't have to go,' I cry. 'Devika, you're *never* going back.'

But she keeps on crying hysterically, repeating over and over, 'I don't want to go back, don't make me go back.' I start to panic that she's having some sort of fit.

There is a knock at the door. She starts, jolted out of her tears. I get out of bed. As I go to the door, I hear a noise and see her slipping down and hiding under the bed. She's convinced the knock signals that the men have come. That she's going to be dragged back to work.

Tears well up in my throat. How long will it take us to rebuild her trust?

And for all I know the knock *could* signal the men are back. I mean, they surely don't know where I am, but . . . There is another, firmer knock. Paranoia grips me and my hand pauses on the handle. Then my mobile beeps. And I realise who it is.

I fling open the door. Liam is standing there,

holding breakfast on a tray. He smiles at me. I swallow, hoping that he might help to make Devika feel safe.

He comes in and looks around. I call out quietly, 'Devika! Liam's here.'

A face peeps out from under the bed. And when she sees him her expression lights up.

Liam puts the tray down on the bed. He pulls her out and up from under the bed. She stands there, suddenly shy, her eyes flitting nervously from me to him. Liam reaches out and gently smooths her hair back from her forehead, as though inspecting her face. He touches the bruise.

'I'm going to kill the bastards who did that to you,' he says. Then he touches her nose. 'You're with us now. You're going to be all right.'

And they hold each other tightly.

Then we all sit down cross-legged on the bed to share breakfast. Liam ordered up some bowls and some spoons and some fresh milk from the hotel kitchen. He winks at me and I grin and go to my suitcase to get the treat I packed before I came. As I take the box out of my case, I have a sudden flashback: packing the case with shaking hands, my terror that I would never find her. Euphoria bubbles up inside me and I turn and dance over to the bed, showing the box to Devika.

'Rice Krispies!'

Finally, for the first time that morning, she lets out a laugh.

I pour them out, trying not to stare too hard as I watch her eat. I see the relief come over her face as she chews on them. She looks soothed.

I think she realises that we're not going to make her go back to work. Maybe we have a way to go before she can wake up in the mornings and feel loved and cherished, feel that the world is a safe place to be, but I will be patient. All I can do is just be patient and love her.

'I fucking hate Rice Krispies,' Liam mumbles through a mouthful of milk.

'Well, why are you eating them then?' I ask.

'Well, I'll feel left out if I don't, won't I?'

I look at Devika and a smile comes over her face and I smile back. And we carry on eating, grinning nervously at each other, hoping everything will be all right.

One week later, all the paperwork is finalised. I make a long-distance call to Angela, who is horrified when I tell her what's happened. She advises us to apply for another visa entry and put in another adoption order the moment we get to England. Mr Charduri agrees that we should take custody of Devika and she is allowed to come back to England with us. All week I daren't leave the hotel with her, terrified a member of the gang might see her; all week I've had a terrible knot of tension in my stomach, scared that something will go wrong, or that we'll be stuck here for weeks. When we finally climb on to the plane in the shivering blue twilight that Wednesday, relief pours over me in waves – oh, thank God, thank God. We get on to the plane and find our three seats and Devika sits in between us.

As the plane rises up from the ground, elation fills me. And then I look down on Delhi and feel a wave of sadness, thinking of all the children we left behind, who will wake up tomorrow morning in darkness and spend years to come in darkness. I try to tell myself that we can all only do so much, and I saved one – one very special girl. It's then that I make a fierce pledge to myself, that every day for the rest of my life I will look after her, I will be the best mother in the world. I reach out and hold her hand tightly as the plane passes into the clouds.

I open the front door and Devika explodes into the house, crying, 'Sophie! Sophie!'

I smile as her coat and lunch box and school bag are flung on to the floor and she goes off in search of the kitten. When we returned to England a month ago, I swear that seeing her new pet brought the biggest smile to her face – bigger than being able to sleep in her bed again, or have Rice Krispies every evening. They fell in love with each other at first sight and since then Devika has practically run home from school every day, eager to find Sophie and play mouse with her or pull her on to her lap in a warm purring ball.

I go into the kitchen and cross to the cupboard and take out a bowl and some Rice Krispies. I notice the new cleaner has left a copy of the *Daily Mail* on the table. I flick through it suspiciously. Will I be left alone for once? Oh, great, there I am on page thirteen. Another article about how wrong celebrity adoption is and how selfish I was to drag Devika back from India, from the loving arms of her natural father, and back to the evils of the Western world. I take the sheet of paper and put it at the bottom of Sophie's dirt tray.

Later that evening, after Devika has done her homework, we sit together and watch TV. And I feel tears beginning to well up. Every so often it happens. I suddenly remember India again, and I feel scared that somehow someone will take her away from me again, or else just such relief that she's with me, that I can feel the warmth of her next to me and her breath close to me, and I can't help having a quick cry. I always hide my tears; I've become very good at crying soundlessly and surreptitiously flicking my eyes.

Today, however, she catches me out.

'Why is Mummy crying?' she asks.

'Oh, it's a very sad programme,' I say, pointing to the TV.

Devika looks confused; it's *EastEnders*. She gives me a look as if to say, my mummy is nuts, and then reaches up and gives me a kiss on the cheek.

'Will Liam come later?' she asks.

'Liam is practising. And no, you can't stay up, you have school in the morning.'

Devika sighs impatiently.

'Maybe in our next lives I will come back as your mummy and then I will look after you,' she says vaguely, and then goes back to watching the TV.

Upstairs, we have a bath together and then I'm meant to sing her a song but we get distracted, talking about all our plans for Christmas. It's only a few days before term ends and then we've got so many things we want to do. It's Devika's first Christmas in England and we're going to *make* it snow – Devika is praying earnestly every night – and then make snowmen and go on a sledge together. We're going to buy our own Christmas tree and Devika is going to make decorations that hopefully Sophie won't try to eat or pull off. We're going to go shopping together and then visit the temple and the church. We're going to learn carols and make chai and hot chocolate.

And then there is New Year . . .

And then the next year and a new term . . .

And then it will be summer. We're getting quite carried away already, talking about holidays and beaches we might go on, but nowhere too hot as Liam doesn't like to get too much sun . . .

And I have no doubt, as I turn off the light and stand in her doorway, watching her, that the years are going to go fast and I will soon be telling her to turn down her music and not stay out late with her boyfriend and saying that no, she can't go into a club . . .

And I smile, thinking of all that we have to enjoy together, all the things to share together, the wonderful life we'll live together, starting with this Christmas.

LOUISE BAGSHAWE

Glitz

'Addictive . . . Louise Bagshawe knows how to keep her readers engrossed' *Heat*

Picture this: you're one of the four fabulous Chambers cousins, blessed with beauty, brains and a lovely trust fund courtesy of your reclusive Uncle Clem. You have:

★ Private jets to take you to lush tropical islands
★ Invitations to the best, most glamorous parties in town
★ An endless supply of clothes, shoes and jewellery

Now picture this: Uncle Clem announces he's getting married. To Bai-Ling, a woman more than half his age . . . And suddenly everything changes. You have:

★ No money
★ No skills
★ And no idea of what it means to stand on your own two feet.

Find out what practical Juno, scruffy tomboy Athena, sassy Venus and flighty Diana Chambers do in Louise Bagshawe's gorgeously addictive new novel, *Glitz*: an irresistible story of glamorous women, powerful men, the price of unearned wealth . . . and the value of making it all on your own.

'A sparkly hit from the never-dull Louise Bagshawe' *Cosmopolitan*

'A brilliantly juicy read – I couldn't put it down *****' *Love It!*

978 0 7553 3607 4

headline
review

WENDY HOLDEN

Filthy Rich

Shire bliss?

When romantic Mary meets Monty, handsome heir to a stately pile, happiness seems assured. But as the mansion crumbles, passion wanes.

Banker's wife Beth swaps Notting Hill for weekends at a bijou cottage. They only offered a smidgeon over the asking price. So why don't the locals like them?

Eco-hag Morag is the terror of the village. She hates incomers, four-wheel drives, slug pellets and anyone between her and absolute power.

Über-WAG Alexandra needs a footballer's mansion – fast. There must be a *Hello!*-tastic palace with pool, gym, champagne bar and helipad somewhere?

When these four face each other in a struggle over sex, power and money – not to mention allotments – village life is never the same again.

The critics loved *Filthy Rich*:

'A modern-day Jilly Cooper, Wendy Holden has made the raunchy romp her own' *Glamour*

'Tasty and explosive ****' *Heat*

'****' *OK!*

'Sparkling ****' *Daily Mirror*

'Another sure-fire hit ****' *Closer*

'Great fun . . . pertly written, fizzing with wit' *Daily Mail*

'The perfect page-turner' *Sun*

978 0 7553 2513 9

headline
review

You can buy any of these other **Review** titles from your bookshop or *direct from the publisher*.

FREE P&P AND UK DELIVERY

(Overseas and Ireland £3.50 per book)

Unsticky	Sarra Manning	£6.99
Changing Grooms	Sasha Wagstaff	£6.99
10 Reasons Not to Fall in Love	Linda Green	£6.99
The Stepmother	Carrie Adams	£6.99
An Offer You Can't Refuse	Jill Mansell	£6.99
The Other Side of the Stars	Clemency Burton-Hill	£6.99
The Sisterhood	Emily Barr	£6.99
Left Bank	Kate Muir	£6.99
An Absolute Scandal	Penny Vincenzi	£7.99
Bad Behaviour	Sheila O'Flanagan	£6.99

TO ORDER SIMPLY CALL THIS NUMBER

01235 400 414

or visit our website: www.headline.co.uk

Prices and availability subject to change without notice.